CHRISTMAS

BY

PATRICIA THAYER

AND

CHRISTMAS MAGIC
ON THE MOUNTAIN

BY

MELISSA McCLONE

MILLS &
BOON

Dear Reader,

So many of you have asked if I plan to give Jarrett McKane his own story. Well, I've finally returned to Winchester Ridge, Colorado, and decided the brooding, live-on-the-edge guy needs a little redemption.

It all starts when he runs into pregnant Mia Saunders and the tenants from Mountain View Apartments. There's widow Nola Madison, handyman and World War II vet Ralph Parkinson, and Joe Carson and other retirees like Emma and Charlie Lowery.

When Jarrett is court-ordered to move into his shambles of an apartment building, he finds himself going beyond landlord duties. He's talked into hanging Christmas lights, making runs to the hospital, painting a baby's nursery and standing in as a labour coach. Oh, yes, Jarrett McKane definitely meets his match.

In creating the characters of Nola, Emma, Ralph and Joe, it made me think back to my own grandparents, John and Lydgia Greiner, and Paul and Loretta Hannan. Their love was unconditional, and time with them was special. I hope this story brings back good memories for you, too.

Enjoy!

Patricia Thayer

DADDY BY CHRISTMAS

BY
PATRICIA THAYER

All the characters in this book have no existence outside the imagination of the author, and have no relation whatsoever to anyone bearing the same name or names. They are not even distantly inspired by any individual known or unknown to the author, and all the incidents are pure invention.

First published in Great Britain 2010
Harlequin Mills & Boon Limited,
Eton House, 18-24 Paradise Road, Richmond, Surrey TW9 1SR

© Patricia Thayer 2010

ISBN: 978 0 263 88841 6

23-1110

Harlequin Mills & Boon policy is to use papers that are natural, renewable and recyclable products and made from wood grown in sustainable forests. The logging and manufacturing processes conform to the legal environmental regulations of the country of origin.

Printed and bound in Spain
by Litografia Rosés S.A., Barcelona

Originally born and raised in Muncie, Indiana, **Patricia Thayer** is the second of eight children. She attended Ball State University, and soon afterwards headed West. Over the years she's made frequent visits back to the Midwest, trying to keep up with her growing family.

Patricia has called Orange County, California, home for many years. She not only enjoys the warm climate, but also the company and support of other published authors in the local writers' organisation. For the past eighteen years she has had the unwavering support and encouragement of her critique group. It's a sisterhood like no other.

When not working on a story, you might find her travelling the United States and Europe, taking in the scenery and doing story research while thoroughly enjoying herself, accompanied by Steve, her husband for over thirty-five years. Together they have three grown sons and four grandsons. As she calls them, her own true-life heroes. On rare days off from writing, you might catch her at Disneyland, spoiling those grandkids rotten! She also volunteers for the Grandparent Autism Network.

Patricia has written for over twenty years and has authored over thirty-six books for Mills & Boon®. She has been nominated for both the National Readers' Choice Award and the prestigious RITA®. Her book *Nothing Short of a Miracle* won a *Romantic Times* Reviewer's Choice award.

A long-time member of Romance Writers of America, she has served as President and held many other board positions for her local chapter in Orange County. She's a firm believer in giving back.

Check her website at www.patriciathayer.com for upcoming books.

To my own little heroes,
Harrison, Griffin, Connor and Finley.

You're the light of life.

CHAPTER ONE

SHE hated relying on a man.

Mia Saunders glanced around the filled-to-capacity community room at the Mountain View Apartments complex. It was already decorated for Thanksgiving and the tenants were hopeful that they would still be living here at the end of November.

At one of the many card tables were Emma and Charlie Lowery. They'd lived here for over twenty years. So had the Nordbergs, along with Second World War veteran and widower, Ralph Parkinson. They'd all come here for the same reason—affordable rent gave seniors on fixed incomes some independence.

At the age of twenty-nine, Mia was an exception, one of the few, younger tenants who lived in the aging apartment complex.

"You've got to help us, Mia!"

She turned to tiny, gray-haired Nola Madison standing beside her. She was a widow who had lived in the complex since her husband's death ten years ago. With social security and a small pension, Nola could survive living alone here without burdening her children.

"Nola, I'm going to try, but I'm not sure how much I can do."

"You're a lawyer," Nola said, her soft hazel eyes seeming larger behind her bifocals.

"Not yet. I've only just started law school." That had been put on hold this past semester and she had no idea when she could start up again.

"But you will talk to the owner for us when he gets here."

"*If* he gets here," Mia added. So far that hadn't happened. They'd tried a half-dozen times to have a meeting with the man to discuss the fifty-year-old apartment complex's crumbling condition. No improvements had been done in years.

"It seems the new owner has been avoiding us."

"Well, he has good reason. He doesn't want to fix things any more than the last owner." Joe Carson, another of the elderly tenants, spoke up behind her. That got the crowd going.

Mia waved her hand and they quieted down. "This isn't getting us anywhere. In all fairness…" She glanced down at the paper. "Mr. Jarrett McKane only took possession of this property a few months ago."

"McKane," Nola repeated. "I wonder if he's any relation to the teacher at the high school, Kira McKane. My granddaughter, Hannah, talks about her all the time."

Joe stepped forward. "I don't care who he's related to, he has to take care of our demands."

Joe's wife, Sylvia, gasped. "What if he evicts us?"

That started more grumbles around the crowded room.

Mia eyed the tenants she'd gotten to know since coming to Winchester Ridge when her brother, Reverend Bradley Saunders, took over as pastor of the First Community Church a half mile away. She'd found a one-bedroom apartment in the affordable complex about three years ago when Brad and his wife, Karen, decided to make the small Colorado ranching community a permanent home. It was a perfect place for raising a family.

All Mia's life, it had been her brother who'd been there for her. Brad had never given up on his little sister, even when she gave up on herself. Over the years, he'd pulled her back from some pretty dark places, and let her know that she was important and loved. When their parents disowned her, Brad stood by her and helped her get her act together and get into college.

She'd do anything for him. Sadness washed over Mia, knowing she would never get the chance again.

Sam Parker hurried into the room and called out, "One of those fancy SUVs just pulled up. A shiny black one."

Those standing scurried to find a seat as if they'd been caught doing something wrong. Mia didn't rush much these days, but she felt the excitement and nervousness as she took a chair at the head table, and then turned her attention toward the door.

Nothing had prepared her for this man.

Jarrett McKane walked into the room as if he owned it. That was because he did. He was well over six feet, and his sheepskin jacket made him look ever bigger as his broad shoulders nearly filled the doorway. There was a brooding look in his ebony eyes that made him look intimidating.

It didn't work on her.

She was Preston Saunders's daughter. No one could intimidate like the CEO of a Fortune 500 company. Though there was no doubt that Jarrett McKane could give good old Preston a run for the title. Intimidator.

She released a breath and put on a smile. "Mr. McKane. It's good of you to come."

Jarrett turned toward her, his eyes showing some surprise and interest, and he returned a smile, showing off a row of straight white teeth. Oh boy. He was going to try to charm her.

"Ms. Saunders?"

"That would be me."

He walked to the table, pulling off his leather gloves then he held out his hand. "It's a pleasure to meet you, Ms. Saunders. I must say I've enjoyed your colorful letters."

She tried not to react as his large hand engulfed hers. *Get down to business,* she told herself and withdrew her hand.

"Well, they seem to have worked. You're here." She motioned to the chair across from her. "Please have a seat and we can begin."

Jarrett McKane didn't like this woman having the upper hand. Well, it wasn't going to last long. He eyed the pretty, long-haired brunette. Even tied back into a ponytail, those curls seemed to have a mind of their own. Her eyes caught his attention right off, a dark, smoky blue. She looked to be in her mid-twenties. He hated trying to guess women's ages, but he knew she was old enough.

He slipped off his jacket and she watched with interest. He liked that. Maybe this would be easier than he thought.

Mia Saunders glanced down at the paper in front of her. "As I stated in my letters, Mr. McKane, there are several apartments that need your immediate attention. The bathrooms in several of the units aren't working properly, and many of the heaters aren't functioning at all. They're outdated and possibly dangerous." She looked up. "The conditions here are becoming unlivable, Mr. McKane." She slid the list across the table to him. "We need you to fix these items immediately."

Jarrett read over the itemized page. He already knew it

would cost him a fortune. "And the previous owner should have taken care of these problems."

"Since you are the current owner, Mr. McKane, it's your responsibility now."

He glared at her.

She ignored it. "I'm sure you bought this property at a reduced price, and a good businessman would know the condition of the place. And since you are the owner now, we're asking that you please address these problems."

Jarrett glanced around at the group. He hadn't expected to find this when he arrived, especially not mainly senior citizens. He pushed away any sentimentality. "I can't fix these problems."

"Can't or won't?" she retorted.

"I don't see how that matters."

"It does to us, Mr. McKane."

"Okay, for one thing, I haven't received any rent payment since I took over the property."

"And you won't until we see some good faith from you. Some of these people don't have hot water or heat. Winter is here."

"Then relocating you all is the only answer." He stood. "Because in a few months, I'll be tearing the place down."

The group gasped, but Mia Saunders still looked calm and controlled as she said, "I don't think so, Mr. McKane."

Jarrett was surprised by her assertiveness. He wasn't used to that, especially not from a woman. No that wasn't true, his sister-in-law, Kira, gave him "what for" all the time.

Ms. Saunders held up another piece of paper. "We all have leases giving us six months to relocate. When you bought the building, your lawyer should have told you about it. Unless you didn't use an attorney."

Dammit, he didn't have an answer to that.

"And you still have to honor our leases."

He shook his head. "Can't do it. I want to start demolition by the first of the new year. And I'm sure the town council will go along with me since this is the site for a new computer-chip plant. It's estimated to bring over a hundred jobs to this town." He saw the panicked looks on the tenant's faces and added, "And I'll help anyone who wants to be relocated, but I can't let you stay here for six months." Finished, he headed toward the door.

"You might not have a choice," Mia called to him.

He turned around, perversely enjoying the exchange. He liked the fire in her pretty eyes, the set of her jaw. He wondered if he could find a way to sway her loyalty. A little dinner and maybe some romancing might help his cause. "I don't think you can win this fight, Ms. Saunders. But I'm willing to discuss it with you, another time."

She rose from her chair and that was when he noticed her rounded belly. Pregnant? Damn, she's pregnant.

Mia Saunders seemed to enjoy the surprise. "You can count on it, when we see you in court."

Thirty minutes later, Jarrett was still thinking about the attractive Mia Saunders as he drove his Range Rover down the highway. He shook his head. What the hell was he doing fantasizing about a pregnant woman? A woman carrying another man's baby.

He turned off onto the road leading toward the McKane ranch. After selling off his part of the family cattle ranch, he hadn't called in here much to start with. He and his half brother, Trace, hadn't gotten along while they were growing up, but the past few years that had slowly begun to change.

Maybe he was getting soft. Of course, his brother's wife, Kira, had a lot to do with it.

Now, he was an uncle and he was crazy about his niece, Jenna. She could ask him to walk over hot coals, and he'd do it, smiling. At three years old, the toddler had his number.

He parked around the back of the house. They hadn't always been a happy family: he recalled just a while back when Trace and Kira were barely surviving a crumbling marriage. Kira's problems getting pregnant had put a strain on them that had nearly ended their five-year relationship. Then a miracle had happened, and now they had Jenna.

Climbing the back steps to the century-old ranch house, Jarrett's attention turned to another pregnant woman, Mia Saunders. It was true what they said about expectant mothers, they did have a glow about them. And unless he had been mistaken, she'd directed that rosy glow toward him.

He knocked on the door and walked in. "Everyone decent?" He peered into the kitchen, knowing he'd be welcome. That hadn't always been true. There was a time he'd tried everything to one-up his younger brother. In their youth, he had wanted nothing to do with the ranch, or with the half brother who'd gotten all the attention. So, after their father died, Jarrett had accepted his share in dollars.

It had taken them years to work out their differences. And with the help of Kira and a sweet little girl named Jenna they'd worked through a lot of their problems, mainly just trying to be brothers.

Kira stood at the stove. "We have a three-year-old. There isn't any time to get indecent." His sister-in-law smiled as she came to him and gave him a kiss on the cheek. "Hi, Jarrett. It's good to see you."

"Hi, sis," he said, returning the hug. He'd used to have

trouble with her being so demonstrative, but she said they were family, and that was how family acted.

Jarrett heard a squeal and little Jenna came charging into the room.

"Unca Jay. Unca Jay," the girl called.

Jarrett caught her up in his arms, swung her around, kissing her cheeks and blowing raspberries. "How's my Jenna girl today?"

The child's tiny mouth formed a pout. "Mommy put me in time-out. I was sad."

Kira arrived on the scene, brushing back her long blond hair. "Tell Uncle Jarrett what you did."

"I got into Mommy's makeup."

Suddenly, Jarrett could see the faint remnants of lipstick on her mouth. "Uh-oh."

"I just want to be pretty, like Mommy." She turned those big brown eyes on him. "Are you mad at me, too?"

"Never." He kissed her. "But you're already pretty, you don't need makeup." He glanced at Kira. "But remember you don't like anyone getting into your stuff, so you shouldn't get into other people's things."

"'Kay." She looked at her mom. "Can I play now? I promise to be good."

Kira nodded, and they watched the child run out of the room. She turned to Jarrett. "Thanks for backing me up."

He nodded. "I don't know how you ever punish her. It would tear me up."

"It part of being a parent."

"That's a job I don't want."

Kira smiled. "You just haven't found the right woman."

He arched an eyebrow. "I've found a lot of women and I like it that way. There's safety in numbers." He winked at her. "Among other things."

She shook her head. "Like I said, you haven't found the right woman."

"But I found mine."

They both looked toward the door to see Trace. His brother went straight to his wife and kissed her. Jarrett hated the envy that engulfed him. To his surprise, his thoughts turned to Mia Saunders again. Well, damn.

"Hi, bro," Jarrett greeted him. "How's the cattle business?"

"If you came out here more, you'd know for yourself."

"If I came out here more, you'd put me to work. You know how I feel about ranching. I'm doing just fine the way things are."

"I take it you're still trying to get by on your looks and your wit. So what brings you out here?"

Jarrett shrugged. "Do I need a reason?"

Trace hugged his wife close. "Of course not. Stay for supper."

Jarrett smiled. "Don't mind if I do." Whatever had happened during their childhood didn't seem to mean much anymore. It had taken years, but Jarrett had finally realized that Trace wasn't competing with him. After they'd found natural gas on McKane land a few years ago, they'd worked together and ensured a prosperous future for them all.

They also found they could be friends.

Kira went to check on Jenna while Trace poured two mugs of coffee. He handed one to Jarrett and the brothers sat down at the large farm kitchen table.

"So, I hear you bought the old apartment buildings on Maple."

Jarrett frowned. He'd been trying to keep the project quiet. "Where did you hear that?"

"It's a small town. There aren't many secrets."

Kira returned. "We heard it at church last Sunday. One

of your tenants, her brother used to be our pastor. Reverend Brad Saunders." She shook her head. "It was such a tragedy about their deaths."

"I don't go to church. What happened to them?"

"A few months ago Brad and his wife, Karen, went on a missionary trip and their small plane crashed in Mexico. Poor Mia."

"What about her husband?

Kira raised an eyebrow. "Mia doesn't have a husband."

Interest sparked in Jarrett, catching him off guard. "Surely the guy responsible for the baby will step up."

Kira exchanged a glance with Trace. "There is no guy to step up. It's not Mia's baby."

CHAPTER TWO

JARRETT stared at his sister-in-law. "Okay, it's been a few years since Biology 101, but I would remember something like this."

"Mia is a surrogate," she explained. "Or maybe I should say she was."

"There's definitely still a baby," he added, recalling the generous curve of her stomach.

"But no parents."

"So what's the story?"

Kira gave her husband a quick glance. "It wasn't exactly public knowledge, but Mia is carrying her brother and sister-in-law's baby."

"The hell you say!"

Suddenly Jenna came running into the kitchen. "Unca Jay, you said a bad word."

Jarrett ignored Trace's disapproving stare. "I'm sorry, sweetie," he told her. "I'll try to be better."

"You got to give me a nickel for the jar." The child held out her tiny hand and smiled. "Pay me."

The little thief. With a smile he dug into his pocket. "Here's a quarter."

"Jenna, go wash up for supper," her mother said.

"Okay, Mommy." She smiled and went and hugged Trace. "Hi, Daddy."

While father and daughter exchanged pleasantries Jarrett tried to wrap his head around this news.

Once the child left, Jarrett turned back to Kira. "Was Mia Saunders going to give the reverend and his wife her baby?"

Kira shook her head. "No, she's been carrying Brad and Karen's baby all along. Surely you've heard of a fertilized embryo being implanted in another woman and she carries the baby when the biological mother can't. In this case, Mia was doing this for her brother and his wife."

Kira got up from the table, went to the oven and checked the roast, then she returned to the table. "But now everything has changed with Brad and Karen's death. Mia will not only be giving birth to her niece or nephew in about six weeks, but now she'll be raising the baby, too."

In the past, Jarrett had always run as far as possible from romantic entanglements. He didn't do relationships beyond a few months, no matter how beautiful or intriguing the woman. It would mean he'd have to put his feelings on the line, to be vulnerable—something he'd avoided since he'd been a kid when his mother had died. Still grieving, he'd soon learned that his father's new wife didn't want to deal with someone else's kid.

He'd concluded a long time ago he wasn't cut out to be a family man.

Yet, this woman caused him to pause. Why was he even giving her a second thought?

A woman with a baby?

He recalled the scene from earlier that day in the community room filled with all those elderly tenants and how Mia Saunders had led the pack. Those amazing blue eyes had dared him to challenge her demands. She'd tried to act tough, but he could see her nervousness.

"Does she have any other family?"

Kira shook her head. "From what I heard there was only her brother. Since her brother was a pastor, Brad and Karen didn't exactly have a fat bank account. Mia had been going to law school, but she had to drop out after the accident. I know she does Web design because she works from home, which is important now with the baby coming. The church is helping as much as possible."

And he was about to throw her out of her home. "When is the kid due?"

"Would you believe Christmas day?" Kira smiled. "I feel that's a good omen. I believe there's a miracle out there for her."

Jarrett hoped it happened before the New Year.

"They have the best food around," Jarrett told Neil Fulton the next afternoon at lunch. "Prime Cut's Barbecue is outstanding. It's all local beef, too. Some of it comes from my brother's ranch."

The fifty-five-year-old business executive looked as if he'd spent a lot of time behind a desk. His skin was pale and his hair thinning. "You own part of that, too?"

"No, I got out of ranching a long time ago." Jarrett hadn't liked all the hard work or a father who drove him to do more than a kid should have to do. For what? To wait out another drought, low cattle prices or a freezing winter without going bankrupt. And you're still poor. He liked the finer things in life, and he'd found a way to get them.

"But my brother is good at what he does. I guarantee you'll love the beef."

"Maybe another time, I usually eat a lighter lunch." Neil looked over his half-glasses at Jarrett. "My wife insists on it."

Jarrett would do everything he could to move this deal along. With the slow economy, he needed to make sure this sale didn't fall through. If only he could find a place for the Mountain View tenants, life would be perfect.

"Why not have the best of both worlds?" he said. "If you lived around here, you could enjoy hearty meals, because there's plenty of hiking and skiing around to keep you in shape. And there's a great gym where you can work out."

Neil smiled. "You've kept in shape well enough since you left football. How do you do it?"

Jarrett couldn't believe people still remembered his college career. But he'd use it if it helped seal the deal with Fulton Industries.

"I have a home gym," he explained. You and your wife will have to come by and I'll show you. It's Robin, isn't it?"

Fulton nodded, then returned to scanning the menu.

"I also want to show you both some houses in the area. There are several estates with horse property. Riding is another great way to keep in shape."

Neil raised a hand. "First, I need to put all my energy into building this plant. Robin will stay in Chicago until we can get things moving along. From past experience, once my wife gets going on a new house, she'll throw herself into decorating it."

"Well, when that happens I'll have one of my top agents help her find the perfect house."

Neil frowned. "You don't know Robin. She's hard to please."

Jarrett bet he could handle her. "Then I'll work with her personally."

Neil laughed. "You may live to regret that offer."

Before Jarrett could respond, a young man approached the table. "Excuse me, sir, are you Jarrett McKane?"

"Yes, I am."

The guy pulled out a manila envelope from inside

his jacket. "This is for you." He smiled. "You've been served."

Jarrett felt his face heat with anger. Then he glanced across the restaurant as the man stopped at a table. He sat down beside a dark-haired woman. Mia Saunders.

"Is there a problem, Jarrett?" Neil asked.

"No. Just a minor disagreement with a client."

Mia raised a hand and waved.

"This doesn't have anything to do with our project, does it?"

Jarrett nodded at Mia. "Like I said it's a minor problem. Nothing I can't handle."

The following morning, Mia drove to her doctor's appointment in Grand Junction, about forty miles away. The roads were clear so far, and she only hoped that northwest Colorado's winter weather would hold off for another month.

Since she was in her last trimester, she had to travel there regularly. Not a problem; she liked her doctor, Lauren Drake. In her forties, the attractive fertility specialist had been there for her from the beginning of the surrogacy. She'd also supported Mia through Brad and Karen's horrible accident and death.

"How have you been feeling?"

"Great," Mia said. "Except the baby is pretty active. He or she is kicking all the time."

The attractive blonde was tall and slender and happily married to her college sweetheart. Mia should hate her for her perfect life, but Lauren was too nice to hate. She had become a good friend. And Mia needed as many friends as she could get.

"I know the pregnancy is going well, but I'm worried about you, Mia. Your life has been turned upside down in the past few months. And now, you aren't even sure about a place to live."

"So what else is new?" Sadness crept in. She missed her brother desperately. He'd been her rock for most of her life. Even with Brad's help, it had taken her years to get her act together. Now, she felt on the verge of falling apart. What kind of mother would that make her? Not a good one.

"I know you've had to deal with a lot," the doctor said. "You only planned to be the aunt to this baby. Now, you're going to be the mother, unless you've changed your mind on that."

Mia shook her head. Well before Brad and Karen had moved ahead with the surrogacy, everyone had agreed that if something ever happened to them, Mia would raise the child. Yet, no one had ever imagined the loss of both parents even before the baby arrived.

"It's a big responsibility, Mia. Even when there's a father in the picture."

Mia added, "A single mother with no money and no apparent means of income isn't the best candidate."

"Don't say that."

Mia hadn't hidden anything from the doctor before the procedure began. Dr. Drake knew about everything in her past.

"There are agencies around to help, too."

Mia shook her head. She had some money set aside. And Brad and Karen had some left-over insurance money. "I just want a job."

"I'd prefer you didn't take any more on your plate right now."

Mia fought her panic. "Is there something wrong?"

Lauren shook her head. "Just watching your blood pressure. It's a little high, but no worries right now." She quickly changed the subject. "Have you picked out any names?"

"No, I haven't thought about it." She had some personal things of Karen's, a baby book that might give her a clue and a letter from her sister-in-law that Mia wasn't supposed to open until the birth of the baby.

"Well, do it. And stop trying to take on everyone's problems. Think about yourself for a change. You won't get the chance after the baby comes."

Mia knew she couldn't walk away from her neighbors. Not now. They'd been so good to her. "We're just trying to stay in our homes for a little while longer. We're going to court next week, and we're hoping the judge will rule in our favor."

Having a place to live was her main concern right now. She couldn't be homeless again. Not with a baby.

A week later, Jarrett walked into the courtroom. What he didn't expect to see were several of the tenants there, too. Of course, leading the pack was Mia Saunders.

She looked professional in her dark skirt and a long wine-colored sweater draped over her rounded stomach. Her rich brown hair was pulled back from her oval face and clipped at the base of her neck. She didn't wear makeup. She didn't try to highlight her already striking blue eyes or her rosy-hued lips. She did nothing to enhance her good looks. She didn't need to.

He wasn't interested in her anyway. She had issues he didn't want to deal with. Yet it seemed he would be dealing with her whether he liked it or not. He hoped today would end any and all future meetings.

That was why he'd brought his lawyer. Matthew Holliston wasn't only his attorney but a longtime friend from high school. And he was damn good at his job.

Although, when Matt had heard that Judge Barbara Gillard was going to hear the case, he'd been worried. She had a reputation as a tough judge, and something else went against Jarrett. Years ago, he had dated Judge Gillard's sister, Amy, in high school. It hadn't ended well, so Matt had suggested that he make a generous offer to the building tenants. They had written up something to appease the judge and, they hoped, the tenants.

"Good morning, Ms. Saunders," Jarrett said.

She nodded. "Mr. McKane."

He was quickly drawn into her sparkling gaze and lost the ability to say more. That was when Matt stepped in and guided him to his seat.

The court deputy soon called their case. "The Mountain View tenants versus Jarrett McKane Properties."

"Here, your honor," Matt acknowledged. He and Jarrett went to the front of the courtroom.

"We're also here, your honor." Mia Saunders walked up with two elderly people.

Everyone waited in silence as Judge Gillard glanced over the case papers in front of her. There were also pictures and estimates for several repairs. The judge's gaze turned to Jarrett. "How can you expect your tenants to live like this?"

Jarrett started to speak, but Matt stepped in. "Your honor, as you read in our deposition, my client only purchased the property three months ago."

The judge just looked at him, then said, "I assume, Mr. McKane, you did a walk-through of the property before purchasing it so you had to know the conditions. And if that wasn't enough, Ms. Saunders contacted you several times. So you should have, at least, begun to make some of the repairs."

"Your honor," Matt tried again. "It would be a waste of time and money. Mr. McKane will be demolishing the building so a factory can be built there—a computer-chip plant that will bring several new jobs into the area."

"Your honor," Mia Saunders interrupted. "The tenants had to sign a lease agreement when they moved in. It states that if the property is ever sold they have six months to relocate." She flashed a cold stare at Jarrett, then went on. "Even with the change of ownership, until each tenant is contacted about their eviction, they still have five months and three weeks to stay in their apartments."

Matt fought back. "Your honor, isn't six months a little excessive? A thirty-day notice is a standard agreement now."

The judge looked at the lease in her hand. "Well, this agreement *is* from 1968." She glanced over her glasses. "But no one thought to change it." She held up the photos. "I'm more concerned that many of these apartments aren't suitable to live in."

Nola stepped forward and introduced herself. "Your honor, I'm Nola Madison, one of the longtime tenants. May I speak?"

The judge nodded. "Yes, Mrs. Madison, you may."

The tiny woman made her way to the front. "Many of us have lived at Mountain View Apartments for a long time. It's our home, and like all of us, it's getting old. With a little work and some minor repairs, we can live comfortably for the winter. Please don't ask us to leave yet."

"You know that in six months you will have to move anyway," the judge told her.

Nola glanced around to her group of friends and neighbors. "Next week is Thanksgiving, your honor. For years a lot of us have spent it together. Christmas, too. If this is our last year, I really would like to be with my friends. My family. And we need the time to find affordable places to live and to save the extra money to move. So staying until March would be helpful."

Seeing the judge blink several times, Jarrett knew he was in big trouble.

"Your honor," Matt tried again. "This is not a good situation, but there is an important business deal pending here. A factory is to be built on this site. A factory that will bring jobs into our community."

The judge straightened. "From which your client will benefit nicely, I'm sure. While these people will lose their homes." She glared daggers toward Jarrett. "Mr. McKane, you knew the conditions of the lease, and you also knew the deplorable condition of the building when you made the purchase."

He didn't agree or disagree. "What I had planned was to help the tenants relocate," he replied.

The judge wasn't buying it. "Seems to me if you'd been sincere you would have answered their letters three months ago," she observed. "Now you're throwing them out of their homes as though nothing matters as long as you make a profit. Well, it's not always about profit, Mr. McKane. My ruling is that you make the necessary repairs to bring the building up to code. I'll waive the fine as long as you begin immediately."

Jarrett bit the inside of his mouth. "Yes, your honor."

"Don't think that's all there is, Mr. McKane. You're to make all repairs so the place is livable." Judge Gillard paused and looked at Mia Saunders. "Is there a vacant apartment?"

Mia nodded. "Yes, your honor, but the apartment is unlivable."

The judge nodded. "Good. What's the number?"

"Two-oh-three-B."

"Jarrett McKane, I order you to move into apartment

203B at Mountain View complex until all repairs are completed. No eviction until March first. Although, I do want to see you back here after the holidays to learn about your progress." She hit the gavel on the block. The sound echoed around the courtroom. "Court adjourned."

"Judge, this is highly irregular," Matt called, but she had already exited the courtroom.

That left Jarrett thinking about everything he was about to lose. No, he couldn't lose this. He'd fix this, like he'd fixed everything all his life. He'd figure out a way to get what he wanted. He always did.

The next day, Jarrett and Matt parked in front of the Mountain View Apartments. "You can't bend any of the rules, Jarrett," Matt told him. "You have to sleep here every night, eat here and even work here. You can only go to your home to get more clothes and food, that's all, or the judge could toss you in jail. You know she means business when she instructed me to escort you here personally."

"Dammit, Matt, you'd better get me out of this mess. If Fulton finds out, he'll walk away from the deal."

"Well, unless he'll wait until April, you're in big trouble. The only alternative you have is talking them into moving out."

Jarrett was frustrated. Thanks to Mia Saunders, he had to figure out something. But honestly there weren't many options since housing was limited in Winchester Ridge.

He looked toward the yellow-and-brown structure with the peeling paint and sagging rain gutters. It seemed even worse with winter-bare trees, but the grass was cut and the hedges trimmed.

"In its day, the place was probably a showcase," Matt observed.

"Well, it's not 1960," he told his friend. "And I'm only

going to do the minimum that needs to be done. It's a waste of time and money."

Jarrett looked out the Mercedes' windshield to see someone coming toward them. It was the older woman, Mrs. Madison. He pressed the button so the window went down.

"Hello, Mr. McKane." She slowly made her way to the car. "I'm not sure if you remember me, I'm Nola Madison."

He got out of the car. "Were you checking up to see if I was coming?"

She smiled despite his rudeness. "As a matter of fact, we were watching for you, but only to warn you about what to expect in your apartment." She shook her head. "It was once the manager's, but he didn't take very good care of it. We tried the best we could to clean it up." She held out a key dangling from a heart keychain. "But I'm afraid it needs more work than any of our places."

Feeling like a heel, Jarrett took the key from her, and pulled his jacket together against the cold. "You shouldn't be out in this weather, Mrs. Madison."

"Please, call me Nola. Let's go inside, but it isn't much warmer."

Jarrett grabbed his duffel bag from the back of the car, asked Matt to have his car brought over from the office, and followed the woman up the walk. They went into a bare lobby. He'd seen this area before and knew how bad it looked, but it hadn't mattered to him, since it was tagged for demolition. He headed for the elevators to find signs that read, Out of Order.

On the walk-through of the property he hadn't noticed that. "There is no elevator?"

She shook her head. "Not in the last year."

Jarrett recalled that day in the community room—two of

the tenants were in wheelchairs. "How do the handicapped get upstairs?"

She led him to the wrought-iron staircase and they started the climb. "Oh, we found two tenants who were willing to move upstairs, and Joe and Sylvia's son, Ryan, built ramps for both Margie and Harold. Now they can get in and out or their apartments. It's important to be independent."

"Who exchanged apartments?"

"Well, Mia was one who moved upstairs, and when her brother, Reverend Brad, was alive he used to help us with a lot of repairs. Many of his congregation did, too."

"Where was the owner? Some of these repairs are required by law."

She shook her head. "He threatened to double our rent if we kept complaining. So we started fixing things ourselves." They made it to the second floor. "But some things we can't fix. We need an expert."

Once again he was confronted with dingy walls and worn carpet. They passed a few doors, then she stopped in front of his apartment. He paused. Hell, he was afraid to go inside.

Suddenly the door across the hall opened and Mia Saunders stepped out. She actually smiled at him and he felt a strange tightness in his chest. "Moving in, Mr. McKane?"

She was dressed in a long blue sweater that went to midthigh, with a pair of black leggings covering those long legs. He looked back at her face. "Seems I am. Looks like we're going to be neighbors."

"Isn't that nice," Nola said, then glanced at her watch. "Oh, my, I just remembered I have a doctor's appointment. I don't know where my head is today. Mia, could you show Mr. McKane around?"

Mia frowned. "Do you need a ride, Nola?"

"No, thank you, dear, my daughter is coming by." With a wave, the older woman walked off.

Mia didn't like Nola's not-so-subtle disappearing act. Why did anyone need to show Jarrett McKane around?

She walked to the apartment entrance. "Brace yourself." She swung open the door, reached in and flicked on the lights, then motioned for him to go inside first. He frowned and stepped into the main room. She heard his curse and couldn't help but smile as she followed him in.

The apartment walls needed paint, but not before numerous holes in the plaster were patched. Under the slipcovers that Nola and her welcoming committee had recently put on, the furniture was thrift-store rejects.

"Joe cleaned the carpet, or what's left of it. It's probably the original. At least the place doesn't smell as if someone died in here anymore."

Without comment, he continued down the hall and peered into the bath. Again another curse.

She called after him. "It might not look very good, but I can guarantee you Nola and Sylvia cleaned it within an inch of its life. And there are fresh towels. And they made up the bed for you, too." Then she murmured to herself, "Why they're being so nice to you, I have no idea."

The good-looking Jarrett McKane came out and stood in front of her. His dark hair had been cut and styled recently. His clothes were top-of-the-line, too. Everything about him rang out success and power. So why was she even noticing him?

Hormones, she concluded. It was just late-pregnancy hormones. She'd learned a long time ago to stay away from men like him.

"Why did they do all this?" he finally asked.

Jarrett McKane was standing too close, but she refused to step back. She refused to let him intimidate her.

"It's their way of being neighborly," she told him. "It's the same with everyone here. Over the years, they've all become a family. Some are alone. Some have family that didn't have time for them so they take care of each other."

"Or it's their way to get me to not tear the place down."

She smiled, not wanting him to see her anger. "It's just some towels and linens and a few home-cooked meals. But yes, they feel it's worth a try. Enjoy your stay." She turned and started to leave when he called her name.

When she turned around, he gave her a sexy grin. "Did you do anything to sway me, Ms. Saunders?"

Her heart began to pound in her chest. "There might be a plate of oatmeal raisin cookies on the kitchen counter."

"I'm looking forward to seeing how far you'll go to persuade me."

Mia arched her aching back, causing her stomach to be front and center. "I'm afraid cookies are as far as I'm willing to go."

CHAPTER THREE

MIA couldn't get out of there fast enough.

She stepped inside her apartment and closed the door. She didn't want Jarrett McKane in her life, or in her space. And he was suddenly in both.

A long time ago, she'd learned about men who thrived on control. Her father was one of those. It had taken her years to get out from under his reign and finally to be free of him.

She walked across her cozy living area. A secondhand sofa and chair faced the small television. A triangular rug hid a lot of the worn carpet underneath. A small table off the galley kitchen was used for eating and for working on her computer.

Her laptop was the only thing of value that she had and the only means she had these days of make a living. Despite her privileged upbringing, she'd never been materialistic. Maybe that was the reason it had been so easy to walk away, or in her case, run away.

To Preston and Abigail Saunders their daughter had always been a problem, a disappointment from the start. An overweight child, Mia had morphed into a rebellious teenager. She had never fitted into her Boston society family. So, once she was of age, she'd just disappeared from their lives.

Even Brad had eventually bucked their father's plans for him. Instead, her older brother had became an ordained minister and had ended up disowned, too.

Now she'd lost her only family. She caressed her stomach, feeling the gentle movement of the baby. At least she'd have a part of Brad and Karen and she vowed to love and protect this child. So she wasn't about to let her parents know where she was. Or let them find this baby.

Mia sat down in the chair, still in awe of the life she carried inside her. Onetime wild child, Margaret Iris Ashley Saunders was going to have a baby. She blew out a breath. She was going to be a mother and D-day was approaching soon. There were so many things she had to get done before Christmas.

She closed her eyes. For months, she'd had to push aside all the feelings she was having for this baby. A mother's feelings. The only thing that had saved her was knowing this child would always be in her life. Brad and Karen would have been the perfect parents and she could be the favorite aunt who spoiled the child.

Now, Mia had to step up and be a parent to this baby. She wasn't sure she was cut out to do it.

That afternoon, with the help of his office staff, Jarrett had made several phone calls. He'd finally found someone to start on the repairs. A local furnace repairman was to come out. He'd also contacted the handyman who serviced some of his other properties to help out with some of the minor fixes.

Flipping his phone shut, he decided to wait downstairs and get out of his depressing apartment for a while. In the hall, the door across from his opened and Mia walked out carrying a large trash bag. She stiffened the second she saw him.

He smiled. "Hello, Mia."

She nodded stiffly. "Mr. McKane."

She was dressed in her standard black pants and over-size blouse, but with an added long sweater for warmth.

"I don't see why we can't be on a first-name basis since we're going to be neighbors."

"You're the man who's evicting us. Why would I get friendly with the enemy?"

He took the bag from her. "It doesn't seem to bother the others." He gave her a sideways glance. "Someone must have really have done a number on you."

She glanced away. "Now you're a psychiatrist?"

"No, just observant."

"Well, observe somewhere else. Thanks to you, I have a lot on my mind."

He wasn't crazy about having to move her in her condition. "I'm not your enemy, Mia. I'm trying to find all of you places to live."

"We can't afford most of the other places."

Was that his fault? "The rent here is well below average for this area. Even if I kept the place and did all the repairs, I'd have to raise the rent."

"Well, you can't yet. Some of us are barely getting any heat or hot water."

"I'm taking care of that."

"I can't tell you how many times we heard that from the last owner."

"The last owner hadn't been court-ordered," Jarrett said. He slowed his pace so she could keep up. He knew little or nothing about pregnant women. Only that Kira had had a rough time with her pregnancy and had had to stay in bed the last few months.

"That's where I'm going now," he continued, "to meet with a furnace guy."

She stopped. "You mean we could have some heat today?"

He shrugged. "I'm paying him extra to start right away."

They continued their way down the stairs to the main lobby. "I would like to ask a favor," he said.

She paused with a glare.

He hid a smile as he raised a hand. "Good Lord, woman, do you mistrust everyone? I only want you to help get everyone together so we see who has the worst problems and fix them first."

"Then come to the community room. It's where a lot of the tenants hang out because it has a working heater."

They stepped outside into the frigid weather. He first tossed the sack into the Dumpster, and then they continued on to the center.

"I hear your baby is due on Christmas day."

She gave him a sideways glance. "Who told you that?"

"My sister-in-law, Kira McKane. You both go to the same church."

She seemed relieved. "How does she feel about you tossing us out of here?"

"I haven't tossed out anyone, and according to the judge, I won't be able to until the spring." Not with Barbara Gillard watching him anyway. If only he could come up with a way to convince everyone to leave a few months earlier.

His only other chance was to get Fulton to hold off on the takeover date. They couldn't begin construction until the ground thawed. But he wouldn't get his money either.

He'd put a lot into this project, buying up the surrounding land, including this place. He had too much to lose.

And it would cost him even more every day Mountain View Apartments stayed open. And now he was being held prisoner here.

While Jarrett went to the community room, Mia knocked on Joe's door and asked him and Sylvia to gather the other tenants and bring them to the community room.

Sending the others on ahead, Mia then went to Nola's place and they walked over together. "We need to make sure you have enough heat, Mia," Nola said. "For you and the baby."

They went through the door of the community room to see a dozen or so tenants already there. "I'm fine for now," Mia answered. Her apartment wasn't too bad. "I wouldn't mind a new faucet for the sink, though. It came off last week."

"You should have told Joe."

"I wasn't going to complain when there are apartments with bigger problems."

Nola gave her a tender look. "You and the baby are a priority."

Mia smiled. Everyone here had rallied around her like overprotective grandparents since they'd heard the tragic news. "He's not even here yet."

"It's a boy?" Joe said, walking over to them.

"I don't know," she insisted. "So you haven't won the baby pool yet."

The older man grinned. "It's a boy all right. He's going to be born at 12:05 on the twenty-fifth of December."

Mia looked up to see Jarrett walk in, followed by a middle-aged man with Nichols Heating and Air printed across his shirt pocket.

"Good, most of you are here," Jarrett began. "This is Harry Nichols. He's here to look at the heating units."

Several of the tenants were already on their feet to greet the repairman. Once the niceties were over, the tenants commandeered Harry and went to start the work.

With everyone gone, Jarrett walked over to where Mia sat at the table. "That seemed to please them."

She studied her new landlord. He was sure proud of himself. "Why not? It's been a while since they've had reliable heat. You'll probably be rewarded with some more baked goods."

Jarrett took a seat next to her, filling the space with his large frame. She inhaled a faint scent of his aftershave.

"I had no idea the extent of the last owner's neglect. I thought it was mostly cosmetic. Now, I'm paying a lot for the repairs."

Mia eyed his expensive clothes, leather jacket and cowboy boots. She'd seen his top-of-the-line Range Rover parked out front. "I doubt you'll starve, Mr. McKane. Besides, this isn't your only property in town."

He arched an eyebrow. "The last I heard, it's not against the law to make a living."

"No. Not unless the properties have been neglected like this one."

He looked at her with those dark, piercing eyes. "In the first place, I wasn't the one who allowed this property to fall apart. Secondly, most of my other holdings are commercial buildings. I've spent a lot of money renovating run-down properties. You can't ask for top rent without a quality product."

Why couldn't he do the same here? "Have you ever considered putting money into this place? You have a whole other section that's vacant. That's twenty-four units that are empty." She shrugged. "Like you said yourself, this town doesn't have enough rental properties. With some remodeling you could sell them as townhomes."

He studied her for a while. "Sounds like you've put some thought into this."

"When we heard that the owner was selling, the tenants tried to buy the complex themselves. They didn't have enough money, or the expertise to do the repairs."

"I doubt if anyone can keep up with the repairs of this old place. No one would want to sink the time and effort into it, without knowing if they could recoup their money. The real estate market has been unpredictable."

He sounded like her father. "Does it always have to be about money?"

He arched an eyebrow. "It does or I go broke."

She'd been both, and she was definitely happier like this. "I can't believe you'd lose everything. You still have family and a home. You might lose a little money, but you'll survive. A lot of these people won't. They can't afford to move and pay double the rent elsewhere."

He frowned. "What are you going to do when the lease is up?"

She blinked, fighting her anger. "Is your conscience suddenly bothering you about evicting a single mother?"

He straightened. "I'm not happy about evicting anyone. But I don't have a choice. This deal has been in the works for months."

"Like I said, it's all about the almighty dollar."

"What about the jobs this factory will create for the town? The economy isn't that great to turn this opportunity away."

"Does a factory have to be built on land that drives people from their homes?"

"I will find them other places to live. I'm not that cruel— I won't put seniors and single mothers out on the street."

"Well, you can stop worrying about me. I don't want your charity."

"Fine. Let's see where your stubbornness gets you."

"I've been able to take care of myself so far."

"Then feel free to continue." He stood and started to leave.

She tried not to let him see her fear. She raised her chin. "I will."

Suddenly she felt her stomach tighten and she automatically covered it with her hands.

He must have seen it, too. "Are you okay?"

She nodded as she moved her hand over her belly and rubbed it, but it didn't help. Then her back began to hurt, too. She tried to shift in the chair, but it didn't help.

"Mia, what's wrong?" Jarrett asked.

She shook her head. "Nothing."

He knelt down beside her chair. "The hell it's nothing."

She shook her head, looking around the empty room. There wasn't anyone else there.

His expression softened. "Mia, let me help you."

A sharp pain grabbed her around the middle. "Oh, no," she gasped and then looked at him. "I think the baby's coming."

Fifteen minutes later Jarrett pulled up at the emergency-room doors. He threw the car into Park, got out and ran around to the passenger side. He jerked open the door. Mia was taking slow measured breaths. Not good.

"Hang on, we're almost there."

She couldn't hide her worried look. "It's too early for me to go into labor. I can't lose this baby, Jarrett."

"And you won't," he promised. He had no idea what was going on, or even if the doctors could stop the contractions. "Let's get you inside and find some help." He slid his arms around her shoulders and under her legs, then lifted her into his arms.

"I'm too heavy," she said.

"Are you kidding?" He smiled, taking long strides across the parking lot. "During roundup, I used to have to hoist calves a lot heavier than you."

"You used to work on your brother's ranch?"

"Back when I played cowboy, it was our dad's place. That was a long time ago."

She studied him. "I can see you as a rancher."

His mouth twitched. "There's the big difference, darlin'. I never did," he drawled as he carried her through the automatic doors.

On the drive over, Mia had phoned her doctor and been told to go to the nearest emergency room, then she'd given Nola a quick call so her friends wouldn't worry if they noticed she was gone.

Winchester Ridge Medical Center was the closest. Once inside, they were met by a nurse who led them into an exam room. Jarrett set Mia down on the bed and stepped back out of the way. Nurses immediately took her blood pressure, asking questions about due dates and the timing of the contractions. All the while, she kept looking at him.

Jarrett tried to give her some reassurance, but he didn't know what to say.

"Excuse me," a nurse said, getting his attention. "Are you the father?"

He shook his head, but hesitated with the answer. "No." Mia didn't have any family.

"Then you'll have to leave while we examine her."

"I'll be right outside," he told Mia. "Just holler if you need me."

Jarrett stepped back behind the curtain and found a row of chairs against the wall. That was as far as he was going.

For the next few hours, Jarrett watched medical personal go in and out of Mia's cubicle.

But no one told him a thing.

Finally they moved her down the hall to a room so they could keep monitoring her. Recalling the frightened look on her face, he knew he couldn't leave her alone. So he followed her and camped outside her room.

He glanced up from the newspaper someone else had left and saw Nola.

He stood as the older woman walked toward him. "Mr. McKane." She gripped his hand with both of hers. "How is Mia?"

"I don't know any more than what I told you when I phoned. And the doctor won't tell me anything because I'm not a relative."

Nola nodded. "I know, I fibbed and said I was her grandmother so I could come back here."

He walked Nola to the sofa and sat down. "How did you get here?"

"One of the parishioners from the church," she said. "Joe can't drive at night, and Ralph doesn't have his license any more." She shook her head. "Mia always takes us places we need to go." The older woman blinked. "Oh, Mr. McKane, what if something is wrong with the baby?" Those watery hazel eyes turned to him. "She wants this baby so much."

He already knew that. He'd never felt so helpless and he hated that. "Nola, the doctors here are good and her specialist is here, too. So try not to worry." He put on a smile. "And will you do me another favor? Please call me Jarrett."

She beamed at him.

He'd broken one of his cardinal rules. Not to get personally involved when it came to business. A week ago if someone told him he'd be sitting here worried about a pregnant woman and a couple of dozen retirees, he'd have told them they were crazy.

An attractive blond woman in a white coat came down the hall toward them. "Are you waiting to hear about Mia Saunders?"

They both stood. "Yes, we are," Jarrett said. "I'm Jarrett McKane, I brought Mia in. This is Nola Madison, her... grandmother. How is she?"

The doctor smiled. "Nice to meet you both. I'm Lauren Drake, Mia's doctor. She's fine for now. We managed to stop the contractions, but I want her to stay overnight as a precaution."

"What about the baby?" Nola asked.

"The fetus is thirty-four weeks, so if Mia does go into labor, she could deliver a healthy baby. Of course the longer she carries it, the better."

"Well, we'll do everything we can to make sure of that," Nola said.

The doctor nodded. "I'm glad, because when she goes home, I want her to stay in bed for the next few weeks. She needs to avoid all stress and just rest."

No stress, Jarrett thought. *Great.* He'd dumped a truckload on her. "Is that what caused the contractions?"

"We all have to agree that a lot has happened to Mia in the past few months," the doctor echoed. "Losing her brother and sister-in-law was traumatic for her."

Nola spoke up. "We've all been trying to help her through it."

Dr. Drake nodded. "I hope that can continue, because she's going to need someone to be around more, or at least within shouting distance to check on her."

"We can be there as much as she needs us," Nola said and turned to him. "Right, Jarrett?"

Great, he was the last person Mia wanted around. "Of course. I live across the hall. I guess I could keep an eye on her."

Thanks to the medication, Mia was feeling groggy. She didn't like that. For years, she'd avoided any and all drugs. But if it kept the baby safe, she'd do whatever it took.

Closing her eyes, she wondered how she was going to manage over the next few weeks. She had deadlines to make, and she needed the money.

Stop! Worrying wasn't good for the baby. She rubbed her stomach, knowing how close she'd come to delivering early. She wasn't ready for the baby. She didn't even have any diapers and very few clothes. The baby bed wasn't set up, either. She sighed. How was she going to do everything? How could she do everything and be a good mother, too? A tear slid down her cheek.

She thought back to her childhood. She'd always messed up. How many times had her father told her that? She couldn't please him no matter how hard she tried. He'd been too busy for her, but the one way she got his attention was being bad. Until he finally gave up on her altogether. No she couldn't let Brad down. She was going to be a good mother to his baby.

Mia glanced toward the door and saw Nola and Jarrett standing there. She quickly wiped away any more tears and put on a smile.

"Hi."

Nola rushed in. "Oh, sweetheart," she cried. "How are you?" Nola hugged her.

Mia relished the feeling, the love and compassion. "I'm doing better now."

The older woman pulled back. "We were so worried about you."

Mia looked at Jarrett. "I didn't want you to worry."

Nola frowned. "Of course we'd worry. You are special to us. We love you." She fussed with the blanket, smoothing out the wrinkles. "And we're going to take good care of you. Aren't we, Jarrett?"

"Looks that way," he said, feeling awkward standing in the room.

"I can't impose on either of you."

"You're not imposing on any of us. We're happy to do it. You need someone around to help you. Jarrett and I volunteered." She clutched her hands together. "Oh, I need to go and call the others. I'll be right back."

"Here, use my phone," Jarrett said, handing it over to her. They both watched the woman walk out of the room.

Jarrett turned back to Mia. "So how do you really feel?"

"Scared, but good."

"You need to stop that. Your doctor said you need to relax and avoid stress."

"Did you tell her that you lived across the hall?"

He fought a smile, but lost. "Yes. Did you tell her that you and your friends brought me there?"

She met Jarrett's gaze. Her heart sped up and the monitor showed it. "So, I guess we're stuck with each other for a while."

CHAPTER FOUR

THE next day, Mia arrived home the same way she'd left. In Jarrett's car. He pulled into a parking spot at the front of the building. There were two heating-and-air-conditioning-repair trucks there, along with several uniformed workers.

"Looks like we'll have heat soon," she said.

Jarrett turned off the engine and glanced out the windshield. "It's just in time. There's a snowstorm coming in tonight." He looked at her. "Soon you'll be tucked into your warm bed. But be warned, Nola is heading a welcome-home committee."

"Oh, I don't want them to go to any trouble."

"I doubt they think you're any trouble. Too bad she and her group don't run this town. A lot more would get done." He climbed out of the SUV and walked around to her side.

He pulled open the door and the cold air hit her. She shivered as she tried to climb out, but he wouldn't let her.

"Remember what the doctor said? Bed rest."

"I will as soon as I get to my apartment."

"No, as soon as I get you to your apartment." He scooped her up into his arms.

"Please, you can't carry me all the way upstairs."

"Of course not. Once I get you inside, Joe's going to take over."

She made a face at him. "Very funny."

Mia refused to admit she liked being taken care of by a big, strong man whose mere presence made her aware she was a woman. The way he smelled, his rock-solid chest and arms. She bit back a groan. Hormones. It was all just hormones.

She had to think of Jarrett McKane as the man who would be kicking them all out of their homes in a few months. Nothing more.

Sylvia held open the door to the building so they could come in. "Welcome home, Mia."

She got more greetings from a group of tenants waiting in the lobby.

"Thank you everyone. It's good to be home."

"Okay, let's get you upstairs." Jarrett continued to the stairway to her apartment.

Nola was waiting there and motioned him toward the bedroom. "Bring her in here."

"No, I can stay out here on the sofa for now."

Jarrett stopped, then said, "Doctor's orders are to put you to bed." He continued through the short hallway and into her room.

Mia blinked as they entered the bedroom. It didn't look like the same room she'd left yesterday. The dingy walls had been painted a soft buttery yellow. The furniture was rearranged and her bed was adorned with a pastel-patterned quilt.

She turned around and saw the white baby bed that had been Brad and Karen's last purchase for the baby assembled. It was decorated with yellow-and-green sheets and an animal mobile hung overhead.

Tears flooded her eyes. "Oh, my."

"Do you like it?" Nola asked. We were going to give you the quilt for Christmas but since you're going to be spending so much time in bed now, we decided not to wait." The older woman pulled back the covers so Jarrett could set her down on the snowy-white sheets.

"Oh, it's beautiful." She examined the intricate work. "How could you get all this done? I've only been gone overnight."

Nola exchanged a look with Jarrett. "We knew we had to. The scare yesterday made us realize that you've been working so hard for us, you put off getting ready for the baby." She helped Mia take off her shoes and put her feet under the blanket. "So we hope this helps you to stop worrying so much." She stood back. "And when you've rested I'll show you all the baby clothes we've collected."

Nola walked to a small white dresser. "Joe found this for you. He sanded and painted it last week and Jarrett helped bring it up. Sylvia and I washed all the baby things and put them inside. If you don't like how we arranged them, you can change it."

"I'm sure it will be perfect." Mia clasped her hands together. "I don't know what to say."

"You don't have to say anything." The older woman came to the bed and hugged her. "Just take care of yourself. We love you, Mia. You're like family."

"I love you all, too."

She'd tried for a lot of years not to get too close to people, except for Brad. Starting with her parents. Whenever she'd let people in, they'd ended up hurting her. She looked across the room at Jarrett standing in the doorway. She definitely had to keep this man away.

"Tell everyone thank you."

"I will," Nola assured her. "Now, you rest and don't worry about lunch. Sylvia will be here to fix you something."

"She doesn't have to do that."

Nola raised her hand. "She wants to. We all want to help." The older woman went out the door, followed by Jarrett. Mia called him back. "Mr. McKane, could I speak to you a moment?"

Frowning, he came toward the bed as Nola left. "Suddenly I'm Mr. McKane again."

"I appreciate everything you've done for me. It's better if we don't become too friendly…given the situation."

He studied her for a moment. "The situation you are referring to is that you've already gotten to stay here until the spring." He shrugged. "But, hey, I won't bother you again."

He turned and walked out. The soft click of the front door let her know she was truly alone. She told herself it was better this way. She couldn't get any more involved with a man like Jarrett McKane. Not that she had to worry that he'd ever give her a second look.

She rubbed her stomach. All she needed to focus on right now was her baby.

Jarrett kept hearing a ringing sound. He blinked his eyes as he reached for his cell phone on the bedside table.

"Hello," he murmured, running a hand over his face. It was still dark outside.

"Oh, I'm sorry, did I wake you?"

It was Mia. He sat up. "Mia? Is there a problem?"

"No. No. I shouldn't have bothered you."

"Wait, Mia. Tell me what's wrong. Is it the baby?"

"No, the baby's fine. I just need a favor, but I'll call back later."

"I'll be right over." He hung up, grabbed a pair of jeans and put them on along with a sweatshirt. He grabbed his keys and phone and headed across the hall. He let himself into her apartment with his master key and hurried to the bedroom.

Mia was sitting on the bed, dressed in a thermal long-sleeved shirt that hugged her rounded belly and a pair of flannel pajama bottoms. Somehow she managed to look somewhere between wholesome and far too good at this time in the morning.

Was it morning? "What's the problem?"

She looked embarrassed. "I'm so sorry I woke you."

"Well, since you have, tell me what you need."

"Could you pull out the table and see if my cable is plugged in? I didn't want to move the table by myself."

"You're on the computer at this hour?"

She shrugged. "I slept so much during the day, I'm wide-awake. So I thought I'd get some work done."

Jarrett went to the bedside table and pulled it out. Seeing the loose battery cable, he knelt down and pushed it back into the outlet. "It's fixed." He moved the table back and stood next to the bed. "You're really not supposed to be working."

"I'm bored. Besides, if I don't work, I don't eat or pay my rent."

The computer screen lit up and he asked, "What are you working on?"

She kept her focus on the screen. "A Web site for a Denver-based company."

He glanced at the home-page logo. "Are you going back to law school?"

As she clicked the mouse and another program opened, she didn't show any surprise that he knew her history. "Not for a while, but I hope I can go back someday. It won't be easy with a baby."

"I'm sure everyone here would love to help you."

"We won't be living here…together," she said.

When she looked up at him with her scrubbed-clean face, large sapphire eyes and her hair in a ponytail, she looked fifteen. "How old are you?"

Mia blinked at his question. "Don't you know you're not supposed to ask a woman her age?"

He shrugged. "You look like jailbait."

"I'm twenty-nine. How old are you?"

"Thirty-seven."

She studied him for a few seconds. "You look it."

Frowning, he combed his fingers through his hair. "What's that supposed to mean?"

"What did you mean when you called me jailbait?"

"I meant it as a compliment. You look young for your age."

"Thank you." She sobered. "Are you really going to try and find us all a place to live?"

"I'm not sure I can find everyone a place, but I'll see what I can do." Was he crazy? Where would he find affordable apartments for them all? He moved away from the bed. "Man, I'd kill for a cup of coffee."

"Sorry, I'm off caffeine for a while," she told him. "But I'd fight you for a jelly donut."

"I guess that's one of those crazy cravings, huh? Well, I'd better go." He walked out, thinking a donut didn't sound so bad.

He retrieved his car keys and a jacket from his apartment and headed down to his car. The ground was covered in a dusting of snow. He climbed into his vehicle, missing the warm garage back at his house. Pushing aside his discomfort, he started the engine and the heater. He was on a quest for one hungry pregnant woman.

In every town there always seemed to be a twenty-four-hour donut and coffee shop and Winchester Ridge was no exception. He picked out a couple of dozen assorted donuts along with a large coffee and an orange juice.

He returned to the apartment building just as dawn was breaking. Funny, this wasn't how he usually spent early mornings. He'd never shared breakfast with an expectant mother, either. With his offerings in hand, he returned to Mia's apartment and gave a loud knock before he walked in.

"It's me, Ms. Saunders. I've got something for you." After hearing Mia's greeting he walked into the bedroom.

She was still working on the computer. "I thought you went back to bed."

"Not after you talked about donuts." He raised the box. "Freshly made." He opened the large box and the aroma filled the room.

Mia groaned. "Oh, my God." She put the laptop aside and reached for one. He pulled back.

"I thought you were going to fight me for one."

She looked confused.

"Of course, if we were on a first-name basis, I'd happily share. Especially if someone had been willing to get up before dawn and help out a neighbor."

Mia was embarrassed by her actions. Yesterday after Jarrett had left, Nola had returned and told her how he'd stayed at the hospital and called everyone with any news. She was even more ashamed when she learned that he'd bought the paint for her bedroom.

"It does seem to be one-sided, doesn't it? I apologize. You have helped me so much. I don't know how I would have made it to the hospital without you."

"Did I say I minded helping you? I just don't want to keep being treated like the enemy here. I can't change things that happened in the past."

"I know. I'm sorry, Jarrett."

He smiled. "What did you say?"

She sighed. He wasn't going to make this easy. "Would you be my friend, Jarrett?"

"You just want my donuts."

She nodded. "And you'd be wise not to get between a pregnant woman and those donuts."

He put the box down and her mouth watered as she eyed the selections. "There are so many to choose from." She rubbed her stomach, feeling the baby kicking her.

He sat at the end of the bed. "Are you all right?" he asked as he nodded to her stomach.

"Yeah, he's just active and hungry."

"Does he move around like that all the time?"

"Well, the baby's bigger now, so I feel it more."

He handed her juice. "Here's something to wash down your donut."

"Thank you." She motioned to the box. "Aren't you going to have one, too?"

"Sure, but ladies first."

"Wise choice." She couldn't help but smile as she bit into the jelly-filled treat. "Mmm, it's so good."

"You might not be able to have caffeine, but you're definitely getting a sugar rush."

Mia watched Jarrett finish off a glazed donut in record time. He looked good even with his finger-combed hair and wrinkled clothes. There were just some men who couldn't look bad. He was one of them.

"I should let you rest." He stood, but his gaze never left hers. "Is there anything you need me to do before I go?"

She hesitated to ask him anything else.

"Come on, Mia. What is it?"

"I can wait for Nola."

"What for?"

"I need to take a shower, but the doctor said someone

should be close by." She waved her hand. "Don't worry about it, Nola's coming in a few hours."

He swallowed. "How close by?"

"Just in the apartment. In case something happens there'll be someone to help me."

He stood there for what seemed like forever, and then he said, "Sure, what are friends for?"

Once Jarrett heard the shower go on, he took out his cell phone and began to check his messages. He had to get some things done today. One was to stop by the office for a few hours and check in with his agents.

Over the last couple of days, between the repairs here and keeping watch on one pregnant lady, he'd neglected his other business.

He was surprised at the next message. It was from Carrie Johnston. He smiled. The pretty blonde from Glenwood Springs he'd met at the real estate conference in Denver last summer had left him another suggestive message. She wanted to see him.

Jarrett should feel a little more excited. During their time together, the two had definitely set off sparks. So why wasn't he more interested in her invitation?

When it came to women, he'd always loved having variety in his life. So why suddenly did it seem too much trouble to make the effort? Maybe thirty-seven was too old to keep playing games.

He thought about what Mia had said, *You look it.*

He wasn't *that* old. Wasn't he considered in his prime? Okay, so most men were married by now, like his younger brother. Trace had found Kira years ago. And it had been love at first sight.

Jarrett didn't believe in that. He wasn't sure he believed in love at all.

Suddenly the bathroom door opened and Mia stepped out. She was dressed in her black stretch pants and a soft-pink sweater. Her dark hair lay against her shoulders in waves. Those big blue eyes looked at him and it became difficult to breathe. Damn. What was wrong with him? This woman came with far too many complications.

"Well, since you're finished, I'll go."

"Of course." She sat down on the sofa. "I appreciate you helping me. Thank you, Jarrett."

"Just do what the doctor told you and stay in bed. He pulled out his wallet and handed her his business card. "If you need anything."

She nodded.

"I mean it. Don't be stubborn about asking for help." He found he wanted to be the one she called.

The snow had been coming down like a holiday greeting card, but by the next afternoon, Mia was getting cabin fever.

She had watched every television talk show and finished up her work on the computer, even cried over an old movie. Neighbors stopped by with offers of help. Even parishioners from her brother's church had called her. She'd taken naps off and on for the past two days and she was still exhausted and totally bored. And no Jarrett.

"You know next week is Thanksgiving." Nola's voice broke through her reverie. "And we have a problem. The oven in the community room is broken."

"You can use mine. It's a little tricky on the temperature, but we could adjust it. It's small though. Don't we usually cook three or four turkeys?"

The older woman nodded. "Remember last year we fed those people from the mission? There were nearly fifty here."

Mia thought back to last year. She'd had family then. Brad and Karen had just begun to research surrogacy as an alternative for a baby. And by Christmas, Mia had volunteered to carry her brother and his wife's child. They all were so happy, and then in a flash she had lost them both.

Tears flooded Mia's eyes and she quickly brushed them away. She looked at Nola. "I'm sorry."

Her friend sat down beside her. "There's no reason to be sorry, dear. We all miss Brad and Karen. They were wonderful people, but they left you a child. A child you get to love and raise as your own. What a special gift."

"I do know. And I love this baby, but I'm scared. What if I can't be a good mother?"

"I have no doubt you'll be a wonderful mother. You know why? Because you're a wonderful person and this little boy or girl will be blessed to have you."

"Oh, Nola. I hope you're right."

"I am. You know what else? We're all going to be around to help you."

She cleared her throat. "I'm so glad because I'm going to need you."

Nola patted her hand. "Well, count on me. Now that that is settled, where are we going to find a big enough oven to cook our Thanksgiving Day turkeys? The ones at the church are already being used, and ours barely work. Too bad Jarrett couldn't replace the one in the community center."

"I'm not going to do that," a familiar voice said, "But I may have another solution."

Jarrett hadn't meant to eavesdrop, but he'd wanted to check on Mia and had found the door partly open.

"I overheard. You're having trouble finding working ovens."

Nodding, Nola stood. "We always feed a large group on Thanksgiving. And this might be the last one that we're all together." Her eyes brightened with tears. "You said you might have a solution."

"I have two large ovens at my house."

Nola immediately smiled. "You do?"

Jarrett stole a glance at Mia. She didn't look impressed by his offer. "Yes. When I built the house I was told it would be a good selling feature. They're like new." He shrugged. "You're welcome to them."

"Oh, my, that's the answer to our prayer." The older woman paused. "There's one condition. You have to come to our Thanksgiving celebration."

In the past Jarrett been happier to stay at home and watch football. He had gone by his brother's house last year for dessert, only because little Jenna had asked him to. He had a weakness for pretty young women. He glanced at Mia. Maybe is it was time to count some blessings. "I'd be honored to come by."

CHAPTER FIVE

HE had to be crazy to have suggested cooking Thanksgiving dinner here.

Jarrett stood back and watched as half a dozen women scurried around his kitchen. He'd told himself earlier that he wasn't going to hang around, but they'd showed up at dawn, ready and eager to begin the baking and cooking.

He had to admit that the place was filled with wonderful aromas. The one disappointment was that Mia wasn't there. It was crazy of him even to think about her at all. She was pregnant, and her life was going in one direction while he needed only to think about one thing—the computer-chip-factory project. And getting out of the jail of his crummy apartment.

Nola walked over to him. "You have a wonderful kitchen, Jarrett. Every modern convenience a woman could ever want. Seems such a waste that you don't have someone to share this with."

Jarrett smiled, but ignored her comment. "I'm glad you like it."

"Just so you know, we'll clean up everything. You won't even know we were here."

"I'm not worried. I have a cleaning service."

"Well, just the same. The place will be spotless when we leave."

Just then his phone rang. He grabbed the extension in the office. It was his brother. "Hi, Trace. Happy Thanksgiving."

"Same to you," Trace echoed. "I've been given orders to call you and see if you changed your mind about coming to dinner today."

Kira couldn't stand for him to be alone. "I appreciate the invitation, bro, but I seem to have a place to go. A few of the tenants have asked me to share the meal with them."

There was a long silence. "You better be careful, no telling what they might put in your food."

"Very funny. I do have a few friends. Besides, the tenants and I are getting along fine."

"Well, that's good."

He didn't want to talk about any apartment troubles. "I take it Kira is fixing dinner today."

"It'll be just us since Jody and Nathan have gone to be with Ben at the army base."

Jarrett remembered Kira's student who'd gotten pregnant in high school. Jody had had the child and Ben had joined the military, but he'd stayed in touch. The couple had gotten married this past summer.

Suddenly the doorbell rang. "I've got to go, Trace. Tell everyone happy Thanksgiving."

After replacing the phone, Jarrett walked across the great room and into the entry. He pulled open the door to find Mia and several other people standing on his porch.

He frowned. "What are you doing out of bed?"

"I'm allowed out now. Some," she added stubbornly. "I just have to stay off my feet as much as possible."

He took her by the arm and led her to the sofa, followed by the other dozen or so tenants. "Why did you come here? We're going to bring the food back to the community room." He folded his arms. "You aren't supposed to do anything."

She nodded. I know, but there's a problem at the community room. It's flooded."

Jarrett cursed. He didn't need another thing that he had to pay for. "How bad?"

Joe spoke up. "I shut off the main valve, but there's about an inch of water on the floor."

Jarrett murmured some choice words as he turned back to Mia.

She suddenly looked unsure. "We didn't know what to do, so we came here."

Nola walked into the room. "Mia, what's wrong? Is it the baby?"

"No, I'm fine, but the community room is flooded." Mia looked back at Jarrett. "We have no place to have our dinner."

Every eye turned toward him. He had no choice. "Well, since everyone is here, I guess it'll be at my house."

Cheers filled the room, then everyone scattered to do their chores. He pulled out his phone and punched in the McKane Ranch number, wondering how he'd gotten into this situation. He glanced at Mia Saunders, those big blue eyes staring back at him. A sudden stirring in his gut told him he was headed for disaster if he wasn't careful. Hell, he'd never been careful in his life.

His brother answered the phone.

"Hey, Trace. Why don't you load up Kira and Jenna and come here? It seems I'm having Thanksgiving at my house."

Two hours later, Mia was still sitting on the large sofa in Jarrett's great room. Although it wasn't her taste, the place was decorated well. A lot of chrome-and-glass tables and black leather furniture filled the room. The most beautiful feature was the huge wall of windows and the French door that led to the deck and the wooded area at the back of the house. Although the trees were bare and a dusting of snow covered the ground, she could picture it in the spring with green trees and wildflowers along the hillside.

She turned toward the open-concept kitchen, looking over the breakfast bar to see rows of espresso-colored cabinets, and marble counter tops. The commercial-size stainless-steel appliances looked as though they were getting a rare workout today.

The dining room was on the other side, the long table already set up for the meal, along with several card tables scattered around to accommodate all the people coming today. Mia didn't even want to count them. All she knew was that her brother and sister-in-law wouldn't be at any table. These people were her family now. She rubbed her stomach. Hers and her baby's.

"Are you okay?"

She glanced up to see Jarrett standing beside the sofa. "I'm fine. Really. Thank you for having us today."

"There wasn't a choice, and you know it."

"It's still very generous that you let us use your home."

He shrugged. "I also get a home-cooked meal."

"You have family. And I bet you could get someone to cook for you pretty easily."

His dark gaze held hers. "I'm pretty selective in choosing my friends." His mouth crooked upward in a sexy smile. "Also who cooks for me."

"Well, you've got some pretty good cooks in your kitchen right now."

"I'm glad about that, because I'm getting hungry just smelling all the wonderful aromas." He sat down across from her. "If your cookies are any indication, I'd say you know your way around a kitchen, too."

The man was too handsome and, when he wanted to be, charming. She scooted to the edge of the sofa. "Could you direct me to the bathroom, please?"

"Of course." He helped her up, but didn't release his hold on her arm. They were walking toward the hall when the doorbell rang.

She looked at him. "I thought everyone was here."

Jarrett pulled open the door to a young couple with a little girl. She recognized them from church.

"Happy Thanksgiving, Unca Jay," the girl cried as she ran inside.

He scooped her into his arms. "Happy Thanksgiving to you too, Jenna. I'm glad you could come today. Welcome, Kira, Trace."

They all exchanged greetings.

Jenna kept her hold on her uncle. "Mama said it must be a really special day because we never get invited to your house. She's really happy because family should be together."

"Jenna," her mother warned.

"Well, you did say that," the child acknowledged, then looked at Mia. "Who's this lady, Unca Jay?"

"Hi, I'm Mia."

Jarrett set her down. "I'm Jenna, and I'm almost four years old. But my daddy says I'm really thirty." The child caught sight of Mia's rounded stomach. "Are you going to have a baby?"

"Jenna." Kira sent another warning glance to her daughter, and then looked at Mia. "Hi, Mia. It's good to see you again."

Trace removed his cowboy hat and nodded. "Hello, Mia."

"Nice to see you, too. I hope you don't mind that we took over Jarrett's house."

The pretty blonde smiled and glanced up at her husband. Love radiated between them just as Mia had seen between her brother and his wife.

"We think it's wonderful," Kira said. "I'm just wondering how you did it."

"I believe a judge did it, along with several of the tenants."

They all looked toward the living room and saw the numerous people. "Welcome to Mountain View Apartment's Thanksgiving Day celebration." Mia turned to Kira. "If you'll excuse me, I need to find a restroom."

Jarrett watched Mia walk down the hall. He wanted to go after her. Why? She was capable of finding the bathroom.

"How is she doing?"

Jarrett looked at his sister-in-law. "She should be off her feet. So would you watch her?"

"Sure. If you and Trace unload the car. I brought a few things for dinner, too. I'll take Jenna to the kitchen and see if they need any help."

"Just ask for Nola."

"I know Nola Madison. I see her at church nearly every week."

"Okay. You'll probably know a few of the others, too."

Once the group of seniors spotted Jenna, they began to fuss over her. His niece couldn't get enough of the attention.

"So tell me about you and Mia Saunders," Trace said.

Jarrett turned around. "There's nothing to tell. She had a scare with her pregnancy and I had to take her to the hospital. The doctor ordered bed rest. She was allowed to come here, but she needs to stay off her feet."

He glanced down the hall. "And if she doesn't come out soon, I'm going in to get her."

Trace arched an eyebrow. "So when did you become her protector?"

Jarrett turned to his younger half brother. Trace stared back at him.

"She doesn't have anyone else," Jarrett reminded him. "Remember, she lost her brother a few months back."

Trace nodded. "Yeah, Reverend Brad was a good man," he said, studying Jarrett. "I just never knew my brother to care much about anything that wasn't about the almighty dollar. You must be getting soft in your old age."

"Hey, I'm not that old." He didn't want to discuss his age or his relationship with Mia. They were neighbors. Temporary neighbors. "But don't go thinking I've bought into the family scene."

"Never say never, bro," Trace challenged. "I've seen you with Jenna. You wouldn't be a bad dad."

Jarrett froze. He didn't want to be a dad at all. His own father had been lousy at the job. "Look, as soon as I make the repairs to the complex, I'm out of there. And I won't be looking back."

On returning from the bathroom, Mia discovered that everyone was taking a seat at the tables. She glanced around for to find one last vacant chair. Next to Jarrett.

Smiling, he stood and pulled out her chair. "Looks like you're next to me."

She caught Nola smiling from across the table. Little Jenna was on the other side of Jarrett and Trace and Kira sat beside her. "I'm just happy we have a place to eat. Thank you, Jarrett, for having us here."

Nola and Margaret stood and went into the kitchen and soon returned, each woman carrying a platter with a large turkey. The group made approving sounds as the birds were placed on the table alongside sweet potatoes, green-bean casseroles, stuffing, gravy and other side dishes too numerous to count.

Nola stood beside the table. "Before we all dig in, we should give thanks for this wonderful day." She turned to Jarrett.

Mia watched as he nudged his brother and said something to him. Trace nodded. "Everyone, take hands and let's bow our heads."

Jarrett reached for Mia's hand. His large palm nearly engulfed hers. She was surprised by the roughness of his fingers, but also by the warmth he generated.

"Dear Lord," Trace began. "We thank you for all the blessings you've given us this past year. There have been some rough times, but sometimes that brings out the best in people. And today, we see that special bond as friends gather together as a family.

"We also ask for your blessing for those who aren't here with us." Trace paused. Mia thought about Brad and Karen. She felt Jarrett squeeze her hand. "We also ask a special blessing for Mia's baby.

"We ask you to bless this food in your name. Amen."

"Amens" echoed around the room.

Mia kept her head lowered, thinking of her brother and his wife. How much she missed them. Brad had always been there to guide her, to spout optimism whenever she wanted to give up. Now, she had to go on without him.

She opened her eyes to see that she was still holding hands with Jarrett. She turned to him to catch him watching her.

"Are you okay?" he asked.

"I'm fine." She pulled her hand away. "I wish people would stop asking me that."

"Then eat a good meal today, and we'll get you home to bed."

His deep voice caused her to shiver. "I can get myself to bed, thank you," she said in a quiet voice.

"Well, one thing is for sure, you're not climbing the steps."

Since when did he become the boss of her? "I wouldn't have to if you'd fix the elevator."

He glared. "That will be Monday. I can't get anyone out before then."

She heard his name called and they both looked up at Nola.

"Jarrett and Trace, would you do the honor of slicing the turkeys?"

The brothers stood, went to opposite ends of the table and began to carve. The side dishes were passed around and Mia put small helpings onto her plate. With Jarrett gone, she dished up food for him, too.

"Are you Unca Jay's girlfriend?" Jenna McKane asked from across her uncle's empty seat.

Mia smiled. "No. We're neighbors in his apartment building in town."

The little girl frowned and turned to her mother. "Mommy, what's an apartment?"

"It's a big building with a lot of houses inside. It's like where Aunt Michele lives."

"Oh." The child turned back to Mia's stomach. "Are you going to have a baby soon?"

"Yes, I am, in just a few weeks."

Jenna grinned. "I have a big brother, Jack. He's old and he doesn't live with us. So my mommy and daddy are trying to have a brother or sister for me."

"Jenna McKane," Kira said, giving her daughter a stern look. "You don't have to talk so much. Now, eat."

Kira looked at Mia. "I'm sorry. Trace and I forget how much she hears."

Mia smiled as the platter of turkey was passed to her. She nodded toward the child eating mashed potatoes. "She's adorable."

Kira looked at her daughter lovingly. "She's our miracle baby. And a very welcome surprise." She looked at Mia. "If you ever need anything, Mia, please don't hesitate to ask. All of us in the church want very much to help."

Mia was touched. "Thank you, Kira. Everyone has been so generous already. I think I'll be fine if I can find a place to live by spring."

Before Kira could say any more, Jarrett arrived back in his seat. For the next twenty minutes everyone concentrated on the delicious food and friendly conversation. Finally the men leaned back groaning at the amount of food they'd consumed.

"There's pie, too," Nola announced as she stood and took several empty plates. She looked at Jarrett. "Jarrett, would you mind helping me with the coffeemaker? I'm not sure on the measurements."

With a nod, he stood. "Sure." He grinned. "If I get first choice of pie."

Nola smiled, too. "You think because you're good-looking, you can charm me into anything, don't you?"

"Hey, I do what I can to get an advantage." He put his arm around her shoulders. "Is it working?"

Mia never heard the answer as they walked off together.

"He's a flirt, but he's a good man."

Mia turned to Kira, but didn't know how to answer that. Was Kira trying to sell her brother-in-law's better qualities to her?

"I wouldn't have said that a few years ago," Kira went

on. "But something in him has changed. And he and Trace are working on being brothers."

She turned and looked at Mia. "I know you're not happy about having to leave your apartment, but I might be able to help with that. We have a guest house at the ranch. It's small, but it has two bedrooms. A friend had been living there during college, and now she's gone to be with her husband in the army."

"Oh, Kira." Mia didn't want to get too excited. "What about Trace? I bet you haven't even asked him."

"Haven't asked me what?" her husband turned toward her.

"About Mia coming to live in the cottage."

He raised an eyebrow as if to think about it. "That's a great idea. The house is sitting empty." He shrugged. "You're welcome to live there as long as you need."

Mia was getting excited. "What is the rent?"

"There isn't any rent."

"No, I would expect to pay something."

Trace glanced at his wife. "I think we owe your brother a bigger debt. He helped us through some rough spots a few years ago. I think Brad would want us to help you and the baby."

"Can I come over to see the baby?" Jenna asked. "I'll be really quiet."

"If I decide to move there, of course, you can." She looked at Kira. "Maybe I could even babysit you so your parents could go out."

A big smile split Trace's face. "That's a deal I'll take."

"What's a deal?" Jarrett sat down next to Mia.

Trace was still smiling. "Mia is coming to live in the guest house at the ranch."

"The hell she is."

* * *

The entire room went silent at his outburst.

"Unca Jay, you said a bad word," Jenna piped in.

Jarrett reached into his pocket, pulled out change and set it on the table for his misstep. "Here, sweetie." Then he turned to Mia. "You can't move all the way out there. Not in the winter."

She glanced around nervously. "I don't want to talk about this now," she said as she pushed away from the table. "Excuse me." She stood and walked out.

Jarrett went after her. He caught up with her right before she got to the bathroom door. She would have disappeared, but someone was using the facility.

"Mia," he called.

"Go away."

"That's not likely." He gripped her by the arm and escorted her down the hall.

"What are you doing?"

"Taking you to a bathroom."

"I don't have to go. I just needed to get away from you and your crazy idea that you can tell me what to do."

He wasn't listening as he took her by the hand, led her to the master suite and opened the door to the large room. He pulled her inside and shut the door.

"Stop this," she demanded. "And stop telling me what to do. You can't boss me around."

He glared at her. "Someone needs to take you in hand. You can't move all the way out to the ranch. If we get a snowstorm—and the possibility is strong that we will—you might not make it to the hospital when the time comes."

"I can take care of myself. And why does it matter to you, anyway? You are my landlord, Mr. McKane, not my keeper."

"Dammit, stop calling me that. It's Jarrett." He leaned closer as her eyes widened. "Say *Jarrett*."

"Jarrett…"

His gaze moved to her full lips. Suddenly, he ached to know how they would feel against his and how she would taste. He couldn't resist and slowly lowered his mouth to hers. He took a gentle bite, then another. Each one a little sweeter than the last.

Her eyes widened, her breathing grew labored.

Finally, he closed his mouth over hers and wasn't disappointed. With a groan, he wrapped his arms around her and drew her closer. She made a whimpering sound and her arms move to around his neck as he deepened the kiss.

Jarrett pressed her back against the door, feeling her body against his, then suddenly something kicked against his stomach. The baby. He broke off the kiss with a gasp, suddenly remembering the situation.

Mia's shocked gaze searched his. "Why did you do that?"

"Hell if I know." He hated that he was so drawn to her. She was a complication he didn't need, but he couldn't seem to stay away from her.

Her hand went to her stomach protectively. Was she having a contraction?

He picked her up in his arms and carried her across the room.

"What are you doing?" she demanded.

"Taking you where you should have been in the first place. To bed."

CHAPTER SIX

MIA was fuming as Jarrett walked out the door, leaving her alone on the bed. His bed. What she hated the most was that she didn't have much say in the matter.

All her life, she'd had to do what she'd been told. Go to the best schools, make the best grades, be the perfect daughter. It had taken years, and although she'd made many bad turns she'd finally gained her independence. She wasn't about to give it up now. Not even for a man.

She glanced around Jarrett's bedroom. Large, dark furniture dominated the spacious room, including the king-size bed with the carved headboard. The walls were a taupe-gray and the floors a wide-planked dark wood. Two honey-colored leather chairs sat in front of huge French doors that led out to a deck and the wooded area beyond. It was definitely a man's room, which reminded her she shouldn't be in here.

Mia's thoughts turned back to Jarrett McKane. What had possessed her to let him kiss her? She shut her eyes reliving the feel of his mouth against hers, his strong arms around her. What she hadn't expected was the way she had reacted to him.

Of course, she would react to the man—any man for that matter. How long had it been since she'd been in a relationship? She couldn't even remember that far back. Not that she was eager to start one now. There hadn't been any time for a man. Then Mr. Hotshot McKane had stormed into her life, with his good looks and his take-charge attitude. No, she didn't need him in her life.

She started to get up when she felt the mild contraction and covered her midsection with her hand.

"Oh, please, no."

After several slow, relaxing breaths she eased back against the pillows and shut her eyes. Why had she come here today? Okay, she'd wanted to come to the party. And Dr. Drake had said she could be out for a few hours if she was careful and didn't overdo things.

Mia caressed her stomach, feeling the tension slowly ease from her body.

There was a soft knock and the door opened and Jarrett came in carrying a tray with a slice of pie. He stopped at the side of the bed, frowning. "You okay?"

"I'm fine," she fibbed. "I'm just resting."

He continued to stare at her. "You don't look fine."

She closed her eyes again. "Then don't look at me."

He sat the plate on the nightstand. "Are you having contractions?"

She opened her eyes. "Just a little one."

Jarrett pulled out his wallet from his back pocket and took out a business card. He grabbed the phone off the table.

"What are you doing?" she asked.

"Calling your doctor."

"You can't, it's Thanksgiving."

"Then we go to the emergency room." He paused. "Your choice."

* * *

Jarrett had worried this might happen if Mia left the apartment. They were lucky that Dr. Drake was on call today, and it only took her minutes to return his call.

The doctor talked with Mia, who didn't look happy when she handed the phone back to Jarrett.

"Yes, Doctor?" he said.

"I instructed Mia not to get out of bed for anything except to use the bathroom, and I want her in my office first thing in the morning. Could you bring her in?"

"We'll be there when your doors open." He ended the call and hung up. "Looks like you'll be staying here tonight."

He watched her eyes widen. "I can't stay here. It's not fair to you."

"Hey, I haven't been staying here anyway."

"But this is your room, your bed."

Smiling, he glanced around at the large space. "I guess we'll have to share."

She glared. "You need to get a life, McKane."

"I have a life, thank you, or at least I did before I moved into the Mountain View Apartments."

There was another soft knock on the door and Kira peered in. "Is everything okay?" she asked.

"It's under control now. Mia's had some contractions. Her doctor wants her to stay in bed and come in tomorrow."

Mia sat up. "I tried to tell Jarrett that I'll be able to rest better in my own apartment."

Kira stood at the end of the bed. "I know this is difficult, Mia, but you really need to stay put. In the last months when I was pregnant with Jenna, I couldn't even sit up to eat."

"See," Jarrett said. "And she delivered a healthy baby. So you stay."

Suddenly two more people appeared at the door, Nola and Sylvia, looking concerned.

"Please don't worry," Mia said. "I'm fine. But I guess I have to stay put for tonight."

Nola came closer and patted her hand. "We're not worried. Jarrett will take care of you." She looked down at the tray of food. "You need to eat."

Jarrett backed out of the room, leaving the women to pamper Mia. He couldn't help but wonder if he was the cause of her problem.

He rubbed his hand over his face. He had no business near her, let alone kissing her.

What happened to keeping your distance, McKane? The woman is pregnant, for Christ's sake.

He looked up to see Trace coming down the hall. "Is everything okay?"

Hell, would the cavalry be coming next? "Mia had a few contractions, but she's resting now."

"That's good." Trace studied him. "You seem to have inherited a lot more than just an apartment building. Need any help?"

Jarrett wasn't surprised at his brother's offer. For years the kid had tried to get close to him, but Jarrett had always rebuffed him. It made him ashamed of his past actions.

"Thanks, but I'm handling it."

Trace smiled. "I never thought I'd see the day my brother entertained a group of senior citizens in his house and had a pregnant woman in his bed."

Jarrett started to argue, but he had no words.

Trace grinned. "Be careful, bro, you're getting soft, or else, Mia Saunders is doing something no other woman ever has."

Jarrett sighed. "I don't want to hear this." He walked out into the great room, seeing the rest of his guests waiting for some news. He hoped he could convince them everything would be okay. First he had to convince himself.

Darkness surrounded her, but Mia knew she wasn't alone. The small room was filled with loud music, a lot of voices trying to be heard. She could smell cigarette smoke. Someone was smoking.

No! It was bad for the baby. She tried to stand, but someone pulled her back down.

"You can't leave, honey," a man with a slurred voice said. "The party's only getting started. Here have another drink." He put a glass in front of her face and she nearly gagged on the stale smell of beer.

"No! Let me go." She managed to break his hold, and get out the door. The night's cold air caused her to shiver as she looked around, but she couldn't recognize anything. She had no idea where she was, but knew she had to get home. But she had no home.

"Margaret!"

She turned and saw her father. She gasped and tried to run, but her legs were too heavy to move fast and Preston Saunders grabbed her arm.

"You can't get away from me," he threatened.

"Let me go," she cried. "I don't want you."

"I don't want you either, but my grandchild is a different matter. If you think I'll let you raise this baby you'd better think again. It's a Saunders."

"No, it's my baby. It's mine! It's mine!" she cried.

"Mia! Mia! Wake up."

She felt another touch. This time it was different. Gentler. Soothing. She opened her eyes and saw Jarrett leaning over her. With a gasp she went into his arms and held on. Tight.

Jarrett felt her trembling. His arms circled her back and

pulled her close and he felt her breasts pressed against his bare chest. The awareness shook him, but he worked to ease her fears.

"Ssh, you were having a bad dream. It's okay, Mia." He felt her tears against his shoulder. "I'm here."

She shivered again and then pulled back but refused to look at him. "I'm sorry."

With the moonlight coming through the French doors, he could see she wasn't all right.

"Bad dream, huh? You want to tell me about it?"

She shook her head, but didn't let go of his hand. "It's just one of those where someone is chasing you."

"Anyone you know?"

She shrugged. "Just someone from a long time ago."

That had him wondering about a lot of things. "A bad-news ex-boyfriend?"

She didn't answer for a long time. He suddenly became aware she was wearing one of his T-shirts, and he was only in a pair of sweatpants, all cozy together on his bed.

"I don't want to talk about it."

He nodded. "Do you want me to get you anything?"

She shook her head. "No, thank you."

"Should I leave?"

She finally looked at him. "Would you mind staying? For a little while?"

He had to hide his surprise. He didn't cuddle with women, not unless it led to something. He was about say, "Not a good idea," but instead he answered, "Not a problem." He changed position, propping himself against the headboard and pulled her back into his arms. "This okay?"

She nodded and then lay back down, her head against her pillow next to him. She blinked up at him with those trusting eyes.

Okay, this wasn't going to work. "Try and get some sleep."

"I don't want to start dreaming again."

He covered her hand with his. "I'm here, Mia. No one will hurt you or your baby as long as I'm around."

Somehow she'd managed to get to him, and he'd just taken on the job of her protector. It was crazy, but he didn't mind one bit.

Mia snuggled deeper into the warmth, enjoying the comfort of the soft bed. She smiled, feeling the strong arms that were wrapped around her back, holding her close.

Slowly, memories of last night began drifting back to her. The nightmare. Her father.

She opened her eyes and was greeted by bright sunlight coming through the French doors. What was more disturbing was the feeling of the bare skin against her cheek. She raised her head to see she was in bed with Jarrett McKane.

Oh, God. What was he still doing here?

She studied the sleeping man who was making soft snoring sounds. He suddenly turned toward her, reaching for her, pulling her against him.

Oh no. His chest was hard and doing incredible things to her out-of-whack libido. But she had a more desperate urge right now. She had to use the bathroom, and quick.

Careful not to disturb him, Mia managed to untangle herself, slide to the side of the bed and escape into the connecting bath.

A few minutes later she returned to find Jarrett awake and leaning against the headboard. His chest was gloriously naked, exposing every defined muscle under his bronzed skin.

"Morning," he murmured, raking fingers through his hair. "We seem to make a habit of this."

She had to put a stop to it. "Well, as soon as I get back to my apartment I won't be bothering you anymore."

Frowning, he got up and came around to her. "First thing, you need to get back into bed," he told her, giving her a little nudge to climb in. Once she complied, he continued, "Secondly, I wasn't complaining, just stating a fact."

Jarrett hadn't had much time for female companionship the past few months. Lately it had all been about business, until Mia Saunders and her group of merry followers had appeared in his life. They might be a costly headache, but he'd found he liked the diversion.

He sat on the edge of the bed. His gaze moved over her soft brunette curls and met her pretty blue eyes. Damn, he could get used to this. "Any more dreams?" He could still hear her frightened cries.

She shook her head. "I slept fine. Thank you."

He smiled and finally coaxed one from her. *Damn, she's pretty*, he thought, suddenly realizing his body was noticing, too.

"Okay, I better get breakfast started." He stood. "Will you eat eggs, or do I need to go on a jelly-donut run?"

Two hours later, Mia sat in the exam room with Doctor Drake, with Jarrett sitting just outside.

After the exam, the doctor pulled off her gloves. "You're doing fine."

"What does *fine* mean?" Mia asked as she sat up.

"You're effaced fifty percent."

"Oh, God. Am I going into labor?"

She shook her head. "You aren't dilated yet. And you haven't had any more contractions, right?"

"Not since last night."

There was a knock on the door and a technician came in pushing a machine.

"I want to do an ultrasound as a precaution," the doctor explained.

"So you are worried?" Mia asked.

"A little concerned. This baby coming early is a very real possibility." She raised a calming hand. "You're thirty-six weeks, Mia. All I want to do is check the baby's weight."

There was a knock on the door. "Yes?" the doctor called.

Jarrett poked his head in. "Is everything okay?"

The doctor glanced at Mia. "You want him in here?"

Mia looked at Jarrett and found herself nodding. "You can stay if you want," she told him.

He looked surprised but walked right toward her as she lay back on the table. Although covered with a paper sheet, she realized that she'd be exposing her belly for Jarrett to see.

Dr. Drake nodded toward the opposite side of the exam table for Jarrett to stand, then she began to apply the clear gel on her stomach.

Mia sucked in a breath.

Jarrett took her hand. "You okay?"

She nodded. "The cream is cold."

The doctor went to the machine and made some adjustments, then began to move the probe over her stomach.

Jarrett had no idea what he was doing here. Then he saw Mia's fear, and knew he couldn't leave her. He eyed the machine, watching the grainy picture, and then suddenly it came into focus. He saw a head first, then a small body.

"Well, I'll be damned," he murmured, seeing the incredible image. "That's a baby."

"What did you think it was?" the doctor chided.

Jarrett was embarrassed. "The way she's craved jelly donuts, I wasn't sure."

The doctor laughed. "Since your weight's okay, I'll tell you to indulge, a little. After the baby comes, you'll be on a stricter diet while you're breast-feeding." The doctor glanced at Mia, then back at the screen. "The baby's in position. So that's one less thing to worry about. This is a 3D machine so let's get a better look at this little one." The picture became a lot clearer and a tiny face appeared.

"Oh, my gosh," Mia cried and gripped Jarrett's hand tighter. "It's crazy but he looks like Brad's baby pictures." Tears formed in her eyes and a sob came out. "I'm sorry."

The doctor patted her arm. "It's understandable. Are you ready to know the sex?"

Mia looked at Jarrett. He shrugged, trying to handle his own emotions. "I say it's a boy."

Mia gave a slight nod and the doctor scanned in for a closer look. He saw all the proof he needed. "Well, hello, BJ."

Mia gave him a questioning look.

"I take it you're naming this little guy after your brother," he said. "Bradley Junior."

During the ride home from Grand Junction, Mia had zoned out, not noticing much of the trip until Jarrett stopped in front of the apartment building.

"We're home," he said, but didn't move to get out of the car. "Mia, are you all right?"

No! she wanted to scream. She hadn't been okay since the day her brother had died. She looked at Jarrett, seeing his concern. "Seeing the baby today made it seem so real." Her voice grew softer, more hoarse. "A boy. How can I raise a boy?" Tears filled her eyes, but she couldn't cry any more. "A boy needs a father. Brad should be here."

He reached across the console and took her hand. Even with the heater going, her hands were still cold. "Hey, this kid's got the next best thing. You."

She wasn't the best. "You don't know that. I've done things, made bad choices."

"I can't believe that, or your brother wouldn't have chosen you to carry this baby."

"But not to raise his son." She sighed. "Besides, I've always had Brad to help me, to guide me in life. Now, I'm on my own. What if I make mistakes again?"

He frowned. "Everyone makes mistakes, Mia, but you can't just give up."

Jarrett had never been the optimistic type, but he was a good salesman. "Don't forget, you have friends to help you. Is there any other family around?"

Mia shook her head. "No. There's no one else." She wiped her eyes. "God, I hate this. I never cry."

"I hear it's normal," he consoled her, hating that he kept getting more and more involved in her life. Not to mention the lives of the other tenants, too.

Once he got off house arrest and they all found other places to live, this time would just be a fleeting memory. They wouldn't be his problem then. They'd move on, and he'd move on. But could he? He thought back to being beside Mia and seeing her baby on the ultrasound.

Damn. He needed to get this apartment building in shape and get the hell out of here. "We'd better get inside and out of the cold so you can rest."

She grumbled. "That's all I've been doing."

"From what Kira tells me you won't get much sleep after the baby comes, so enjoy it now." He started to climb out of the car when she stopped him with a soft touch on his arm.

She nodded in agreement. "Thank you," she said softly. "Thank you for being there with me today."

He caught her pretty blue eyes still glistening with tears and something tightened in his chest. Dear Lord. He was in big trouble.

CHAPTER SEVEN

BY the next week, Jarrett had accomplished several things. He'd finally gotten one of the elevators repaired and a plumber had replaced the rusted pipes in the community room. Somehow, he'd even been talked into helping put up some Christmas decorations. Joe convinced him that since this would be Mia's baby's first Christmas, they should celebrate it.

The major thing he'd wanted to do was keep his distance from Mia. He'd gotten too involved with the expectant mother.

Thanks to Nola, Jarrett knew how Mia was doing, whether he wanted to or not. By afternoon, he'd seen several women going into his neighbor's apartment carrying presents for a baby shower.

Kira and Jenna stopped by his place afterward to see him and tell him all about the gifts Mia had gotten for the baby. His niece also had several things to say about the condition of his temporary home. None were good.

"Unca Jay, I like your other house better."

"I still have my other house, sweetie. I'll move back there soon."

She smiled, then looked thoughtful. "But you have to take care of Mia until she has her baby. Promise you will."

What was going on? "Okay, I promise as long as I live here I'll watch out for Mia and the baby."

That seemed to satisfy the three-year-old and she smiled. "Then you can come see her at the ranch. She's going to move in with the new baby." She turned to her mother and was practically jumping up and down. "I can't wait. I get to hold the baby, too."

Jarrett looked at his sister-in-law. "So, it's definite?"

Kira nodded. "I'm pretty sure I have her convinced it's best for her and the child."

"Isn't that neat, Unca Jay, she's gonna be in our family? It's almost going to be our baby, too."

"That's great," he said.

The girl's eyes lit up more. "Maybe if you ask, Mia will share her baby with you, too."

Jarrett looked at Kira for help, hoping she didn't read anything more into his relationship with his neighbor. "Where does she get this stuff?"

Kira only smiled. "Sounds like a pretty good idea to me."

The next day Jarrett drove to his office, McKane Properties, and started two of his staff working on finding affordable apartments for some of the tenants. He needed to get this over and done with.

He needed everyone to move on, but if Mia and the baby moved out to the ranch, he'd still see her. Would that be so bad? With Kira and Trace looking out for her, at least he wouldn't worry about her so much.

That way he could go back to business as usual and a life without Mia in it. He turned his thoughts to the day at the doctor's office and seeing the ultrasound. He'd had no business sharing that with her. Just as he'd had no business kissing her Thanksgiving Day.

He had to stay away.

There were other things he needed to think about, like the Fulton plant project. It had been a big cause of his loss of sleep. He'd been working on some changes, changes to the factory site that might help everyone.

For him to survive financially, Jarrett knew he had to finalize this deal, or he might be living in the Mountain View Apartments permanently.

A few days later Jarrett was awakened in the middle of the night by his ringing phone. He grabbed it off the bedside table.

"Hello," he groaned.

"Jarrett," a familiar voice said. "I'm sorry to bother you, but could you come over?"

"Sure." He hung up, got out of bed, pulled on jeans and shirt along with boots. He crossed the hall, but before he could knock she opened the door.

At 3:00 a.m. in the morning, she looked fresh and dressed for the day. Her dark hair lay in waves around her shoulders and she even had on makeup. "I take it the call wasn't for a donut run?" he joked.

"I need you to take me to the hospital. My water broke."

He froze, then his heart began to race. "You're in labor?"

She nodded. "I've only had some light contractions, but Doctor Drake said I need to come in now."

"Of course." He pointed to his apartment. "Let me grab my car keys." He rushed back, slipped on a coat and hurried back to find her waiting with a small bag.

"I hated to ask you, but Nola's daughter is sick and she's helping with the grandkids," Mia apologized.

He took her by the arm and they slowly made their way

to the elevator. "I'm glad you asked me, I don't want Nola to drive at night." He gave her the once-over. "You okay?"

She smiled. "Outside of being a little scared, I feel pretty good."

"I think it's normal to feel scared."

They rode down one floor and the doors opened. "Thank you for helping me out, Jarrett. I know this isn't in your landlord duties."

"Hey, I told you it's not a problem." They stepped off the elevator and walked outside. "Is there anyone you want me to call?"

Mia shook her head. "Nola was supposed to be my coach, but I can't take her away from her grandkids."

"Is there a backup?"

She stopped and looked at him pleadingly. "You?"

"You're kidding?"

"Do you think I like asking you again?"

"I didn't say I mind doing it, I just don't know what to do." He wasn't making any sense.

"Join the club. This is my first time, too," she began, then suddenly groaned.

He saw the pain etched across her face, but it was her fingernails digging into his arm that told him what was happening. Labor had begun.

"Looks like you're getting an early Christmas present."

Thirty minutes and five labor pains later, Jarrett pulled up at the emergency-room door. An attendant brought out a wheelchair, and Mia took the seat. Then Jarrett drove off and she was wheeled inside to get admitted.

After minimal paperwork, she was taken up to the maternity floor and into a labor/delivery room. Once dressed in a gown and in bed, she was hooked to monitors to watch her progress.

"Looks like you lose the bet for a Christmas-day baby."

Mia looked up as Dr. Drake walked in and nodded to the other doctor leaving. "December fifteenth seems like a fine birthday to me."

"How are you doing?" Lauren asked, checking the monitor.

No sooner were the words out than Mia felt a contraction begin to build.

"Breathe," the doctor instructed her as she came to the bedside. "It's almost over. There. Take a cleansing breath."

Mia sighed and lay back against the pillow. "That was stronger than the others."

"They're going to get even stronger before the baby comes. Don't worry, the anesthesiologist should be here soon with your epidural." The doctor glanced around. "Do you have someone here with you?"

"Will I do?"

They both turned to find Jarrett standing in the doorway. He hadn't gone back home.

"Jarrett, you don't have to stay. This could take all night."

He came in anyway. "I called Kira and she's on her way. So how about I be a stand-in until she arrives?"

"Kira's coming all the way here?"

"I didn't ask her to, she just said she's coming to help you."

Mia had to blink back tears. She wasn't going to be alone. She managed a nod at Jarrett. "Thank you."

"I know my limitations. My only experience is birthing calves." He shook his head. "And that was a long time ago."

"I'd like to see you all decked out in Western gear, cowboy hat, chaps." Mia found herself saying, feeling oddly relaxed in between pains.

"Hey, I didn't look bad." She knew he was nervous about his role as coach and trying to distract her. "I had a few girls following me around when I did some rodeos. Calf-roping was my event. I was known for my quick hands."

Mia couldn't hide her smile. "I bet you were," she said as another contraction grabbed her. "Ooh…"

The doctor looked at Jarrett. "Do your job, coach," she told him.

Jarrett took Mia's hand as Lauren instructed him on what to do.

Over the next hour, Mia's contractions grew more frequent and more intense. It helped if she focused on Jarrett's encouraging words and gentle touch, even his humor. She did her breathing, and he wiped her brow.

After another series of strong contractions had eased, she noticed him watching her. She had to be a mess. Her hair was matted down and she was sweating as though she'd run a mile.

His dark eyes locked on hers. "You're amazing. And you haven't even complained once." He spooned her some ice chips that soothed her throat. "You're going to make a great mother."

"You're not doing so bad yourself. A great stand-in coach." She started to say more when the door opened and the anesthesiologist walked in.

It didn't take the doctor long to work his magic, and soon Mia was relaxed and feeling no discomfort, just pressure from the contractions.

Jarrett stood beside the bed. "Is it better now?"

Smiling, she nodded. "Isn't medication wonderful?"

He laughed. "I'd still have to be knocked out to go through what you're doing."

Over the next hour things began to move a lot faster. Mia's contractions started coming faster and harder, and they were different. She felt more pressure, lower.

Dr. Drake came in and checked the monitor. "Could you step outside a minute, Jarrett?"

He squeezed Mia's hand. "I'll be right back," he promised as he walked out.

The doctor checked her. "You're close, Mia," she told her. "It won't be long now."

"Really?" She glanced at the clock. She'd only been here a few hours.

Lauren smiled. "Sometimes it happens like this, short labor is rare with the first baby."

Mia's thoughts turned to Brad and Karen and sadness swamped her. They should have been here.

Outside the room, a nurse handed Jarrett some paper scrubs. "But I'm not her coach. My sister-in-law is supposed to be here."

The nurse frowned. "Well, if someone plans to be with her, they'd better get inside because she's ready to go."

Jarrett paused momentarily. He didn't want to leave Mia to do this alone. She hadn't complained, but there wasn't anyone else here. He quickly slipped on the scrubs and walked back into the room.

"If you want me to leave, I won't be offended. Just say the word."

Before Mia could speak a contraction seized her and she grabbed his hand. Things happened quickly after that. The doctor instructed him to stand behind Mia. He continued to coax her through each contraction, and held his breath with each push. When she became exhausted, he made her focus.

The next thing Jarrett knew he was witnessing a miracle as Mia's son made his noisy entrance into the world.

"Here's your son, Mia." Doctor Drake held the baby up for inspection.

Jarrett found he was counting fingers and toes and other male body parts. He swallowed hard. "Well, I don't think you're going to have any trouble hearing this guy."

He looked down to see Mia's tears. "He's so beautiful, don't you think?" she asked.

"Well, he runs a close second to Jenna, so yeah, he's a good-looking kid."

A nurse took the baby, carried him to a table and began to clean him up. "He's seven pounds and ten ounces and twenty-one inches long," she announced.

Mia gave him a tired smile. "Jarrett, thank you."

He leaned closer to her. "Hey, you did all the work," he said, brushing back her damp hair. He suddenly felt the urge to kiss her. To signify this special moment.

"Yeah, I did, didn't I?" She looked sleepy. "I hate to ask, but would you call Nola? Let her know that I'm okay?"

Jarrett expected she wanted some privacy. He nodded and left. Outside the room he saw Kira hurrying toward him.

"Sorry I'm late." She studied his face and smiled. "I take it the baby's arrived."

He could only nod, feeling his emotions rushing to the surface. "Yeah, it's a boy. Mia and the baby are fine."

She nodded. "And it looks like you did a good job as a stand-in."

He didn't even bother to deny it. "I couldn't leave her."

Kira took his hand. "Be careful, Jarrett. People might mistake you for a good guy," she teased.

"I don't think I have to worry about that." He turned away, wondering when he could see the baby again. "Mia will probably want to see you." He stripped off his cap. "I need a cup of coffee." He started to walk away, but stopped. "Tell Mia I'll be back in a little while."

His sister-in-law studied him for a long time, then said, "Don't look now, brother-in-law, your feelings are showing. It's about time."

Thirty-six hours later, Mia was nearly ready for the trip back home. She and her baby had been checked out, deemed healthy and could be discharged from the hospital.

There was one thing left. She had to put a name on her son's birth certificate. During the night, she'd taken out the letter her brother and sister-in-law had left for her, not to be read until after the birth of their baby.

Mia sat up late to read it and let the tears fall—for the parents who would never know their son, and for the baby who wouldn't have the chance to know them, either.

She opened the envelope.

Dear Mia,

Words can never express the joy and love we feel for you at this moment—the moment we learned that you were pregnant.

Joy and love not only for your unselfish act, not only for giving up a year of your life, but for carrying our child. For that Karen and I will be eternally grateful.

We don't care if this baby is a boy or a girl. But like all mothers, Karen has chosen names for the child. Bradley Preston for a boy or Sarah Margaret for a girl.

Our son or daughter will know what a special person you are. To make sure of that, you will always be a big part of his or her life. Karen and I would like you to be the godmother to little Brad Jr. or Sarah.

If, God forbid, anything should ever happen to either of us, we want you to be the child's guardian. After all, you carried this little miracle in your womb and in your heart for nine months. So who better? Our only other wish is that you find the happiness you truly deserve.

Love always, Brad and Karen.

Mia had sobbed most of the night after that, then the baby was brought to her to be fed. The second she held him in her arms, she knew that she loved him. Yes, BJ was her heart. And he was her son now.

Two hours later, Jarrett parked outside the apartment building and Mia glanced back at the baby. She still had trouble thinking of herself as a mother.

It didn't take long for a welcoming party to open the door and wave. "Looks like everyone is anxious to see the new resident," Jarrett announced.

That made Mia smile. "BJ's going to have many surrogate grandparents, that's for sure."

"Let's get him inside before they start the inspection," Jarrett said.

He climbed out and came around to the passenger side. He opened the back door and unfastened the baby carrier from its base. "Come on, fella. You've got people to meet."

He raised the carrier's hood and used a blanket to protect the baby from the cold, then lifted him out of the car.

Mia was waiting and took his offered arm as they made their way up the shoveled walk to the door and went in.

"Welcome home, Mia," Nola called along with several other tenants as they walked inside.

"Thank you. It's good to be back."

She glanced around the large entry to see it had been decorated for the holidays. A large tree sat in the center of the area and lights and garlands had been strung along the wrought-iron stairway.

She went to one of the grouping of sofas and Jarrett placed the baby down on one of the now slip-covered sofas. Mia pulled back the blanket and everyone gasped.

"Oh, he's perfect," Nola cooed and glanced at Mia. "And so handsome, like your brother. What's his name?"

Mia swallowed. "Bradley Preston Saunders, Junior. That's the name Brad and Karen chose. I'm going to call him BJ."

Nola smiled. "It's perfect."

She felt Jarrett's presence behind her. It seemed so natural for him to be there. Too natural.

"I think these two need some rest," Jarrett told everyone.

Normally, Mia wouldn't like him making decisions for her, but she was tired. "Maybe you can come up later."

"Of course, but you need to rest now," Nola added. "If you need someone to watch this little guy, I'm available."

Jarrett picked up the carrier and placed a hand on her elbow as they made their way to the elevator. She was glad she didn't have to climb the stairs. They stepped into the small paneled compartment. He punched the second floor button and the doors closed.

"This is nice," she said.

He frowned. "What, the elevator?"

She nodded. "You have to remember it's been a while since we've been able to ride upstairs."

The doors opened and Jarrett motioned for her to step out first. "Well, only one's working," he said. "The other has multiple problems. I'm going to have to mortgage my home just to fix it."

"You're kidding?"

He suddenly grinned and her heart tripped.

"Almost. These old parts aren't easy to find. But all I need to do is make sure it runs for the next few months."

They reached her apartment and she unlocked the door. Once inside, she tried to take the baby, but Jarrett had already walked into the other room. Her bedroom.

She went after him, knowing it would be best to end this…dependency. She had to do this on her own. No distractions. And Jarrett McKane was definitely a distraction.

"I can handle it from here." Besides she wanted time with her son. Alone.

He set the carrier on the bed and stepped away. "I just didn't want you to lift anything yet." He shrugged. "You just got out of the hospital."

"The baby isn't heavy. Besides, I need to get used to carrying him." She worked to unfasten the straps and he began to stir, then made a little whimpering sound. She lifted him into her arms, feeling the tiny body root against her shoulder. If Jarrett would just leave.

Even though they had shared the birth, she had to draw a line at having an audience while breast-feeding.

"Not a problem."

"I'm sure you have plenty to do. And I need to feed him."

He looked embarrassed as he quickly glanced at his

watch. "Sure, I have a meeting anyway." He started out and stopped. "If you need anything…"

"I know, you're across the hall," she echoed, knowing how easy it would be to depend on him. To care more and more for this man. But she had to stand on her own and raise her son. "Jarrett, I could never begin to thank you for everything you've done."

"Hey, what good are landlords if they can't step in as labor coaches?" He glanced at the baby. "Be good to your mom, hot rod." He turned and walked out.

Mia heard the door shut and it sounded so final. But it had to be. She couldn't get involved with Jarrett McKane.

She laid BJ down on the changing table. Startled, the baby blinked open his eyes and looked at her. Something stirred in her chest as his rich blue gaze stared back at her.

"Hey, little guy," she whispered, almost afraid he would start crying. Instead, he stilled at the sound of her voice. Her throat tightened. "Welcome home, son." She swallowed, knowing there could be only one man in her life.

"Looks like it's just you and me now."

CHAPTER EIGHT

A FEW nights later, Jarrett got off the elevator on the second floor after a friendly poker game with Joe and friends in the community room.

Friendly, hah. They were card sharks. All of 'em. They had set him up, and by the time Jarrett had figured it out, it had cost him nearly a hundred bucks. Nothing to do but cut his losses and go home.

Fighting a smile at how the old guys had tricked him, he unlocked his apartment door. Before he got inside he paused, hearing a sound coming from across the hall. A baby crying. BJ. He checked his watch. It was after midnight. He waited a few minutes, but the crying didn't stop. Concerned, he went to Mia's door, and the sound got louder and angrier.

"Mia." He knocked, and after a few seconds the door opened.

A tired and anxious-looking Mia stood on the other side. Dressed for bed, she had on a robe, but by the looks of her, she hadn't gotten much sleep.

"Is everything okay?"

She didn't answer, instead she handed him the baby wrapped in a blanket. "Here, you make him stop. I've tried everything."

He quickly grabbed the bundle, then she turned and walked across the living room.

Jarrett looked down at the red-faced infant with his tiny fists clenched, waving in the air. "Whoa, there, little guy." He closed the door and followed after the mother. "It can't be that bad."

The answer was another loud wail. Not good.

He looked at Mia. "Did you feed him?"

She sent him a threatening look. "Of course I fed him. And I diapered him, bathed him, burped him, but he won't stop crying." Tears filled her eyes, her lower lip trembled. "I'm lousy at this."

"Stop it. You're just new at it."

He readjusted the squirming baby in his arms. Hell, he didn't know what he was doing either. He raised the baby to his shoulder and began rubbing his back. The baby stiffened, but Jarrett didn't stop.

"Has he been eating good?"

Mia nodded, but looked concerned. "Maybe he's not getting enough. I feed him every two hours."

"Maybe he's got an air bubble," Jarrett said.

He went to the sofa and sat down, laying the screaming baby across his legs. He remembered seeing Kira doing this with Jenna. After a few minutes a burp came from the little guy and the loud crying turned to a few whimpers and then, finally, silence. He kept patting the baby's back until he fell asleep.

He smiled at Mia who still looked close to tears. "Hey, BJ is fine now."

She didn't look convinced.

He lifted the baby into his arms and caught the clean sent of soap as the tiny bundle move against his shoulder, then finally settled down again. Protectiveness stirred in him as he carried the infant into the bedroom.

There was a night-light on over the crib, and he placed BJ down on his back. He made room as Mia adjusted the baby's position and covered him with a blanket. The kid stirred but didn't make another sound. The silence was golden.

They stepped away from the baby's bed. "He's so exhausted, he should sleep for a while," Jarrett said encouragingly.

"Thanks to you," Mia said, then added, "I couldn't even figure out it was gas."

Jarrett took her by the arm and led her across to the queen-size bed. They sat down side by side.

"So now you'll know," he said, seeing the dark circles around her pretty blue eyes. He brushed back wayward strands of hair that had escaped her ponytail. His heart pounded at the surge of desire that shot through him. He needed to leave, but he already knew nothing could draw him away from her.

"Call Kira. She had trouble with Jenna, too. That's how I knew what to do. And the next time you'll know, too."

She swiped at the last of her tears. "You're lucky to have family."

He glanced away. "Trace and Kira didn't always think so." He'd made so many mistakes with his brother.

"You and your brother haven't always been close?" she asked.

"Try never," he admitted. "It was mostly my fault."

"You two look pretty close now."

"Sometimes damage can't be fixed. But thanks to Kira, we've been working on it."

She watched him, waiting for more. "You're half brothers?"

He nodded. "Different mothers. I lost mine at six." He

shrugged. "My dad remarried, and his wife had a baby, Trace."

"Was she a good stepmother?"

"Alice? She didn't have much time for me, so I don't know much about her mothering skills. My dad just dealt with the ranch business, and that included taking me along." He glanced away. "I hated it. I can still smell the stink of the cattle, the burning hide of the steers during branding. And it's damn hard work, for damn little money. And as soon as I could, I got out. Straight into college."

She smiled. "Bet they were proud of you."

"Yeah, sure.

"Brad was my cheering squad. My best friend. Whether I wanted him to be or not." She glanced away. "All I gave him was trouble."

"I can't believe that. I bet you were a good kid."

She shook her head. "I was resentful, headstrong, but mostly stupid. An overweight girl who did anything to fit in. I turned out to be a big disappointment to a lot of people." She released a breath. "So I ran with a crowd that accepted me."

Jarrett could only nod, but he wanted to know so much more about Mia. What had hurt her so much she couldn't talk about it?

"Sometimes we can't see what's right in front of us." He began. "I took out resentment for my father on Trace. And it was well over thirty years before I figured out he wasn't my enemy. We're still working on it."

She brightened. "I bet little Jenna helps."

He tried not to smile but failed. "Okay, the little squirt has my number. But look at her. She's too cute to tell her no." *So are you,* he nearly confessed, trying to fight the attraction he felt.

"I agree. You are so lucky to have them."

"I'm realizing that." He eyed her closely. "When was the last time you slept?"

She shrugged. "I nap when BJ does."

He breathed a curse. "It's not enough, Mia. You haven't even been out of the hospital a week." Had it been that long since he'd seen her? Since he'd been purposely avoiding her? He'd worked late at the office, staying away to finish the repairs. Anything not to get any more entangled in her life. Trace was the family guy, not him.

Tonight, he realized how much he'd missed her. His gaze went from those brilliant blue eyes to her full mouth. God, he had to be crazy, but he couldn't stop himself as his head lowered to hers.

"Jarrett…"

"I like the way you say my name, Mia. A lot." He reached for her, pulling her to him until his mouth closed over hers. She released a sigh as her fingers gripped his arms and she leaned into him.

Only the sound of their breathing filled the room as his mouth moved over hers in a slow, sensual, drugging kiss, taking as much as she was willing to give. And he wanted it all.

Hungry. He was hungry for her. His tongue slid past her parted lips and tasted her, but it wasn't enough. He never could get enough of her.

He broke off the kiss and they both drew in needed air. He knew he had to stop, it was too soon for her.

Yet, it was already too late for him.

Mia stirred in the warm bed. It felt so good as she pressed deeper into her pillow. Sleep. She loved just lying in bed. Soon her thoughts turned to last night and Jarrett. The kiss. Smiling, she opened her eyes to the morning light coming through the window, then reality hit her, as she registered her tender breasts.

"BJ," she whispered, throwing back the covers to get out of bed. The crib was empty. Her heart pounded in her chest and she raced out to the other room. That was when she heard a familiar voice in the kitchen. Nola.

She stood in the doorway. "You are getting to be such a big boy," the older woman cooed at the baby in the plastic tub. BJ's tiny arms waved in the air as he enjoyed his bath.

Nola glanced at her. "Well, good morning."

"Good morning, Nola." She brushed her hair back. "What are you doing here? And why didn't you wake me to feed him?"

"He slept most of the night until five o'clock, which is when Jarrett called me and asked about using the bottle of breast milk in the refrigerator. I instructed him on how to heat it and he fed BJ. That was an hour ago, when I came up to relieve him. So I decided to steal some time with this guy while you got some more sleep." She grinned down at the baby, who was cooing. "BJ and I are getting to know each other."

Mia glanced around the empty apartment. When she'd dozed off last night Jarrett was still here. She suddenly recalled several things from their evening together. The things she'd told him about herself. Things she hadn't told anyone.

"If you're looking for Jarrett, he had a meeting to go to. He said he'd be back later today. I hope in time for our Christmas party."

"Who said I was looking for Jarrett?" She hated that she was so easy to read. "Why did he call you instead of waking me?"

"Because we're both worried about you." She nodded

for Mia to hand her the towel. She lifted the baby out of the water and Mia wrapped her son in the hooded terry cloth. "New mothers can get burnt out."

Mia hugged BJ to her. "I need to be able to take care of my son."

"You are a good mother, Mia," Nola assured her. "You're also doing this alone. But you have what's most important, a good heart and a lot of love for this little boy."

Together they walked into the bedroom and dressed BJ in one of his new outfits with a shirt that said, Chick Magnet.

Before Mia could pick him up, Nola did. "You need to eat something first. And I figure you have just enough time for some breakfast and a shower before this guy wants his mommy's attention."

She smiled. How lucky she was to have friends. "Thanks, Nola. I don't know what I'd do without you."

"We owe you a lot, too. We'd all be homeless without your help."

"We'll all be homeless soon anyway. So I didn't help that much."

The older woman pushed her bifocals back in place. "It's not over yet. I have faith in our handsome landlord. I also see the way he looks at you, Mia." She smiled. "And you should have seen him with BJ this morning. He's a natural."

Mia tried not to think about Jarrett McKane. He wasn't the man for her. He was the kind who only thought about the financial bottom line. Business before family. It was all about profit. The money. "He's counting the days until we're all out of here."

Nola watched her. "Yeah, that's the reason he had us all out to his house for Thanksgiving. And helped Joe paint your apartment. And stayed with you at the hospital during the birth of this little one." She glanced down at the baby, but quickly looked back at Mia. "Jarrett has a few rough edges, but that just makes him interesting." She lowered her voice. "And sexy."

Mia felt heat rise to her face. He had always been the one who'd showed up to help her. She recalled the way he made her feel when he kissed her last night. She hadn't wanted him to stop. That was a problem. If she got involved in a relationship with a man, she had to think about BJ, too. They were a package deal.

Worse yet, could she share all her secrets about her past? Even the lies she'd told to protect herself. What happened when Jarrett discovered who she really was?

Just a little before noon, Jarrett walked into the restaurant for his meeting. He hoped his lack of sleep last night wouldn't hinder him from convincing Fulton of his new plans. If he kept thinking about Mia and their kiss, it would. Or the fact that he'd left a beautiful woman's bed and gone into the other room to sleep on the sofa. That had been a first for him. There had been a lot of firsts with Mia, including being a babysitter for her son.

When Nola had relieved him from his duties early this morning, he'd had time to shower at his apartment and then go to the office where he'd finished up the presentation for today.

Over the past week or so, he'd been working on new plans for the Fulton factory. He hoped he'd come up with some changes to the construction that would be beneficial to everyone.

And save this deal for him.

If this new idea didn't go over with the CEO, he could lose a lot more than just a sale. Business ventures like this just didn't come down the road every day. It could take years for him to unload this property.

He walked across the restaurant behind the hostess to find Neil at the table by the window. The man didn't look happy, but Jarrett was hopeful he could convince him to make a few concessions.

"Neil, glad you could make it on such short notice."

They shook hands then sat down. "I hope you have some good news. I'd like to finalize this before I fly out tonight."

Jarrett released a quiet breath to calm his nervousness. *Don't let them see you sweat,* his college football coach had always told him. "Then let's get to it," he suggested.

The waitress came by and took their order.

"Now, tell me what's so important." Neil checked his watch. "I have to get on a plane and be back in Chicago tonight for a Christmas party. Robin will kill me if I'm late, especially since we're hosting it."

"It's what I want to show you." Jarrett pulled out the sketches for the plant site. "As you know, I have two apartment buildings located on the property." He took a breath and rushed on. "Because of airtight lease agreements, the remaining tenants aren't moving out until March."

Fulton frowned. "I thought you said you had it handled, that the building would be demolished by the end of January so we could break ground by early spring." Fulton was visibly irritated. "You assured me there wouldn't be a problem."

"Well, a judge stepped in and said otherwise." Jarrett raised a hand. "So I have another idea that might work even better."

Jarrett opened the folder and presented a sketch of the factory structure. "There's enough land to move the location of the new factory to the back of the property, and put the parking lot in front, leaving the existing apartment buildings."

"And why would I want to do that?" Fulton asked.

"Well, there's a couple of reasons," Jarrett began. "For one thing, it's a better location, a little further from town. So it won't be a traffic nightmare at rush hour."

"It would also cost more for extra materials for laying the utilities," Neil argued.

Jarrett pushed on, hoping his idea would work. "But if you use one of the existing apartment buildings for your corporate offices, you'll save on construction costs."

Neil's brow wrinkled in thought. "You can't be suggesting I use those dilapidated buildings?"

"Use *one* of the buildings," Jarrett corrected. "Why not? They're solidly built. They might have been neglected, but a remodel is a hell of a lot more cost-efficient than brand-new construction, even if you gut it entirely. You'd be recycling and it's better for the environment. And best of all, the building is already vacant. You could start the inside remodel after the holidays. No delay waiting for the ground to thaw."

Jarrett pulled out another drawing. "I had a structural engineer check out the building. It has the fifties retro look, but that can be changed, too. The main thing is it's large enough to house the plant's executive offices. Overall, you'll save money on this project. The shareholders will have to be happy about that."

Fulton didn't say anything for a while as he went over the new plans, then he looked at Jarrett. "There's no way you can remove the tenants?"

Jarrett shook his head. "I can't and won't. The majority are seniors on fixed income and two are disabled. I promised them they could stay until the spring." Then he said something that he never thought he would. "If possible, I'd like them to stay in their apartments for good."

Fulton leaned back in his chair. "You know that there are other locations the board of directors are looking at for this project, don't you?"

Jarrett's gut tightened as he nodded, seeing everything he'd worked for going down the drain. "Yes, I do. But you know this is the best location."

Fulton arched an eyebrow. "These people mean this much to you?"

Jarrett sat back. He hadn't thought about it until now, but these people been more accepting of him than his own father had. Truth was, they were starting to matter to him. Too much. He thought of Mia and BJ.

He eyed Neil Fulton's expectant look and shrugged. "Hey, I'm just trying to stay out of jail."

Later that evening, when Jarrett returned to the apartment building, he was exhausted. Fulton wouldn't give him an answer, but he had promised to talk it over with the board. Jarrett couldn't ask for any more.

He walked up the sidewalk toward the double doors. If Fulton went along with the new plan it meant Jarrett would keep the apartment building open. Of course, he'd have to put more money into the place, starting with paint. A lot of paint.

He shook his head. It was too soon to get excited. In these economic times nothing was a sure thing.

So Jarrett was in limbo. He thought about last night. Mia Saunders had stormed into his life and begun messing up his perfect plans. He'd liked things his way. Most of his life he'd been able to get what he wanted, until everything started to change, thanks to a blue-eyed do-gooder and her merry band of followers.

Hell, he'd never been a follower, and now look at him. Even worse, he was anxious to see her.

He pulled open the entry door and walked in, surprised to hear the sound of singing. A group of about two dozen tenants stood around an upright piano singing Christmas carols.

Standing back, he watched the people he'd come to know over the past few weeks sharing the joy of the holiday. This was hard for him. He couldn't remember when Christmas had been a happy time. Not since he was a small boy.

Then he spotted Mia across the room and felt a familiar stirring in his gut. She looked pretty, dressed in a blue sweater and her usual black stretch pants. Her dark hair was pulled back and adorned with a red ribbon. Smiling, she waved at him.

Maybe it would be a happy holiday after all.

CHAPTER NINE

MIA caught sight of Jarrett when he walked into the open lobby. It was hard not to notice the man. In a charcoal business suit with a crisp white shirt and a striped tie, covered by a dark trench coat, he looked more Wall Street than small-town Colorado.

"That's one good-looking man."

Mia glanced at Nola who was holding BJ. "Both the McKane men are handsome."

Her friend smiled. "But you're only interested in the older brother." She nudged Mia. "Now, go talk to him before someone else lays claim to your man."

She glared. "He's not mine."

"And he won't be if you keep ignoring him."

Nola gave her another gentle push, sending her off in Jarrett's direction.

Mia hadn't seen much of him, so there hadn't been a chance to invite him to the impromptu party. She couldn't blame him for keeping his distance. He was probably tired of taking care of her.

Besides, why would a man like Jarrett McKane be interested in her? Why would he want to take on a woman with a baby? Yet he'd done so many things for her. He'd been there when she'd needed him the most. How could she not care about a man like that?

Mia discreetly moved around the back of the crowd as Nola watched over BJ. Heart pounding in her ears, she walked up behind him. "You're expected to sing along," she managed to say.

Jarrett turned around to face her. Immediately, she caught the sadness in his eyes before he could mask it. "Everyone will be sorry if I do. My voice is so bad I don't even sing in the shower."

"I can't imagine you doing anything badly." Great. She was acting like an infatuated teenager, and she had never been any good at flirting.

"You'd be surprised at all the things I've messed up." His dark gaze held hers. "Did you get enough sleep last night?"

"Yes, thanks to you," she said, wondering if he'd thought about their kiss. Her gaze went to his mouth, then she quickly glanced away. "And thank you for not bringing up my meltdown."

Jarrett couldn't stop looking at Mia. Blue was definitely her color, bringing out the richness of her eyes.

"What meltdown?" he said, trying hard to focus on what she was saying. "You were just exhausted from lack of sleep and worried about your baby."

He couldn't help but remember how, during the night, he'd kept going in to watch her sleep. How strange was that? "I hope you got enough rest."

She nodded. "Plenty. And you're a good neighbor for coming to my rescue."

He tensed. Neighbor? *What neighbor kisses you like I did?* "That's me, just the full-service landlord," he said, trying to keep the sarcasm out of his voice. He started to leave, but she put her hand on his arm.

"Jarrett, what I meant was you went beyond helping me." Her eyes searched his face. "I've asked far too much of you. BJ and I weren't part of the deal when you were ordered to move in here."

"Did you hear me complain?"

She shook her head. "You should. I feel like I've taken advantage."

"Like I said, I haven't minded."

"And I'm grateful for everything—"

Grasping her hand on his arm, Jarrett leaned forward. The memory of last night's kiss had him aching for another. "I didn't do it for your gratitude, Mia."

He watched her swallow quickly, but before she could speak, the singing stopped and someone called to him.

"Unca Jay! Unca Jay!" Jenna came running toward him. "You're here."

He swung the child up in his arms. She had on a pretty sweater with snowflakes and dark pants.

"I have to go to work," he told her. "What are you doing here?"

"It's a Christmas party, silly. We got invited to come and sing." Her big blue eyes rounded. "You know what else?"

He played along. "No, what else?"

"It's only two more days 'til Christmas, and Mommy and Daddy asked everybody to come to our house for Christmas dinner. Even Mia and her new baby, BJ. And I got to hold him."

Jarrett looked across the room and saw his brother and Kira walking toward them. "How nice."

He got a hug from Kira and a handshake from Trace. "So, the festivities are at your house?"

Trace nodded. "Same as every year, but with Jody and Nathan gone, Kira's a little lonely. So why not have a big crowd?"

Jarrett looked at his sister-in-law.

"I love to cook," Kira said. "Besides, Nola and the others are bringing food, too. It's not much different than the group we had at your house on Thanksgiving."

"And now we have baby BJ," Jenna added as she patted her own chest and looked at Jarrett. "Unca Jay, did you know that BJ drinks milk from Mia's breasts?"

"Jenna…" her mother said with a warning look.

Everyone bit back a chuckle while Jarrett exchanged a look with Mia that felt far too intimate. Oh, yeah, he knew that.

His niece drew his attention back to her. "Look, Unca Jay." She pointed up to the sprig of greenery hanging overhead in the doorway. "Mistletoe."

Great. "It sure is." He leaned forward and placed a noisy kiss on the girl's cheek.

That wasn't the end of it; Jenna wiggled to be put down. "Now, you gotta kiss Mia."

Jarrett looked at a blushing Mia. "Sure." He leaned forward and placed a chaste kiss on her cheek. Their eyes met as he pulled back.

"No, not like that," Jenna insisted. "Like Mommy and Daddy do it. Put your arms around her and you have to touch lips for a long time."

Jarrett eyed his brother as Trace shrugged, trying not to smile. He got no help as he turned back to Mia. Without giving her a chance to protest, he reached for her and pulled her into his arms. His gaze locked onto her mesmerizing eyes, and, once his mouth closed over hers, everything and everyone else in the room faded away. It was all Mia and how she made him feel. How she tasted, how her scent drifted around him, how he was barely keeping himself in control.

Finally cheers broke out, and he tore his mouth away. "Did I do it okay?" he asked his niece.

A smiling Jenna nodded her head. He turned back to the woman in his arms. "Suddenly, I'm getting into the Christmas spirit."

Mia glanced at her kitchen clock and debated whether to attend the services tonight. For the first time in ten years, it wouldn't be Reverend Bradley Saunders standing at the pulpit delivering her Christmas Eve sermon. The last three years he'd been the pastor here in Winchester Ridge.

Mia had only been nineteen when Bradley had rescued her from self-destruction and got her on the road to recovery. From then on she'd sat in the front pew, grateful she had the love of family, and a future.

She glanced down at her son in the carrier. BJ would have the same; she would make sure of that.

"It's just us now, kid." She smiled as BJ, dressed in his dark-green holiday outfit, reacted to her voice with a cooing sound. "I might be new at this mother stuff, but no one could love you more." She wished she could give him a traditional family. Every kid deserved a mother and a father.

"I guess we'd better get going, or we'll be late."

She checked her own Christmas outfit, her standard black stretch pants and a long red sweater she'd found in a drawer.

After putting on her coat and BJ's cap and tucking a blanket around him, she picked up the carrier and walked out. She glanced across the hall to Jarrett's apartment.

As much as she tried not to, she'd thought about Jarrett a lot over the last few days. Okay, so it had been from the day he'd moved in. Not that she'd wanted him in her life; he'd just sort of barged into it.

At first, she'd even tried to compare Jarrett to her father, but she quickly realized they were nothing alike. Preston

Saunders would never open his home to a bunch of strangers for Thanksgiving dinner. Nor would he give up his time to help paint a room for her baby son, or even stay and play coach as she gave birth.

Mia touched her lips thinking about the shared kisses. Even though Jarrett had been goaded into the one under the mistletoe, he hadn't acted as if he minded at all. Yet he hadn't exactly shown up at her door the past thirty-six hours wanting to continue what had been started either.

Suddenly the elevator doors opened and Jarrett got off. He immediately smiled. "Hello, Mia."

"Jarrett," she said, trying to act casual. He looked too good in his jeans and sweater with a sheepskin jacket hanging open and his cowboy hat cocked just a little. "Merry Christmas."

He raised his arm to check his watch and she noticed the big shopping bags. "Is it that time already?" He eyed her closely. "I guess I'd better finish up my wrapping." He glanced at BJ. "Where are you two headed?"

"To the Christmas service at the church."

His smile faded. "Give me a second and I'll drive you."

"Jarrett, no. I can't let you do that. I can drive myself. We're not going that far."

"There's a lot of snow still on the roads, and your tires aren't in that great a shape."

He was right, but she hadn't had a chance to replace them. "It's only a few miles."

"And you have precious cargo." He nodded at her son and pulled out his keys. "Then at least take my SUV. It's four-wheel drive."

He was letting her drive his car? She looked at him, telling herself not to read anything into it. It was for her ten-day-old son. She decided to test him.

"Okay, I'll let you drive us, but only if you stay for the service."

He frowned. "You're kidding, right?"

She shook her head.

"It's been a long time since I've been inside a church."

"It's not going to crumble down around you. C'mon, you can handle it. You're a big strong guy," she challenged him.

He hesitated and finally relented. "Okay, just let me drop these presents off in the apartment."

She hadn't really thought he'd come, but suddenly she was glad she didn't have to face this night alone. Nor did she mind spending Christmas Eve with this man.

Nearly two hours later, Jarrett stood in the back of the church, watching as the parishioners fussed over BJ. Mia was enjoying showing off her son. She'd put up a brave front, but he knew it had been hard for her to come back here without her brother, her family.

He glanced around the ornate stone building with the stained-glass windows and high ceilings. He remembered another church across town where his stepmother had insisted they go to services weekly. And the Sunday school teacher who swore that a young Jarrett's bad attitude would send him straight to hell.

That hadn't been a good time in Jarrett's life. His mother had died suddenly when he was barely six, and within a few months his father had another wife. The following year his baby brother, Trace, had been born. And the struggle between the McKane brothers had begun. The father he'd so badly needed after the loss of his mother, turned away and found another family. Jarrett had been told he had to carry more weight and help out. Suddenly there wasn't any time to be a kid, or time to be with the father he'd needed so desperately.

He quickly pushed aside the bad memories. Tomorrow was Christmas, and, thanks to Kira, he and Trace were finally working on liking each other.

Family wasn't the only thing that gave him trouble; he was still hoping to hear from Fulton.

He'd closed the office early today, but Neil had his cell phone number. If the land deal crashed, *no one* would have a happy holiday. He might even end up being a permanent resident in the Mountain View Apartments.

He glanced across at Mia. Not that he would mind being her neighbor. If he was honest, he was happy that he got to spend time with her tonight. He tried to tell himself it was only because he felt protective of the new mother. But he was attracted to her, big-time. As much as he'd tried to stay away, she kept drawing him back into her life. He sure as hell wasn't putting up much resistance, either.

Mia walked over to him. "I'm sorry I kept you waiting. Everyone wanted to see BJ."

"Well he's a cute kid, and you should be a proud mama. It's okay if you want to stay."

She shook her head as she pulled the carrier hood up and covered the baby. "I really need to feed BJ. Could we go home?"

"Sounds good." He took the carrier from her and escorted her through the doors. Once outside they were greeted by a strong wind and snow flurries. He pulled Mia close against his side, trying to shield her from the biting cold.

At the SUV, he helped Mia get in and quickly latched BJ's safety seat in the back, then he climbed in the driver's seat and started the engine.

Glancing out the window, he waited for the cab to warm up. "I was afraid of this."

She was shivering. "I'm sorry. I didn't think the weather would turn bad. It's supposed to be clear tomorrow."

Her coat wasn't heavy enough to keep her warm. He flipped the heater on high and took a blanket from the back seat to drape over her legs. "We're lucky it's not a big storm, just the tail end of it. But I'll feel better when we're back at the apartment."

Jarrett pulled out of the parking lot cautiously. He glanced at the baby in the back seat; he was starting to fuss.

"Hang on, BJ. We'll be home soon."

Jarrett turned off the main street onto a back road, thinking he could shave off some time. First mistake—the road was deserted. Secondly, it hadn't been cleared of snow. Even with four-wheel drive, traction was nonexistent.

"Sorry, this was a bad idea. I'll turn back."

BJ began to cry louder.

Jarrett found a wide spot in the road and slowed more as he began to turn the wheel. He cursed when the back of the vehicle began to slide. "Hang on," he called to Mia. He gripped the wheel tighter, turning into the slide, but he couldn't gain control. When he got the car stopped they were off the side of the road.

Jarrett cursed under his breath and BJ let out a wail. Shifting into Reverse, he backed up, but nothing happened. He tried going forward again, but the only thing he got was the spinning of the tires as the car slipped sideways, deeper into the snowbank. Although angry with himself, he remained calm. "I'll go see if I can dig us out."

"Be careful," Mia called over the screams of the baby.

Placing his hat on his head, Jarrett got out and made it through the ankle-high snow to the back of the car. He opened the hatch and took out a shovel. He began digging, but soon discovered it was useless. He made his way back to the driver's side and climbed in. Pulling off his gloves, he took out his phone. "We need a tow truck." He punched in his roadside assistance. By the time he hung up, he wasn't happy. "She put us at the top of the list because of the baby, but it still could be an hour."

"Long as we're warm, it's okay," she said. "Do you have enough gas?"

"Yeah, a full tank."

"Good. I need to feed BJ. I'll go in the back."

"No, stay up here, it's warmer." He flipped on the interior light, leaned into the back seat and managed to unfasten the crying baby's straps.

"Come on, little guy, settle down," he coaxed. "You'll have your mama in a minute." He lifted the small bundle and handed him to Mia who had already removed her coat, leaving it draped over her shoulders.

She looked at him and paused. "Would you mind turning off the light?"

"Oh, sure." Of course she didn't want an audience.

In the dark, he could see her tug up her sweater. All at once there was silence. Jarrett looked over at Mia as she leaned over the child at her breast, stroking him.

His chest tightened at the scene. Finally turning away, he concentrated on the snow blowing across the front window, but he could still hear Mia's soft voice as she talked to her son. Leaning back against the headrest, he closed his eyes and tried not to think about how much he wanted to wrap his arms around both of them and protect them. Yeah, he'd done a great job of that so far.

Restless, he sat up. "Life is pretty simple to him, food and Mama." He looked at her as she moved the baby to her shoulder and began to pat his back.

"Sometimes it scares me that I have someone who's so dependent on me," she admitted.

"You're a natural at this."

She paused. "How can you say that when you've seen me at my worst?"

BJ gave a burp and she lowered him to her other breast. This time Jarrett didn't turn away from the silhouette of mother and son. He'd never seen anything so beautiful. Leaning across the console, he reached out and touched the baby's head. "I've only seen a mother who loves her child." His chest tightened at the sight.

Their gazes met in the dark car. "I do love him. At first I was so frightened, but he's become my life. I know technically he's my nephew, but—"

Jarrett placed his finger against her mouth to stop her words. "In every way that counts, Mia, he's your son. You carried him in your womb, now you nourish him from your body." His fingers moved and grazed her breasts. "It's beautiful to watch you with him."

"Oh, Jarrett."

At the husky sound of her voice, he shifted closer. He felt her breath against his cheek.

Suddenly a bright light shone through the windshield, illuminating the front seat. He drew his hand away, but continued to hold her gaze.

"It seems we've been rescued," he said, knowing he wasn't so sure about his heart.

CHAPTER TEN

It was after eleven o'clock by the time the tow truck pulled Jarrett's SUV out of the snowdrift and they'd driven back to the apartment. The night had been long, but still Mia didn't want their time together to end.

Jarrett walked her to her apartment door. "I'm sorry about tonight. I never should have taken that back road." He glanced at BJ in the carrier. "I would never do anything to endanger either one of you."

"Of course I know that. You didn't cause the bad weather, Jarrett."

He watched her a moment, then he finally said. "I probably should let you get some sleep."

She put her hand on his arm when he started to step back. "Won't you come in for some coffee?" Did she sound desperate? "I have something for you."

He looked surprised. "Okay, but let me grab something from my place first. I'll be back in a few minutes."

With a nod, Mia went into the apartment, leaving the door unlocked. She quickly dressed her son in his sleeper and put him in the crib, knowing in just a few hours he'd be awake and hungry. She checked her makeup and went back into the living area, quickly picked up several baby items scattered around and tossed them into her bedroom.

She'd finished plugging in the lights on her tabletop

Christmas tree when there was a soft knock. She tugged on her sweater and brushed back her hair before answering the door.

"Oh, my," she gasped as Jarrett walked in carrying several presents. "What did you do?"

He set the packages down on the table. "I took Jenna shopping yesterday and she convinced me that BJ had to have all these things." He raised an eyebrow. "You should have seen what I talked her out of."

Mia eyed the boxes, but picked up the stuffed bear. "He isn't even sitting up yet."

"Then put some away for his birthday." He smiled and her heart tripped.

She glanced toward the present under her tree. Before she lost her nerve, she grabbed the tissue-wrapped gift and handed it to him. "This is for you."

He looked touched. "Mia, I didn't expect anything."

She shrugged as if it were nothing. "It's probably silly."

He tore through the paper and uncovered the charcoal-gray scarf she'd knitted. As he examined it she wondered if he could see the mistakes.

He stared at her, his brown eyes tender. "Did you make this?"

She managed a nod. "Nola taught me while I was on bed rest. I'm not very good."

She didn't get to finish as he leaned forward and placed a sweet kiss on her mouth. Chaste or not, she felt dizzy.

"Thank you. I've never received anything so nice."

Jarrett had trouble holding it together. He hadn't enjoyed the holidays for a long time. His mother's death only days before Christmas had left a little boy devastated with grief.

"You're welcome," she said, her voice hoarse.

He finally stepped back and draped the scarf around his neck before he lost all control. "I have something for you."

"Did Jenna pick it out, too?"

"No, I did." He pulled a small jewelry box from the bag. "So I can't blame her if you don't like it."

She blinked seeing the store name on the box. "Oh, Jarrett, you shouldn't have done this."

He smiled at her. "You haven't even seen it. Maybe you won't like it."

She gave him a stern look. "Of course I will." She opened the box to see a sterling-silver chain with a round charm engraved with BJ's name and his date of birth.

She glanced at him. "I was wrong, I don't like it. I love it. Oh, Jarrett. It's perfect. You couldn't have gotten me anything I wanted more."

He released a breath. He'd bought women gifts before. Why did he care so much about this one? "I'm glad."

She took it out of the box. "Will you help me put it on?" She gave him the necklace and turned around. Moving aside her rich brown hair, she exposed her long slender neck to him. Somehow, he managed to fasten the clasp, but she was too tempting not to lean down and place a kiss against her exposed skin.

He felt her shiver, but she didn't move. He slid his hands around her waist, pulling her against him. He whispered her name and after a few seconds, he turned her in his arms. "This isn't a good idea. In fact it's crazy. You just had a baby, and I shouldn't be thinking…"

"Oh, Jarrett." She shook her head. "I don't see how… I'm having enough trouble trying to handle my life. You've seen me at the worst times, and you have to be tired of rescuing me."

"Maybe I like rescuing you." He didn't let her go. He

had no business wanting her. He was all wrong for her. But all he wanted was to be with her.

"I want to be self-reliant."

"We all like to be. But there are some things that are fun to do with someone else, someone special."

He dipped his head and captured her mouth. His arms circled her and he pulled her close as he deepened the kiss, tasting the addicting sweetness that was only Mia.

With the last of his control, he broke off the kiss, and pressed his forehead against hers. "You're big trouble, lady."

Before she could say anything, the clock chimed. Midnight.

"Merry Christmas, Mia."

Even though the air was brisk, the day promised to be bright and sunny. A perfect Colorado Christmas, Mia thought as she fingered the charm on her necklace.

She glanced across the SUV at Jarrett. Christmas Eve had already been wonderful and this morning had started out close to perfect, too. Jarrett had showed up with a box of jelly donuts and they'd shared breakfast together. Just the three of them.

It could give a girl ideas. Ideas she had no business thinking when she should only be thinking about her son.

Although the man was definitely making this holiday memorable, especially when he'd insisted on taking her and BJ out to the ranch today. Were they a couple? No. She shook away that crazy thought.

"We're here."

Jarrett's voice drew her attention as he turned off the main highway and drove under an arch announcing the McKane Ranch.

Mia felt the excitement as a large two-story house came into view. She smiled at the snowman in the front yard, then her attention went to the wraparound porch and the dark shutters that framed the numerous windows.

Jarrett bypassed the driveway and went around the house. "We're pretty informal here," he said. "I don't think the front door has been opened in years. Everyone has always used the back door."

That would never be allowed in her parents' home. The service entrance was only for the hired help. "Sounds like my kind of place. I bet you had fun growing up here."

His smiled faded. "Ranching is a lot of work. One of the reasons I left and went away to college."

He parked next to Joe and Sylvia's car at the small porch that overlooked the barn and corral. "So now the place belongs to Trace."

He turned off the engine. "After our parents died, I was happy to sell him my half."

She smiled. "You can still come back whenever you want, and the best part is seeing your family."

There was a long pause, then he said, "There was a long time when I wasn't exactly welcome. But a few years ago, Trace and I became partners in a natural gas lease. The money helps him keep the ranch and not worry about having to run cattle. And I can invest in business ventures. Anyway, then Jenna came along, and somehow I ended up calling by more and we sorted some things out."

Mia was surprised by Jarrett's admission. "Well, I'm glad you and your family have reconciled your differences."

He nodded and turned toward the house. "Oh, look, here comes the welcoming committee."

Kira and Trace stepped onto the porch. "Welcome and Merry Christmas."

Mia got out and the cold breeze brushed against her cheeks. "Merry Christmas," she called back.

Trace came down the shoveled steps and greeted his brother first, then walked around the car to her. "Welcome, Mia."

"Thank you for inviting us. Your place is beautiful."

"We think so." He glanced at his brother. "There's plenty of time before dinner so you can leave BJ with us while Jarrett shows you around." He pointed toward a group of bare trees. "The cottage is just over there, if you're still interested in seeing it."

Mia turned around to see a small white structure about fifty yards from the house. "Oh, yes. I'd love to."

Jarrett got BJ from the back seat while Mia handed a large poinsettia plant to Trace.

When Jarrett's brother started to protest, citing the no-gift clause, she quickly said, "It's from BJ."

With a smile, she retrieved a salad and a pie and carried them into a huge country kitchen with maple cabinets and granite countertops filled with food. Several mouthwatering aromas surrounded her, making her hungry.

Nola and Sylvia were already there helping Kira with the meal. "Just put those things down, if you can find a spot for them."

Kira beamed as she came up to Jarrett and gave him a kiss on the cheek, and then looked down at the carrier. "I'd love to get my hands on this little guy, if I could."

"Sure," Mia told her. "He loves being held."

It took only seconds before Kira had BJ in her arms. "Now you two run off and see the cottage. We can handle things here."

Jarrett came up beside Mia. "They seem to be trying to get rid of us."

"Not at all, but I would love to have this little guy around more." Kira smiled down at the baby and cooed, "Oh, yes I would."

"Let's go." Jarrett escorted Mia out the door and across the yard, but she was distracted by the horses roaming around in the corral.

"Oh, what beautiful animals."

Jarrett changed direction as they detoured to the corral fence. "Trace has been doing some horse-breeding the past few years. This guy is Thunder Road." When he whistled, the horse trotted over as Jarrett climbed up on the fence railing so he could pet the spirited animal. "Hey, Roady." He rubbed the horse's face and neck briskly, then glanced at Mia. "This guy was sired by Midnight Thunder, a champion cutting horse."

"He's beautiful." She could see how much Jarrett loved animals. "He seems to like you, too."

"He knows me. I come out here sometimes."

There was so much about this man she didn't know, that he kept hidden. She glanced around. "I still can't see how you'd want to give this place up. I love the peace and quiet."

He shrugged and released the horse and they watched him run off. "When I was younger, I called it boredom. I wanted excitement and fun." He looked toward the horses. "After my mother died, my father and I didn't get along much."

Mia understood that. "He's gone now?"

"Yeah. When his wife died, he wasn't much for living alone."

"What about your mother?"

He continued to stare toward the corral. "She's been gone since I was a kid."

"I'm sorry, Jarrett. How old were you?"

"Six."

"Oh, God, you were just a child."

He turned toward her. She could see the pain before he quickly masked it. "I grew up fast."

"What about your stepmother?" She wanted him to tell her that she'd been a caring and loving woman. "Did she help you through that time?"

"I don't remember much." He shifted. "She was just there, and soon, so was Trace."

"At least you had a brother to share things with."

"Yeah, right. I did everything possible to let him know how much I hated him."

Jarrett stepped up to the small cottage porch and turned to see if Mia needed help. Damn, he hated that he'd spilled his guts to her. He'd never told anyone about his childhood. Why her?

He inserted the key into the lock. "I know Trace and his foreman, Cal, redid the entire inside."

"The outside is well-maintained, too," she said, coming up beside him. "I can't wait to see the rest."

He swung open the front door, and they stepped into a living room that had a small sofa and two chairs. An area rug covered part of the shiny hardwood floors.

"Oh, this is nice."

He gestured with his hand to go on, and she walked into a galley-style kitchen. All the stained-wood cabinets were new, as were the egg-shell-colored solid-surface counter-tops. The white appliances gleamed. Jarrett had no doubt Kira had been out here cleaning.

"This is so nice. There's even a table and chairs." Mia walked through to a small sunroom that looked toward the open pastures. "This would be a perfect work area. Plenty of light and space for a desk and computer."

She beamed as she walked ahead of him and down the

hall. She stuck her head into the bathroom that also had a stackable washer and dryer. "Okay, I've died and gone to heaven." She went on to check out the two bedrooms. When she came out she looked about to burst.

Her dark hair was bouncing against her shoulders. And he noticed how slim she was becoming, and how long her legs were. Yet, it was her eyes, those blue eyes of hers that made his gut tighten in need.

"This is three times as big as my apartment," she said, bringing him back to the present.

"And thirty miles out of town." But closer to his house. "In the winter that could be a difficult drive."

"But I know I can afford this place," she insisted. "Obviously, if I stay here, I plan to pay rent to Kira and Trace."

He studied the stubborn woman in front of him. She was beautiful and no doubt capable of doing anything she set her mind to.

"Okay, but you have to let me take you to look for a dependable car. That sedan of yours is in bad shape."

Her eyes widened. "I can't afford a new car."

"Not new, but at least an upgrade from what you're driving now. I can get you a good deal, one with decent tires."

She smiled slowly. "You're a fraud, Jarrett McKane. You try to get everyone to think you're this ruthless business-man with no heart, but you're a nice guy."

He stood straighter. "If you think I've gone soft because I'm fixing the apartments up, think again. I have a good reason for doing it. The judge ordered me to."

Her look told him she wasn't buying it.

"Ah, hell. At least while you're living there I can keep an eye on you."

"You're not responsible for me, Jarrett," she told him

sternly. "I can take care of myself, and have for a lot of years."

"I know that." He couldn't help wondering about other men in her life. "What if I just want to help you?" He tested her. "Say if I want to come around to see if you and BJ need anything? I mean, I do visit my brother and sister-in-law out here."

"And Jenna," Mia added.

"And Jenna," he repeated, watching the light play off her hair. Her skin looked so soft.

Her eyes met his. "Aren't you going to be too busy with the new factory project to bother with us?"

He shrugged. "That's not a done deal, yet. I'm still going over things with Fulton Industries."

"It's because of the tenants, isn't it?"

"Things could work out better." He didn't want to tell her his idea to keep the apartment building. "Hey, what's the worst that can happen? The deal goes south and I get to live in the hellhole apartment 203 forever."

"Well, BJ and I would be your neighbors."

He stepped closer. "I thought you were moving in here?"

"Not if the apartment is still available. I like paying my own way. Would you raise the rent on us?"

He smiled at her. "Maybe we can work out a special deal."

An hour later, with BJ asleep in his carrier in the living room, the Christmas dinner could start.

In the McKanes' dining room, there were two long tables dressed with red and green tablecloths and holiday china. A row of delicious food dishes crowded the sideboard, not to mention the overflow waiting in the kitchen, along with a dozen pies and assorted desserts.

Mia carried her heaping plate to the table to find a seat. It was no surprise Jarrett had saved one next to him.

"This is the best Christmas ever." Jenna climbed into a booster seat next to her uncle. "And you know what else, Unca Jay?"

The youngster didn't wait for prompting. "I'm glad you bringed BJ and Mia. And that you aren't mad at Daddy anymore."

Mia caught the exchange between the two brothers who sat across from each other.

"Yeah, well it's Christmas," Jarrett said. "Everyone should get along."

"It's a time for peace and goodwill," Joe added. "And we should think about those who aren't here with us today."

"Like Jody and Nathan," Jenna said. "And Ben, 'cause he's protecting our country."

"That he is," Nola said. "We need to pray for all servicemen who are away from their families, too. And to keep them safe."

Everyone bowed their heads as Trace led them in the blessing. Mia was surprised when Jarrett took her hand in his. It was warm and reassuring. She was glad that she had someone to share this day with.

"Now, let's eat," Jarrett announced after the prayer. And it began. Lively conversation and good food.

"Mia, how did you like the cottage?"

She looked across the table at Kira. "Oh, I love it. It's beautiful and so roomy."

Kira exchanged a look with her husband. "Does that mean you plan to move in?"

"If you still want us, I'd love to move out here."

A big smile spread across Kira's face. "That's wonderful." She looked at her brother-in-law. "And it's not so inconvenient living out here. We have good neighbors. How far away is your place, Jarrett? Five miles?"

Jarrett's fork paused on its way to his mouth. "Something like that."

His sister-in-law was grinning now. "See, there's a McKane around if you need one, and also we have Cal here, too."

The foreman looked up from the other end of the table and nodded. "It would be nice to have another little one around the place."

Trace stood up. "Speaking of little ones." He glanced down at his wife and exchanged a look that showed everyone in the room how much they loved one another. "We have some news, and we thought that this would be a perfect day to share it. Kira and I are expecting our second child next summer."

Jarrett watched as the room erupted in cheers and congratulations. He suddenly felt the old jealousy creeping in. Why would he be jealous of a baby? He'd never wanted a family.

He turned to Mia, who was watching him.

"Isn't that wonderful news?"

"Yeah, it is." He glanced at his brother. "Hey, Trace. Congratulations."

Jenna finally got into the act. "Am I going to have a baby sister? I asked for a sister."

Everyone laughed.

"We don't know if it's a girl or boy, yet," Kira told her daughter. "But I know you'll be happy with either."

Before Jenna could speak, the sound of BJ's crying drew everyone's attention.

"Someone's hungry. Excuse me," Mia said as she left the table.

Jarrett wanted to go with her, but he had no right to

share this time with her and her son. He saw Kira direct her upstairs to a bedroom.

Again he was on the outside looking in, where he'd been for so many years. He didn't want to be there anymore.

Mia sat in the rocking chair in the McKane nursery. Once the room had been Jenna's, but the toddler had been moved to another bedroom and a big girl's bed. How convenient that Trace and Kira already had a beautiful room for their next baby.

She smiled down at her son, and her heart nearly burst with love. She could no longer see her life without this child. He was everything to her, and she would do everything she could to give him a good life. She'd find a way to finish law school and make a home for him. She ran her hand over his head. "I promise you this, BJ, I'll be the best mom I can."

Her thoughts turned to Jarrett. Would he be a part of their lives? Would he come around once she moved out here? Once the apartment building was demolished, he'd be so involved in the factory project she doubted there would be time for her.

Mia fingered the chain around her neck. She was a realist, and couldn't lie to herself. Jarrett wasn't the type of man who took on a woman with a baby. Yet, she recalled him telling her about his mother's death, and his stepmother's neglect. She thought back to her own youth. Seemed they weren't so different after all.

BJ stiffened and began to fuss. "I think you need a burp." She brought him to her shoulder and began to pat his back gently. BJ cried louder. "Sshh, honey. Relax." She continued the rubbing, but it wasn't working.

There was a knock on the door and Jarrett peered in. "Sounds like someone isn't happy."

Mia was both confused and relieved as Jarrett walked in. "You want to try?"

He took the infant from her. He placed her son against his large chest and began to walk and pat. After about thirty seconds, the crying stopped when a burp erupted from the infant.

Jarrett smiled at her. "Looks like I still have the touch."

"Then I'll give you BJ's feeding schedule and you can come by and do the honors."

She didn't hide her smile at his surprised look.

"You know I will if you need me," he said sincerely.

"Don't, Jarrett. I can't keep relying on you to help me." Even if she wanted nothing more than to have him around all the time. "BJ is my responsibility."

He came closer, but wouldn't relinquish the baby. "Why, Mia? Why do you think you have to do this all by yourself?"

She glanced away from those velvet-brown eyes. "It's safer that way, Jarrett. And no one gets hurt."

He touched her chin and turned her back to him. "Who hurt you, Mia? What man broke your heart?"

She stiffened and shook her head. "It's not important. It was a long time ago."

"It's important to me. You're important to me, Mia."

She wanted so much to believe him, but she wasn't good when it came to trust. "Oh, Jarrett. I don't know what to say."

He stepped in closer. "Good. I'd rather do this." Even with BJ against his shoulder, he leaned down to capture her mouth and quickly had her heart racing and her body stirring, wanting more.

He broke off as BJ began to complain. "Maybe we can

talk more about this later." He gave her another peck and straightened up just as Kira walked in.

"I hate to disturb you both, but there's someone here to see you, Mia."

"Who?"

"He says he's your father."

CHAPTER ELEVEN

MIA had been dreading this day for ten years. Why did he have to find her? Why now? She saw the confused look on Jarrett's face, not surprising as she'd told everyone she had no family.

As far as she was concerned, since Brad's death, there hadn't been anyone. Putting a sleeping BJ in the crib, she finally looked at Jarrett. "Please, don't say anything about the baby."

He stared at her a moment, but his expression didn't give anything away. "I'll follow your lead."

They walked out and down the stairs, grateful that Kira had put the unexpected guest in the living room, away from everyone. She glanced at Jarrett. "I need to talk to him alone."

He nodded. "I'll be close by."

With a sigh, she walked into the room. Preston Elliot Saunders stood in front of the massive stone fireplace. Since his back was to her, she took the opportunity to study him. Still tall and trim, his once thick dark hair was now nearly white and there was a slight slump to his shoulders. He turned slightly and she could see he wore a dark wool coat over a business suit.

Had she ever seen him when he hadn't been in a suit? As a child she'd only seen him when she needed to be disciplined. She'd been the daughter who couldn't seem do anything right, so that had been a lot.

Preston finally turned around and she saw that the last decade had added lines to his face. She hoped to see some emotion from him, but, once again, she was disappointed.

She fought off all the old fears and insecurities and stepped fully into the room. "You wanted to see me?"

He frowned. "After all this time that's all you have to say to me?"

"Ten years ago I was a disgrace to the family and was destroying my life. You disowned me and sent me away. So excuse my surprise when you show up here now. There must be a reason." She knew exactly the reason. Somehow he'd learned about her baby.

"No matter what happened between us, you should have had the decency and compassion to tell me about Bradley's death. Your mother and I were heartbroken when we learned about it recently."

Mia noted he didn't mention his daughter-in-law's death. Not only had Preston and Abigail disapproved of their son's chosen profession, they had made their disdain at his choice of a wife perfectly clear. Karen hadn't come from the right family. "It's been years since you disowned us, so why would I think you wanted to know about Brad's death?"

Her father looked sad. "For God sake's, Margaret, we're family."

"Since when? We weren't a family. A family man comes home. You were never there, and when you were, all you did was criticize."

Preston straightened. "You know perfectly well why I did what I did. You were out of control. An embarrassment to yourself and everyone else. We tried to warn Bradley."

Mia tried to hide her surprise. Her brother had contacted their father? "Did you expect him to send me away, or have me locked up in a place where I lived like a prisoner?" She shivered in memory. "Like you had?" She spread her arms. "I've gone to college, and I can support myself. Well take a good look, I'm perfectly fine. Have been for years. So now that you've checked on me, you can go home with a clear conscience." She turned to leave, praying this would be the end.

"Not so fast, Margaret. There's some unfinished business to do with my grandson."

Mia swung around as a fierce protectiveness took over. "He's not your grandchild. You didn't want to be a part of my life or Brad's because we refused to do what you wanted. So you have no claim on this baby."

Preston Saunders frowned. "You're wrong, Margaret. My family has always come first, which is why I'm here." He glared at her. "You can't possibly think you can give Bradley's son the life I can. I've seen where you live. You have nothing to offer him. The boy would be much better off with your mother and me."

"That's not true. Besides I can give him love, which is more than you and Mother ever did. Brad and Karen wanted me to raise their child if something happened to them."

Her father's gaze moved over her. "I don't want my grandchild living in that slum apartment."

"Not that it's any of your business, but I'll be moving soon into a two-bedroom house. I have income and I'll be going back to law school. I can support BJ. And that's all that you need to know."

He studied her for a long moment. "I know more than you might think. And I don't want you moving in with this Jarrett McKane."

She was shaking. "My personal life is none of your business."

Her father stood his ground. "You're wrong. I've asked around. Your ex-football player may have had minimal success during his college career, and even in this small town, but things can change quickly."

Mia hated that this man could still get to her. And he was planning to use her friendship with Jarrett. "What is that supposed to mean?"

He shrugged. "These are hard times, and business deals can easily fall apart. Just recently I was discussing this with Neil Fulton. What a coincidence that his wife, Robin, and your mother were sorority sisters." A smug look appeared across his face. "From what Neil tells me, it's still up in the air about where their new factory is going to be built."

Mia felt sick to her stomach. "This has nothing to do with Jarrett. It's between you and me."

"Then all you have to do is give me what I want."

Jarrett stood in the hallway. If Mia had let everyone think that her parents were dead, there had to be a reason, and he couldn't wait to hear it.

"Is there a problem?" Trace asked coming up to him.

"Not sure." Jarrett had no idea what was going on. "But I plan to find out." When he heard Mia tell her father goodbye, he went into action. He walked into the living room.

"Is everything okay?" He went over to Mia, slipping a possessive arm around her back.

She looked surprised to see him. "Yes. My father was just leaving."

The man didn't move, just turned his attention toward Jarrett. "I'm Margaret's father, Preston Saunders." He held out a hand.

Jarrett shook it. "Jarrett McKane. You should have let us know you were coming to town."

"This was a sudden trip for me." Saunders glanced back at his daughter. "Mia and I have been estranged for…a while."

Jarrett felt Mia stiffen. "It's been years," she insisted. "You disowned me and Brad, and you have no right to this child."

Saunders seemed surprised by his daughter's backbone. "We're still family. And this child is a Saunders which is the very reason I'm here. To help you." He glared at her. "Margaret, you can't possibly think you can give the child the kind of life he deserves." He shook his head. "You and the boy would be much better at home with your mother and me."

Mia was still trembling, even after her father left. Once the front door closed, she wanted to disappear. Instead, she hurried up the stairs to check on BJ. Anything to keep from having to face Jarrett. To have to explain. But he wasn't letting her get away, and followed her.

"Mia," he called to her.

She stopped in the upstairs hall, but didn't turn around. "I can't talk about this right now."

She started for the nursery, but he took her by the arm and led her into a guest bedroom. After the door closed, he pulled her into his arms.

She didn't resist. Shutting her eyes, she let herself revel in the secure sound of his beating heart, his warmth. She fought the tears, but lost as a sob escaped and she began to cry. She cried for the years that her parents weren't there for her. For herself because she couldn't be the daughter they wanted her to be. For the relationship she wanted with this man that now was lost too.

The only thing that mattered now was BJ.

She pulled back and wiped her eyes. "I'm sorry."

"How long since you've seen your father?" Jarrett asked as he pulled out a handkerchief and handed it to her.

"Ten years. It was a few days before my nineteenth birthday." Wiping her eyes, she raised her head. She might as well tell him everything.

"I'd just gotten released from the rehab clinic he'd had me committed to. I was excited because he came to bring me home. Instead, he handed me five thousand dollars and said he'd paid a year's rent on an apartment in Atlanta, Georgia. He felt it would be better for everyone if I didn't return to Boston."

Mia moved across the room toward the bed. She needed space. "Funny thing was, the pills I'd become addicted to were ones prescribed by a doctor my parents insisted I see to help me lose weight."

Jarrett walked over to her. "I can't believe you were ever overweight."

"I had crooked teeth, too."

His finger touched her chin and made her look at him. "And incredible blue eyes, and hair the color of rich coffee," he told her as his gaze moved over her face. "I could go on and on."

She swallowed hard. "No one has ever said that to me."

"Maybe you never gave them a chance."

She shrugged. "I've been kind of busy lately. But Jarrett, as a teenager, I gave my father plenty of reasons not to trust me."

"Didn't we all." He smiled. "I was no angel, either. That doesn't mean you aren't a good mother now."

She gasped. "BJ." She started to leave, but he pulled her back.

"He's sleeping," Jarrett said. "You know that kid's got a strong pair of lungs, so we'll hear him when he wakes up." He paused a moment then said, "Back to you. How did you end up in Colorado?"

"I used the money my father gave me and flew to Denver. Brad was a junior pastor there. He and Karen had just gotten married, yet they opened their arms and took me in. He probably told our parents, but I think Preston was just happy I was out of his life."

"Seems that Brad wanted you," Jarrett acknowledged.

She nodded. "At first I gave him a lot of trouble. But he got me to finish high school, then college. For the first time, I felt good about myself." She felt a surge of panic. "I owe it to Brad and Karen to raise their son with love and compassion for other people. I'll do anything to keep my parents from taking BJ."

He reached for her. "It won't happen. I won't let it."

No! She couldn't let her father destroy Jarrett, too. She shook her head. "No, Jarrett, you have to stay out of this."

"Mia, listen to me. You're going to need some help."

The last thing Mia wanted was for this to go to court. She was doubtful she could win against the power of the Saunderses' money. She shook her head. "I can't let my father scare me off. I have to prove to him I can handle things on my own." She pushed past him and out the door.

More importantly, she had to get Jarrett McKane out of her life. It was the only way she could protect him.

This had been Jarrett's best Christmas in years until the unwelcome guest showed up. Although dessert was being served, he knew that for Mia the celebration was over. Using the excuse that BJ was fussy, he drove her back to town.

Mia's silence continued as they walked into the apartment building. Jarrett tugged on the glass door, hearing the scrape of metal before it gave way and opened. Inside, Jarrett glanced around the large lobby. Even with the elaborate holiday decorations, the place was still a dump.

It needed a lot of work, especially if he was going to rent to more tenants. Whether Fulton finalized the factory deal or not, he should get a contractor out here to look over the building.

Saunders must have come here first. How else would he know that Mia was at the ranch? What if he'd taken pictures? If he was going to fight for custody, would he show them to a judge?

Damn. He needed to get Mia out of here and moved into the cottage. Honestly, he wanted her at his house, but Ms. Independence would never go for that.

At the apartment door, Mia unlocked it and they went inside. She carried the baby into the bedroom.

"I'll bring up the rest of the things," he called to her.

Jarrett hurried back outside in the cold. He opened the back of his SUV and grabbed the box of leftover food and presents. That was when he noticed the car at the end of the car park. With the help of the overhead security light, he saw the shadow of a man leaning against a dark vehicle.

He didn't like a stranger hanging around. He thought about the older tenants, then Jarrett thought about earlier today and couldn't help but wonder if Saunders had something to do with it. Had he hired someone to watch the place? Would he go that far? The man he'd met today didn't seem like the type who gave up easily.

Jarrett carried the box back inside the lobby. He took out his cell phone and called the sheriff's office, asking his old friend from high school, Danny Haskins, to come by and check out the situation. He wasn't going to make it easy for Saunders.

Call made, Jarrett returned to Mia's apartment. When she came out of the bedroom, she didn't hide her surprise that he was there.

"Jarrett, I didn't realize you were still here."

He put the box on the table. "I brought up the rest of the things from the car."

"Oh, I'll put them away, you don't have to stay."

He was discouraged by her rejection. "Look, Mia, I saw a stranger hanging around the parking lot." He took off his hat and coat. "I'm having it checked out, so I'm not leaving here until it's cleared up. Could be your father is having someone watch you."

She looked panicked, but quickly covered it. "I have a good lock on the door. He's not getting in here."

"I want to help you."

She shook her head. "I don't want you involved in this."

He went to her. "I'm already involved, Mia."

"No, Jarrett. You can't keep rescuing me."

Before he could answer there was a knock on the door. Jarrett checked the peephole, then pulled open the door. "Hi, Danny."

The sheriff removed his hat and stepped inside the apartment. "Hey, McKane."

"Thanks for stopping by, Danny."

"Not a problem." He looked at Mia and nodded. "Hello, ma'am."

"Mia, this is Sheriff Danny Haskins. Danny, this is Mia Saunders."

"Nice to meet you, Ms. Saunders. I'm sorry to have to bother you on Christmas."

"It wasn't necessary for Jarrett to call you."

"It's my job to protect our citizens." Danny turned to Jarrett. "There was a dark sedan leaving when I pulled in, but I got the license plate. It's a rental." He pulled out a small notebook. "The name of the customer is Jake Collins of Collins Investigation. He's a P.I. out of Denver and he's been here over a week."

Haskins turned to Mia. "Jarrett told me that your father, Preston Saunders, came to Winchester Ridge after no contact with you for years."

Mia nodded. "He has a P.I. watching me to see if I make any mistakes," she said to Jarrett. "He'll use anything he can against me."

Jarrett saw not only her fear, but the sadness. Damn Saunders. "We're not going to let him," he assured her.

He walked Danny out the door. "Thanks, friend. Is there any way you could keep an eye out for this car? I'll bet my next deal that Saunders is trying to find something against his daughter so he can get custody of his grandson and it's my guess he'll do anything to get him."

"Since he isn't breaking the law, I can't do much, but I'll alert my deputies to keep an eye out. I'll also have them patrol this area." His friend smiled. "I take it you have more than a passing interest in that very attractive brunette."

"Yes, I do. So don't get any ideas."

Smiling, Danny raised a hand. "Enough said, friend. You always had all the luck when it came to the ladies. I'll let you know if I find anything."

Jarrett said goodbye, then went back inside to find Mia in the kitchen putting away leftovers.

He walked up behind her. "I don't want you to be alone tonight. I don't trust Saunders."

She closed her eyes a moment. "My father just wants me to know that he's there, that he's a threat if I don't do what he wants. I can handle this on my own."

"Like you did in the past," he said, regretting the harsh words. "Why are you being so stubborn?"

She stiffened. "Because if you stay it will only infuriate him. Believe me, you're not the type of man Preston Saunders wants his daughter to associate with. You're not successful enough, not from the right family or the right school."

"So a poor country boy isn't good enough for a Saunders?"

She glared at him. "That's correct. It's strictly eastern blueblood."

Jarrett hadn't done too badly for himself, but suddenly he felt like the kid with dirt under his fingernails.

"I'm that poor little rich girl," she told him. "I'll do whatever it takes to keep my son. So please, I need you to leave… And I mean for good."

Mia woke up the next morning, fed BJ and tried to eat but her stomach couldn't handle food. She hadn't gotten much sleep last night, either. All she kept seeing was the look on Jarrett's face.

How could she have said those things to him? The hurt she'd caused nearly killed her, but she couldn't let him get mixed up in her fight. He would lose everything.

So many things rested on her playing nice with her father. Even if she was miserable and lost the man she loved.

There was a knock on the door. She didn't open it until she heard Nola's voice.

"I was worried about you," the older woman said.

"Why? I'm just tired from the long day yesterday."

Nola watched her. "Your father showing up out of the blue might have had a lot to do with it, too."

She nodded. "I'm sorry I never told you about my parents."

Nola shook her head. "We all figured if you didn't want to talk about them you had your reasons."

Tears welled in Mia's eyes. "My father's threatening to take BJ."

Nola took hold of her hand. "He can't do that, you're a good mother. All of us can attest to that."

"But Preston Saunders has money and a legal team on his payroll that I can't compete with. He's a successful businessman, and I'm a law student who can barely make ends meet."

"What about Jarrett? He could help you."

She shook her head. "I can't let him get involved in this. You have no idea what my father could do to him. He'd destroy him without a backward glance. No, this is my fight. And I told him so last night."

Nola nodded. "That explains the man's grumpiness when I greeted him this morning. A bear, he was."

"It's better this way, Nola. He has to stay away from me."

"Why don't you let Jarrett decide if you're worth it or not? He's a big boy. He'd probably go a few rounds with your father and still be standing afterward."

"No. This is my fight. All my life, I've let everyone else do things for me. First my parents, even Brad. Jarrett has already done too much."

"I know you can fight this. You're a strong woman who handled the tragedy of her brother's death with grace and strength. You've fought hard to get into law school. And don't you forget all the times you helped us. I remember a feisty gal who took our landlord to court so we could stay in our homes."

And fell in love with him, Mia thought. "I was only helping out my neighbors."

Nola took Mia's hands in hers. "Did you forget the most unselfish gift of all? You carried your brother's and his wife's baby."

She smiled. "Oh, Nola, that wasn't a sacrifice, that was pure joy for me. BJ is a miracle."

Nola agreed. "And no one could love him more. BJ belongs with you. What's most important, it was your brother's wish. He trusted you enough to raise his child. That should say it all. So somehow we've got to make sure that little boy stays with his mother. That's you. Nothing will ever change that."

CHAPTER TWELVE

THE next morning, Jarrett got out of bed in a bad mood. He left the apartment early so as not to run into Mia, then went in to the office, hoping to get some work done. Not possible. He couldn't clear his head of the stubborn woman.

"Ah, hell." He stood up from his desk and went to the large window looking out over the snow-covered ground. The Rocky Mountains off in the distance were magnificent against the blue sky. The view did nothing to improve his lousy mood.

How was Mia doing today? Dammit! She couldn't cave in to her father's demands. She had to stand her ground, everything would be all right. He needed to be there....

"Hey, you busy?"

Jarrett glanced over his shoulder and saw Trace peering into the office. "If I said yes, would you go away?"

He walked in. "Sorry, big brother. Your bad attitude doesn't scare me anymore. What happened with Mia yesterday?"

It had taken a lot of years, but he finally realized that Trace and Kira wanted to be the family he'd longed for. "Nothing happened. She sent me packing last night when I offered to help her. So I don't know and I'm not sure I care."

His younger brother placed his hat on the chair and

joined him at the window. "Now, that's a lie. And your way of helping is about as subtle as a bulldozer."

Jarrett glared, but Trace didn't budge. "Thanks a lot."

"I know you mean well, but it's true," Trace told him. "So what's going on with Mia's father?"

"We're pretty sure that Saunders has had a P.I. watching her this past week. He came straight out and told Mia he wants to take BJ away from her."

"What kind of a man would do that to his daughter?"

"You don't want to hear my answer to that. Besides, I told you I'm not involved in this anymore. Mia doesn't need or want my help."

"Poor Jarrett." Trace shook his head. "Ain't getting any lovin' these days."

"It isn't that way with Mia." Damn, if he didn't want it to be though. "She's a new mother."

"And a very attractive woman."

Jarrett studied his brother. "I thought you only had eyes for Kira."

"Kira has my eyes, plus my heart and soul and my fidelity. But that doesn't mean I don't notice a pretty woman. I'm not dead yet. As I remember, a while back you had eyes for my wife, too."

That seemed so long ago. Now he couldn't think of Kira as anything else but a loving sister. "Bite your tongue. She's the mother of my favorite little girl."

"I think you just found the right woman for you."

Jarrett couldn't deny it, nor could he confirm it. Mia was different from anyone he'd known.

He glanced at Trace.

"What?"

"I want to ask you something, but you'll probably think it's stupid."

"Just ask me."

"How did you know that you loved Kira?"

His brother acted surprised by the question, then he turned serious. "Honestly, I can't remember a time I didn't love her, even when our marriage was falling apart."

Trace raised his hand. "Here are a few of the symptoms if you have doubts. When Mia looks at you, you get tightness in your chest, like you can't breathe in enough air. Your heart rate isn't ever normal when she's around. And when she smiles at you." He shook his head. "It's like everything is right in the world."

Jarrett groaned. "Damn!"

There were voices in the outer office, and then his secretary, Marge, came in followed closely by Nola Madison and Joe Carson.

"Sorry, Jarrett," his secretary apologized. "I told them you were busy, but they said it's important they see you."

"It's okay, Margie." He had no idea why they would come here.

As Marge left, Nola hurried across the office. "Hello, Trace." Then she turned to him. "Jarrett, this is important. It's about Mia."

He saw the worried look on the older couple's faces. "Did something happen to her? To BJ?" He came around the desk. "Is her father causing trouble again?"

Nola looked at Joe, then turned back to him. Her large glasses made her eyes look huge. "No, she's fine for now. I would tell you, but I promised Mia I wouldn't say anything."

Jarrett frowned. "Am I supposed to guess?"

Nola shook her head. "No. I did tell Joe and Sylvia, but Sylvia is at the apartment watching BJ so Joe drove me here. He didn't promise Mia anything, so he came along to talk to you."

"Talk about what?"

Joe took over. "Mia's considering moving home with her father, so she'll be guaranteed to be a part of the boy's life."

"What? She can't do that." Jarrett started for the closet and pulled out his jacket. "How is she expected to have a life of her own? And what about BJ? We all know what Mia and Brad thought about their father's parenting skills. No, it isn't gonna happen."

Trace stopped Jarrett at the door. "Hold on there, bro. I think you need a plan before you go rushing in and playing hero."

"My plan is to stop him."

"Bulldozer," Trace reminded his brother.

"What if I tell her how I feel?"

Trace didn't look happy. "Okay. So you're ready to take the next step? The big question is, what are you going to offer her?"

Jarrett swallowed the dryness in his throat. It had been all he'd thought about it. He'd never felt about anyone the way he did about Mia. "I care about her. But you know everything is pending on this Fulton deal. I could be broke in a month."

Nola nodded. "Does that really matter? We all know the way you feel about her."

"Yeah," Joe agreed. "That was some kiss under the mistletoe."

"Thanks."

Nola pushed her way to the front. "But is it enough to commit to her?"

"Stop pushing the guy," Joe said. "He can't think."

"He doesn't have time to think about it," Nola argued. "Besides, how long does it take to know you love someone? If it's for real, you know it." The older woman turned back to Jarrett. "You know she's leaving town because of you?"

His chest tightened. "I don't want her to leave."

Joe spoke up again. "Mia's only leaving to save the factory project. Seems Mr. Saunders knows Neil Fulton and he's threatened to ruin you if she doesn't play his game."

Jarrett looked at Trace for help.

"Okay, maybe it's time we help out a little," his brother said.

Jarrett had never let anyone get this close. He thought of Mia's pretty blue eyes, her smile. Somehow she'd gotten through all his barriers. Now, nothing mattered if he couldn't be with her.

Jarrett looked at the group. "You know, this means I could be living in the apartment from now on."

Joe smiled. "Hey, Mountain View is a great place."

"Just make sure you tell that to the judge when I go back to court."

The next day, Mia walked into the hotel lobby. With each step, she had to fight the urge to turn and run. Run so far that no one would find her or BJ. She detested being here. Even as a child she'd hated that awful feeling that came when she was summoned by her father.

Nothing had changed. She was still sick to her stomach. Of course she was older and hopefully wiser. Bound and determined to stand up to the man, she had a list of rules for if she did return to Boston.

First and most important, she would never give up custody of her son. BJ would be a Saunders, but she would be his mother. So, needless to say, there were a lot of things to be ironed out before she committed to anything. She had to protect her son and herself.

She would never trust Preston Saunders. That had been

the reason she left BJ with Sylvia. He wasn't getting his hands on her grandson, yet. Suddenly she was sad, thinking about leaving this town and all her friends. They'd been like family to her and BJ.

And then there was Jarrett.

She swallowed the ache in the back of her throat. She'd never wanted to hurt him, or herself, but by leaving she'd manage to do both. She knew Preston Saunders well enough to worry that he would destroy Jarrett's factory project. Perhaps even the man himself.

She also had to think about the people in town who needed those jobs created by the project. Not just in the building of the factory, but finished, it would employ a lot of workers.

She went to the desk clerk. "Preston Saunders, please."

The young man looked the name up on the computer screen. "Mr. Saunders is in one of our small conference rooms." He gave her directions.

Mia walked along the carpeted hallway and found the room. The door was ajar and she heard her father's voice. She peered in and saw that he was on his cell phone, looking out the window.

He didn't see her. "I told you it will all be taken care of by the end of the month. Yes, the money transfer will be there by the thirty-first." He nodded. "You have my word."

Mia was only half listening, but she wondered if her father could have money troubles. It wasn't a good time for a lot of businesses. She knew little about the family finances, except that both her parents came from money.

Her mother's wealth came from Ashley Oil and Textiles. Her father's from banking. Their marriage had been more of a merger than a love match.

Since she and Brad had been disinherited, she didn't concern herself with any of that. She only cared about BJ. And she would do anything to keep him. Even sell her soul.

Preston ended his call and turned around to see her. "Eavesdropping isn't polite, Margaret."

She walked up to the table. "You're the one who set up this meeting. Besides, you're the one who's been sneaking around. I don't think I want to stay if you're going to be condescending."

She started to leave and he called her back. With hesitation, she turned around and waited.

"Maybe we both got off on the wrong foot," he said.

"That's what you call destroying my life?"

"I want to be a part of my grandson's life. Is that so awful?"

"You keep saying that." She paused. "What about Mother? Is she here with you?"

He shook his head. "No, your mother stayed home. She didn't want to get her hopes up if this didn't work out."

Mia had realized a long time ago that Abigail was just what Preston wanted her to be. A society wife. She did charity events, but raising her children was just too difficult for her. Nannies had always taken care of her and Brad. Mia was afraid that would happen with BJ. She couldn't let history repeat itself. She reached inside her purse, took out an envelope and handed to her father.

"What's this?"

"The list of conditions you have to agree to if you want me to return to Boston."

"You're in no position to demand anything."

She straightened her back. "If you don't want a court battle, Father, we need to come to terms. I will never hand over my son to you. I'm BJ's mother and that isn't going to change." She still needed to work out the legal adoption agreement. "So we're working on my terms. You've got twenty-four hours to give me an answer."

She swung around and marched out, praying he wouldn't stop her. She'd crumble for sure. But just thinking of BJ gave her strength. He was all she had. She'd lost everyone else, she couldn't lose him, too.

Later that day, Trace and Jarrett were at the office doing research on Preston Saunders. Thanks to his Internet whiz, Margie, they'd been able to learn a lot about the Saunders family, including the fact that Saunders Investments was a Fortune 500 company.

"How much to do you want to bet Mia is a shareholder?" Jarrett glanced at Trace. "I wouldn't put it past Preston to have another reason besides his grandson for showing up here. Could it have something to do with money? Mia's money?"

"Wait, this is all speculation," Trace said.

"You didn't talk to this man—I did," Jarrett assured him. "By Mia's own admission, he's been a lousy father. And on Christmas, he made no bones about trying to use his authority over his daughter by showing up and trying to regain that control and take his grandson. There's got to be a reason why he's here." He stood. "And I'm going to find out what it is."

"Where are you headed?"

"To see Mia. Whether she likes it or not."

That evening, Mia was still shaken from the visit with her father. Of course, this time she'd done a lot of the talking, but he'd definitely had enough to say.

She looked down and watched the baby at her breast and

smiled. She began to calm down. No way did she want to relay her anxiety to BJ.

She knew Preston would be upset with her demands. She'd insisted she have her own apartment, refusing to live in the large house she was raised in. She refused to let her father control her life again. But as long as she had BJ, life would be good.

She heard a knock on the apartment door. "Come in, Nola, it's unlocked," she called from the bedroom.

When she looked up, she saw Jarrett standing in the doorway of her bedroom.

"It's not Nola," he told her.

She tried to cover herself, but BJ was having none of it. He began to fuss. She raised him to her shoulder and quickly made an adjustment to rearrange her blouse.

"Jarrett, I'm busy right now. So if you'll—"

He walked toward the bed. "Leave?" he finished for her. "I will, but first we need to talk, Mia. And we need to be honest."

Mia stared at the man. He looked so good she felt a stirring that made her ache. "We've said everything already."

"No, we haven't." He sat down on the bed. "Look, Mia, I know why you're doing this. It's because of what your father threatened to do to me."

She couldn't answer him. "Who told you that? Did my father say something to you?"

He shook his head. "I wish he had, because I'd have let him know that he couldn't scare me off."

She rubbed the baby's back as he squirmed in her arms. "That's not it. I decided that I need my family around me. It'll be good for BJ."

He leaned closer. "You have family here, too." Those

dark eyes held hers. "You deserve a good life, Mia. I don't believe you'll have that if Preston is running the show."

"I just want to keep my son."

BJ let out a cry.

"Seems the little guy isn't happy," Jarrett said and reached for the baby. "Let me."

Before Mia could stop him, he'd lifted the infant off her shoulder, but Jarrett's focus was still on Mia. She quickly pulled her blouse together, covering her exposed breast.

He put the baby against his shoulder and began to pat his back. He spoke in a soothing voice and, after a burp, the baby calmed down. He returned him to Mia's outstretched arms.

"He should be able to finish his supper now."

Jarrett's gaze held hers and she couldn't look away, nor did she want to. They'd shared so many things in the past few months. He'd been a part of BJ's life from the beginning. She opened her blouse, moved her son to her other breast, and he began to nurse again.

Jarrett drew an audible breath. "I don't think I've ever seen anything so beautiful."

She looked at him, feeling tears building in her eyes. "Please, don't do this. It's hard enough…"

He placed a finger against her lips. "It's going to be okay, Mia. I promise you." He leaned down and brushed his mouth against hers. She sucked in a breath and he came back for more. The slow, lingering kiss wasn't enough, but she couldn't take any more.

With a shuddering sigh he pulled back. "I don't want to let you go."

She swallowed hard. "Oh, Jarrett, there's not a choice."

"There's always a choice, Mia," Jarrett told her and stepped back, away from temptation. "Now, to return to why I stopped by— I believe your father's sudden appearance has to do with money, your money and your brother's money."

She looked confused. "We don't have any money."

"You're listed as a stockholder in the family business."

"No, he took the money away from us when we left home."

"Your father doesn't run Ashley Oil and Textiles. Your maternal grandfather, Clyde Ashley, began that family business. Did you know your grandfather?"

She shook her head. "Not really, I was five when he died."

"It's only speculation, I'm going to bet Clyde had made provisions for his grandchildren in his will. Did you or Brad ever get any money from him?"

"We never wanted anything from the family."

"I understand, but you're entitled to it, Mia. More importantly, you could use it for BJ and his future. And if your brother had his trust coming, it would definitely go to his son."

Mia's eyes rounded as things started falling into place. "That's why Preston wants BJ?"

As if the baby heard his name, he paused and looked up at his mother. She smoothed her hand over his head, and coaxed him back to her breast.

Jarrett glanced away a moment to gather his thoughts away from Mia. How incredibly beautiful she looked with her child. "Have you noticed any correspondence concerning insurance policies, or where your brother's financial records might be?"

"I've already collected Brad's insurance. Every other piece of paperwork that my brother had I put in a file box." She raised BJ to her shoulder and began to pat his back.

"It's in the hall closet." This time, BJ burped like a pro. She got up and carried the infant to the crib. Buttoning her blouse, she went to the hall and retrieved the box.

She carried it to the coffee table in the living room. "I put everything in here after the accident. If it didn't need to be paid, I didn't really look at it."

"You had enough to deal with." He arched an eyebrow. "Do you mind if I have a look now?"

Mia shook her head. She would do anything that might stop her father.

She watched as Jarrett shuffled through the file for a few minutes, then he extracted an envelope and took out the letter. He scanned it. "Bingo. I think I found it."

Jarrett handed the paper to her. The letterhead was that of a law firm, Knott, Lewis and Johnston. It was from James Knott, addressed to Brad and dated a year earlier.

The lawyer said that he was the executor of Clyde Ashley's estate. Since Bradley had reached his thirty-fifth birthday he was now entitled to his inheritance. No amount was given. Just to contact him as soon as possible, and a phone number.

Mia was in shock. "Why hadn't Bradley gone to claim his money?"

Jarrett shrugged. "Maybe he didn't have a chance."

Mia thought back. "He turned thirty-five not long before his and Karen's trip to Mexico. Maybe he was going to contact the lawyer when he returned home."

"And he never got the chance," Jarrett finished. "Maybe the lawyer contacted your father and that sent Preston searching and he found out about his son's death. And since no one has kept it a secret that BJ is Brad's child, your father learned about a grandson."

That didn't stop Mia's worry. "So now he's going to try

and have me proved an unfit mother to get the money. He doesn't have enough?"

"And we can't let him have it. This money will secure BJ's future."

"Not if he proves I'm a bad mother."

"Hey, where's that feisty woman who came after me? Mia, you're a great mother. Besides, you've got the most important thing on your side—your brother wanted you to raise his son. So much so, he put it in writing."

CHAPTER THIRTEEN

LATER that afternoon Jarrett paced his office. Mia was on her way to the hotel to see her father, while Fulton was on his way here to discuss his board of directors' decision about the factory project.

Hell. He didn't want to think about business right now.

What he wanted was Mia as far away from Preston Saunders as possible. That wasn't going to happen today. He'd wanted to go with her, but she'd insisted that she needed to confront the man by herself. Her only concession had been to let Nola go to help watch BJ.

Still Jarrett didn't trust Saunders. He wouldn't put it past him to kidnap them both and drag them back to Connecticut.

"The hell with this." He headed for the door just as Neil Fulton walked into the outer office.

"Hey, Jarrett. How was your holiday?"

"It was busy. And yours?"

Neil seemed to be in a good mood. "The same. I didn't know if I could get away early. I'm glad we could get together on such short notice."

"About that, Neil. An emergency has come up and I need to leave."

The man frowned. "I'm sorry. Can I help?"

Jarrett wasn't planning to mention Saunders but what did he have to lose? He didn't care about the project unless he had Mia. "Maybe you can. I hear you're a friend of Preston Saunders, but the guy's a real bastard."

"Whoa, whoa." Neil raised a hand. "Who told you we were friends? I've only met him a few times at fundraisers."

Jarrett was puzzled. "Aren't your wives sorority sisters?"

He nodded. "They went to the same eastern college, but that doesn't mean they're friends. There's no connection between us, I haven't seen the man in probably five years." Neil frowned. "Rumor has it he's lost a bundle on sub-prime mortgage loans."

Jarrett cursed, and filled Fulton in on the details of what had been going on since Saunders came to town. "He said he'd talked to you about putting a halt to the factory project."

Neil shook his head. "Even if Saunders and I were friends, I would never let personal issues interfere with my business decisions. It never works out. Although I do listen to my wife, and she's definitely a fan of yours. She likes a man with integrity. You didn't toss your tenants out on the street, even though it could mean losing this deal."

"Yeah, even I have a heart."

"That's not always a bad thing. It actually helped you win this deal. Several of the board members are inclined to agree with my Robin." Neil smiled. "She's looking forward to meeting you."

Jarrett blinked. "Meeting me? You've decided to build the factory here?"

Neil nodded. "You were right, your location is the best and there's plenty of room to expand. And as long as the

PATRICIA THAYER   161

business offices are going into your retro apartment building, Robin wants to help decorate them."

Jarrett knew he was grinning like a fool. "I'll have it
put into the contract. Could we talk about this later?" He
slipped on his coat. "I need to let someone know I want to
be a part of her future. And boot a certain someone else
out of town."

"Would you like some backup? I wouldn't mind helping
bring Saunders down."

"It could get nasty."

Neil straightened. "I can hold my own. I want to see you
get the girl, too."

"Not as much as I do."

Mia pushed BJ's stroller into the hotel. She hadn't wanted
to come back here again, but she didn't want her father
anywhere near her apartment.

All she wanted was to finish this for good. She wanted
Preston out of her life. More importantly, out of her son's
life.

No matter what it cost financially.

"Mia, I wish you would think about this for a few
days," Nola said as she walked alongside her. "I don't
trust the man. You shouldn't, either. Maybe you should
call Jarrett."

Two months ago she hadn't even known Jarrett McKane.
And now she was hopelessly in love with the guy. She
thought about all the things he'd done for her, for BJ. How
he'd been there for her when she'd really needed him. He'd
coached her through her son's birth. When she was exhausted, he walked the floor with BJ so she could sleep.

"Nola, I can't let Jarrett suffer at my father's hand. This
is my problem. I should've stood up to my father years ago,

but this is going to end today." She couldn't let Jarrett lose everything because of her. Not for her past sins.

That was the reason she'd just give Preston what he wanted. Money. Then he would leave town, and she and BJ could have a peaceful, loving life.

"I know Jarrett doesn't mind helping you." The older woman walked next to the stroller. "You have to know he cares about you and BJ."

"Yes, he's been a good friend." She wanted more.

"Friend?" The older woman gave her a sideways glance. "I think you'd better open your eyes and see how that man looks at you. Even you can't be that blind."

No, she wasn't blind. "Okay, I've seen him watching me." They continued along the hall to the small conference room. "But Jarrett McKane watches a lot of women."

"All men look—until they find the right one. You're Jarrett's right one, Mia. Don't let your father spoil your chance at happiness. Jarrett is a good man." Nola smiled. "He reminds me a lot of Reverend Brad," she rushed on. "Maybe Jarrett has a slightly rougher side, and he curses a little too much, but he has the same good heart."

Mia stopped. "I know all this Nola. It's one of the reasons I'm doing this."

Her friend pursed her lips and shook her head.

"I don't need the money. What Jarrett's doing for this town by creating jobs is much more important. I can work. I plan to finish school and make a good life for BJ. I won't ever let my father hurt the people I care about."

Mia released a breath, and pushed the stroller through the conference-room door to see her father standing by the window. Dressed in his tailored gray suit, he took his time to come to greet her.

"Margaret."

She gripped the stroller handle tighter. "Hello, Father."

He nodded and turned to Nola. "We haven't had the pleasure."

"Nola Madison, Mr. Saunders. I'm a *very* good friend of Mia's."

Mia watched her father look down at the stroller, studying the sleeping child, but he didn't comment on his grandson. "Maybe we should get started."

"Yes," Mia agreed. "We have a lot to cover before you leave town."

At the front desk, Jarrett and Neil got directions to the conference room and headed across the lobby. Their pace picked up when he saw Nola with BJ in the stroller.

"Oh, Jarrett," she cried. "I'm so glad you're here."

"Of course I'm here. Nola, this is Neil Fulton. Neil, Nola Madison. He's going to help us."

The two exchanged pleasantries, then Jarrett nodded toward the door. "Is Mia inside?"

"Yes, she's with her father. I'm worried, Jarrett, she's trying to protect everyone but herself." The baby started to fuss, and Nola rocked the stroller. "See, even BJ's upset."

Jarrett directed Nola to a lounge area a short distance away, and promised her everything would turn out okay. Then he partially opened the conference-room door to hear what was going on. He saw the father and daughter across the small room, their backs to him.

"You can't have BJ," Mia insisted. "And I'm not returning to Boston with you, either."

"You're making a big mistake, Margaret. I hate to go to court and spill all the family secrets, but you know I will. I have to protect my grandson."

"And I have to protect my son from you. Come on, we're

alone, you can admit you only want BJ because of Bradley's trust fund."

Saunders tried to act wounded and failed. "How could you accuse me of something like that? Besides, you should know that any money would stay in trust for Bradley's son. I couldn't get my hands on it."

"As the child's guardian, you'd have access to the account. It must be a sizable amount for you to come all this way."

"I can't touch it. Your grandfather made the trust airtight." He studied her. "You, on the other hand...you have something I want."

After all this time, she'd thought she was immune to his ability to hurt her. She wasn't. "What is that?"

"Your grandfather Ashley was very generous to you in his will. Not only with a trust fund, but with company stock. You can't touch the money until you're thirty-five or married. But there is the question of the stock."

"You want my Ashley Oil stock?"

"I've earned it. I've been voting your shares for years."

"How? You shouldn't have had access once I turned twenty-one."

He smiled. "You don't remember signing power of attorney over to me? When you got out of rehab?"

She hated to think about that time of her life. She did remember her signature had been her ticket out. All she had to do was give Preston Saunders what he wanted, and she'd get her freedom. "So what else could you want?"

"Your grandfather was overprotective. I only had a temporary power of attorney and it's expired."

After all these years, her father had only tracked her down to get money from her. "Why don't I just hold out my arm and you can take all my blood, too."

"Don't act so dramatic. For years, your mother and I had to explain away your indiscretions."

She wasn't going to let him bring her down. "I was your daughter," she stressed, then calmed down. "You never once accepted me for who I was. When I had a problem, you were never there for me.

"You had the Saunders name and money, more advantages than a lot of kids. So it was expected you'd do well. Bradley Junior will have to do the same."

"No, you won't do the same thing to my son."

Preston glared at her. "He's not your son, Margaret. He's your nephew. And he needs to be raised as a Saunders."

"Never," she insisted. BJ was hers. She'd already started legal procedures.

Jarrett watched Mia stand tough. Yet, Preston wasn't relenting, either. "I changed my mind on one of the conditions of our new agreement. Along with your stock, I want to see my grandson periodically. Say, four times a year. And I'll need the stock signed over immediately."

She shook her head. "That's not our deal. You get the money. You walk away."

"You're not dictating to me. Secrets could leak out. There's a certain factory project that hangs in the balance."

Jarrett couldn't stand back any longer. He glanced at Neil as he swung open the door and walked into the room.

Preston Saunders was the first to notice him. "So you brought your cowboy along to save you."

Mia turned around. He could see her shock and some relief. "Jarrett. What are you doing here?"

He came up to her. "I thought you might need some support."

"I don't want you involved in this. I can handle it."

He leaned closer and whispered, "Woman, as far as I'm

concerned, you could handle anything. But if you think I'm going to stand by and let this guy hurt you, you'd better think again." He gave her a quick kiss, then placed his arm around her shoulders and faced the problem.

"Your words are touching, Mr. McKane," her father said, "but this doesn't concern you."

"I think it does, Mr. Saunders. I don't like that you've threatened Mia."

"As I said, this doesn't concern you." He looked at Mia. "Does it, Margaret?"

She looked at Jarrett. "He's right. This isn't good for the factory project."

"You think I care about the project more than you?" He smiled. "I can't tell you how much it means to me that you're willing to sacrifice your future for me. But there's no need."

He turned to Preston. "Okay, Saunders, here's how it's going to be. You're going to leave town *today*. Mia is going to stay here, finish law school and raise her son. Oh, and if I'm lucky, I get to be a part of their lives."

"Well, you're going to have to live off her money, because your future is looking bleak at the moment. You're about to lose everything."

"I think you're wrong about that, Saunders."

Everyone turned toward the door as Neil Fulton walked in. He went to stand beside Jarrett and Mia.

"Neil," her father stammered. "It's good to see you again."

"I don't think so, Saunders. First thing, I don't like you tossing my name around as if we're friends." He glared at Preston. "Secondly, Jarrett McKane and my company just agreed on a rather lucrative property deal. Nothing you say is going to change a thing." He took a step closer to Preston. "So I suggest you do what Jarrett asked, because

I also heard you threaten your daughter. And believe me, you don't want to mess with me."

Her father looked at Mia. "Margaret, are you going to allow this?"

Mia knew he wouldn't stop trying to control her. "Yes." She fought tears that it had to come to this. "Please don't contact me again."

If Preston was surprised, he hid it. "Your mother is going to be so disappointed."

"Please tell Mother that she's more than welcome to visit her grandson."

Preston Saunders started for the door, but stopped and looked back at her. "I wouldn't act so smug if I were you, Margaret, not with your past. There's a lot of things that could come out I'm sure you'd like to keep buried." He nodded to Jarrett. "I'm sure your friends would be interested to know their sweet Mia isn't so innocent." He turned and walked out the door.

Mia felt the heat climb to her face and those dark years came rushing back, threatening to consume her, take away everything she'd made good in her life.

"Mia, are you okay?"

She nodded and put on a smile.

Neil looked at Jarrett. "I think I'll leave you two alone to talk." He turned to Mia. "It's a pleasure to meet you, Mia. I hope we get a chance to talk later." With a nod, Neil Fulton walked out, leaving her with Jarrett.

She looked at him, saw his questioning look, then burst into tears and ran out of the room, too.

Two hours later, Mia was back at her apartment. She fed BJ, and, after putting him down to nap, she dragged her suitcase from the closet and began to pack.

Okay, she was a coward. But when it came to a protecting

her son, she'd do anything, go anywhere. She wasn't sure if her father would bring her past out in court. Would he even take her to court?

Mia sank to the sofa. After all these years, all the things she'd accomplished, she'd turned her life around, and still her past had caught up with her. And she couldn't trust anyone to love her if they found out the truth about her.

She brushed away a tear. "Brad, I wish you were here to help me."

She stood and looked around. There wasn't much worth taking with her, except the baby things. She needed some boxes and went to the stairwell to get some. She found two. As she returned to her apartment, Trace McKane got off the elevator. She couldn't avoid him.

He smiled. "Hey, Mia. Have you seen Jarrett?"

She shook her head. "Not since earlier."

Trace played with his cowboy hat in his hands. "I hear you talked with your father. I hope that went well."

"He's leaving town, and I hope it's the end of it." She motioned to her apartment. "I'd better get inside to BJ."

He glanced at the boxes as he walked with her. "So you're getting ready to move out to the cottage? Maybe I can take some things out today."

She couldn't make eye contact as she backed up to her apartment door. "Look, Trace, I appreciate you and Kira offering us a place to live, but I've decided to move back to Denver for school."

Before Trace could say anything, the sound of BJ's cry distracted them. She hurried inside and got her son back to sleep, then returned to the living room. Trace was waiting.

"I know it isn't any of my business, but are you leaving because of my brother?"

She shook her head. "No, it's me. I feel it's for the best."

He watched her. "I'm not buying it. I know you have feelings for Jarrett, and the guy's crazy about you. What's the real reason?"

She couldn't deny it. She was totally in love with Jarrett. "I don't think it will work out. My father will probably try and cause more trouble." She glanced away. "There are things in my past." She shook her head. "A time in my life when I didn't care much about myself. I did things I'm not proud of."

"All of us have those times. Jarrett and I have a lot of bad history. We really haven't been brothers until the last few years." He studied her. "And Kira and I had our share of rough times, too. It took her years to tell me she'd had a baby when she was fifteen. She gave him up."

Mia remembered Jenna saying she had an older brother. "That must have been hard for her."

He nodded. "I was married to her and she never told me. When I finally found out, of course I was hurt. Not over what she did at fifteen and alone, but because she didn't trust me enough to tell me. We almost split up over it."

She couldn't imagine Trace and Kira not together. "I just have so much baggage. I can't keep dumping it on Jarrett."

Trace smiled. "Do you see the man complaining? He's crazy about you and BJ. Besides, Jarrett isn't an angel, either. There's plenty of women around town that will attest to that."

She wasn't sure what to say, then suddenly she blurted out. "I love him too much to hurt him."

He turned serious. "A few years ago, I would have told

you to walk away from Jarrett, that you were too good for him. But he's changed. Give him a chance to prove that he's the man you need."

By about five that night, Jarrett wasn't sure what he was doing. Things hadn't turned out as he'd planned. He'd charged in to help, but in the end he didn't get the girl.

He knew that talking with her father had taken its toll on Mia. But he also thought that she'd rush into his arms when it was over. Instead, she'd run out the door, right out of his life.

He'd tried calling her several times, but she didn't answer. How could he tell her how he felt in a phone message?

After Mia's rejection, he'd spent the day with Neil going over the changes in the project. That was the reason he'd called this meeting of the tenants. They were going to be a big part of this and he wanted to make sure everyone agreed to his proposal.

He'd hoped to see Mia when he walked into the community room, but she wasn't there. As he made his way to the front, the room grew quiet and everyone turned to him.

"Good evening, everyone." He glanced around, realizing how many of the tenants he'd gotten to know these past months. He'd shared meals and holidays with these people.

"I know you've all wondered why I called this meeting. Well, as of a few hours ago, I finalized and signed the contracts for the new factory to be built. So the construction is scheduled to start in the early spring." The tenants exchanged glances, but didn't say anything. "Since we last gathered, there have been some changes to the plans. Neil Fulton has agreed to build further back on the property. I feel this is a better solution for all of us."

"You mean for you," someone said.

"Just hear me out." He took a breath. "First of all, when I say the factory will be relocated on the back of the property that means the apartment buildings won't be torn down. Instead, the vacant building will be used to house Fulton's corporate offices, and this building will be remodeled and left as Mountain View Apartments."

Jarrett raised his hand to quiet the suddenly noisy group. "Of course, there's going to be a lot of construction noise during the remodeling. So I'm going to compensate you all with lower rents for the next six months."

Joe stood. "Wait, we don't have to move out by March?"

"No. Unless you want to. But it's a better investment for me to keep the building open. We're in an era of recycling, so I want to bring these apartments back to their original state by painting and repairing the structure. The kitchens and baths will be updated, of course, with new appliances and fixtures. So what I need to know is, how do you feel about continuing to live here?"

Cheers went up in the room.

Joe got out of his chair again. "How much more will it cost us in rent?"

"Since you all lived here at the worst time, you shouldn't have to pay any extra once things improve. So there won't be any increase in rent for any of the tenants living here now."

"We'll need to get it writing," a familiar voice called out from the back of the room.

Heart pounding, Jarrett looked toward the doorway. Mia was standing there behind BJ's stroller. She looked tired, but as beautiful as usual.

"I can do that," he offered. "Anything else you need?"

Mia didn't take her eyes off Jarrett as she moved along

the side of the tables. She had so many things she needed to say to him. Maybe this wasn't the place, but she had to see him. She had to give this one last chance. For both of them.

"A good handyman on the premises," she went on. "Someone who can take care of emergencies." Nola came over, took the stroller as Mia continued to the front of the room. She stopped in front of Jarrett. "Someone we can count on."

He studied her for a moment and nodded. "Do you think you'll need someone just during the day or around the clock?"

Those dark eyes locked on hers, and she wondered if he could read her mind, her heart. She could barely speak. "Oh, definitely around the clock. Do you know of anyone?"

"Yeah, I've got just the guy for the job." He took a step forward and she could feel everyone in the room hanging on their words.

"Does he like children?"

Jarrett didn't even blink. "He loves children." Then he smiled. "And pets." He inched closer. "Does this suit you, Ms. Saunders?"

She could only manage a nod.

"Maybe we should go somewhere and discuss this further."

"Just kiss her," someone yelled.

A smile appeared across Jarrett's face. "I'm also good at taking directions."

His head lowered to hers and he captured her mouth. This time whistles and cheers erupted. He kept it light, but he told her everything she needed to know. They might just have a chance.

CHAPTER FOURTEEN

JARRETT wasn't exactly crazy about having an audience when he was trying to talk to Mia. That was the reason he'd hurried her and BJ out of there and into his SUV.

He ended up taking Mia to his house. Guaranteed privacy. He pulled in to his long driveway, opened the garage and drove in. Once the door shut behind the car, he reached for her hand.

"We need to talk without being interrupted." He brushed his lips across hers, then got out, took BJ out of the back and they walked inside through the kitchen.

He looked down at the sleeping baby. "How soon before he needs to be fed?"

"We have a few hours."

"Good." He took her into the living room, only the outside light on the patio illuminating the space. Setting the baby's carrier down on the rug at one end of the sofa, he turned on the gas fireplace and some soft music.

"I haven't been home much lately," he told her. "I don't have much to offer you."

"I don't want anything."

He moved to turn on a lamp.

"Please leave it off," she asked. "It's nice like this. It's peaceful and the view is incredible."

With a nod, he took her hand and they sat down on the

sofa. For a long time, they stared out the French doors watching the wintry scene. The snow on the ground lightened the area, illuminating the rows of bare trees that dotted the landscape.

He began. "Tell me I haven't messed up everything by coming after you today."

Mia squeezed his hand, trying to relay how she felt. She couldn't look at him. Her father had nearly destroyed a lot of people and maybe the future of the town. "No. I'm just sorry you got caught in this mess."

"I don't care about your past, Mia. Meeting your father explained a lot to me. I came to the hotel to support you. When Nola told me the truth about what your father had threatened, I couldn't stand by and let him blackmail you."

"It's only money," she insisted. "I don't care about that. It's BJ I care about. I just didn't want my son raised the way Brad and I were. In a house without love."

"You should have told your father to take a hike. My failure on the project would have saved the apartments."

"I couldn't do that. You've worked too hard on bringing the factory to town. I didn't want my father to destroy you." She took another risk and confessed, "I care about you."

He reached for her, and she didn't resist as he turned her in his arms so she was facing him. He pressed her head against his chest and she could feel the rapid beating of his heart.

"And I care about you," he informed her. Not just you, but BJ, too." He touched her face, tilting her head back so she had to look at him.

"I more than care, Mia. I love you."

Her breathing caught as her throat tightened with emotions. She couldn't speak.

"Crazy, huh?" He placed a soft kiss on her forehead,

then on one eyelid, then the other. "I don't know how or when it happened, I'm thinking the second I saw you." He continued kissing his way down her cheek. "All I know is I couldn't seem to stay away. I used every excuse I could to see you." He placed a kiss against her ear and she shivered, resting her hand against his solid chest, trying to resist. "Then all those precious moments—when we shared the ultrasound of the baby, BJ's birth."

Every word he spoke made her yearn for more. She wanted everything from this man. "I'm glad you were there with me, too."

He ran his mouth over her jaw. "All I know is that when I thought you were leaving, I couldn't let you go."

She gasped. "Oh, Jarrett," she breathed, her body responding to his touch.

He raised his head. "Hey, I'm pouring out my heart here and that's all you have to say."

Tears filled her eyes. "I love you, too."

"You don't sound happy about it." He sat her up, stood and walked to the French door. "Maybe I've read the wrong signals here."

She hated seeing his hurt, but she wasn't sure she could handle his rejection. She went to him. "You might change your mind when you learn about the things I've done."

"We've all done things. So you were hooked on prescription drugs, you already told me that. It's not a problem now, is it?"

She shook her head. "I didn't tell you all of it. There was more."

He waited for her to speak.

"I ran with a wild crowd in high school. You know how bored rich kids go out partying? We drank so to forget our rotten lives. A joke, huh?"

"Not after meeting Preston."

Here was the hard part for her. "I had a drinking problem, Jarrett. My father was right, he helped me get out of several messes. The worst was one night when I left a party so drunk I ran my car into a tree. I wasn't hurt, but my passenger was."

"How bad was he hurt?"

"Thank God, it was nothing permanent, but he was in the hospital for a while. My father rescued me, paid off his family and the local police. Otherwise I might have gone to jail and have a police record, not be working on becoming a lawyer."

"How old were you?"

"Seventeen."

"I was nineteen when I was stopped for drinking and driving. And because I was the local football star, I got off, too." He took a step closer to her. "We were kids, Mia. We were given a second chance. What happened after that?"

"Even that scare didn't stop me. That's when my father put me into rehab and I finally got sober."

"How long?"

"It's been ten years." She released a breath. "I can't drink alcohol, Jarrett."

"Do you feel the need to?"

"I haven't for a while, maybe when Brad died, and then when my father came to town…" She stopped. "I need to go back to meetings. It's been a while."

The last thing Jarrett had expected was to hear Mia say she was an alcoholic. His chest tightened as he tried to imagine what she had gone through. Her brother had been her only support. Now he wanted to be. "If you'd like, I'll go with you."

She blinked and a tear fell. "Why, Jarrett?"

"I've been trying to tell you, Mia Saunders. I love you.

But for some crazy reason, you think you don't deserve that. I guess I'm just going to have to prove it to you."

Jarrett lowered his head and captured her mouth. He swiftly deepened the kiss, drinking in her sweetness that made him so hungry for more. He ran his hands over her body, folding his palm over her lush breast. She moaned and moved against him.

He broke off the kiss on a ragged breath. "Nothing matters but this. Not your past nor mine. It's how I feel when you're close to me. How wonderful it's going to be when we finally make love. I love you, Mia."

She touched his jaw. "I love you too."

He smiled against her mouth. "Now those are the words that get my attention. And I never get tired of hearing them." He kissed her again, and again, until he was desperate for her. "I want you, Mia."

She drew a needed breath. "I want to make love with you, too, Jarrett, but I can't—"

"I know it's too soon." He leaned his forehead against her and groaned. "It's killing me, but I can wait."

She laid her head against his chest. "I may die before then," she added, enjoying him touching her.

"Then we'd better get married fast."

Jarrett felt her tense and she pulled back. "You want to get married?"

He swallowed. "Did I forget to mention that?"

She nodded.

"I guess I should be more direct." Of course, he hadn't exactly been prepared for this moment. He didn't even have a ring. Then he remembered his mother's.

"Just give me a second." He gave her a quick kiss and hurried off down the hall to his bedroom. He opened the top drawer of his dresser, digging through some things until he found the keepsake box he had since he'd been a kid.

Inside was a ring, a small sapphire circled in tiny diamonds. It had belonged to his mother and she gave it to him before she died.

It probably wasn't worth much by today's standards. But it meant a lot to him. He returned and saw Mia standing by the French doors.

He came up behind her and hugged her. "Are you planning your escape?"

She shook her head. "I love it here. It must be wonderful to live out here."

He hadn't realized how wonderful until he'd seen it through her eyes. "I saved five acres before I sold the rest of my share of the ranch to Trace. So neighbors aren't too close."

"I'm glad, and if we have neighbors, it's your family."

He turned her toward him. "Do you want to live out here, Mia?"

She rose up on her toes and kissed him. "Anywhere you are, Jarrett McKane."

That was all he needed. He went down on his knee. "I love you, Mia Saunders. You'd make me so happy if you'll agree to be my wife."

"Yes, oh, Jarrett, yes. I'll marry you."

He stood and took the ring out of his pocket. "It belonged to my mother," he told her as he slipped it on her finger. It was too big. "We can get you something else."

"No, all I want is to have this sized, then it'll be perfect."

He kissed her, sweetly and tenderly. "I have one more request. I'd like to adopt BJ. I don't want to replace his real father, but it's important that we're a true family. I don't want him ever to feel left out, or that he doesn't belong."

"I think Brad would like that." She kissed him. "You're a good man, Jarrett. How lucky BJ and I are to have you."

"I think we make a great team," he said, knowing they were getting what they all wanted—to be a family.

Mia began to look around. "Just think how wonderful this house will look decorated for the holidays."

Jarrett drew her back into his arms. "As long as there is plenty of mistletoe, I'll be happy."

EPILOGUE

IT was January.

A new year, a new beginning, but not before he closed
one last chapter of his life. Today Jarrett returned to court
and Judge Gillard. He hoped it was for the last time. He
glanced at his soon-to-be bride next to him. In three days,
she would be his wife, and soon after that, he hoped BJ
would be his son.

"It's going to be okay," she whispered. "The judge will
be happy with the way things turned out."

He thought so too, but he loved having her positive
reinforcement.

Suddenly the court was called to order by the deputy,
and Judge Gillard walked up behind the bench and sat in
her chair. She glanced over her first file, then looked at
Jarrett.

"Case number 4731," the deputy began, "Mountain View
Apartment tenants vs. Jarrett McKane."

"Here, your honor," Jarrett said.

"We're here, too, your honor," Mia said and glanced
back at Nola, Joe and Sylvia who'd come today, too. Trace
and Kira were there too, holding BJ. Sometimes, Jarrett
found it hard to believe they were rooting him on.

"Your honor," Mia began. "We'd like to drop the charges
against Mr. McKane."

The judge looked over her glasses at Mia. "It's too late for that. I gave Mr. McKane a job to do, and for his sake, I hope it's been completed."

"It has been, your honor," Jarrett said. "I have the sign-off from code enforcement, saying everything was completed as asked."

The judge glanced over the sheet, then looked at Mia. "Are the tenants happy with the results?"

Mia smiled. "Very much so. Right now, Mr. McKane is in the process of remodeling the property."

The judge frowned as she turned to Jarrett. "I thought the building was going to be torn down."

"There's been a change," he told her. "With a slight modification to the building plans, the apartments are no longer interfering with the factory construction. So I've decided to keep it as an investment."

Judge Gillard leaned back in her chair and studied him for a moment. Then she turned to Mia. "Is everyone happy about the situation?"

Nola stood up. "May I speak, your honor?"

"It's Mrs. Madison, isn't it?," the judge asked, then, at Nola's nod, she waved her up to the front. "Please, tell us how you feel."

Nola came up next to Jarrett. "It's been wonderful. We're all getting new apartments and Jarrett isn't even going to raise our rent. We're getting a new neighbor, too. Fulton Industries is opening their business office in the other building, and Mr. Fulton said that maybe some of us can work there part-time." She smiled. "This is all thanks to Jarrett McKane, your honor. He gave us a home when no one else cared. Now he's our friend and he's going to marry Mia and be a father to her baby."

The judge looked overwhelmed. "Well, that's more information than I needed," she said. "But I'm glad it all has worked out for everyone."

She looked at Jarrett. "When is the wedding?"

"Excuse me?"

"The wedding?"

Jarrett caught Mia's attention. "This Saturday at the First Community Church, one o'clock. The reception afterward is in the Mountain View's community room. You're welcome to come, your honor. You did play a big part in getting us together."

She gave him a half smile. "Glad I could help. I might surprise you and show up. I wouldn't mind checking out an apartment for my mother. I like how everyone at Mountain View watches out for each other."

"We do," Jarrett assured her. "And there's a full-time handyman and around-the-clock security on the premises. We'll have some vacancies in another month. Joe and Sylvia Carson are going to be the managers."

Joe stood and waved to the judge.

"I'll have to look into it," she said and glanced over the paper again. "Well, it looks like everything is in order."

Barbara Gillard eyed the couple. "I wish all my cases ended like this. Congratulations," she said and smiled. "I guess there's nothing more to say. "Case dismissed."

The following Saturday evening, Mia sat beside Jarrett in the SUV as they left the wedding reception that had been filled with friends and family. Now they drove toward their home. She couldn't believe it, just a few hours ago they'd got married.

"Have I told you how beautiful you looked today?"

"Yes, but I like hearing it."

"You look beautiful." He kissed her.

She still wore the strapless, ivory satin tea-length dress,

with a fitted bodice covered in tiny crystals. Her bare shoulders were covered with a short matching jacket. Her new sister-in-law had taken her shopping in Denver.

She felt beautiful, too. "Yes, but I like hearing it."

He raised her hand and kissed it. "Then I'll have to say it more often."

Her husband looked incredible in his black Western-cut tuxedo. "You look mighty handsome, yourself. I saw a few women eyeing you too."

"The only woman I care about is you." He took his eyes off the highway and glanced at her. "I'm going to show you how much you mean to me tonight."

She took a shuddering breath. They'd decided to delay any honeymoon, not wanting to leave BJ. But Nola and Sylvia were going to watch BJ for this night, giving her and Jarrett time to be alone. Even though she'd gotten the all clear from Dr. Drake last week, they'd decided to wait until they were married to make love.

He went up the drive, then into the garage and pressed the button to shut out the rest of the world.

Silently, Jarrett got out of the car and walked around. Hell, he was as nervous as a teenager. He'd been wanting Mia so much the past few months, and now he wanted this night to be perfect.

He opened her door and surprised her by scooping her into his arms and carrying her into the house. He didn't stop until they were inside the dimly lit great room. He stood her in front of the French doors, but didn't let go, just leaned down and kissed her.

A kiss that soon had them breathless when he eased his mouth away.

"I love you, Mia. I can't seem to tell you enough how much I want you, tonight, and every night to come."

"I love you, too, Jarrett." She couldn't believe everything they'd gone through to get here.

How Jarrett stepped in to help her with her father. She had decided to sign over part of the company stock, but to her mother. Whatever Abigail wanted to do with it was her business. Maybe it would give her mother the courage to stand up to her husband. Even to rebuild a relationship with her daughter.

"Any regrets that I rushed you?" he asked.

"No. Have you?"

He shook his head. "Not me, but I didn't give you much chance. I've known from the beginning you were special."

"I was attracted to you, but I blamed it on hormones."

He cupped her face and kissed her again. "Oh, yeah, mine are definitely working overtime. But there's one last thing I want to give you." He went to the desk and returned with a piece of paper. "I've contacted my lawyer, Matt Holliston. I introduced you to him earlier today."

"And I remember him from when we took you to court."

Jarrett nodded. "Well, I've asked him to start proceedings to adopt BJ."

Tears welled in her eyes. She found it hard to speak.

"If you think it's too soon—"

She touched her finger to his lips. "I can't see any reason not to give my son—our son a loving father as soon as possible."

Jarrett seemed to be the one at a loss. She loved the man who'd trusted her enough to reveal the bad memories of his childhood. Despite all that, or maybe because of it, he was going to make a wonderful father for BJ.

"I love the little guy, Mia, and I love you. I can never tell you how much."

She raised up and kissed him. "Then show me."

There wasn't any hesitation as he swung her up into his arms again and headed down the hall. Mia knew that with Jarrett she didn't need to run away anymore. She had him to ground her. They'd found what they needed in each other's arms.

They were home.

CHRISTMAS MAGIC
ON THE MOUNTAIN

BY

MELISSA McCLONE

First published in Great Britain 2010
Harlequin Mills & Boon Limited,
Eton House, 18-24 Paradise Road, Richmond, Surrey TW9 1SR

© Melissa Martinez McClone 2010

ISBN: 978 0 263 88841 6

23-1110

Harlequin Mills & Boon policy is to use papers that are natural, renewable
and recyclable products and made from wood grown in sustainable forests.
The logging and manufacturing processes conform to the legal environmental
regulations of the country of origin.

Printed and bound in Spain
by Litografía Rosés S.A., Barcelona

Dear Reader,

You know how certain people intrigue you? How some places draw you back again and again? That happened to me writing about Sean Hughes and Hood Hamlet, Oregon. Both first appeared in *Rescued by the Magic of Christmas*. I fell in love with the quaint mountain town, and I wanted to give the handsome team leader of Oregon Mountain Search and Rescue his own story.

My original idea had heartbreaker Sean and his loyal Siberian husky rescuing my injured heroine. I submitted a brief storyline to my editor and was good to go. And then I heard from the sister of a friend about Michael Leming, a member of Portland Mountain Rescue and one of my go-to guys for research questions.

Michael had been climbing a twelve-foot vertical piece of ice just below the summit of Mount Hood. A chunk had sheared off. He fell back on a fifty-degree slope and slid over two hundred feet. He was taken off the mountain by helicopter with two injured ankles. Fortunately Michael's injuries weren't life threatening, but he did require rehab and physical therapy. Thirteen weeks later, however, he climbed Mount Hood—a tad slow—and snowboarded down from 9500 feet. A year after his accident his ankles are at ninety percent.

Once I knew Michael would be okay, the writer in me took over. I kept thinking about a rescuer needing to be rescued. Suddenly I knew I had to change my story. The changes kept getting better when my editor asked me if I could set the story during Christmastime.

I had so much fun writing about Sean Hughes and Zoe Flynn Carrington and revisiting Hood Hamlet. It's a story about hope, family, and of course love!

Enjoy.

Melissa

With a degree in mechanical engineering from Stanford University, the last thing **Melissa McClone** ever thought she would be doing was writing romance novels. But analysing engines for a major US airline just couldn't compete with her "happily-ever-afters". When she isn't writing, caring for her three young children or doing laundry, Melissa loves to curl up on the couch with a cup of tea, her cats and a good book. She enjoys watching home decorating shows to get ideas for her house—a 1939 cottage that is *slowly* being renovated. Melissa lives in Lake Oswego, Oregon, with her own real-life hero husband, two daughters, a son, two loveable but oh-so-spoiled indoor cats and a no-longer-stray outdoor kitty that decided to call the garage home. Melissa loves to her from her readers. You can write to her at PO Box 63, Lake Oswego, OR 97034, USA, or contact her via her website: www.melissamcclone.com

For Virginia Kantra, my critique partner extraordinaire, and Michael Leming, who patiently answers all my questions.

Special thanks to Erik Denninghoff MD, Brook Holter PA-C, John Frieh, Porter Hammer and Steve Rollins. Any mistakes and/or discrepancies are entirely the author's fault.

CHAPTER ONE

THE FAMILIAR sound of the crunch of traction tires against packed snow filled the cab of Sean Hughes's truck. He inhaled the crisp air laced with the scent of pine and the smell of wet dog. Denali, his Siberian husky, panted on the seat next to him.

Winter on Mount Hood was their favorite time of year—boarding, climbing and snowshoeing. Sean grimaced wryly. Too bad Thanksgiving and Christmas had to get in the way of all that fun.

A snowplow heading west passed him.

No doubt the early morning road crews working hard to clear the overnight snowfall from Highway 26. Portlanders would be driving up in throngs today to spend Thanksgiving on the slopes or eating turkey at Timberline Lodge's Cascade dining room.

Sean wished he could be one of them.

A well-cooked dinner served by an obliging wait staff at a nice restaurant where quiet conversation was de rigueur would be better than the chaotic holiday meal at his parents' house where everyone poked their noses into everybody's business. Especially his. No one listened to his "let's eat dinner out" suggestion—not even when he offered to pay for all thirty-eight of them. Make that thirty-nine. One of his cousins had given birth to another baby a couple of months ago.

"A good thing we don't have to be at Mom and Dad's until later." Sean glanced at Denali. "I'd rather spend this bluebird day on the mountain than be stuck inside listening to people tell me what's missing from my life is a wife."

Denali nudged his arm with her nose.

"They don't seem to understand you're my number one girl." Sean patted the dog's head. He had nothing against marriage per se, but he didn't have the time necessary to make a relationship work. He had too many other things going on in his life to make any woman a priority. In the past, he'd somehow given women the wrong idea about his commitment level so now he only dated casually. Much to his family's dismay. "No worries. We'll make the most of the time we have on our own this morning."

The dog stared out the windshield and barked.

At the base of the road leading up to Timberline Lodge stood a snowboarder. A large, overstuffed backpack set at his feet along with a board.

Around here, no one thought twice about hitchhiking up to the ski area or giving a skier or snowboarder a lift.

Sean remembered hitching rides up the hill from locals and strangers when he'd been a teenager. Back then he'd worked all summer for his dad to pay for a season pass. He'd pack a lunch since he couldn't afford to buy a cup of hot chocolate, let alone food. Times and his circumstances sure had changed since then. But seeing the kid made Sean remember the joy and freedom of those days.

Flicking on his left turn signal, he tapped the brakes to slow down. The image of the kid hoping for a ride made a great visual. He would have to mention that to the advertising firm his snowboard manufacturing company used. They were already talking about next season's promo campaign.

He turned off the highway, pulled over to the right and rolled down the passenger window.

A burst of frigid air rushed in. Denali stuck her head out.

The snowboarder straightened. "Hi."

Not a kid. A woman. Even better.

"Hey," Sean said to her.

SAVE OVER £41 25% OFF

Sign up to get 5 stories a month for 12 months in advance and **SAVE £41.70** – that's a fantastic 25% off
If you prefer you can sign up for 6 months in advance and **SAVE £16.68** – that's still an impressive 20% off

FULL PRICE	PER-PAID SUBSCRIPTION PRICE	SAVINGS	MONTHS
£166.80	£125.10	25%	12
£83.40	£66.72	20%	6

- **FREE P&P** Your books will be delivered direct to your door every month for FREE

- **Plus** to say thank you, we will send you a **FREE** L'Occitane gift set worth over £10

  Gift set has a RRP of £10.50 and includes Verbena Shower Gel 75m and Soap 110g

What's more you will receive ALL of these additional benefits

- Be the FIRST to receive the most up-to-date titles
- FREE P&P
- Lots of free gifts and exciting special offers
- Monthly exclusive newsletter
- Special REWARDS programme
- No Obligation –
  You can cancel your subscription at any time by writing to us at Mills & Boon Book Club, PO Box 676, Richmond, TW9 1WU.

MILLS & BOON

Sign up to save online at www.millsandboon.co.uk

S0KIT

A wool beanie hid her hair. The fit of her jacket made him wonder what curves lay underneath.

"Beautiful dog," she said.

"Thanks." The woman was pretty herself with pink cheeks and glossed lips. Her outerwear coordinated with the graphics on her board. Not one of his snowboards, but she looked like the type of rider more interested in fashion than in function. He didn't mind. Sean had a soft spot for snow bunnies, especially ones who boarded. "Heading up for a taste of the fresh powder?"

"I hear it's light and fluffy. My favorite kind." Hopeful, clear blue eyes fringed with thick lashes met his. "Have room for one more?"

She was young. Early twenties, maybe. But cute. Very cute. She'd be turning some heads on the slopes today the way she had turned his.

He shifted the truck's gear stick into Park. "I'll put your stuff in the back."

A wide smile lit up her face. "Thanks, but I've got it."

Independent. Sean liked that. Much better than the women who wanted him to do everything for them.

In the rearview mirror, he watched as she put her things into the back. He appreciated how careful she was to avoid his splitboard and the prototype bindings he'd been working on. She kicked the snow from her boots, climbed in the cab and closed the door.

"I can't tell you how happy I am you stopped." She pulled off her mittens and wiggled her fingers in front of the dashboard vents. "Oh, the heat feels so good."

She smelled good. Like vanilla. He wouldn't mind seeing if she tasted as good as she smelled. "Been waiting long?"

"It felt like forever." Her fingers fumbled with the seat belt until she managed to fasten it. "But it was probably only twenty minutes or so. There isn't as much traffic as I thought there'd be this morning."

"Most people won't head up until later." He shifted gears,

pressed on the gas pedal and drove up the curving road to Timberline Lodge. "The lifts don't open until nine."

"That explains it." She rubbed her hands together. "I'm Zoe."

"Sean Hughes." Walls of snow from the plow lined each side of the road. "This is Denali."

"Nice to meet both of you."

Denali rubbed her muzzle against Zoe's cheek.

"Off," Sean ordered, his gaze focusing for a moment on Zoe's high cheekbones. The dog obeyed. "She's very friendly."

"I see that." Zoe glanced at the window behind them. "I noticed an OMSAR sticker on the window."

"Oregon Mountain Search and Rescue."

She fiddled with her mittens on her lap. "You guys are on TV a lot."

"When something happens on the mountain, the media flock to Timberline, but otherwise they pretty much leave us alone."

"I suppose really bad things happen up there."

"Sometimes." He thought about fellow OMSAR member and good friend Nick Bishop who had died almost seven years ago climbing on the Reid Headwall. "Accidents can happen to the best climbers."

"I'd like to climb a mountain someday."

"There isn't much in this world that beats standing on a summit," he encouraged. "But it's all about getting to the top and back down safely. You need to be ready, prepared."

With a nod, she rested her left hand on a contented-looking Denali.

Sean noticed her bare ring finger. He'd bet she had a boyfriend. Still, awareness buzzed through him.

"Before I forget," she said. "Happy Thanksgiving."

"Same to you." At least Thanksgiving was only one day. That made the holiday a hundred percent better than Christmas, when the chorus of "When are you settling down?"

questions drowned out the carols from the stereo. "You're not from around here."

She stiffened. "Why do you say that?"

"A local would know what time the lifts open."

"Oh, right."

Her cheeks remained pink, even though it wasn't cold in the truck. The women he went out with rarely blushed, but Sean found it charming.

"I got a ride up from Portland yesterday and spent the night at the Hood Hamlet Hostel. I wanted to get an early start this morning." She rubbed Denali. "Spending the day on the slopes before Thanksgiving dinner is a family tradition, but I think I may have started a little too early. I suppose getting up before the sun should have been a clue."

He smiled. "Are you meeting your family later?"

"No." She stared out the window. "I'm on my own this year."

Interesting. Maybe there wasn't a boyfriend in the picture. At least not a serious one.

"Lucky you." Sean negotiated the truck around a tight curve. "I wish I were on my own today."

Zoe turned toward him, her eyes wide. "But it's Thanksgiving."

He smiled. "Exactly."

"The holidays are a time to spend with family."

"I know," he admitted. "That's why I'll be at my parents' house this afternoon with more than three dozen extended family members. Picture total chaos with cooking in the kitchen, football blaring on the TV in the living room, kids running around screaming and my uncle Marty snoring in the recliner. It's so crazy, you can't keep track of the score of the game."

"It sounds wonderful to me."

Zoe sounded wistful, a little sad. Maybe she wasn't as keen on spending Thanksgiving by herself as he would be. Sean couldn't deny his attraction. Truth was, he wouldn't mind spending time with her. "You want to come?"

Uncertainty filled her eyes. "I don't know you."

"You want references? I can probably get 'em for you."

"I know."

He looked at her, not understanding what she meant.

"The OMSAR sticker," she explained. "And you gave me a lift. Obviously you're used to rescuing damsels in distress."

"Rescue is my specialty." That earned him a smile. "So dinner?"

She shook her head.

"Is it my family? Because my relatives make me nuts, but not in an ax-murderer kind of way. The rugrats are pretty cute, and the pies are really good. Ask anyone at the ski area about the Hughes family. We've lived in Hood Hamlet forever."

She laughed, as he hoped she would. "No, I meant… You can't spring an unexpected guest on your mother at the last minute."

Pretty and polite. Not too shabby. "My mom lives for holidays. She makes enough food to send leftovers home with everyone, including Denali."

"That's really kind of you, but—"

"You have other plans."

"No," she said. "I wouldn't want to impose."

"You wouldn't."

"Last-minute guests are always impositions."

Sean should let it go, except he didn't want to. He could tell she was considering his invitation. She obviously didn't want to be on her own for the holiday. He didn't want her to be alone, either.

Besides, he was the last unmarried cousin. His relatives close to his age, some much younger, were all chasing after kids or holding babies now. He didn't have anything in common with them anymore. It had been his choice to remain single, and he really did enjoy his lifestyle—running a successful company, boarding, climbing, mountain rescue. But a part of Sean felt as if he'd been left behind, and his cousins—make that all of his relatives—were trying to get him to catch up.

Bringing home a pretty girl in need of a family Thanksgiving dinner tonight would not only help her, but deflect the personal questions about his sex life from male relatives, and questions about who he'd been seeing from the female ones.

"It'll be fine." Dinner at his folks' would be good for Zoe's morale. His, too. "You can ask my mom yourself."

"No, I couldn't."

"Then I will."

Zoe stared at him. "Do you really feel comfortable invit-ing a total stranger to have Thanksgiving dinner with your family?"

He didn't want to explain how her presence would take the heat off him or how being with Zoe might actually make to-night fun instead of a chore. If things went well during dinner, maybe they could spend more time together afterward. At his house. Alone. "I can take you if you pull any funny stuff."

"You think?"

Sean's blood pressure spiked. He'd been around the block enough times to know when a woman was interested. Zoe was. Her flirting suggested tonight would turn out way better than he'd thought when he woke up this morning.

"Definitely." He flashed her one of his most charming smiles, the one that had melted his share of female hearts. "Besides, one of my cousins is married to a sheriff's deputy, and another is a martial arts instructor. You wouldn't stand a chance against us."

She laughed. "No funny stuff, I promise."

"So you're in."

"Only if it's okay with your mom."

Sean didn't want Zoe to change her mind. He hit the button on his cell phone and called his parents' number. His mother answered on the second ring with a cheerful "gobble, gobble."

"Hey, Mom, I'm bringing someone with me to dinner tonight. Okay?"

"Honey, you know your friends are always welcome," she said. "We have more than enough food."

"Thanks. I'll tell her."

"Her?" His mother's voice shot up an octave. "You're bringing a girl?"

"Her name's Zoe. She's going to be boarding at T-line while I'm up on the hill trying out a new binding."

"And then you're bringing her home for Thanksgiving dinner. That's wonderful, Sean. Of course Zoe's welcome to come."

Something about his mother's tone set off alarm bells in the back of his head. "I don't want you making a big deal out of this and scaring her off, Mom."

His mother laughed. "Of course not. I'll be discreet, I promise. Let me talk to her."

He frowned and looked over at Zoe. "She wants to talk to you."

A puzzled expression crossed Zoe's face. "Me?"

"Maybe she wants to give you references," he joked.

"Hello?" Zoe said into the phone, almost shyly. "Yes, this is Zoe…Zoe Flynn… Thank you, Mrs. Hughes. Okay, Connie… No, my family isn't… I've been out here on my own for a while.…"

The way she spoke made Sean smile. He knew his mom's interrogation skills all too well, but Zoe was holding her own when she could get a word in. He was curious to see how she handled everyone at the dinner tonight.

"Yes, holidays are hard alone," she said. "I appreciate it… I understand. I just didn't want Sean to spring an extra guest on you at the last minute.… Yes, he is.… Thanks again.… I look forward to meeting you, too.… Yes. Yes, I'll tell him."

Zoe handed the phone back to him. "Here you go."

He was about to say goodbye, but the line was already disconnected. His mother had hung up. That was…odd.

He tucked the phone in his pocket, both relieved and puzzled. "What are you suppose to tell me?"

Zoe drew her eyebrows together. "Your mother wants me to remind you about your grandmother's present. It's in the safe-deposit box. She said she could pick it up from the bank for you on Monday morning."

His grandmother's present. His grandmother's...

"Oh, hell," Sean said.

"What is it?" Zoe asked.

His grandmother's engagement ring, intended for Sean's future bride. And now his mother thought... His mother planned...

"Damn. She thinks it's serious."

"Your grandmother? Is she ill?"

"She's dead," he explained. "No, it's my mother. She thinks we're serious. You and me. That I invited you to dinner because we're in a relationship."

Lines creased Zoe's forehead. "Why would she think that?"

Because his mother was a hopeless romantic who wanted her son to get married so she could have grandchildren. "Because I'm bringing you to Thanksgiving dinner."

"That doesn't make any sense."

"My family never makes much sense."

"Haven't you ever brought anyone to Thanksgiving dinner before?" Zoe asked.

"Not in a long time." Sean tried to keep his personal life as private as he could. Not easy living in a nosy, small town full of close friends and a large, demanding family. "That must be how she got the wrong idea."

"You have to admit it's kind of sweet."

"Imagine if it was your mother."

Zoe winced. "Okay, not sweet at all."

"My mom's probably calling my aunts who will call my cousins..."

"It's not a problem, Sean. It's just a little misunderstanding." Zoe smiled. "We can tell everyone the truth when we arrive and have a good laugh about it."

He stared at the snow on the side of the road. "Right."

"You're not laughing," she said gently.

"Nope."

"I don't have to go," Zoe offered.

"You're not spending Thanksgiving alone." Sean wasn't going to let her get away that easily. He blew out a puff of air. "My mom's expecting you now. It would disappoint her if you didn't show up. She looks forward to the holidays all year. I don't want to ruin her day."

"She's going to be disappointed anyway when we tell her the truth."

"Yeah."

"Unless…" Zoe's voice trailed off.

"What?"

"We could pretend to be dating," she suggested. "Just for today."

That would solve his problem. Problems, actually. His mom's Thanksgiving would be salvaged, his opinionated family would be off his back about settling down and he would get to spend time with Zoe. A win-win situation for everyone.

"Bad idea?" Zoe asked.

Probably.

"No." He liked that she was both helpful and a little daring. He also liked the idea of what might happen while she was playing his girlfriend. "But it's a lot for me to ask. Are you up for it?"

"I know what it's like to disappoint your family."

The sincerity in Zoe's voice covered him like a soft, warm quilt. He wasn't used to a woman making him feel like that. It made him…uncomfortable.

Still, she was willing. Why not? "I owe you."

"You gave me a lift up here, and I get a free Thanksgiving dinner out of the deal." Zoe smiled. "I'd say we're even."

Not even close once she met his crazy family, but he'd make sure she had a good time. At dinner and afterward. He grinned. "Okay, thanks."

"You're welcome."

Funny, but Sean was looking forward to Thanksgiving for the first time in years.

They arrived at Timberline. The lot was almost empty. He parked the truck close to the WyEast day lodge and turned off the engine.

"Would you mind if I leave my pack in the cab?" Zoe asked. "It would save me paying the locker fee."

"Not a problem." That was the least he could do for her. "Denali and I are going to head up the mountain a ways so I can try out some new bindings. You want to come?

"Thanks, but resort runs are more my speed."

He was unexpectedly disappointed she wasn't up for it. He liked being with her. "I can hang with you down here."

"I'll just slow you down," she said. "Have fun riding the freshiez up top. I'll see you later."

Sean wanted to see how his new design performed, and he didn't want to push her too much. He would have plenty of time to charm her later at the Thanksgiving dinner. "Okay."

She reached for the door handle. "When should we meet back here?"

"Two o'clock," he answered. "That will give us plenty of time to get to my parents' house."

"Sounds good, but this is my first day out this season." Zoe looked up at the summit. He followed her line of sight. The snowcapped peak contrasted sharply against the blue sky. "I might be finished before then."

"Do you want my cell phone number?" he asked.

"I don't have a phone with me."

"I'll leave the keys on the top of the rear left tire so you can get into the cab whenever you want."

"Thanks." She studied him. "It's not often you meet someone who is so trusting of strangers."

"I could say the same about you."

"Yes."

"But don't forget you're not a stranger," he said playfully. "You're my Thanksgiving-day girlfriend."

She grinned. "Mustn't forget that."

Sean sure wouldn't. He was really looking forward to tonight. "Besides you don't look like the type who would steal her boyfriend's truck."

"What type do I look like?" she asked.

Sean gave her the once-over.

She dressed the part of a snow bunny, but with her cap pulled down over her hair and little to no makeup on her face, she had the fresh-faced-girl-next-door look down. Sean didn't normally go for that type, but something about Zoe intrigued him. Still he didn't want to appear too interested. He was imposing on her enough already.

He smiled. "You look like the type of girlfriend a guy brings home to meet the family."

Around a quarter to two, Zoe Flynn Carrington made her way past the WyEast day lodge toward the parking lot. Her muscles ached from all the snowboarding. Even though she'd had fun on the slopes, she kind of regretted not taking Sean up on his offer to go up the mountain with him.

Thinking about his thoughtful hazel-green eyes, easy smile and the brown strands of hair poking out from under his ski hat warmed her cold insides right up.

A mountain rescuer to the rescue. Zoe grinned.

She couldn't wait to see him again.

The guy was gorgeous—a yummy piece of eye candy who would fit into one of the trendy new hotspots in L.A. as well as he did here on the mountain. He probably had women throwing themselves at him. Yet she got to be his girlfriend for the rest of the day.

Anticipation rippled through her.

He seemed as interested in flirting with her as she was with him on the drive up. Tonight could get interesting.

She felt an unfamiliar prick of caution.

Not interesting, Zoe corrected.

Her suggestion to be his pretend girlfriend had been nothing but impulsive, something she'd vowed not to be anymore. But the idea of having a home-cooked family Thanksgiving dinner tugged at her lonely heart, and the thought of spending more time with handsome Sean filled her tummy with tingles. She'd spoken without thinking. She hadn't been able to help herself even though she had no room in her life for romance at the moment.

Zoe located his truck in the now-full lot and made her way toward it.

She would have to be more careful, more vigilant. She couldn't afford not to be. Not that she was in any position to afford anything right now.

As she waited for an SUV to drive by so she could cross the road, her boots sank in the slush of melted snow.

With the end of the month approaching and her allowance almost gone, she'd only had enough money to do one of two things: buy a lift ticket or eat Thanksgiving dinner. Obviously she'd made the right choice because now she would get both.

Thanks to Sean Hughes.

With a smile pulling at her lips, she crossed the road.

Maybe her luck was finally changing.

What type do I look like?

You look like the type of girlfriend a guy brings home to meet the family.

She'd wanted to hug Sean for saying that, even if he might be the only person in the world who thought so. Maybe what she felt for him wasn't really attraction, but gratitude. Being with Sean made her feel different, better than she'd felt in a long time. A good thing since the past few months had been so bad, so hard on her.

Wild Child. Party Animal. Homewrecker.

She cringed at the memory of the tabloid headlines written about her. Headlines that everyone believed even though they were lies. Headlines that had ripped everyone she held dear from her. Headlines that had ruined her life.

You are an embarrassment to me, to your brothers and to the Carrington name. You need to learn responsibility. And I can think of only one way for that to happen.

Zoe sighed.

No matter. The past was behind her. She was on the other side of the country from her family. All she had to do was remain out of sight, stay away from the media spotlight and keep out of trouble until after the special election for the vacant U.S. Senate seat her mother, Governor Vanessa Carrington, wanted more than anything in the world.

If Zoe failed to do any of those three things, her mother, the executor of her father's will, would tie up Zoe's access to her trust fund until she was forty. Sixteen years from now. The same length of time her mother had been governor. Her mother was serving her fourth term and couldn't seek reelection, which explained her fixation on winning the Senate seat.

A dog barked.

Denali ran around the side of the truck and nearly knocked Zoe over with excitement.

"Hi, pretty girl." Zoe hugged the dog. "I missed you, too."

Denali panted. The dog's hot breath hanging in the air like little puffs of clouds.

Zoe placed her board in the back of Sean's truck. Funny, but she didn't see his board. That seemed weird. Especially since Denali had her leash on. Had Sean tied her to the truck? "Where's—?"

"You must be Zoe."

She cringed. With her helmet and goggles, no one should be able to recognize her. "I am."

A tall man wearing a black-and-red jacket with the initials OMSAR written in white on the front and Rescue on the sleeves held on to the end of Denali's leash. "Jake Porter. I'm a friend of Sean's."

She raised her goggles onto the front of her helmet.

Intense blue eyes stared down at her. Like Sean, he wore a ski hat, and that emphasized his ruggedly handsome features. He wasn't as gorgeous as Sean, but he was still good-looking. Were all mountain rescuers hotties?

Speaking of which… She glanced around the parking lot. "Where is he?"

"There's been an accident."

"Oh, no." She touched Denali's head. "I saw a helicopter earlier and wondered if someone had been injured. Is Sean helping out?"

"Sean's been hurt."

"Sean?" Zoe's stomach clenched. Her hand dropped to her side. "How?"

"He fell."

Accidents can happen to the best of climbers.

A chill inched its way down her spine. "Is he okay?"

Jake looked at Denali. "He was unconscious when he was found, but was conscious when we placed him in a vacuum splint to immobilize his spine."

She trembled. "His spine?"

"We do that as a precaution. With his head injury we couldn't clear his cervical spine of injury."

A head injury sounded really serious. Really bad. "Did he hurt anything else?"

Jake hesitated.

"Please," she urged.

"His left leg is broken. We couldn't tell if his right ankle is or not," Jake explained. "Fortunately, he was lower on the mountain so easier to reach. The rescue happened a lot quicker than normal. He should be at the hospital in Portland by now."

Sean had seemed so vibrant, so strong this morning. Zoe couldn't imagine him lying helpless on the snow unconscious. She shivered. "I can't believe he was the one in the helicopter. Have you called his parents?"

Jake nodded. "Hank and Connie are on their way to the hospital. She wants me to drive you there."

Connie. His mom. Who thought Zoe was Sean's serious girlfriend. And now Sean was seriously injured.

Zoe felt light-headed.

Jake touched her arm. "You're pale."

"I'm…" She wasn't fine, that was for certain. She only prayed Sean would be okay.

"This has to be a shock," Jake said compassionately.

No kidding. She took a deep breath.

"We should head out," he added.

She didn't know what to say. Going to the hospital seemed like a really bad idea. She was supposed to stay out of trouble, not dive headfirst into it. But what else could she do?

Zoe reached under his truck, removed the keys from the top of the left rear tire and handed them to Jake.

She wanted to know how Sean was doing. No way could she leave him in the lurch after he'd come to her rescue at the side of the road this morning. She remembered his not wanting to disappoint his mother and upset her plans for Thanksgiving.

Now he was in the hospital, and Zoe felt as if she had to take care of this for him. She would have to explain to his worried mother their supposed relationship was all a big joke.

Oh, dear.

Zoe's heart lodged in her throat.

Talk about a ruined Thanksgiving…

CHAPTER TWO

MOUNT HOOD lay far behind Zoe. Each passing mile brought her closer to the hospital, closer to Sean. He'd been on her mind for the past hour and twenty minutes. No matter how hard she tried, she couldn't stop thinking about him.

"We're almost there," Jake said from behind the wheel of Sean's truck.

Seeing the hospital's emergency department sign, she scrunched her mittens in her hand. Her concern over Sean doubled, but she was also a little worried about what she'd gotten herself into. How was she going to explain to his family that she didn't belong here with them? With Sean?

"This hospital has one of the best trauma centers in the Pacific Northwest," Jake said over Denali, who sat between them.

Zoe swallowed around the lump of fear in her throat. At least Sean was in good hands. "Thanks for driving me down here."

"Anything for Sean." Jake parked, cracked the windows and turned off the ignition. "I'll put your board in here."

As he opened the door, she looked down at the dog that stared back at her with big, reproachful eyes. Zoe bit her lip. "Um…what about Denali?"

"She'll be fine in the truck. It's cool enough for her. I'll bring her some water."

Zoe didn't know a lot about dogs, but that sounded good

to her. The dog seemed to mean a lot to Sean. She patted Denali's head.

Jake placed her snowboard in the cab and shut the door.

"Everything's going to be fine," Zoe said to the dog. She hoped. She would just get an update on Sean and tell his family…tell his family…

Denali nudged her arm.

"Stay," Zoe said firmly, remembering the way Sean had spoken to the dog on the drive up to Timberline.

The dog stayed.

Zoe glimpsed her board and backpack behind the front seat. She could grab both and be out of here in minutes. Seconds, really. She didn't have any real responsibility for Sean. Flirting aside, they were only tied by a crazy ruse they'd cooked up to satisfy his need for a holiday date to appease his mother and Zoe's need for a holiday family dinner to appease her heart.

Should she stay? Or go?

Zoe stared at the double-glass-door entrance to the emergency department. Apprehension shuddered through her. The last time she'd been to a hospital had been for her father. He'd gone in and never come out.

She remembered Sean's smile. The way laughter had lit his eyes.

Zoe had to stay. At least long enough to assure herself he would be all right. She forced herself out of the truck and closed the door.

Denali's sad stare followed Zoe accusingly as she backed away from the truck. Her breath hitched.

"Hang in there," Jake encouraged when he met her around the back of the pickup. "Sean's tough. Nothing will keep him down for long."

She knew nothing about Sean Hughes except he didn't seem to like his family's holiday get-togethers all that much. Still, she found herself nodding, hoping.

Zoe wanted Sean to be okay. He seemed like a good guy,

one who cared enough about his mother's feelings that he hadn't wanted to ruin her Thanksgiving.

"There could be a lot of Sean's family and friends here," Jake warned. "More will show up once the word gets out."

A close-knit group, she imagined. One of them would know she wasn't Sean's girlfriend, and if that person said something…anything to Sean's family before Zoe got the chance that would make matters worse.

Not that they weren't bad already.

She took a deep breath, trying to settle her already frayed nerves. It didn't help.

"Do you need anything from your pack?" Jake looked anxious, the way she felt. "Your purse?"

"No." Zoe shivered. From the chill in the air or cold feet, she didn't know. "We should probably get in there."

Even if it was the last place she wanted to be.

Jake nodded once.

The glass doors opened automatically. She stepped inside. Warm air surrounded her, yet she longed for the fresh, cold air outside.

On Zoe's right, a man sat behind a window. He took one look at Jake in his OMSAR jacket and waved them past. She walked through another set of doors.

The sterile, antiseptic hospital smell reminded Zoe painfully of her father's heart attack. Memories of being in the emergency room, waiting for word on her father's condition, brought a lump to her throat. She had sat on an uncomfortable chair, wishing she could see her father, but she'd never gotten that chance. He'd died surrounded by a team of medical professionals. Not family.

Zoe still regretted not being with her father at the end. But her father had been in his sixties, a victim of his lifestyle and diet choices. Sean was young, a victim of an accident. He might be a stranger, but she would help him if she could. The way she hadn't been able to help her dad.

She focused on the crowded waiting room in front of her.

The noise level surprised her. Conversations, commotion,

crying. A television set tuned to a twenty-four-hour news channel hung from one corner. Below it, a man coughed while a woman held his hand and comforted him. Next to them, a baby cried while a woman cradled her and rocked, humming a lullaby. Across from them, a teenager iced her ankle while a man paced near her.

In the opposite corner, a group of healthy-looking men and women filled seats while others stood. They spoke quietly amongst themselves, ignoring the chaos around them. The wide range of ages made Zoe think this had to be Sean's family and friends. All had one thing in common—worried expressions on their faces.

"That's Sean's family." Jake pointed to the group and led her over there. "Any word?"

"They've cleared his spine," a uniformed sheriff's deputy answered.

The relief on Jake's face matched the way Zoe felt inside. Now to find out about his head and his legs.

"They're doing a head CT now," the sheriff deputy added.

Tests were good, Zoe thought. Tests meant Sean was alive.

She noticed an OMSAR jacket hung on the back of one of the chairs.

A middle-aged woman, her brown hair sprinkled with gray, rose from one of the chairs. She wore a pumpkin-orange apron covered with pilgrims over her stylish brown pants and a chic matching tunic. She wiped at her red, swollen eyes with a tissue. "Zoe?"

The distress on the woman's face hurt Zoe's heart. She nodded.

"I'm Connie." Her slight smile faltered. "Sean's mom."

"I'm so sorry." Zoe didn't know what else to say.

Connie took a tentative step toward her.

Zoe did the same.

Suddenly she was enfolded in the woman's arms, engulfed in her warmth and the scent of cinnamon and cloves.

Connie let go. "When you love someone who lives to be in the mountains, you always know in the back of your mind this is a possibility, but the reality of it—"

The way the woman's voice cracked brought tears to Zoe's eyes.

"Sean's strong." He looked strong, so Zoe felt safe saying that much. "I'm sure he'll pull through this."

"You're right. I know you're right." Connie took a deep breath as if trying to compose herself. "Hank, Sean's dad, went to check with the nurse."

Zoe smiled. "Let's hope he has some good news to share."

Gratitude filled Connie's eyes. "Everyone, this is Sean's Zoe."

Oh, no. Zoe forced herself not to cringe as the group's attention focused on her and the temperature in the waiting area shot up by twenty degrees. Surely someone here would recognize her as a fraud.

Sweat trickled down Zoe's back, but her discomfort was nothing compared to what had happened to Sean. A few minutes of awkwardness over her and Sean being strangers was minor, nothing really, compared to what he and these people were going through right now.

She waited, but no one said a word. "Everyone" simply nodded as if they already knew who she was, as if being "Sean's Zoe" was enough for them.

People surrounded her. Names and hugs were exchanged like candy at Halloween. She kept waiting for someone to question her, to ask about her relationship with Sean, but no one did.

The sheriff's deputy handed her a cup of coffee.

"I'm Will Townsend," he introduced himself. "I'm married to Sean's cousin, Mary Sue. She and a couple others are at Connie and Hank's house cooking and watching kids." His cell phone rang. "Excuse me."

Zoe looked to see if anyone new had joined the group.

She wanted to know what Hank had found out about Sean's condition.

"I'm Leanne Thomas." A pretty but serious looking woman stepped forward. "I'm a friend of Sean's. I'm also a member of OMSAR and a paramedic. Right now they are doing a noncontrast head CT scan to see the extent of his head injury. Once that's done, they'll take X-rays of his legs and any other extremity where they might suspect an injury. We should get another update as soon as they're finished and can evaluate them."

"Waiting is the hardest part," Zoe said.

"You've been through this before."

The coffee cup warmed her cold hand. "With my dad."

"It never gets any easier, does it?" Leanne gave her a Hershey's candy bar. "I don't know about you, but chocolate always makes me feel better."

The woman was so nice. "Thanks."

Zoe stared at the candy bar. She was surprised at how anxious and worried she was to hear about Sean's condition. But receiving all this genuine sympathy from his friends and family made her feel lower than pond scum. They all thought Zoe cared because she was his girlfriend, because of a romantic attachment. She really needed to tell them the truth.

A middle-aged man she hadn't seen before walked toward her. He had the same athletic build and eyes as Sean, but lines of worry etched his face.

"I'm Hank, Sean's dad." His gaze rested on Connie, who was motioning to Zoe as she spoke with one of the OMSAR guys—Tim? No, maybe it was Bill.

"I'm sorry about Sean, Mr. Hughes," Zoe said sincerely.

"Hank," he corrected. "Don't worry about me. How are you holding up?"

"I'm fine." She was sweating from a combination of nerves and concern. She really should have stayed in the truck with Denali, but Zoe wanted to hear how Sean was doing. "Truly."

"Should have known Sean would pick himself a strong girl," Hank said approvingly.

She blinked. "No, I—"

"Let me tell you." He lowered his voice confidingly. "Connie was about to lose it before you arrived. Now she can fuss over you instead of sit here and worry until it makes her sick."

This is Sean's Zoe.

Guilt coated her mouth. Zoe hated deceiving these nice people, but they were so worried about Sean. She shouldn't— she couldn't—add to their troubles. That meant only one thing. She would have to be Sean's Zoe today.

Wrong, yes, but telling his family the truth when they were so upset seemed worse, even though their pretend relationship was nothing compared to Sean's injuries.

"I'm glad I'm here," she whispered. "Connie's free to fuss all she wants. Tell me what I can do to help, and I'll do it."

The corners of Hank's mouth curved. "You're going to fit right in."

That would be a first. Zoe smiled up at him.

An older, blue-haired woman, Aunt Vera if Zoe remembered correctly, studied her with an assessing gaze. "You're wearing snowboarding clothes and boots."

Zoe glanced down at her jacket, insulated cargo pants and boots. No wonder she felt so warm and was sweating. "I came straight from Timberline."

Unlike most of the others here. The OMSAR people were dressed for the mountains, but the Hughes men wore a mix of khakis and jeans. Long sleeved button-downs seemed to be the shirt of choice. The women wore dress pants or skirts with coordinating blouses. All were dressed for dinner. She obviously was not.

This wasn't the first time Zoe had been called out for what she was wearing. This wouldn't be the last once she returned home.

Home.

Thoughts of returning to her old life, partying with her

friends and using her Visa Platinum card had kept Zoe going these past weeks, but all that seemed suddenly foreign and empty compared to how these people were banding together over one of their own.

"Zoe has more on her mind than what she's wearing, Aunt Vera." Connie eyes softened when she looked at Zoe. "You must be burning up. Let me hold your coffee and candy so you can get rid of that jacket."

Zoe shrugged out of her jacket. She pulled off her ski cap, shoved it in her jacket pocket and brushed her fingers through her hair.

Connie tucked the coat under her arm and handed back the cup and bar. "I'll hang this on the back of a chair."

That must be what Hank meant about fussing. "Thanks."

She led Zoe to an empty chair. "Sit. You can drink your coffee and eat your candy bar. I have a feeling we're going to be here for a while."

Time dragged. New patients arrived. Others left. Jake checked on Denali. Hank kept bugging the nurses for news, but could get none.

More of Sean's friends and family members arrived. One of them, Jake's pregnant wife, Carly, brought a container of chocolate chip cookies. Zoe ate one, but only to be polite. Her appetite seemed to have disappeared even though she hadn't eaten lunch.

She looked around at the crowd that had gathered. On Thanksgiving, no less.

If friends were the measure of the man, not many could match Sean Hughes. Her instincts about him had been right. Zoe had never met nicer, more generous people in her life. Talk about being there for someone in good times or in bad.

She longed for the same kind of connection with her family and friends. But her family was too busy and her friends were more interested in partying and shopping. The realization left her feeling a little hollow.

The tension in the waiting room kept rising while they

waited for more information. Connie shredded her tissue. Zoe got her another one as well as a home magazine for Connie to read.

"Want to see if there are any good recipes or decorating ideas for Christmas in here with me?" Zoe asked.

"I'd love to," Connie said.

Together they pored over the articles and pictures, but the distraction only went so far. Each time the doors leading to and from the emergency department opened, everyone stared. They wanted—needed—to hear more about Sean's condition.

"Would you like me to talk to the nurse?" Zoe offered.

"Thanks, but let Hank keep trying," Connie said. "He's not one for sitting still long. Besides, I'd rather keep you to myself."

Her words made Zoe feel good inside. Accepted. She really liked Sean's family and all his friends. She would have felt better, however, if they knew the truth.

A man dressed in surgical scrubs walked out of the two double doors leading to the emergency department. Silence fell over the waiting area. Several people stood.

"Mr. and Mrs. Hughes," the doctor said.

Hank stepped forward. Connie rose. She reached a hand for Zoe, clutching her forearm and dragging her forward with her.

Zoe didn't belong with them, but she could not deny that desperate grip on her arm. She held her breath, hoping for the best.

"Whatever you have to say to us, the others can hear," Hank said, a slight tremor to his voice. "We're all family here."

"I'm Dr. Erickson," the man said. "Sean's head CT is negative for a serious injury. No skull fracture or internal bleeding, but he has suffered a closed head injury. A concussion. Sean is being admitted by the trauma surgeon."

Hank opened and closed his mouth several times.

"But you said it wasn't serious," Zoe said. As soon as the

words were out of her mouth, she realized she never should have spoken.

"The concussion is mild." Dr. Erickson's eyes darkened. "I'm more concerned about his left leg. Sean has a tib-fib fracture. Tibia and fibula. It's an open fracture so he's being given Ancef, an antibiotic."

"A broken leg can't be that bad," Connie said.

Hank put his arm around her.

"Certainly not life threatening," the doctor agreed with a tired smile. "But he will need surgery tonight. An orthopedist will use a plate and screws. It's called ORIF. That means open reduction, internal fixation. Basically the fracture is closed and the fracture immobilized or fixed with hardware."

The more the doctor said, the tighter Connie held on to Zoe.

Zoe wished she could ease some of the worry. This wasn't her place, but she wanted to help Connie. "Isn't this a pretty common procedure?"

"Yes," he said. "This method has been used often and quite successfully."

Connie sighed and loosened her grip slightly.

"Sean also has an ankle sprain on the contralateral side."

Zoe blinked. "The what?"

"He sprained his right ankle," Dr. Erickson explained. "If you'll come with me, you can see him now."

Sean's parents followed the doctor. Connie still had hold of Zoe and pulled her with them.

Her snowboarding boots felt as if they were filled with cement. Zoe had already said enough. Too much really. "I'll stay here. Sean will want to see you."

Connie didn't release her.

Hank smiled. "I'm sure he'd rather see your pretty face."

Zoe let herself be dragged forward.

She wanted to see Sean, but he had a concussion. What if he didn't recognize her?

It was just a mild concussion, but still…head injuries could make people forget things. She remembered the professional football player—a quarterback—she'd dated a couple of times. He'd gotten concussions being sacked on the field and had some memory issues.

What if Sean didn't remember she was supposed to be his girlfriend? What if he didn't remember her at all?

Her insides quivered.

Okay, the odds of that were slim, but with her string of bad luck anything was possible. Zoe's heart pounded so hard she thought it might burst out of her chest.

That would be such a cruel way for his parents to discover the truth. These nice people didn't deserve that. If only she'd had the guts to tell the truth when she arrived, but she hadn't. She didn't mind paying that price, but she minded if the Hughes did.

Maybe if Zoe stood in the back, far away from the bed and kept her mouth shut or rather said as little as possible, Sean wouldn't even notice her. Maybe…

Sean felt as if he were floating. He felt a pressure in his left leg and in his head. Far-off pain like the distant rumble of thunder. Threatening, but nothing like the lightning jabs that had seared him earlier.

Beeps, machines. Footsteps sounded.

He was in a hospital in a large room with surgical lights. He had been stripped naked. A huge number of people had evaluated him, a posse of medical professionals, but it was quiet now. Someone had covered him with a gown. Another had laid a warm blanket across his chest.

That was what he knew about his situation.

But he was too out of it to care.

He probably should care, but all he wanted to do was drift off on the cloud of whatever medication they'd pumped into him.

"Oh, honey."

The sound of his mother's voice forced Sean to open his eyes. The light blinded him. He blinked. It didn't help. He closed his eyelids, thankful for the darkness once again. "Mom."

His voice sounded different. Husky. Disembodied, almost.

She kissed his cheek. "Thank goodness you're in one piece."

Was he in one piece? He didn't feel all here. Everything seemed fuzzy. His left leg was immobilized. His right ankle had been elevated.

Sleep. He wanted to sleep.

"That had to have been some fall, son," his dad said. "I hope the mountain is as beat up as you are."

"I…" Sean forced himself awake. "I don't remember."

He'd been riding down on his board. Something had snapped, and he'd felt as if he were flying. Someone—Sean couldn't remember who—had mentioned a broken binding, but he hadn't a clue what actually happened out there except… he hadn't been alone.

Panic bolted through him. His chest tightened.

He tried to sit up, but couldn't. The dull ache in his head sharpened to a knife's edge.

"Denali?" he croaked.

No one said anything. He thought he heard his mom tell someone to speak.

"Denali?" Sean repeated, firmer this time, even though it hurt.

"Denali's fine," an unfamiliar feminine voice said. "She's in your truck in the hospital parking lot."

The woman's words brought instant relief.

He cracked open his eyes, straining to see her, but couldn't see past the lights and equipment. They'd connected some annoying monitor to him that beeped at regular intervals.

"Jake told me she stayed with you and kept you warm until help arrived," the woman added.

"She's my good girl." The medication took the edge off the pain in his head. Denali was fine. Now he could sleep.

"She's a very good girl," the mystery woman agreed.

He'd heard that voice before. Somewhere.

"Are you in a lot of pain?" Connie asked.

Sean wiggled his right hand where they had inserted an IV for medication. "Whatever they're giving me makes me not care so much about the pain."

"You'll be headed to surgery shortly, Sean," the doctor said. "An open fracture needs immediate attention. A good thing your tetanus vaccination is up to date or you would have needed a shot on top of everything else."

"He never liked shots," Connie said.

Sean should let it go, but couldn't. "I was a kid, Mom."

"You're still my kid, Sean."

He wasn't about to argue that would make him a thirty-three-year-old kid.

"You'll meet the orthopedic surgeon in pre-op holding," the doctor said.

Sean struggled to focus. "How bad is it, Doc?"

"You took quite a fall, but with time and rehabilitation you shouldn't have any permanent damage. You'll be able to snowboard and climb again," the doctor explained. "You're a lucky man, Sean."

"Lucky," he repeated with his eyes still closed. He was happy to be alive, but he wondered when he could get started on rehab, when he would be able to climb and board again. He needed to get back up the mountain.

Thinking hurt. He squeezed his eyes shut more.

"The lights seem a little bright in here," the woman who Sean couldn't quite place said. "Is it okay if I turn them down, Doctor?"

"Go ahead," the doctor said. "Try opening your eyes now."

Sean opened his eyes slowly. The lights had been dimmed. Better, but he still felt as if his brain were stuffed with cotton. He looked around the room. The doctor in scrubs. His mom in her trademark pilgrim apron. His dad with his hands shoved in his pockets. Monitoring equipment with blinking lights and digital numbers. A pair of female breasts.

Sean blinked. The breasts were still there. High, perky, round.

At least his eyesight hadn't been affected by the head injury. Maybe this wasn't a hospital, but heaven. A heaven full of female breasts sounded about perfect to him.

"See, Zoe." Connie sounded less worried. "It's a good thing you came with us. You made him smile."

"And sent his pulse rate up, too," Hank added.

Zoe. Sean knew that name. He looked up from her chest to find a brown-haired woman staring at him from behind some sort of medical equipment. The angel breasts matched an angelic face. Young. Cute. Concerned. "Zoe?"

Maybe he'd rattled his brain even more than he thought. He had no idea who she was, but she sure was easy on his eyes.

"Don't you worry, honey," Connie said to him. "I had Jake drive her down in your truck. We're all taking really good care of your Zoe."

Your Zoe.

His Zoe.

Zoe.

It all came back to him in a harsh, painful rush.

That face, pink-cheeked, peering up at him from the side of the road with her snowboard and pack at her feet. He'd offered her a…ride, he remembered. A ride and turkey dinner at his parents' house. But there was more.… He searched his hazy brain. His grandmother's ring in the safe-deposit box at the bank. His girlfriend meeting the family for the first time.

Oh, hell.

His girlfriend.

"Zoe," he repeated, this time with a hint of urgency. "You okay?"

"Yes." She approached the bed tentatively and touched his left hand gently. Her skin felt warm, the pads of her fingers soft against his skin. "I'm so sorry about all of this."

She wasn't only talking about his fall. He squeezed her hand. "More than you bargained for."

"It's okay." Her eyes clouded. "Are you…all right with this?"

He glanced at his parents who were watching them with satisfied looks on their faces. She really was a trooper for continuing the charade. "Fine."

"You should rest." She glanced at his parents. "Get better."

"Yeah."

She wet her lips. "Is there anything you need?"

Actually he could think of something that would make this crappy day a little better.

Sean stared at her mouth, at her full, glossed lips. Yes, he knew exactly what he needed to see him through surgery and recovery. She was his "girlfriend" after all. "Come closer."

Zoe leaned over him. Strands of her below-the-shoulder brown hair swung forward.

He raised his hand to touch her hair. Brown. Silky. "Nice," he whispered.

She smiled at him, her cheeks flushed.

Sean knew Zoe was trapped. Still, he couldn't resist taking advantage of the situation to steal a kiss. He could blame it later on his head injury or the pain medication, but he was going to kiss her if it was the last thing he did.

He reached up and drew her head toward him.

Surprise filled her eyes. Her mouth parted, but she said nothing.

With an extreme amount of effort, he raised his head slightly off the pillow and kissed her on the lips. She tasted like chocolate and when she kissed him back something else. Heaven. The way he felt standing on a summit.

The surprising realization jolted him. He felt as if he'd hit his head again. Sean rested his head on the pillow. He closed his eyes with a smile on his face for what he'd gotten away with and for her kissing him back. He kept hold of Zoe's hand, as much for his sake as his parents'.

"After his surgery he'll be taken to a room upstairs."

The doctor's voice cut through the darkness in Sean's brain. "There's a surgical waiting area for family members."

"We'll wait there," Connie said. "Right, Zoe?"

"Yes," she said to Sean's relief. "What about Denali…?"

Zoe truly was an angel to think of his dog.

"Jake can take her to Hannah's," Sean muttered.

"Hannah and Garrett Willingham have dogsat for Sean before," Connie explained to Zoe. "They won't mind, and their kids will love having Denali around."

"That settles it, then," Zoe said.

"This isn't the Thanksgiving you expected, Zoe," Connie said.

"I don't think this was the Thanksgiving any of us expected, but that doesn't matter," Zoe replied. "We all have something to be very thankful for today."

Sean couldn't imagine what she was talking about. He forced open his eyes once again. "What's that?"

Her tender gaze met his. "You're going to be okay."

The warmth of her words wrapped around his heart the way they had earlier. Only this time it didn't feel as uncomfortable.

He was going to be okay.

A part of him just wished she would hang around until he was better. He kind of liked having her pretend to be his girlfriend.

CHAPTER THREE

THE AROMA of Thanksgiving dinner filled the air, making the atrium lobby area smell more like a restaurant than a hospital. Nurses had rolled in a cart to hold the dinner delivered by Sean's cousin, Mary Sue Townsend, wife of the sheriff's deputy.

Zoe sat at a round table with Sean's parents. All three were eager for an update on the ongoing surgery, but so far no word. She poked at the food on her paper plate with a plastic fork.

"Please eat something, Zoe," Connie encouraged. "I know you're worried, but Sean wouldn't want you to go hungry."

Zoe stared down at her rapidly congealing gravy. She appreciated the dinner and the thought behind it even more. Slices of turkey jostled with stuffing and mashed potatoes. Homemade cranberry sauce ran into the green-bean casserole. It smelled delicious, but her appetite was gone.

All she could think about was…Sean.

How was the surgery on his leg going?

Why had he kissed her?

And why did her lips still tingle from his kiss?

"It could be a long night," Hank added. "You'll need your strength."

The concern in his voice made Zoe take a bite of stuffing. Warm, but a little soggy.

"That wasn't so bad, was it?" Connie asked.

"Delicious." The satisfied smiles on Hank's and Connie's faces made Zoe ignore the lump in her stomach. She would eat whether she wanted to or not. They had enough on their minds. She didn't want to add to their real worries for their son.

She forced the moist stuffing down her dry throat.

Connie exchanged a relieved glance with Hank.

Zoe sipped from her bottle of lemon-lime soda. The cool liquid quenched her thirst, but did little to calm her churning stomach. Her tummy had felt all fluttery since the touch of Sean's lips against hers.

What was going on?

She had kissed a lot of guys over the years. More than her mother would want her to admit. More than Zoe could even remember.

Yet Sean's kiss disturbed her. As much as she would like to dismiss it as a combination of his pain medications and a show for his parents, the glint in Sean's eyes right before he kissed her, and the way he kissed her, clearly wasn't an innocent gesture. Zoe had been surprised at the heat considering he was banged up and hurting. She'd also been shocked by her reaction.

Sean's kiss had shot straight to Zoe's heart, leaving her bothered and confused. The way he'd flirted with her in the truck had been fun, but the way he invited her to dinner and up the mountain with him had made her feel special. Very special.

She wanted to kiss him again.

Stupid, stupid Zoe.

She shoved a piece of turkey with some gravy into her mouth as if food could make this better.

Allowing a second kiss to occur would be beyond dumb and totally irresponsible. Her mother was right. Zoe was too impulsive. She hadn't always acted responsibly, especially in matters of the heart. More than once, she'd been taken advantage of, and even lied to.

The stakes were too high to allow herself to be taken in again. No more plunging headfirst and heart first into relationships. Her heart had to remain immune to kisses, to handsome men, to…everything.

Including Sean Hughes.

Zoe liked him more than she should for knowing him for so short a time. As great as Sean seemed, she couldn't trust herself not to mess things up somehow.

She ate her dinner roll.

"Do you want another roll?" Connie asked.

"No, thank you," Zoe said. "But all the food is delicious."

"We'll have to see about having a makeup Thanksgiving dinner once Sean is out of the hospital." Connie picked up her iced tea. "A welcome-home-get-well celebration."

"I'm sure he'll appreciate that." Zoe tried a bite of the homemade cranberry sauce. It tasted bittersweet.

She wanted to help Sean out, but at what risk? Her own feelings? Her heart?

If her mother found out what she was up to, Zoe would lose access to her trust fund. And for what? A cute guy, who offered a ride up the mountain, invited her to dinner with his family and kissed her so tenderly and with such emotion she couldn't think straight?

Zoe slumped in her chair.

Somehow she forced herself to continue to eat. She ate a slice of pumpkin pie topped with whipped cream, but she barely tasted one of her all-time favorite desserts. All Zoe could think about was the smile on Sean's face and the gleam in his eye when he was telling her about the really good pie on their drive up to Timberline. If only she hadn't told him to go on when he said he'd board with her at the resort…

Once dinner was finished, they made their way to the surgical waiting room. The tension seemed to escalate. She glanced at the clock on the wall, mindful of the time since they'd wheeled him away. She wasn't the only one. The clock became everyone's prime focus. Zoe could almost feel each minute tick by.

She hated waiting. It reminded her too much of her experience with her dad.

Goose bumps prickled her skin.

No, she told herself. Sean was going to be okay. The doctor had said so.

Connie paced. "It's taking a long time."

"He had to go to pre-op first. Then there's the anesthesiologist. I'd imagine putting in a plate and screws takes a little time," Zoe said, as much for her own benefit as Connie's.

Hank nodded. "Better they go slow and get it right, than have them rush and need to go back in."

The words didn't stop Connie from pacing.

"You're going to wear yourself out," Hank said finally.

"I hope so." Connie's voice sounded tired, strained. "Sleep would be better than worrying."

Half an hour later, the orthopedic surgeon, Dr. Vandenhoff, entered the waiting area. He wore sweat-stained green surgical scrubs.

Connie clutched Hank.

"The surgery went well," Dr. Vandenhoff said. "We washed out debris from the fracture. Inserted the plate and screws. Sean is in recovery."

Connie sighed. "Thank goodness."

"Thank you, Doctor," Hank said.

Relief welled up inside of Zoe. Tears stung the corner of her eyes. "Yes, thank you."

She was thankful, because the sooner Sean was feeling better, the sooner she could leave.

The sooner she would be safe.

Sean felt as if a white-noise machine had replaced his brain. He had no idea how long he'd been asleep or what had occurred while he was sleeping. The familiar pressure in his head and legs remained, as did the far-off ache.

Pain.

You're a very lucky man, Sean.

Yeah, right. He wondered if that was what the doctor said to everyone who passed through the E.R.

A loud snore ripped through the air. Sean forced open his heavy eyelids.

The lights in the hospital room had been dimmed, but he could make out a sleeping figure in a chair. Another deep, familiar snore sounded.

His dad.

Sean grinned and winced at the same time. It was great his dad was here, but man, the snoring sounded like his chain saw.

Sean noticed something different in this room—the smell. The scent of flowers masked the typical, sterile hospital scent.

"You're awake," a woman said.

He struggled to place the voice, fighting the fog inside his head. Not just a woman, he realized, pleased. Zoe.

His Zoe.

"Would you like some water?" she asked.

He felt as if he'd swallowed a bag of cotton balls or his throat had been scoured with sandpaper. "Please."

A straw sticking out from the lid of a plastic cup poked at his lips. "The nurse said you should take little sips," Zoe cautioned.

Sean fought to raise his head. He didn't care what the nurse had said. She didn't know how thirsty he was. He sucked the water, choked and coughed. Somehow he managed not to spit it out. He cleared his throat. "Nurse was right."

Zoe supported the back of his neck with one hand, handed him a tissue with another and eased him back onto his pillow. "That's what you said before."

Before. He didn't remember.

Sean focused on Zoe standing next to the bed. Her clear, blue eyes looked at him with such compassion his breath caught in his throat. Her long-sleeved T-shirt fit tight across her chest and raised his temperature ten degrees. Her jeans clung to her hips, showing him he'd been right about the curves hidden beneath her snowboarding jacket.

He smiled. "You're still here."

Which made him feel unexpectedly relieved.

She glanced over at his dad and back at Sean with an uncertain smile. "Where else would your girlfriend be?"

"In bed. With me." He tried to wink, but wasn't sure he managed one. Right now he couldn't manage much of anything.

She shook her head, her smile growing. "There isn't room."

Not to mention he couldn't fool around with her. But the idea of her curled warm against his side was surprisingly appealing.

"I don't mind being cramped," he said.

"I might hurt you."

"Promise?"

She laughed. "Okay, you're feeling better."

"I'm not feeling much at all."

Zoe patted his hand lightly. Her touch soothed and comforted him. "That's probably a very good thing right now."

"I'll be fine."

"I'm sure you will."

"What about you?" he asked.

She glanced at his dad once again. "I'm fine, too."

Fine, huh? Zoe looked tired. Sean didn't like that. "What time is it?"

"Four o'clock."

"In the morning?" he asked.

"The afternoon."

Sean noticed gray light streaking through the window. A mylar balloon floated from a red string and two bright floral arrangements sat on the counter. He remembered none of those things. He must have been out of it awhile.

"Where did you sleep last night?" he asked.

She looked down at the IV in his right arm. "Here."

He looked at his dad asleep on the recliner. "Where's my mom?"

"At a nearby motel," Zoe explained. "Your mom's been through a lot in the last twenty-four hours. She needs to rest and relax away from the hospital for a little while."

"You're giving her a break."

Zoe rubbed the small of her back. "Your dad is here, too."

As if on cue, his father let loose another snore.

"My dad's working real hard."

The corners of Zoe's mouth curved.

In spite of her smile, she had to be tired sitting and sleeping upright. This was going above and beyond the call of phony girlfriend duty. Sean couldn't let it continue. "I can come clean to my folks about us."

"And your family and friends, too?"

Sean had forgotten about them. He tried to think of how to handle this. It wasn't easy. "Breaking up might be easier than trying to explain things." Although the fallout over his supposed breakup with a girl his family obviously approved of could be worse than their comments about settling down. That wouldn't make for a very nice Christmas. "Actually there might be less drama if I tell the truth."

"Whatever you think best."

Best would be her body next to his. He'd settle for another kiss. His father stirred awake.

"I'll explain everything to them once I'm out of the hospital," Sean said.

"That's fine."

"You'll stay?" he asked, knowing the answer he wanted to hear.

Uncertainty filled her eyes.

"Until I'm out of here. The hospital," he clarified.

Time seemed to slow while he waited for her answer.

Say yes.

"Until you're out of the hospital," Zoe said.

Sean smiled. That was good enough for him.

* * *

Zoe couldn't remember what day it was. She stared at her exhausted eyes and pale skin in the mirror of the women's restroom. She looked as if she'd been up half the night. Which she had. Again.

Zoe yawned. She was running on fumes. Not even caffeine would help at this point. She had spent another night at the hospital while Connie and Hank slept at the motel. They'd decided to split into shifts. Zoe had offered to take the night shift to limit her interaction with Sean's family and friends. There was only so much pretending she could take. She didn't like misleading people. The sooner everyone knew the truth the better. She didn't know how much longer she could keep up the charade.

Sean's parents were up in his room now. They had arrived minutes ago to relieve her. A tag team of family and friends would spell them throughout the day.

Zoe splashed cold water on her face. It didn't help. She couldn't wait to return to the motel. Connie had generously rented a room with two queen-size beds and handed Zoe a key so she, too, would have a place to sleep outside of the hospital.

She dried her face with a paper towel from the dispenser above the counter and tossed it into the trash. She would give the Hughes a few more minutes alone before Hank drove her to the motel. They needed time together as a family.

And Zoe needed time away from Sean.

She applied lip gloss. The rest of her makeup as well as her backpack were at the motel.

She liked Sean. He wasn't just a pretty face with a hot body. His injuries hadn't dampened his sense of humor. He hadn't complained or seemed all that down. In fact, he'd been handling his situation with a courage and attitude she respected.

Too bad respect wasn't the only thing she felt for him.

The way Sean looked at her when he woke up from one of his naps made her feel special even in the middle of the night. He wanted her at his side. She wanted to be there for him. Feeling wanted was a whole lot better than feeling like a screwup.

For once she was no longer oopsie-baby, the nickname given to her by her older brothers, or Zany Zoe, which her friends had called her after all her trouble with the tabloids. She preferred being simply Zoe.

Zoe Flynn, she reminded herself. Zoe Carrington had all but ceased to exist the past few weeks. Maybe that wasn't such a bad thing.

The more time she spent with Sean, his family and friends, the more she liked them and the less she missed her old life. She could never imagine Connie or Hank sending one of their kids away so they would learn responsibility and wouldn't cause any problems. Zoe wished the Hughes were her family and she'd be spending Christmas with them, not alone in a strange town somewhere far away from home.

She felt a pang in her heart.

Stop. Now.

Thinking like that was too dangerous. And not possible. December twenty-fifth was too far away.

Sean was handling his pain better. He'd been visited by a physical therapist and an occupational therapist. He would be out of here before Zoe knew it, and so would she.

She wasn't his real girlfriend. He didn't really need her. Nor did Connie and Hank or any of the other family members or friends Zoe had met.

The realization made her heart drop to her feet with a resounding splat. She was all alone and had to remain that way until after the special election.

Feeling sad and even more tired, she returned to Sean's room. He had fallen asleep again.

She glanced around.

Crayon drawings by the children of his extended family and friends hung on the walls. One was a picture of Denali. Another was a mountain surrounded by space ships. More flowers and balloon bouquets had been delivered along with cards. A part of her wished she could send Sean one of the lovely flower arrangements, but all she could afford at the moment was a single rosebud without the vase. Zoe sighed.

"Would you mind running down to the gift shop with Connie before I take you to the motel?" Hank asked quietly. "She wants to pick up some things for her shift."

"Not a problem," Zoe said.

"I'll stay here in case Sean wakes up," Hank added.

Downstairs in the gift shop, Connie tucked a newspaper under her arm and studied the candy selection. She had a real sweet tooth. "While you were gone, the occupational therapist stopped by. She gave her recommendations to the discharge planner."

Relief Sean was doing well enough to be discharged pulsed through Zoe. "That's wonderful news."

Good news for Sean and his family. As for her...

It was best if she moved on.

"I just hope Sean doesn't fight their recommendations," Connie said. "He can be stubborn sometimes."

"He also has a concussion, a sprained ankle and a broken leg." Zoe scanned the newspaper headlines. She hadn't watched much TV in Sean's hospital room because she hadn't wanted to disturb his sleep. She'd been too tired when she got to the motel. She felt as if she were emerging from a cocoon and needed to catch up on what she'd missed the last couple of days. "Stubborn will only take him so far."

"He may need you to tell him that."

She flashed Connie a supportive smile. "If he does, I will."

That was the least Zoe could do, even if Sean wouldn't listen to her. She owed the Hughes family big-time. They had provided a warm place for her to sleep and shower, dropped off food for her at Sean's hospital room and given her rides back and forth to the motel. She hadn't spent a dime since buying her lift ticket on Thanksgiving morning. She now had enough money to make it until her monthly allowance would be deposited into her checking account on the first of

December. She would find a way to repay their generosity somehow, someday.

Zoe glimpsed the cover of a tabloid and did a double take. She reread the words in the top corner of the front page.

Party Animal Zoe Carrington Caged?

Her heart plummeted to her feet.

She glanced at the name of the tabloid. *Weekly Secrets*.

Anger burned. They were one of the worst gossip rags out there, the first to publish the photos of her at that club with Lonzo the liar. They'd only gone on two dates, but he'd made it out to be the love affair of the century. The lying, married jerk.

She saw Connie shuffling through greeting cards. Zoe wanted to ignore the headline, but curiosity made her reach for the paper. She opened the tabloid. A file photo of her, with blond highlighted hair, a ton of makeup and an expensive designer cocktail dress, greeted her. She cringed.

Party Animal Zoe Carrington Caged!
Garrett Malloy and Fred Silvers

Political insiders claim Governor Vanessa Carrington, currently embroiled in a special election for a coveted U.S. Senate seat, has banished her youngest daughter, Zoe, from the state, possibly the country. The move is not surprising given the scandal that erupted when photos of the lovely socialite and heartthrob actor Lonzo Green surfaced two months ago.

Zoe claimed Green told her he was divorced, but he countered her statement by saying, "Young women have a tendency to hear only what they want to hear when they are in love."

When asked about his missing ex-paramour, Green replied, "No comment."

His indifference is surprising since the publicity resulting from the scandal is widely credited with Green landing a lead role in the highly anticipated blockbuster *Tsunami*. No doubt he hopes to ride the wave straight to the A-list. As for Green's wife, soap opera actress Britt Bayer, she has been at his side ever since the story of her husband's torrid affair broke.

Sources close to the governor claim twenty-four-year-old Zoe simply wanted a break from her hectic social schedule. But if that's the case, why has no one seen or heard from Zoe?

"A break means a short trip to Paris or New York or Milan," gossip blogger and hanger-on Charlotte Rafferty said. "There are always parties. Appearances. Photos. Zoe constantly sent tweets until her disappearance, and her Facebook page hasn't been updated in weeks. Something has definitely happened to her, but the governor keeps shutting down any attempts at an official investigation into Zoe's whereabouts."

There is speculation the governor may have committed her wild child to a mental health or rehab facility to avoid more embarrassing headlines that would compromise her senate run.

If you know the whereabouts of Zoe Carrington, please contact us here at *Weekly Secrets*. She's one of our favorite headline makers, and we'd like to make sure she's safe.

Safe. Yeah, right. Zoe grimaced. The only thing tabloids cared about was selling more papers. She only interested them when she was doing something scandalous or glamorous. Nothing else rated with them.

She glanced at Connie who still stood at the card display.

Disgusted to be touching such trash, Zoe shoved the piece of garbage back into its slot on the rack. If they were looking for her, others would be, too. Not good.

Okay, she no longer had blond hair and wasn't wearing much makeup now. She barely recognized herself, but that didn't mean someone else might not put two and two together.

The longer Zoe stayed in a city the size of Portland, the better the chance of being discovered. She needed to find a place to hide away. A small, cheap town with an ATM where she could access her checking account.

A cell phone rang. Connie's.

One of the many family members calling or something about Sean? Zoe's muscles bunched.

Connie answered the phone before the second ring with a strained hello, but soon her eyes lit up and she smiled.

Thank goodness. Zoe relaxed.

"That's great, Hank," Connie answered, animated. "Yes, he must be feeling more like his old self. No, we'll be right up."

Zoe waited until Sean's mom had hung up. "Are they discharging him?"

"Not yet, but the press is on their way to Sean's room to interview him about his experience. A rescuer being rescued by his own unit." Connie set three candy bars, a get-well card and a newspaper on the counter. She pulled out her wallet. "We need to get up there."

The air rushed from Zoe's lungs. Every single nerve ending went on alert. Being in the same building as the media was bad enough. No way could she risk being in the same room. "I'm too tired."

"Sean will want you there."

No, he wouldn't. Especially if he knew the truth about her. Zoe forced a smile. "I'm not the story. He is."

Connie didn't look convinced as she paid the elderly cashier wearing a pink jacket.

Zoe would try another tack. "There's going to be a lot happening up there, and the room's not that big. I'm going to stop by the cafeteria for a coffee. Maybe I'll make it back before they're finished."

Emphasis on *maybe*.

"Okay." Connie picked up her bag of purchases from the counter. "But if Sean asks—"

"I'll tell him you wanted me up there," Zoe interrupted. "You'd better hurry so you don't miss anything."

"You're sure?"

"Yes." Zoe had never been more certain of anything in her life. "Now go."

The camera crews were gone. The last reporter had left.

Where was Zoe?

Sean felt cranky and deflated.

The news from his discharge planner wasn't making him feel any better. He was used to taking care of other people, not needing someone to take care of him.

"I'm sorry, Sean." Meghan, a well-dressed thirtysomething woman with bright red hair piled on top of her head, spoke gently, as if her soft voice would ease his frustration. "An independent discharge is not possible. You cannot ambulate safely with both your fracture and a sprained ankle."

"I understand the OT's assessment." He was still on pain medication, but not even that was going to make him go along with this nonsense. "But really, I'm used to living alone. I can take care of myself. My ankle will be fine. I'll hire a physical therapist to help me with the recommended exercises. I have friends to help with my dog. It won't be a problem."

Zoe entered the room quietly. Relief washed over him. Now he might have an ally and—

"Problem or not, you're going to be using a walker for the first couple of weeks," Meghan said. "You'll need help preparing meals and bathing. Living alone in your current condition is not possible."

"You don't know me."

Connie opened her mouth. Hank tapped her thigh. His mother pressed her lips together.

"I don't," Meghan said patiently. "But I'm required to follow what OT recommends. A recommendation your orthopedic surgeon agrees with."

Sean gritted his teeth.

Zoe walked toward his bed. "What are Sean's options?"

"The first is a sniff," Meghan said.

"A what?" Connie asked.

"Skilled nursing facility, also known as a SNF," Meghan explained. "Hiring homecare is another option. But usually the best solution, especially with a head injury, is for Sean to go home with someone capable of caring for him."

"He can stay with us," Connie said without a moment of hesitation.

Hank nodded. "That's the best option for our son."

Sean forced himself not to grimace. He didn't want to hurt his parents' feelings. "Mom. Dad. I appreciate the offer, but I'm a little old to move back home."

His mom glanced at his dad. The determined look in her eyes told Sean she wouldn't change her mind without a fight.

He had friends and family who would gladly stay with him, but Sean didn't want to put anyone out.

"Would you mind if we discussed this in private, Meghan?" Hank asked.

"Take your time." The woman rose. "I'll be at the nurses' station."

"Thank you," Connie said.

"Would you like me to leave?" Zoe asked.

"Stay," Sean said.

"Of course you should stay," Hank said.

Connie nodded.

Silence descended on the room. Meghan closed the door behind her.

"I know you're independent, Sean, but you won't be at home with us forever." Connie spoke as if the decision had already been made. Not good. "Only until you're back on your feet and can take care of yourself."

"I can take care of myself now," Sean countered. "I can order takeout when I'm hungry. I've been on climbing trips where I haven't been able to shower."

Hank shook his head. "Your mother's right, son. Coming home with us is your best option."

Only option was what his dad meant.

Sean had to be careful here. He'd put his parents through enough these past few days. "December is a busy time of the year for both of you. I don't want you to have to take care of me on top of everything else you do at Christmastime."

"You're our son. Caring for you is not a burden." Connie's chin jutted forward. "We aren't about to let a stranger take care of you."

Sean's gaze locked with Zoe's, pleaded with her to help him out.

As if reading his mind, she walked to the side of his bed and patted his hand, the way she'd done many times before. Despite his frustration, despite the fact that she probably made the gesture to fool his parents, Sean was oddly comforted. Reassured. He spread his fingers so hers fell between his.

She smiled at him.

He smiled back.

"Unless…" Connie's voice faded.

Sean's gaze narrowed. He was willing to consider any alternative to going home with his parents. "What?"

"Zoe," she said.

"Zoe?" Sean repeated, confused.

"Me?" Zoe sounded puzzled.

"Great idea," Hank approved.

"It took me a minute to understand why you didn't want to come home with us, but I finally figured it out," Connie said with a pleased smile. "You want your pretty girlfriend to take care of you while you recover. Not your mother. And honey, I'm perfectly fine with that."

CHAPTER FOUR

Take care of Sean?

Panic ricocheted through Zoe.

Connie might think that was a good idea, but Zoe didn't. Sure, she felt good helping the Hughes family. But she needed to say goodbye to them, not entangle herself deeper in their lives. Time to get out of here, except…

With Sean holding tightly on to her hand she wasn't going anywhere.

"I don't know how much time you've spent in Hood Hamlet, but everyone will pitch in and help with Sean's recovery," Hank said to her. "You won't find a more supportive community."

"The way Sean's friends have rallied around him since his accident makes it seem like a very friendly place," Zoe admitted.

"Nothing beats living near family," Connie piped in.

Hank nodded. "I wouldn't want to live anywhere else."

Sean smiled at Zoe. "It's friendly, definitely. Your typical small town. I gave living in Portland a try once, but I prefer the mountains."

The Hood Hamlet Chamber of Commerce would be proud of the Hughes for championing the town. Too bad their sales tactics were wasted on her.

"Who knows, Zoe?" Connie grinned. "You might just fall in love."

Love? The air whooshed from Zoe's lungs.

Sean's lips thinned. "Mom."

"What?" Connie feigned innocence. "Zoe might fall in love with Hood Hamlet. It's a very nice place to live."

Maybe for them, but not Zoe. She was used to city living. On her own. Not caring for someone who needed more help than she knew how to give.

Her shoulders sagged, a combination of exhaustion and frustration. They spoke as if this were a done deal, as if she would be staying in Hood Hamlet. "About taking care of Sean…"

"Yes," he said. "About that…"

"My son isn't the best patient." Connie smiled at Zoe, as if sharing a family secret. "I remember when he had chicken pox. You would have thought his world was ending."

"I was nine." Sean's chin jutted out. "Two feet of fresh powder to ride, and I was stuck in bed."

"I'm sure he'll behave better with you," Connie said.

Whether he behaved or not didn't matter. Zoe started to tell them this was a really bad idea, but stopped herself.

What could she say without giving everything away?

She would have to wait for Sean to say something, to tell them why she shouldn't be the one to take care of him.

Zoe waited. The seconds on the clock seemed to tick as slow as minutes.

Please, Sean.

Her gaze bounced between him and his parents.

What was taking him so long?

There was no point—no need—to drag out the charade any longer. He was clearly recovering. With the worst of his parents' worries allayed, it was time for Sean to tell them the truth about Zoe and his nonrelationship.

But how?

That question made her realize why Sean was hesitating. He must be trying to figure out what to say to his parents and how to explain all of this to them.

A mix of emotion churned inside Zoe. Relief at not having to continue the lie. Regret at the thought of hurting the people she'd come to care about these past few days. But in her heart, Zoe knew this needed to be done, now, no matter what the fallout.

Connie and Hank didn't want a stranger looking after their son. Well, Zoe was a stranger. Even though she liked feeling needed by his family and by Sean, she was the last person they would want to care for him.

She looked at Sean.

He lay covered with a blanket in the hospital bed, so different from the man she'd met a few days ago on the side of the road. Stubble covered his face. A cut near his chin had scabbed over. The dark bruise on his cheek was fading. His hair was sticking up all over the place.

Oh, he was still handsome. A few cuts and purple blotches didn't change his amazing bone structure and his warm, hazel-green eyes. But his physical weakness, his vulnerability struck at her heart and her insecurities.

Zoe's chest ached.

Sean needed someone who knew what they were doing, someone who could make sure he had everything he needed while recovering.

That wasn't her. She had the necessary skills to be his personal shopper, not his caretaker.

Besides, no matter how vulnerable Sean Hughes might look at the moment, he wasn't a man to play doctor or house with. She shouldn't play with him period.

She was vulnerable, too.

Careful and cautious, remember?

Zoe toyed with the edge of his blanket with her free hand. "Sean…"

His gaze met hers.

Something passed between them. She chewed on the inside of her cheek. They were in this little ruse together, but it had morphed into something neither had imagined.

He squeezed her hand. "Mom, Dad, would you mind giving me and Zoe a few minutes alone?"

Connie jumped to her feet. "Of course."

"We'll wait outside," Hank added.

Sean's parents exited the room. As soon as the door latched, he grimaced. "I'm sorry about all this."

"We have to tell them the truth."

"I know," he agreed. "You must have some place else you need to be."

Zoe had no set itinerary, simply a list of places she couldn't go: home, Los Angeles, New York, London and Paris. "Not really, but that's beside the point."

"Your family and your boyfriend must be expecting you home at some point."

"Traveling was actually my mother's idea. My brothers are older than me. We're not very close. I'm actually estranged from my family right now," Zoe admitted. "And I don't have a boyfriend. A real one, that is."

"Where do you live?"

She thought about the apartment in Los Angeles she'd been forced to give up before setting off on her own. "I don't have a permanent address at the moment."

He studied her with an unreadable expression on his face. "What about a job?"

"I'm between jobs."

His eyes locked on hers.

She knew exactly what he was thinking. "No way."

"Why not?" he asked.

"We're not in a relationship." She kept her voice low in case Hank and Connie walked back in. "We're strangers."

"We're past the point of being strangers, Zoe."

"Your family and friends have been so nice to me," she said. "They've made me feel welcomed and accepted. I don't like lying to them."

"You've helped them get through this, Zoe. Me, too. We all appreciate that."

She liked feeling useful, but she had her trust fund, her future to consider. "If they knew the truth…"

"They'll never have to know."

"I can't stay here forever."

"I'll take care of it."

"That's what you said before."

He smiled, as if a charming grin could make everything better. "I haven't left the hospital yet."

Okay, his smile did help. A little. But she needed to be smart about this. She hadn't been smart about so many other things in her life. "It's too complicated. I haven't dealt well with complications in the past."

"You're selling yourself short."

"I'm not. If you knew…"

"I know this is a better deal for me than you," Sean admitted. "I'm willing to do whatever it takes. You'll be paid a salary. You'll also get room and board."

She didn't know whether to be insulted or reassured. "You want to pay me to take care of you?"

"Yes," he said. "I'd have to pay for home health care."

"Insurance would cover that."

"I'd rather have you there." He squeezed her hand again.

Zoe's heart bumped. That only added to her rising doubts. "I don't know."

"There are easier ways to earn money," he said. "You heard my mom. I'm not a good patient. But I'll try to be better."

Zoe could try, too. She could—

No, wait.

She should forget about this. Going along with Sean's proposal wasn't a smart idea. She should say no and walk away, yet curiosity wouldn't let her.

"What would I have to do exactly? If I took the job," she qualified.

He eyes brightened at her apparent weakening. "Walk Denali. Pretend to be madly in love with me in front of my parents. Drive me to work and appointments. Wait on me hand and foot."

A couple of those didn't sound too difficult.

In fact, the job sounded perfect given her need to stay out of the spotlight for the duration of her mother's campaign. A small town like Hood Hamlet might be the perfect place to hide. If she could live off her salary, her mother would see she had learned to manage her money. This sounded almost too good to be true. And in Zoe's experience, that meant trouble.

She'd learned nothing was ever as good as it sounded, but that hadn't kept her from hoping, wishing, it would be. All she ever wanted was to be accepted for who she was—loved—and that had often led her to ignore warning signs and even her own gut instinct. She didn't want to repeat the same pattern.

Restlessly, she moved away from the side of his bed. Zoe couldn't think when Sean was watching. She walked along the row of colorful, fragrant bouquets lined up on the windowsill. Roses, a mixed bouquet of fall-colored blossoms and Stargazer lilies. Reading the feminine names on many of the cards made her feel strange.

Not that his social life was any of her business.

"Why me?" she asked.

"My family thinks you're my girlfriend. Who else would I ask?"

"How about Chelsea or Grace or Lulu?" Zoe read the names from the cards. Reading between the lines of one of the cards seemed to indicate a close, probably intimate, relationship. The knowledge unsettled her. "Seems to me, one of them would be more than happy to help you out."

Unexpected color appeared on his cheeks. "They don't know my family. And they would have certain expectations if I asked them to help me. You won't."

"Because anything between us is pretend."

"Because we're friends," Sean said. "I don't know too many people who would go to the lengths you've gone to for a person they'd just met. I'd tie in with you any day."

"Tie in?"

"Climber term," Sean explained. "It means I'd climb with you anytime, anywhere."

The compliment made Zoe tingle all over. She felt a little breathless. "Thanks, but you helped me first."

"You've done way more for me since then."

The sincerity in his voice brought a rush of warmth flowing through her. She returned to the side of his bed.

Sean pushed a strand of hair behind her ear.

Zoe's heart stuttered. His gesture felt so intimate, so natural, so right. The impulse to agree to take care of him was so strong she pressed her lips together. She couldn't give in that easily. Sean Hughes wasn't just some guy who needed help. He was dangerous to both her senses and her hormones. And his family had already touched her heart.

"What are you thinking?" he asked.

She liked him enough, trusted him enough, to tell the truth. Or as much of it as she could.

"My mother thinks I'm too impulsive. She wants me to be more responsible."

"What could be more responsible than taking care of an injured friend?"

Not even her mother could find fault with Zoe taking care of a friend. Except that Sean's kiss on Thanksgiving before his surgery hadn't been at all friendlike. "It might cramp your style."

"Huh?"

"If we're supposed to be having a relationship, you won't be able to date."

"The same goes for you."

She shrugged. "I'm not looking for a relationship."

"That makes two of us."

She thought about his kiss, about the way he touched her. A part of her wanted to read more into his wanting her to stay. Then she remembered all the flowers from various women. "You sure about that?"

"Dating is not the same as having a relationship."

Zoe bit the inside of her cheek. "I'm not qualified."

"You've been the perfect pretend girlfriend."

"I mean I've never taken care of anyone before unless you count Popcorn, my hamster when I was nine," she explained. "He died."

"I'm going to be a lot harder to kill than a hamster."

"I don't know about that." She thought about growing up in the governor's mansion with a cook and a housekeeper. "I'm not, uh, very domestic. I feel it's fair to warn you I'm cooking and cleaning challenged."

"I don't care if you burn water," he said.

"I've never burned water, but I ruined a pan trying to heat up soup," she admitted, trying to discourage him. "I didn't know you had to add water."

"We can order takeout every night. I'll get a housecleaner to come twice a week if that makes you feel better."

"That will be expensive."

"I can afford it."

Still the cons seemed to outweigh the pros. She wished he would realize that so this would be easier. "I don't have any references."

"I don't need references," Sean said. "You've showed me the kind of person you are these past few days."

Guilt coated her mouth. He had no idea who she was. He didn't even know her real last name. Yet he was trying awfully hard to get her to stay with him.

"You're the one I want to take care of me." His earnest tone tugged at her conscience. "You're exactly what I need, Zoe."

No one had ever needed her before. Well, besides her hamster. And look how that had turned out.

Still Sean's words made Zoe feel as if she mattered, as if she wasn't as useless as people had accused her of being.

"Will you please come home with me?" he asked.

Home.

Emotion clogged her throat. If only she could go home...

But Zoe no longer knew what home meant. The place she'd grown up seemed to have drifted farther and farther away. She felt rootless, adrift, alone.

This time with the Hughes had given her a taste of both family and community. Something she hadn't really experienced since her dad died. Every day since then, Zoe's family life had been more like a job, one long PR event. That was why she'd tried to do more—to go places, see new things and bond with friends. But even then she never really felt like she was in the right place.

Was this the right place for her? The right move?

She needed to put her emotions aside and think about things logically. He was offering her a place to stay and a salary. Where else was she going to find those things without needing some sort of background check?

If she accepted Sean's offer, she could hide away in Hood Hamlet and help him out. She could show her mother she had changed, and at the same time spend Christmas with Sean's loving, accepting family.

She stared at him.

A ball of warmth settled in the center of her chest.

Christmas in Hood Hamlet with the Hughes family might help her figure out what she wanted and where she belonged. That appealed to her on multiple levels.

"Okay," Zoe said finally. "I'll do it."

Damn walker. Sean hobbled from his mother's minivan to his house. His mom had offered to drive him home while his dad took Zoe in the truck.

Sean owed a six-pack to whoever had cleared the path to his front porch this afternoon. Making his way through the snow wouldn't have been easy. It was hard enough with two bum legs and a device senior citizens used.

He glanced at his mom. She walked at a snail's pace next to him. No sense telling her to get inside before she got cold. She would only say no.

Like it or not, Connie Hughes knew what needed to be done. She'd nursed his father back from spinal surgery and her mother after a hip replacement.

"Who plowed?" Sean asked.

"Jake."

Of course, Jake Porter would make sure the path was

plowed. The guy did everything for everybody while running the Hood Hamlet Brewery, one of Sean's favorite haunts.

He glanced down at his legs and grimaced. Too bad he wouldn't be stepping in there for a pint anytime soon.

"Jake left some bottles of Twelfth Night, his new winter brew, for you in the fridge," Connie added. "But I wouldn't mix alcohol with pain medication."

Ever since the accident, people kept telling Sean what he should and shouldn't do, as if he couldn't figure things out for himself. He was a Wilderness First Responder, dammit. He had EMT training. He knew his family and friends meant well, but the constant admonitions only increased his feeling of helplessness. He wished they would keep their mouths shut. "I know, Mom."

Sean already felt off balance due to the boot on his left leg and the air cast on his right ankle. He hated feeling so fuzzy and wobbly, not knowing when a wrong step with the walker might send him flat on his ass. Falling had always been a risk when he climbed, but he'd never feared falling as much as now. He didn't want to hurt himself more.

"Sometimes pain medication can lead you to make bad decisions," she said.

Like cajoling Zoe to continue as his pretend girlfriend?

Nope, that was a good decision even though his desire to have her stick around had surprised him. He wanted to chalk it up to attraction or desperation at wanting to be home, but wasn't quite sure what compelled him. Sean had gone with his gut, and it still felt like the right move. Keeping Zoe around made him feel better. "Don't worry, Mom."

"I'm your mother," Connie said. "It's my right to worry."

Too bad, because he was worrying enough for the both of them.

Sweat beaded on Sean's forehead, even though he was wearing shorts and the temperature was in the mid-thirties. Each step took concentration, as if he were climbing in the death zone on Everest, not the front steps of his house.

He grunted. His warm breath rose on the cold air.

His mother stayed at his side, making him feel more like a four-year-old at a crowded mall than a grown man. "Sean—"

"I've got it."

With a deep breath that chilled his lungs, he managed another shaky step.

Almost inside.

"There's no rush," she said gently.

"I don't think I'll be rushing anywhere soon."

Unfortunately.

The doctor had told Sean he would need the walker before moving on to crutches. He'd laughed, thinking he could ditch the walker as soon as he arrived home. Sure he could ditch the stupid thing, but only if he wanted to crawl.

The realization was both humbling and disheartening.

He'd been an athlete his entire life and suffered his share of injuries, but nothing this serious. Now he couldn't even walk on his own.

Sean exhaled on a sigh. A lifetime of ignoring discomfort in his athletic and rescue pursuits tempered his grousing.

He was alive. He needed to concentrate on the positives.

Sean took another step. All he had to do was string a bunch of these together. No different than a steep ascent, except without using the rest step.

"You're doing great, honey," Connie encouraged, sticking close to him.

"Thanks, Mom."

Sean was glad she was here with him instead of Zoe. Maybe he would feel less wrung out by the time she arrived.

Standing on his front porch, he waited while his mom unlocked and opened the door.

He crossed the threshold and stepped onto the hardwood entry. Sean expected Denali to pounce on him, but he heard no barking, no sounds of four paws against the hardwood floor. Then he remembered. She would stay with Hannah and Garrett until Sean was steadier on his feet.

"Happy to be home?" Connie asked.

He nodded. "But I miss my girl."

"Zoe will be here soon." Connie removed her coat and hung it on the rack next to the door. She slipped off her shoes. "They were stopping by the motel to check out."

Zoe. Sean bit back a smile. He'd meant Denali, but he wouldn't mind calling Zoe his girl, too.

She might mind, however.

Sean wasn't going to do or say anything to upset Zoe. That included keeping his fantasy about her wearing a sexy nurse costume to himself. He still couldn't believe she was going to take care of him. Granted, he was paying her well, but not many people would interrupt their travel plans for a total stranger. Even fewer would pretend to be his girlfriend. He knew she'd been close to saying no. Thank goodness she hadn't. Sean hated to think how this situation would have played out without Zoe around. He would probably be settling in at his parents' house instead of his own home.

He wavered slightly and clutched the handles of the walker.

Concern clouded his mom's eyes. "You look pale."

Sean took another step. "I just need to get used to the walker."

"Take your time."

As if he had any other choice.

Slowly, molasses-in-January slowly, he made his way across the floor. The walker made a lot of noise. Maybe it was him with all the herky-jerky movement.

Finally, he reached the leather couch, turned around and sat. He settled back against the cushions. This would be his bed until he could negotiate the stairs safely. Too bad he hadn't put a bedroom on the main floor when he designed the house. At least the couch was comfortable and the television nearby.

His mother hovered over him. "Let's get that jacket off before you get too warm."

He unzipped his fleece and shrugged out of it himself.

"I appreciate the help, Mom, but my leg's broken, not my hand."

"I'll hang up your jacket and get you a glass of water." She took the coat and tucked it under her arm while she nudged the ottoman closer with her foot. "Elevate your legs."

A minute later, Sean watched her in the kitchen. She filled a glass with filtered water from the stainless-steel refrigerator, one of those French door types with the freezer on the bottom his cousin Mary Sue had suggested.

"Do you need anything else?" Connie asked.

Sean couldn't remember the last time he'd needed someone to get him a glass of water. He was coming to realize how little he could do on his own right now with his injuries and the pain medication. "No thanks, Mom."

She handed him the cup of water. "I don't mind."

But he did.

Sean took a sip and placed the glass on the end table. He heard the front door open, footsteps, voices.

Zoe.

Relief flooded him. Many women had walked into his house the same way, but none made him smile like Zoe. "Hey," he said.

"Hi." Zoe hesitated a moment before crossing the great room to stand in front of him. Leaning over, she brushed her lips over his in an awkward yet thoughtful gesture.

For his parents' sake, he realized with a stab of regret.

"How does it feel to be home?" she asked.

"Good." He cleared his dry throat. "Especially now that you're here."

Sean noticed the pleased glances exchanged by his parents. Funny thing was he wasn't pretending. He'd meant what he said.

Zoe smiled. "I'm happy to be here."

Yet he knew she wasn't as happy as he was at the moment. How could she be?

That made him feel…strange. Truth was, he needed

Zoe more than she needed him. He didn't like being in that position. Sean adjusted his legs on the ottoman.

"You need pillows," Connie said. "Zoe, dear, run and get Sean some pillows."

Zoe's startled gaze met his.

Pillows, he realized. She wouldn't know where the pillows were. She had no idea where anything was.

"Take the pillows off my bed. The blue ones," he said. Would that be enough of a hint?

"Oh, right." Gratitude filled her no longer panicked eyes. "Sorry, I'm a little tired."

"You were up all night," Hank said. "You should be tired. I'm surprised you didn't nap on the drive home."

"I enjoyed talking with you," she said.

Sean wondered what they'd talked about.

"I'll come with you, Zoe," Connie offered. "We can put your backpack in Sean's room."

Zoe's panicked expression returned, only this time she looked more uncomfortable than ever. "I, uh, can do it."

"I want to help," Connie said. "As Hank said, you're tired."

Sean inhaled sharply.

His mother was only trying to be open-minded. Modern. It was endearing, yet annoying since the one place Zoe wouldn't be sleeping was his room. He liked the thought of her in his bed, but she looked thoroughly embarrassed with her pink cheeks. "Zoe's staying in the guest bedroom, Mom."

Connie looked between him and Zoe. "Honey, there's no reason to pretend with us. You're both old enough to decide—"

"Guest bedroom."

His mother hesitated.

Hank picked up the backpack. "I'll take it upstairs."

"I'll get the pillows." The words were barely out of Zoe's mouth before she sprinted up the stairs.

Connie stared at Sean strangely. "You and Zoe—"

"She's not like other women, Mom," Sean admitted.

"I see that." Amusement and warmth reflected in his mother's eyes. "You know you're going to need help bathing."

He couldn't believe he was having this conversation. "We've got it covered, Mom."

"Your dad could always help."

Sean nodded, though sponge baths played a big role in his Nurse Zoe fantasy.

Connie opened the refrigerator. "Aunt Vera made you a casserole. I'll stick it in the oven for Zoe."

"Thanks, Mom." He remembered what she had said about her lack of cooking skills. "That will be really helpful since Zoe's so tired."

And he was hungry for something other than hospital food.

As his mother put the pan into the oven, Sean leaned his head back. The interviews, coming home. He was wiped out.

Zoe returned downstairs with her arms full of pillows. "Here you go."

Sean straightened. He could only see her jean-clad legs. Not a bad view actually. "I didn't realize I had that many pillows."

"I wasn't sure how many you needed," she said. "You might like a couple for your back so you don't get uncomfortable."

He smiled, knowing he could get away with more with his parents here. "That's what back massages are for."

"Massages, huh?" Zoe asked.

"Unless a sponge bath sounds better," Sean teased. He noticed his mother watching with interest. He'd behave when they were alone, but he would take advantage of their "relationship" when they were with his family and friends. A fair deal, he decided.

Zoe set all but one of the pillows on the couch next to him. She eyed him warily. "I'm hanging on to this in case I need to keep you in line."

"You wouldn't hit an injured man."

She narrowed her eyes playfully. "Are you willing to take that chance?"

Most definitely. He winked. "I can't forget about Popcorn."

Zoe blushed and lowered the pillow.

"Do you want some popcorn, Sean?" his mom asked.

"No, thanks."

"You don't play fair," Zoe whispered.

"I do when the odds are more even."

"When will that be?"

"Soon." He hoped.

As Zoe carefully placed pillows under his feet, his mother watched them. More than once she started to speak, but changed her mind. Sean felt as if he was fifteen again and bringing a girl home after school. It wasn't a good feeling.

"The timer will go off when Aunt Vera's casserole is ready," Connie announced. "I'll just get a salad and a couple of sides—"

"Come on, honey," Hank interrupted. "We've done our job here. It's time to go home and let the kids handle this."

Connie's gaze drifted to Sean. "But—"

"We'll be fine, Mom."

"He's in good hands, honey," his dad said gently.

Hank put his arm around Connie and led her to the door. She glanced back. "Call if you need anything."

"We will," Sean said.

His dad practically dragged her out of the house. The door slammed with a resounding thud.

"We're finally alone," Sean said.

"Massage or sponge bath?" Zoe teased.

His pulse picked up speed. "Can I have both?"

Mischief twinkled in her eyes. "If you're good."

"Oh, I'm very good."

"I'm sure you are." Zoe shielded herself with a pillow. "But don't forget I'm armed and mobile so watch out."

He smiled. "Trust me, I'm watching."

That was one homebound activity he was looking forward to.

She glanced toward the front door, her lips pressed together. "Do you think your parents are gone?"

The worry in her voice made him realize her flirting and playfulness had all been an act. Disappointed, he leaned against the couch. "They won't be back tonight. Relax. Make yourself at home."

She set the pillow on the couch. "Your house is lovely. Craftsman-style?"

He nodded.

"All the wood, glass, openness." She looked around. "The architecture fits the setting perfectly."

"Thanks." Sean was happy she liked the house. He patted the cushion next to him. "Sit."

She did.

"You did great," he said.

Zoe rolled her eyes. "Except for the pillows."

"Not a problem," he said. "People see what they want to see."

"What do your parents want to see?" Zoe asked.

"Grandchildren."

"So that explains why Connie wanted to put my backpack in your room."

"I'm not sure what explanation I have for that since she'd prefer a wedding to come first."

"Experience?"

He looked at her blankly.

"Lulu, Chelsea, Grace."

Sean wasn't going to touch that one. He didn't want to sound like a player. "My mom likes you."

"I like her." Zoe's eyes softened. "Connie loves you a lot. So does your dad."

"I know," Sean admitted. "They might drive me crazy, but I wouldn't trade them for anything."

"The feeling's mutual."

Sean shrugged. "Unfortunately for them."

Zoe laughed. "You're not that bad."

"Guess you'll find out."

She tilted her chin. "I'm looking forward to it."

So was he, Sean realized. A lot more than he should be.

CHAPTER FIVE

THE NEXT morning, gray light filtered through large wood-framed windows along the back wall of the house. Zoe yawned as she walked down the stairs. Afraid she might miss giving Sean his medication on time, she'd hardly slept. She hadn't wanted to make a mistake.

This was her first job. Zoe wouldn't let Sean down, or herself. So what if she was a little sleepy? She would grab a nap once Sean was awake and fed. That was why she hadn't changed out of her pajamas.

As Zoe stepped from the carpeted stair to the hardwood floor, she winced from the cold. It wasn't just the floor underneath her bare feet. The air temperature felt ten degrees cooler. She needed to adjust the thermometer. The last thing Sean needed was to catch a cold.

He lay asleep on the couch.

Zoe studied him.

The dawning light streamed down on his hair. His facial stubble made him look more rugged. His legs, elevated on pillows, were no longer covered. The blanket pooled on his chest. Still handsome, but he also looked a little…helpless.

She felt a pang.

Who was she kidding? He was helpless. Sean really needed someone. He needed her. The thought both pleased and terrified her at the same time.

She hadn't understood how much assistance he needed until helping him into the bathroom yesterday. Maneuvering his heavy, muscular body and the walker into the small space and waiting on the opposite side of the door for him to finish or call for help had been the definition of awkward. Sean had been even more embarrassed than her. The next time had been easier, but no less uncomfortable. Maybe in another day or so it would feel normal.

Zoe sure hoped so. She wanted Sean to feel normal again.

She'd never broken a bone in her body. She imagined it hurt both physically from the pain and emotionally due to the limitations forced upon a person. The limits had to be the hardest thing for Sean. Or would be shortly. He didn't seem like the type of guy to sit around all day. Last night, he'd almost damaged the remote channel-surfing to find something—anything—he was interested in watching.

She would have to keep him entertained, but how?

Zoe loved to snowboard. She worked out doing Zumba and Pilates, too. She was a decent athlete, but not the caliber of Sean, who climbed mountains and rescued people. Making his life during recovery less boring was going to be difficult. Her typical activities, at least before her banishment, had been shopping, dancing and partying.

What was she going to talk to him about? Suggest they do to keep him from getting restless being off his feet?

A lump the size of her Hermès coin purse formed in Zoe's throat. She took a deep, calming breath.

No reason to panic. Freaking out wouldn't help her get the job done. She shouldn't get ahead of herself. One day at a time. All she needed was a plan for this morning. She quickly decided what she should do: check on Sean, brew a pot of coffee and fix breakfast, give him his medicine, help him clean up and feed him. The only iffy thing was breakfast. Everything else she could handle. Even a sponge bath if that was what he needed.

A sponge bath.

The thought of touching a nearly naked Sean with a soapy sponge raised her temperature by fifteen degrees. She noticed the dark hair covering his leg and imagined running the palm of her hand over it.

What was she thinking?

Sean was her patient, her responsibility. Nothing more.

With her resolve and plan firmly in place, she walked quietly to the couch. Zoe adjusted the blanket so Sean's legs were covered. She expected him to bolt upright, but he didn't stir.

His eyes remained closed, his breathing even. The almost serene expression on his face made him look a decade younger, even with the appealing stubble. So handsome. She fought the urge to brush the hair hanging over his eye. No way did she want to risk waking him up and having to explain her actions.

Slowly, quietly, she backed away from him.

He continued sleeping.

See, Zoe told herself, her confidence gaining a needed boost. She could handle this.

In the kitchen, she checked the sheet of paper listing the doses of medication she'd given Sean. She still had time before his next round.

She had looked inside the cupboards last night so knew where to find the coffeemaker, filters and coffee. She opened a new package of coffee, scooped the already ground French roast beans into the filter, poured in the water and turned on the machine.

As the coffee brewed, Zoe stood at the kitchen island trying to figure out what to fix for breakfast. She glanced at Sean, who continued to sleep soundly.

Something moved in the backyard. She couldn't tell what, but it looked to be an animal of some sort.

A dog?

Oh, no. Zoe hoped it wasn't lost. The temperature had plummeted last night. Trying to get a closer look, she leaned over the counter until the granite counter pressed into her abdomen.

Not a dog. A deer. Make that two deer. They pranced across the yard like characters from *Bambi* come to life.

Excitement rushed through Zoe. She couldn't remember the last time she'd seen deer up close.

She raced to the back door, opened it slowly so the noise wouldn't startle the deer or wake Sean and stepped out onto the snow-covered deck.

The cold pierced her bare feet and seeped through her body. Zoe shivered, but she wasn't about to let the temperature send her back inside with the deer down below in the yard. She crossed her arms in front of her and wiggled her toes.

The scent of pine permeated the cold air. The smell brought back memories of Christmases past, of her father dressing up as Santa Claus and passing out gifts. She had always received the first gift from the large sack, as well as the last.

Tall evergreens, Douglas firs if she wasn't mistaken, formed an arc around a patch of snow dotted with hoof prints. A deer with velvet-covered antlers nibbled on some sort of vegetation. It might have even been bark.

She gasped in delight. Smiled.

The deer raised its head and looked at her. Its eyes looked cautious, yet bright.

So pretty.

Zoe stood transfixed, holding her breath. This wasn't something she saw, living in Los Angeles or even back home on the east coast. She was used to living in the city. Walking down Rodeo Drive in stilettos was the definition of hiking in her world. But this...

This was simply beautiful. The fresh air. Wildlife. Snow.

In spite of the cold temperature, warmth flowed through her. She'd forgotten how much she loved the mountains, a place her father had introduced her to before she could walk.

The setting here in Sean's backyard reminded Zoe of something out of a holiday movie. People in Hood Hamlet must feel like it was Christmas all winter long here. That must be so nice.

The deer broke eye contact and continued to chew. A doe, however, edged toward the trees, but stayed within sight.

Zoe watched in awe as the two explored the yard and ate. She couldn't believe she was experiencing this in person on Mount Hood and not sitting on the couch watching the scene unfold on the Animal Planet channel.

Talk about special.

As if on cue, large, fluffy snowflakes fell from the sky, spinning and dancing in their own choreography. Laughing, she raised her palms and caught an intricate flake. It melted almost on contact. Undeterred, she stuck out her tongue to catch another.

One landed in her mouth.

Nature's own snowcone. No flavoring needed.

Almost as tasty as Sean's kiss.

She grinned, wanting more, more snowflakes, more kisses. But kisses were too complicated. Sticking with snow was the smarter, safer option. She looked up at the sky and opened her mouth.

Warmth cocooned Sean as he lay on the sofa. He kept his eyes closed, ignoring the pressure in his legs and the crick in his back. He rarely slept in late, but drifting back asleep sounded like a good idea this morning. He'd been dreaming of riding powder with a pretty brunette with long hair.

Zoe.

As he pulled the blanket up under his chin so he could return to his dream, something tickled his nose. Coffee. Good coffee based on the robust aroma. After days of awful hospital sludge, the scent teased him fully awake. His dream would have to wait.

Sean opened his eyes.

Leave it to Zoe to know exactly how to kick off his first full day at home. A smile tugged at the corners of his lips.

Rising slightly on his elbows, he glanced toward the kitchen. No lights were on, but he saw the coffeemaker on the counter. Zoe wasn't there. He felt a twinge of disappointment. She must be upstairs.

The boot felt awkward. He adjusted one of the pillows beneath his left leg to get more comfortable.

The play of light and shadow through the wide glass windows snared his attention. He glanced outside at the falling snow and saw Zoe.

Zoe…dancing?

In her pajamas, a thin lavender tank and a pair of flannel bottoms. With her arms outstretched, she dipped and twirled.

Surrounded by falling snowflakes, she reminded him of a ballerina in a snow globe. Snow clung to her wet hair. She was barefoot, too.

He sat upright, ignoring the ache in his legs.

Showtime was over. She had to be freezing out there. That deck got slippery when wet. What if she fell?

"Zoe," he shouted, but she didn't hear him.

Sean reached for his walker. He wasn't comfortable using it yet, but Zoe needed to be inside where it was warm.

Standing up proved harder than Sean thought it would be. Twice he fell back on the couch, wincing. On the third try, he found his footing.

He ignored the dull throb in his legs. He tried to move faster, but couldn't. The muscles in his forearms strained as Sean supported himself with the walker. He steadied himself with one hand and opened the back door with the other.

Her bare feet stood on the snow-covered deck. Wet flannel clung to her skin, accentuating the curve of her hip and round bottom.

Sean grimaced, a combination of pain and arousal. "Zoe."

She swirled around, her eyes sparkling with excitement. Her wet lavender tank plastered against high, round breasts and beaded nipples. "Sean."

Desire hit hard and fast. The pressure in his legs was nothing compared to the ache in his groin. "Get inside before you freeze."

His voice sounded rough, on edge.

Zoe hurried into the house, closing the door behind her. Goose bumps covered her bare arms. The cotton, sticking to her body like a second skin, left nothing to his imagination.

She looked…really hot. And cold. Her wet feet left damp marks on the floor.

"Careful," he said huskily. "Don't slip."

"I didn't realize you were awake. You shouldn't be up." Concern filled Zoe's voice. "Are you in pain? You still have about fifteen minutes before you can take your medicine."

No medicine was going to help him now. His gaze continued to linger, his body responding to the memory of his dream and the closeness of her body. She smelled like woman and snow…

Cool it, Hughes.

She was living with him. She worked for him. He shouldn't leer. "Grab the blanket off the couch and warm yourself up."

"Let me make you breakfast—"

"Please, Zoe." Desperation filled his voice. Blood was rushing where he didn't want it to go. "For both our sakes."

Zoe wrapped the blanket around her shoulders. "Standing can't be good for you."

Lusting after his caretaker wasn't good for him, either. Sean hobbled to a chair, trying hard not to lose his balance, and sat. He felt immediate relief in his legs. If only he could get the same relief in other parts of his body.

Don't think about that, he told himself.

"You shouldn't be outside dressed like that." Sean put on his team leader face. "It's too cold. You could become hypothermic."

She raised her chin. "I appreciate the concern, but I wasn't out there that long."

"Long enough. Your pajamas are soaked through." And practically see-through, he thought.

Zoe opened the blanket and glanced down. "Oops."

He would have used another word.

She met his gaze with a rueful grin. "Well, I guess since I'll be seeing you half-dressed it's only fair you got to see a little of me."

He wanted to see a lot more. She had a killer body. She also had an easy confidence and humor that he liked a lot.

She shivered.

"You need to warm up," he said.

"A cup of coffee will do the trick." She retreated into the kitchen with the blanket around her. "Would you like one?"

"Please." He watched her pour coffee into two mugs. "What were you doing out there, anyway?"

"There were two deer in your backyard."

"Deer?"

"You know, Bambi," she explained.

Sean hadn't thought of Bambi since he was six. "There are lots of deer around here."

"Well, I'm not used to seeing them, so I went outside to get a closer look." A thoughtful smile formed on her lips. "Oh, Sean, you should have seen them. Velvety horns and dark eyes. Simply beautiful. And then all of a sudden, it started to snow. These perfect little snowflakes just floated down. I half expected to hear music play. It was that…"

Her wistful tone intrigued him. "What?"

She looked outside where snowflakes fell in a sheet of white. "Magical. The way Christmastime should be."

Zoe sounded like a Hallmark greeting card. Normally he hated sappy sentiments, but he found the words attractive coming from her.

"I'm sorry you had to come after me," she added.

"But you're not sorry for going outside to see the deer."

She pursed her lips. "No, I'm not."

He appreciated her honesty. "When Denali's here, deer keep their distance. But you should see a few more before she gets home," Sean said. "But next time you go outside put on shoes and a coat. A hat and gloves, too."

She nodded. "Do you want your coffee at the chair or couch?"

"The couch," he said. "But I'm going to wash up first."

As Sean stood, he felt off balance and nearly fell.

Zoe ran from the kitchen to his side. "I'll help."

"I've got it."

"I'm sure you do, but you have to be sore and your medication is wearing off. Don't forget, you're paying me to help. It wouldn't be right to accept a salary if I wasn't doing my job."

He'd hired her to keep his parents off his back more than to play nursemaid. "Suit yourself."

Zoe didn't say a word, but remained with him. When he reached the bathroom, Sean negotiated himself inside with less effort than it had taken last night. Not a lot of progress, but he'd take it.

At the sink, he stared at the row of toiletries laid out conveniently on the counter: washcloth, towel, shaving cream, razor, toothbrush, toothpaste and comb. He stared at Zoe. "You did this."

She nodded. "Last night."

Her actions touched him. "Thanks."

"Let's get your shirt off."

His temperature spiked higher. He gripped the handles of the walker. He wanted her to undress him. And he wanted to undress her. But...

"Don't be modest," she said.

Sean pressed the walker and himself close to the sink. She must have no idea what she was doing to him. Or maybe she did. He glanced at her. No, she didn't seem the type to purposely tease a man. All she wanted to do was help him.

Maybe her help would extend past her caretaker duties. He'd be game. "Go ahead."

Zoe tucked the blanket under her arms. As she raised the hem of his T-shirt, her knuckles grazed his skin. His tingling nerve endings stood at alert.

"Let's try one hand at a time," she suggested.

He let go of the walker with his left hand and pulled it through the armhole.

"Other one," she said.

He did and soon stood shirtless with Zoe right behind him.

She tilted her chin. "Was that so hard?"

He shook his head, not trusting his voice.

Awareness buzzed through him. He tried to think of something to kill his attraction, but all he could see was Zoe in her wet pajamas. He swallowed.

"What's next?"

"I can handle the rest," Sean said between clenched teeth. Not even the blanket was keeping his fantasies at bay. He needed her to go away and get dressed ASAP.

"Go change into dry clothes," he added. "And can you grab me some clean clothes to put on while you're upstairs? Shorts and T-shirts are in my dresser."

"I can't leave you alone."

"I'll be fine."

"I don't—"

"I need clothes to wear." He was losing his patience.

"Okay." She lowered the toilet seat cover. "I'll run upstairs if you promise to sit here until I return."

"Zoe."

"Sean."

He needed to get her out of here before she realized the effect she was having on him, so he sat.

"I'm leaving the door cracked," she said.

She acted as if she was his babysitter, not a woman attracted to a man. "Is that necessary?"

"Yes, and I promise I won't peek," she said lightheartedly.

"You're more polite than me."

Smart, Zoe, really smart.

Upstairs, she peeled off her wet pajamas. She really needed to think before she acted.

Zoe dried off with a towel from the upstairs bathroom, stepped into a pair of panties and clasped her bra.

Seeing the deer had made her happy. Sean, however, didn't look happy with her at all. At least he hadn't chastised her like her mother had when those photos of her topless at a beach on the Côte d'Azur made the rounds in the tabloids and on the Internet this summer.

She pulled a sweater over her head.

Still, this wasn't the impression she wanted to make with him. Sean hadn't hidden his interest. She was interested in him, too. And she hadn't had to take off his T-shirt and see his muscular chest and abs to realize it.

But she would have to ignore the physical attraction between them. She had to be responsible. She was Sean's caretaker, his pretend girlfriend. Anything more would be a really bad idea.

She only hoped he agreed.

Sean.

Zoe needed to get back downstairs pronto. She wiggled into a pair of jeans, pulled on a pair of socks and rushed into Sean's bedroom. She'd been in such a hurry getting the pillows and later his toiletries, she hadn't taken a good look at his room before.

A navy blue comforter covered a king-size bed. The nightstands and dresser matched the slotted headboard. A painting of Mount Hood hung on the wall. A digital alarm clock and lamp set on one of the nightstands. Books—*Freedom of the Hills, Classic Climbs of the Northwest*—and a snowboarding magazine were stacked on the other.

Masculine, yet comfortable.

A lot like Sean.

Zoe opened his top drawer to find neatly folded underwear—boxer-briefs and boxers. She grabbed a pair of green plaid ones. The next drawer contained socks, which she took even though he hadn't asked for any. Another had T-shirts so she grabbed a white one. In the bottom drawer, she found a pair of navy shorts.

She returned downstairs.

Things had not gone well so far. Zoe had to put the morning behind her and show Sean she could take care of him. Looking on the bright side, at least things could only go up from here.

Sean sat in the bathroom, waiting. His heart pounded against his ribs.

Forget the injuries to his legs and head. Zoe was the one who would do him in.

Ignoring her order to stay seated, he awkwardly positioned himself in front of the sink and splashed cold water on his face. A cold shower would be better, but he didn't have that option. At least washing off would cool him down and help get himself back together.

A mix of emotions swirled through him.

Anger, annoyance, arousal.

You know, Bambi.

Amusement.

Sean laughed. He couldn't be upset at Zoe. She'd admitted she was impulsive. He'd just experienced it in action. Life would never be boring with her. That was for sure.

He liked her. He appreciated her thoughtfulness at setting out his toiletries. He liked the way little things, such as wildlife or snowfall, excited her. She made him smile and feel better. He wanted to return the favor though he wasn't sure how to do that.

Maybe in a couple of days when he felt better he could convince her to play doctor. He grinned. Her impulsiveness could turn out to be a good thing in the long run.

He caught his reflection in the mirror and frowned.

Damn. Even after three weeks of climbing in Patagonia, he hadn't looked *this* grungy. Sean combed his fingers through his hair. It didn't help.

Forget playing doctor. Zoe wasn't going to want to be anywhere near him. Ignoring the throbbing in his legs, Sean brushed his teeth.

No pain, no gain. The phrase summed up ice climbing, where scaling a waterfall of ice in the biting cold made calves whine and shoulder and back muscles burn. The words fit his situation now.

Sean balanced his weight by resting a hip against the walker. He rubbed shaving cream on his face and ran the razor across the whiskers.

"You're supposed to be sitting down."

Uh-oh. Zoe didn't sound happy.

Sean turned to the sound of her voice. She stood in the doorway with his clothes in the crook of her arm. A green V-neck sweater fit tightly across her chest and her jeans accentuated the curve of her hips.

The air in the bathroom seemed to crackle with attraction.

Forcing himself not to stare, Sean rinsed his razor. "I have to look in the mirror to shave."

"You shouldn't be standing."

"You shouldn't be peeking."

She gave his bare chest the once-over. Approval filled her eyes. He stood taller.

"I couldn't help myself," she said after a long moment.

That brought another smile to his face. Maybe Zoe liked scruffy, rugged types. "Irresistible, huh?"

Her assessing gaze made him feel as if he were under a microscope. "Not really."

He nearly nicked his face. Women usually flocked to him. "You like pretty boys."

"If you were any prettier, you'd have to change your name to Shauna," Zoe said. "It has nothing to do with how you look. I know being injured must be hard, but if you're not careful you could fall and hurt yourself more. I don't want that to happen."

"I can take care of myself," he said stiffly.

"Then you don't need me."

She was stronger than he expected. Smarter, too. He'd played right into her hand.

"I do." He repositioned the walker and sat. "I just…" The concern on her face made him feel like a jerk. "I'm used to being the one helping people."

"You are helping," she said. "You're helping me."

He looked down at his useless legs. "Yeah, right."

"It's true."

Sean didn't need her pity. "I have no problem relying on climbing partners when I'm on the mountain or at a crag. There I can pull my own weight. But here…"

In his own home. In the bathroom.

He shook his head.

"Let's talk about here. At your house and at the hospital. You gave me a job." Zoe touched his shoulder. Her warm, soft skin sent a burst of heat rushing through him.

"A job to keep me from having to live with my parents."

She shrugged. "That's one way to look at it. We might be using each other, but we're also helping each other. The day we met, Thanksgiving, I only had enough money to buy a lift ticket or food, not both. I had no idea where I would go next or what I would eat that day."

"Yet you decided to ride."

Zoe nodded, her eyes dark. "I chose one family Thanksgiving tradition over another. Not the most financially responsible decision I've ever made."

"It's a decision I would have made if I'd been in your shoes," he admitted. "Actually I have made that same decision when I was younger."

Except Sean had a family he could fall back on, a family that would have never let him go hungry even if he spent every dollar he made on snowboarding and starting his own company.

He remembered what she'd said about being estranged from her family. She must really miss them if she wanted to keep their traditions alive so badly she would go hungry. "So what's the deal with your family?"

She shrugged.

"You miss them."

"Sometimes," she admitted. "But I don't miss being judged. My mother and brothers…"

Sean wondered about her father. "What?"

"Nothing."

He didn't press, even though he was curious. He respected her privacy. She would tell him more when she was ready.

"Anyway," she continued, "I'm really happy I chose to ride that day because I got to meet you. You gave me a lift, an invite to dinner, a job and a place to stay. H-E-L-P, in case you need me to spell it out for you."

Sean hadn't thought of it that way. "I can see your point."

"Good." Her smile widened. "Now maybe you'll let me do something for you."

Her generosity of spirit—and her offer—took his breath away. He could think of lots of things he wanted her to do for him. "What did you have in mind?"

She blushed. "How about breakfast?"

Baby steps. That was what the doctor had said. The same strategy applied to Zoe. Sean grinned. "I am hungry. Maybe you could fix us both something while I finish washing up."

Zoe pursed her lips. "Promise me you won't get up again."

"Promise."

She placed his clothes over a towel rack. "Give me a shout out when you're ready to get dressed. I'll leave the door cracked so I can hear you."

Remaining seated, Sean washed off. He heard pans bang together in the kitchen. Not wanting to be an even bigger burden, he struggled to change out of his clothes.

He managed to get his basketball shorts and boxers off, but getting dressed wasn't so easy. With the boxers tucked inside the shorts, he brought the waistband over his feet, but he couldn't get his foot through the leg openings.

He cursed, tried again, swore. His elbow hit something off the counter. The shaving cream can clattered against the floor.

"Sean?" Zoe called.

Damn. He was naked. Sean covered his lap with a towel.

She poked her head into the bathroom. "Are you okay?"

He pointed to the shaving cream on the floor. "I knocked the can over."

Zoe stared at the clothes lying on the floor. "You were trying to get dressed yourself."

Looking down, he nodded.

"This is a two person job." She kneeled in front of him. Quickly she rolled his shorts and boxers into a roll. "It's no different than putting on panty hose."

"I wouldn't know."

"A good thing you have me then."

She was eye level with his knees. As she bent over, he had a perfect view straight down the neckline of her sweater. He could see the V of her breasts, ivory skin, white lace.

Sweat broke out on his upper lip.

One leg at a time she brought up the shorts. Her hands brushed his feet. Her hair caressed his leg. "See, this isn't so bad."

Maybe not for her.

She raised the roll up to his knees. "Almost there."

No kidding. Sean swore under his breath. He was getting turned-on. Again. He placed his hands on his lap. "I can take it from here," he said, desperate for her to leave him alone again.

"Now the socks," she said.

"I don't wear socks in the house."

"Your feet will get cold."

"I could slip."

"You—"

A loud squeal sounded. An obnoxious sound that hurt his brain. What the—

Panic crossed Zoe's face. "Breakfast."
She ran out of the bathroom.
The smoke detector.
Oh, hell.

CHAPTER SIX

SEAN ripped off the towel, lifted his hips off the seat and tugged up the waistbands of his shorts and boxers. In spite of the blare of the alarm, he heard clanging and doors opening.

"Ouch," Zoe cried.

Clutching the handles, Sean threw the walker in front of him. He stood only to be forced down again by the pain in his leg. He tried again, but this time focused on Zoe. It worked. He stayed on his feet.

When he reached the doorway, Sean smelled smoke.

Adrenaline shot through his veins.

Out of the bathroom, he noticed the front door wide open. He hobbled into the great room. Zoe used a towel to fan the smoke out the back door and windows.

"Zoe?"

She looked at him. "I've got everything under control."

The alarm silenced.

He made his way across the floor and eased onto the couch before his legs gave out. "What happened?"

She continued fanning. "Cooking challenged, remember?"

"Yeah, I remember." Something smoldered in the kitchen sink. "Is that...breakfast?"

"It was, but caught fire when I was—"

"In the bathroom with me."

"I'm sorry." She sounded frustrated. "This really hasn't been a good morning."

"Zoe."

Instead of looking at him, she kept waving the towel, trying to clear the smoke.

"You must be freezing." She closed the back door. "You need a sweatshirt and a clean blanket—"

"Zoe," he repeated. "Slow down. It's okay."

"But it's not. I should be handling this better. My mother really was right."

"About you being impulsive?"

"And a few other things."

"I'm willing to take my chances."

"What if the fire had been worse?" Zoe glanced toward the kitchen. "You might not have been able to get out."

"It wasn't that bad."

She bit her lip. "This time."

Sean hoped it was the last time. He rubbed his aching leg.

"Oh, no." She sprinted to the kitchen, filled a glass with water and opened pill containers. "It's past time for your meds."

"I'm fine."

She returned to the couch, handed him the water and medicine. "The doctor said you're supposed to stay ahead of the pain."

He swallowed the pills. "How late am I taking the medicine?"

"Twelve minutes."

"No worries."

Tears glistened in her eyes. "I really wanted to do well here."

Something twisted inside of him at the regret in her voice. He shoved a pillow off the couch. "Sit."

She did.

"It's okay," he said.

"Okay?" She stared at him. "If the rest of the day continues like this morning, you'll catch pneumonia and be dead by nightfall."

"I'll give Popcorn your regards."

Tears fell from the corners of her eyes.

Damn. He'd wanted to make her smile, not cry.

Sean wrapped his arm around her. She felt nice and warm against his bare chest. But this was about Zoe, not him. "Don't worry about it."

She sniffled.

He pulled her closer.

"It's your first day. First days are always the hardest." The scent of grapefruit filled his nostrils. Sean felt dizzy. He wasn't sure if it was Zoe or the medicine. "Remember what I said about ordering takeout?"

He felt her nod.

"We can get breakfast to go."

Zoe looked up at him with a confused look in her eyes. "You're not angry at me?"

"Not at all."

"But so much has gone wrong. You're supposed to be off your feet, not running around and catching a chill because of me." The words tumbled from her mouth in a rush. "I'm really not quali—"

Sean pressed his lips against hers. Zoe stiffened, no doubt as surprised by his kiss as he was. But it was the only way he knew how to stop her from talking and getting more upset.

He expected her to back away. She didn't. Instead, Zoe kissed him back. Her soft breasts pressed against him, heating the blood pounding through his veins.

He moved his lips over hers, tasting and touching and exploring. Something he hadn't been able to do at the hospital. Something he enjoyed doing now. She fit so nicely against him.

As Zoe wove her fingers through his hair, she took the kiss deeper.

Wow. She really was a good kisser.

A noise sounded. Lots of noise actually, but Sean didn't

want to stop kissing her. He would be happy to spend the rest of the day with her on the couch.

"What the…?"

The sound of a male voice made Sean jerk back from Zoe. He looked over and saw members of the Hood Hamlet Fire Department standing in his kitchen and great room.

"Looks like the fire's out," Bill Paulson, also an OMSAR member, said.

Leanne Thomas grinned. "I'd say it's just heating up."

Sean had climbed with both of them during OMSAR missions and for fun. Great climbing partners and even closer friends. He knew them well enough to know they were never going to let him live this down. Rightly so, since Sean would do the same if he was standing in their places.

"Did you dial 911?" he asked Zoe.

Red-cheeked, she shook her head.

"No one called," Bill explained. "Remember that state-of-the-art alarm system I told you to install?"

"Damn."

Leanne nodded. "A neighbor heard the alarm and saw smoke so she called, too."

More firefighters entered.

Zoe cringed. "I'm so sorry."

Sean squeezed her shoulder.

"What happened?" Bill asked.

"I tried to cook breakfast," she answered before Sean could. "I don't cook."

Bill gave her an appreciative once-over. "Cooking's overrated."

Christian Welton and John Keller nodded.

Leanne rolled her eyes.

"Sorry about the false alarm," Sean said. "You guys must have better things to do with your time."

Christian, who was the rookie at the station and could redpoint 5.13 routes at Smith Rock, stared at Zoe like a lovesick puppy. "I'd rather be here than sitting at the station."

Sean wanted him and all the rest of the crew gone so he

could be alone with Zoe and kiss her again. "Do what you need to do so you can get out of here."

"May I see your hand, Zoe?" Leanne asked.

Her hand? Sean looked at Zoe.

She hid it behind her back. "Oh, it's nothing."

Sean's muscles tensed. "What's wrong with your hand?"

She smiled at him. "Just a little burn."

Oh, hell. A burn. He hadn't even thought... "Let me see."

"I'll take care of it." Leanne led Zoe away.

He tried to stand, but Bill stopped him. "Don't get in the way, Hughes. You know she's in good hands."

Leanne had patched Sean up more than once, but that didn't make this any easier. He was used to being in the center of the action, usually in charge of a rescue team. He didn't like being on this side of things. He hated not being able to see what Leanne and the other paramedic, Marc, were doing to Zoe.

"Status?" Sean asked as soon as they had finished.

The other firefighters surrounded Zoe. Bill dealt with the smoldering mess in the sink.

"Nothing serious. A first degree burn." Leanne walked over to Sean and lowered her voice. "It's obvious the two of you are crazy about each other, but Zoe needed First Aid more than she needed a kiss. Even one of your kisses, Hughes."

Okay, his mind had been on other things, but why hadn't Zoe told him she'd burned herself? "I'll pay more attention to her."

Leanne laughed. "Any more attention, and you'll enter creepy-stalker zone."

Sean frowned.

"Kidding, and you should know that." Leanne's forehead creased. "I had no idea you were seriously dating someone, but it's about time. Does Zoe climb?"

"No, but she wants to."

"You going to teach her to cook, too?" Leanne winked.

"Though I'm guessing the kitchen is the last room you want Zoe to spend her time."

"Guilty as charged."

"Just don't add her to the long list of hearts you've broken." Leanne was one of the guys, but every once in a while her feminine side peeked out. "I talked to Zoe at the hospital. She seems sweet. Nice. I like her."

Leanne wasn't the only one. The guys swarmed around Zoe as if she was the queen bee and they were her drones.

"And you look better already," Leanne added. "She's good for you."

"I'd like to keep her around." He understood the attention Zoe was receiving, but he didn't like it. Time to send Hood Hamlet's finest back to where they came from. "You think you can get all these babe-magnets away from my girl?"

"They're filling out the report."

"All of them?" he asked.

"They like pretty things."

"Tell you what," Sean said. "If you can clear them out of here, I'll let you have the first lead when I'm back climbing."

"You're on." Leanne grinned with anticipation. "Come on, boys. Finish up the paperwork. It's time to head back to the station."

The firefighters shuffled out of the kitchen with a chorus of goodbyes and long glances back at Zoe. The front door slammed shut.

She blew out a puff of air. "So…"

He focused on her bandaged hand. "Why didn't you tell me you were burned?"

She shrugged. "I want to do a good job."

"But if you're hurt…"

"It's nothing," she said. "You must be starving."

Zoe was trying to change the subject. Again.

"I am." But not for breakfast. In spite of her burn, he wanted to kiss her again. The way her gaze kept drifting to his lips made him think she wanted the same thing. Good, another thing they agreed on. Not that he usually had a lot in common with the women he went out with. Casual dating didn't require that. "Come over here so we can get back to what we were doing."

The thought of kissing Sean again filled Zoe's stomach with butterflies. Kissing him made her forget all her troubles. It also made her forget all the reasons she couldn't get involved in any sort of relationship with him.

Thank goodness the Hood Hamlet Fire Department had showed up. They had stopped her from making another impulsive mistake.

Yes, she liked kissing Sean. He made her feel special. But even bruised and with both legs injured, he was dangerous to her new resolve.

She had to stand her ground. "I...we can't."

He flashed her a dazzling grin that made her knees go weak. "Yes, we can."

"I mean, it's not a good idea," she said firmly. "You need me to help you more than you need me to kiss you."

"I know what I need. I have a pretty good idea what you need, too." Mischief gleamed in his eyes. "Trust me, we can do both."

She could—a part of her was tempted to give in to his charm—but... "More kisses would complicate things."

"What things?" he asked.

"Us. Not that there's an 'us,'" she backtracked, not wanting to read anything more into the kiss than what it had been. She liked him. But earlier, when she'd talked about them using and helping each other, kissing was not what she had in mind. "We can't get physical. Whatever we've told your family and friends, we're practically strangers."

"I don't think of you that way," he said. "But even if I did, what better way to get to know each other?"

The anticipation in his eyes made her pulse quicken. She felt her resolve weakening.

Zoe squared her shoulders. "What if we did get involved, and it didn't work out? It would be awful. I'd have to leave."

"You're going to be leaving anyway."

"When you don't need me anymore." The thought made her sad for reasons she didn't want to examine.

Sean eyed her warily. "Is that a problem?"

"Leaving, no." She needed to get a grip. "As long as my job is finished here, and we're not personally involved."

"We're both adults," he countered.

"So we have to act like adults." She cringed. "Oh, no, I sound just like my mother."

"And that's a bad thing."

"Usually, because my mother is a very controlled, cautious, responsible person."

"Then don't be like your mother and come here."

Temptation grew. But as Zoe took a step toward Sean, her mother's warnings about men and love returned with renewed force. She had never listened before and look where that had gotten her. She stopped five feet from Sean. "You know, sometimes my mother is right. She only has my best interests at heart. And I only have yours."

He stared at her, in disbelief or confusion Zoe couldn't be certain, but she knew what she had to do.

"No more kissing," Zoe said in case he didn't get the point.

From the set of his jaw, she could see Sean did, and he didn't like it.

No more kissing.

Sean wasn't happy about not kissing Zoe, but he had to respect her new rule. And he did. Sort of. He didn't kiss her again when they were alone. But when people dropped by to visit often during the next two days, and whenever they had an audience, he snagged as many kisses as he could.

A jerk move? Probably.

But he liked kissing Zoe. And even though he knew she

was playing a role for others, she seemed to like kissing him, too.

He couldn't understand why she didn't want to take things between them to the next level. They already spent all their time with each other. Why not be together in every sense of the word?

Her restrictions chafed. He was already frustrated. His energy was improving. He didn't need as many pain pills. And he was desperate to get back to work.

At least he had his laptop.

Sean stared at the screen. The words blurred. Must be glare from the screen. He squinted. It didn't help.

He'd been going through the hundreds of e-mails that had piled up in his in-box. Maybe he should do something else.

He opened a file about the Rail Jam Extravaganza, an upcoming PR event he needed to attend at New Year's.

As he read the information, a sharp pain sliced through his head. He massaged his forehead.

"That's enough." Zoe walked toward him. "You said you wanted to check e-mail, but you've been online working for three solid hours."

She grabbed his laptop.

He reached for it, but she was too quick and backed away. "Hey, I need that," he said.

"You're squinting and have a headache. In case you forgot, you have a concussion. I'm going to have to restrict your computer usage so you won't overdo it again."

"I won't overdo it."

She hugged the laptop to her chest. "You won't now."

"I have a company to run."

"I have a job to do," she said. "You can ask your doctor about working full-time when you have your sutures removed."

"That's—"

"How it's going to be." Zoe moved toward the built-in shelving unit. "I'll put this away, then we can watch that DVD your mom dropped off."

Knowing his mom, it would probably be a love story, a romantic comedy where the guy proposes at the end. Subtlety was not in Connie Hughes's vocabulary.

Zoe bent over to set the laptop back in its place. Her scoop top provided a great flash of her round, high breasts. Was that a hot-pink bra?

Sean blew out his breath. He needed to show her that kissing each other would be a lot more fun than playing games and watching movies. He shifted to get a better view and elbowed a can of soda onto the floor. Brown liquid splattered on the hardwood floor.

Zoe straightened. "You okay?"

"Fine, but I made a mess."

She grabbed a roll of paper towels. "I'll clean it up."

He hated that his leering had been the cause of all this. "It would be easier with a mop."

"A mop?"

"In the laundry room."

"The laundry room," she repeated. "Where else would a mop be?"

Zoe returned in a few minutes with a mop and a bucket. She filled the bucket with water at the kitchen sink. "Do you use soap on the floor?"

Hadn't she mopped a floor before? Maybe not hardwoods.

"My mom says a little dishwashing soap goes a long way," he said.

"Right."

Sean turned on the television set and flipped through the channels. So many stations yet nothing good ever seemed to be on. Truth was, he'd rather watch Zoe.

She carried the bucket to the spill. As she stuck in the mop, water cascaded over the edges. "Guess I put in a little too much water."

He didn't say anything. It was his fault she had to mop the floor in the first place. He changed the channel again so she wouldn't think he was staring at her.

She tucked her hair behind her ears, pulled the mop out of the water and swabbed the spill. Water flew everywhere, making an even bigger mess.

First a fire, now a flood. Sean bit back a smile. It was always entertaining with her around.

Staring at all the water, Zoe leaned against the mop with a dejected look on her face.

He remembered what Zoe had said to him at the hospital.

I'm not, uh, very domestic. I feel it's fair to warn you I'm cooking and cleaning challenged.

In spite of his headache, Sean tried to piece together the clues she'd given him about her past. Snowboarding on Thanksgiving with her family. That would be expensive. Her board and outfit weren't cheap, knockoff brands, either. Yet Zoe had told him she'd been running low on funds and didn't have a place to live. She couldn't cook or clean, either. Zoe Flynn might not have money herself, but he'd bet her family did. Sean wanted to know more about her.

"Sorry you have to clean up after me," he said.

"That's okay."

"I'm not used to it," he said. "Somebody else cleaning up my mess."

She didn't reply.

He tried again. "I guess you're used to having a housecleaner."

A smile broke over her face. "In college, I even paid my roommate to clean and do my laundry."

Definitely from money, Sean realized. That explained a few things.

She bit her lip, as if realizing she'd said too much. "So where did I go wrong? With the floor?"

Apparently more revelations would have to wait. "You need to squeeze the water out of the mop before you try to wipe the floor with it."

"So that's what that thingy at the bottom is for."

He grinned. "Yeah."

She put the mop over the bucket and wrung the water out of it with the lever. "You learn something new every day."

Sean nodded thoughtfully. He couldn't wait to learn more about Zoe. Most women didn't shut up about themselves, but Zoe diverted his questions. That raised his curiosity and his concern.

What was she hiding? Or who was she hiding from?

A few days later, Zoe pushed her stack of poker chips forward. "All in."

Her move didn't seem to surprise Sean. Well, if it did, she couldn't tell. His expression remained exactly the same as it had been all through the game. He studied the flop, turn and river cards lying between them on the couch.

On the radio, Mariah Carey sang "All I Want For Christmas Is You." Zoe knew what she wanted. Not for Christmas, but right now.

She wanted to win.

Sean reminded her of a border collie, a high energy animal that didn't like being kenneled or leashed or, in Sean's case, stuck on the couch. He'd been right saying this wasn't an easy job. Helping Sean and not letting him try to do too much was a full-time job. Not to mention doing chores around the house.

Worse, she'd been struggling to keep him from getting bored. Bored equaled grumpy so she'd tried to keep him busy playing video games, board games and anything else she could think of. He'd been counting the days until he could get his computer back. But when she'd found a silver case full of poker chips and cards in the coat closet, her job had gotten easier because Sean loved playing poker. That improved his mood.

His healing seemed to be taking care of itself, but everyone from Connie to Jake Porter said Zoe was the reason. She wasn't going to take all the credit, but the compliments filled her with pride. She was finally doing something right and being responsible. Her mother would be pleased, but that didn't matter as much to Zoe now. She was necessary to Sean in a way she'd never been necessary to anyone before. She'd never felt so valued or valuable and didn't want it to end anytime soon.

Zoe studied her cards. "You could always fold."

Sean raised an eyebrow. "Having second thoughts?"

"None whatsoever."

And Zoe didn't. She was going to win. Finally. She had three aces—two in her hand and one in the river position.

"Such confidence," he said.

She searched for any kind of tell that would give away his cards, but nothing in his mannerisms and facial expression told her if he was bluffing or holding a winning hand. "It's all in the cards."

Sean's gaze met hers, probing yet secretive. She stared back, as if she could will him to call her bet.

The air sizzled between them.

Slowly, his fingers inched toward his stacks of chips that towered over hers.

Zoe's heart beat faster. The game, she told herself, not him and how much healthier and happier he looked today. If she didn't win this hand, she would be out.

He matched the amount of chips she'd put in. "Call."

With a smile, she turned over her cards. "Three aces."

Sean flipped his. A two, three, four, five, six.

Her shoulders sagged. "I don't believe it. A straight."

Using his hand, he swept the pile of chips toward him. "We're different kinds of players."

She gathered the deck of cards. "Yeah, you win."

Sean's smile crinkled the corners of his eyes.

Butterflies flapped in her stomach. She focused on this pile of chips.

"That's not quite what I meant," he explained. "You play by instinct. That means you'll win big, but you'll also lose big. It's an exciting way to play if you don't mind taking the risks."

"You're the risk taker, not me." Zoe tucked the cards

into their box. "You climb mountains, snowboard, rescue people."

"I take calculated risks. Ones I'm prepared for."

"And I just go all in."

"That makes you fun to play with," he said.

"Easy to beat."

Laughter gleamed in his eyes. "That, too."

"So how do you decide when you're going to bet?"

He sorted the chips. "I only bet when I'm going to win."

She thought about the times he folded or checked. "So if you don't think you can win…"

"I don't play."

"And I only play harder," she said. "We do approach the game differently."

He nodded. "The way a person plays cards says a lot about them."

No kidding. Sean played to win. His MO extended beyond poker and reaffirmed her decision not to kiss him again. Well, except for pecks on the cheek in front of his family and friends. Losing a card game was one thing, but having her heart broken was something to be avoided at all costs.

"Want to play again?" he asked.

"Not now," she said. "You know all my secrets."

He grinned. "I wouldn't say all of them."

Sean was right, and Zoe had to keep it that way. She chewed the inside of her cheek.

"But I'm hoping to discover a few more," he added.

Panic bolted through her. "You might be disappointed by what you learn."

"No way. Not after all that you've done for me."

Thank goodness. A way to change the subject. Talking about herself made Zoe uncomfortable. She didn't want to lie to Sean, yet couldn't tell him the whole truth, either. "You're doing so much better."

"Thanks to you."

Her cheeks warmed. "Just doing my job."

"A good job, but I can't wait until I can shower."

"I could try taping plastic bags over your feet and legs."

"That's okay," he said. "I'm still working on negotiating the stairs with the walker. The sutures come off soon. I can wash up at the sink a few days longer."

She couldn't do much about his desire to shower, but she could make one thing easier for him. "Want me to wash your hair?"

"I don't mind ducking it under the faucet."

"But I mind. Please let me do this for you."

"I'd rather play another round of poker."

"If you let me wash your hair, I'll play another game after dinner."

Not that she had much to do to prepare the food. Once word got out about her lack of cooking skills, meals appeared every day. Zoe only had to order takeout occasionally now. She would have liked to learn to cook for Sean, but this was better for him and kept the fire department away.

"Deal," he said.

Zoe was relieved he was up for something new. She only hoped this activity would go off without a hitch unlike some of the others. She stood. "I'll be right back."

CHAPTER SEVEN

TEN MINUTES later, Zoe had everything in place. Towels padded the edge of the granite counter. A bar stool set in front of the sink. A bottle of shampoo was within arm's reach. "Ready?"

"Not really." He made his way toward her using the walker. "Playing beauty salon isn't really my thing."

"You have no idea what you're missing out on." She helped him sit in the chair and moved his walker out of the way. "Take off your shirt."

"Is being shirtless a prerequisite for getting your hair washed?"

"It'll keep your shirt from getting soaked."

His eyes brightened as he pulled off his T-shirt. "Do I get to wash your hair next?"

"No."

He shrugged. "A guy sometimes has to try."

"And a girl sometimes has to say no." Even when she had to force her gaze from drifting downward to his bare chest and abs. She adjusted the towels to better cushion his head. "Comfortable?"

"Fine."

Zoe removed the nozzle, hit the spray button and tested the water against her wrist. "Relax."

"I'm relaxed."

The moment the warm water hit Sean's head, his eyes widened. She ran her hand over his hair. Strands of hair slipped through her fingers. Slowly, his eyelids drooped.

"Feel good?" she asked.

"Mmm-hmm."

She squeezed shampoo onto her palm and rubbed it on his head. Slowly she worked the shampoo into his hair. The rise and fall of his chest became more even, calm.

Leaning over to reach the back of his head, her breasts brushed his arm. She jerked back. "Sorry."

"No worries."

Zoe wished she could say the same. The water temperature matched the heat emanating from Sean's body. She felt as if the thermostat had been turned up fifteen degrees. The turtleneck she wore only made her hotter.

"So this is what I've been missing by going to a barber all these years," he said, his eyes nearly closing. "No wonder women get their hair done so much."

She rubbed her fingertips against his scalp to work up a lather. The scent of coconut filled her nostrils. "I love going to the salon. A new cut. A different color. It's like I'm a new person when I walk out the door."

Sean's gaze fixed on her face. "I like the person you are just fine."

His words would have pleased her, except he didn't know the truth about her. "You don't know me very well."

"Well enough." As if sensing her discomfort, he lightened his tone. "So what's your natural color?"

Water spurted. "Oh. Um. I hardly remember. I've been coloring my hair since I was fifteen."

"Fifteen?"

She nodded. "My mother didn't want me to so I couldn't go to a salon. A friend and I did it by ourselves. My hair turned green."

"I can't imagine you with green hair."

"I once streaked it with hot-pink-and-blue stripes," Zoe admitted. "That was my alternative rock stage. I also went through a Goth stage in high school. The jet-black hair drove my mother absolutely insane."

Sean studied her face. "I don't see any body piercings."

"My mother would have killed me if I'd done that. I had to make do with black nail polish and temporary tattoos."

Zoe massaged his scalp. His wet hair slid through her hands. His scalp felt smooth beneath the pads of her fingers.

"You're way too sweet to be into that look," he said.

She shrugged. "Sometimes I wasn't so sweet."

Sean raised a brow. "Are your brothers as rebellious?"

"Not at all."

"How many brothers?"

"Three. Older," she added, forestalling his next question. "And they always did, still do, what Mother wanted."

Clean-cut and conservative, her brothers had accumulated advanced degrees, high-paying jobs, beautiful wives and perfectly groomed children in the appropriate order and according to their mother's timetable. Maxwell, the oldest one, had recently run and won a seat in the state legislature.

Zoe grimaced. "I haven't been so good at meeting expectations."

"Me, either," Sean said.

She looked down at him in surprise. No one could say Sean wasn't successful. "In what way?"

"Well, my dad would have preferred if I'd gone into the construction business with him. And let's not even mention children. Rather the lack of them."

She laughed.

"You haven't mentioned your father," Sean said.

Remembered warmth settled around Zoe's heart. "My father was the greatest. Friendly and fun—that was my dad."

"He sounds like you."

"My mother says I'm a lot like him." She ran her fingers over his scalp again. "He died when I was twelve. A heart attack."

"I'm sorry."

Zoe nodded. "Things were never the same after he was gone. But I think he would have liked all my different hair colors. Even the wild, crazy ones."

Sean reached up and tucked a strand of hair behind her ear. "I like your hair now."

"Thanks." She picked up the spray nozzle. "My mother actually suggested it."

"Before you were estranged?"

Zoe nodded.

"You said you missed them."

"Yes, but…" How could she explain to him that she needed this time away? Not only to spare her mother's campaign, but also to figure out what she wanted. "I'm happy I'm here with you."

"So am I."

His words gave her a boost of confidence.

"So you're the youngest," Sean prompted. "And the only girl."

She eyed him warily. She wanted to be careful how much she told him. "That's right."

"I'm surprised your family isn't keeping closer tabs on you."

"Well…my mother has a pretty high-powered position that takes all her time and energy. My three brothers are male versions of her."

"But not you."

"Nope," Zoe admitted. "Which drives them all crazy. I don't understand why since none of them ever has any time for me."

"Do they have any idea where you are?"

"No, but it was my mother's idea for me to…"

"What?"

"See the world. Learn responsibility. Stay out of trouble."

"How is that going for you?" he asked.

"Only time will tell, but it seems to be working out okay."

"I think you're doing great."

"Thanks."

As she rinsed the soap from his hair, Sean closed his eyes. A satisfied smile settled on his lips. He was enjoying his shampoo.

So was she.

A little too much.

Her suggestion to wash his hair had been totally innocent, one more way she could care for him. But touching his hair, his head, was much too intimate.

Zoe felt guilty.

For the shampoo and for not being able to tell him the truth. Sean liked the person he thought she was. So did Zoe.

She gave his head a final rinse to make sure all the shampoo was gone.

Too bad she couldn't leave Zoe Carrington behind and just be Zoe Flynn.

"I guess I should have figured out you are one of those workaholic types."

Sean glanced up from his computer, the one he'd been dying to use for the past week, to find Zoe standing in front of him with a cup of coffee in her hand. "What?"

"You're like a kid playing video games." She set the steaming mug on the end table. "We might have to rethink your allotment of screen time. You're completely obsessed with your computer."

"Not obsessed, just checking e-mail. I've been out of touch with people at the office for a while."

She went into the kitchen. "Whose fault was that?"

"Mine, but it's a busy time. I need to get caught up," Sean explained. "Custom orders are streaming in because of the holidays. We've got a huge PR event coming up at New Year's, the Rail Jam Extravaganza, that could increase our exposure and distribution significantly."

Zoe returned with a cup of coffee for herself. "Is it ever not busy?"

"No, this is pretty typical."

"How do your girlfriends feel about that? When you have one." Her cheeks heated. "A real one, I mean."

"I don't have time for a real girlfriend. Between work, climbing, riding and rescue work, there isn't a lot left over for the women I date."

"You like playing the field."

"Well, yeah," he admitted. "That keeps things casual. I figured out a couple of years ago that no one gets hurt that way."

"So you used to be a heartbreaker."

It wasn't a question. Sean shrugged, uncomfortable with the turn the conversation had taken. "Let's just say I'm careful not to create expectations now."

She sat cross-legged on the floor, cradling her mug in the palms of her hands. "What changed?"

"I grew up."

"But not enough to settle down."

"Ouch."

"Kidding," she joked. "I'm just surprised how focused you've become on work."

"My company is important to me. My employees, too. I owe it to them to make sure everything's running smoothly."

"What do you do when you have a rescue mission to go on or a vacation?" Zoe asked.

"Excuse me?"

"I'm sure this isn't the first time you've been out of the office for an extended amount of time."

"No, it's not," he admitted. "I have a capable staff. Very talented and trustworthy."

"So you should let them do their jobs and take care of things while you recover," she urged. "If they need you, you're only a phone call away."

Zoe made it sound so easy. Maybe it was.

Sean hadn't had this much spare time in eight years. Not since he'd started his snowboarding company at the age of twenty-five. He'd hired the best people he could find and trained others to do what he wanted. His company had survived not only rescue missions, but also climbing expeditions to Denali and Patagonia. No doubt, Hughes Snowboards would survive this.

A part of him wasn't ready to jump back in with both feet. He liked being with Zoe, playing games and watching television with her. He didn't want to have to give that up completely just yet.

Sean closed his computer. "I can do that."

Her eyes widened. "Really?"

"Yeah."

A satisfied grin settled on her lips.

"What do you want to do?" he asked.

"That's usually my question."

"Let's shake things up a little," he suggested.

"Let's shake things up a lot."

The mischief gleaming in her eyes filled Sean with hope. Maybe she was having second thoughts about no more kissing.

"Why don't we pull out your tree and decorate your house for Christmas?" she suggested.

Sean never put up a tree until his mother's nagging got to be too much to bear, but Zoe's excitement made decorating for Christmastime a little more appealing. "I have decorations, but I don't have a tree to pull out. I cut one down each year."

She leaned forward. "With an ax like they do in the movies?"

Smiling, he nodded.

"That must be so much fun to do."

He heard the longing in her voice and remembered how she'd been humming "It's Beginning to Look a Lot Like Christmas." Except his house looked as if the holidays were months away. He felt bad because she was so eager to please and working so hard, he wanted to return the favor. "Would you like to cut down a tree for us, Zoe?"

"I'd love to, but I don't know how."

Unfortunately, he wasn't in any shape to go with her. "A good thing I have a few friends who do."

"Got your permit?" Sean asked two days later.

"The tree-cutting permit is right here." Zoe patted her coat pocket. She was dressed, like his friends, in a down jacket, waterproof pants and boots. Only she wore borrowed gear. Still, he couldn't scrub the image of her dancing half-naked in the snow from his mind. "The ten whatever you called them are in the backpack."

"The ten essentials," he said tightly, running through the list in his mind. Map, compass, firestarter, waterproof matches, first-aid kit, knife, flashlight, sunglasses, extra clothing and extra food and water.

Damn, Sean wished he were going with them. He glanced at his legs. Not happening.

Bill Paulson grinned. "So Zoe, did you pack your toothbrush and dental floss, too?"

Lines creased her forehead. "My—?"

"Relax, Zoe. Just some ribbing," Jake explained. "Sean acts like a mother hen whenever we go out on a mission."

Tim Moreno, another OMSAR member and climbing partner who also worked for Hughes Snowboards, nodded. "We have to go over our checklist."

"And review our objective," Bill added.

Jake smiled. "But it is Hughes's job to keep us safe up there."

"And get our sorry asses back down the hill in one piece," Tim added.

"I haven't lost anyone yet." Sean didn't mind poking fun at himself. "At least I haven't lost anyone, except people leaving my team in sheer disgust."

Jake's mouth quirked. "I wonder who that might have been."

"Not now." Even with two useless legs, Sean couldn't help falling into his usual role. He looked at Zoe. "You charged up my cell phone and packed it, right?"

"Dude, Zoe told you. We're set." Jake pulled out a candy bar. "I even brought chocolate."

She laughed. "The eleventh essential."

"You're going to fit right in," Tim said.

She zipped her backpack. "I really appreciate you guys taking me out."

"Even Ebenezer Scrooge needs a Christmas tree," Jake joked.

"Scrooge?" Bill furrowed his brows. "I always thought Hughes was more of a Grinch type."

"Green?" Jake asked.

"Jealous," Bill said with a nod. "Because we get to spend the morning with Zoe."

"Sean's not jealous." A pretty blush colored Zoe's cheeks. "And he's no Scrooge, either. He's the one who suggested I get the tree."

"Sean?" Jake asked.

Tim made a face. "You're kidding."

"I get a small tree every year." Sean's friends continued to stare at him in disbelief. He didn't blame them. "Okay, I do it to appease my mom."

"Your sad excuse for a tree last year made the Charlie Brown Christmas tree look great," Jake joked.

Sean's idea to send Zoe out to cut a nice one down seemed really stupid now. This was totally out of character for him.

"That was last year," he said. "Zoe wanted to decorate the house for Christmas and asked if we could pull out the tree. I discovered she's never cut down a tree before."

She grinned. "It sounds like a lot of fun."

"Well, Zoe," Tim said. "You're in for a treat today. Nothing beats cutting down your own tree."

Jake nodded. "Damn straight."

The doorbell rang.

"I'll get it," she said and walked toward the front door.

"You must really like her to go to all this trouble for a Christmas tree," Tim said.

"Well, you three have to do all the work." Sean lowered his voice. "So here's the deal. Zoe's a city girl. She's not used to being out in the woods. I went over numerous scenarios with her. She knows if she gets separated from you to stay put, but—"

"We're not going to let anything happen to her," Jake said.

Bill nodded. "I'll take extra special care of her for you, dude. I can even short-rope her to me if you like."

Sean eyed him warily. The guy had a reputation with the ladies. "Maybe Leanne should tag along."

"Don't worry, Hughes." Tim nudged his shoulder. "Us married guys will keep the single guy in line. Your girl's safe with us."

Your girl.

That was how Sean was coming to think of Zoe even though nothing physical was going on between them. On second thought, hair washing ranked right up there with back rubs when it came to foreplay. Not that he could even get to second base with Zoe.

Still, the more time he spent with her, the more he liked her. She was always bright, always warm, like the sun on a cold day or a fire in an empty room, even when she was upset and scolding him for overdoing it. He was getting to know her in a way he seldom got to know his here-today-gone-tomorrow dates. He liked the woman he was getting to know. She wasn't just his caregiver. She was a friend. He wished she could be more.

But if he acted on those desires, he risked losing her. Any sort of romantic fling would mess things up. Sean didn't want to do that to her. She needed the job. She needed a place to stay.

The last thing Sean wanted was to hurt her. Once he healed, he wouldn't have time for her anyway.

Better to settle for the quick kisses in front of his family and friends, the card games and surprisingly intimate talks, her smile when she looked at him and her fingers against his scalp when she washed his hair.

The din of conversation and laughter pulled him from his pleasant fantasy of Zoe leaning over him, her chest at eye level.

"Carly and the kids must be here," Jake said.

The familiar sound of paws against hardwood widened Sean's smile. "Denali."

His dog rounded the corner, sliding a little on the floor. Her clear, blue eyes met Sean's. She sprinted toward him, a bundle of energy and excitement.

"Whoa, Denali." Jake grabbed her by the collar before she could pounce on top of Sean. He led her over to the couch as Zoe entered the great room. "Go easy on him, girl."

"Welcome home, baby." Sean patted the couch, and Denali jumped up. She nuzzled and licked his face. He hugged her. "I missed you, too."

"The kids thought you might want to see her. And they wanted to see you." Carly Porter walked in with her ten-year-old niece Kendall and eight-year-old nephew Austin in tow. "Hannah, Garrett and Tyler went Christmas shopping."

"Denali missed you, Sean," Kendall said.

"But we kept her busy so she wouldn't miss you too much," Austin added.

Sean grinned and rubbed the dog. "Thanks."

The two kids were so much like their late father, Nick Bishop. Kendall had his no-fear personality, and Austin looked exactly like him. Nick would be proud of his kids. Sean sure was.

"Denali and I appreciate that." The dog circled then lay against Sean's side. He exchanged a smile with Zoe. "Hey. Did you guys meet Zoe?"

Austin nodded. He looked at her. "Are you one of Sean's models?"

The room went quiet.

"Zoe is a friend of Sean's," Carly said. "I told you that, Austin."

"But Sammy Ross said Sean only dates models," Austin said.

"Sammy Ross says too much," Jake murmured.

"I'm not a model," Zoe answered with an amused smile.

"But she is Sean's girlfriend. That's why she's here taking care of him," Kendall explained as if she knew all the answers. She looked at Zoe. "Mrs. Hughes said once he's better you'll get married. Do you know how many flower girls you're going to have?"

Zoe blushed.

Sean sighed. He would have to have a talk with his mother.

"Let's save the wedding talk for later, Kendall," Carly said to his relief. "They need to get Christmas-tree hunting. And we have lots we want to do with Sean."

"We're going to play video games." Austin jumped from foot to foot. "And build Lego."

"Don't forget baking cookies," Kendall added.

"I can see I'm leaving you in good hands." Zoe pulled her wool beanie over her hair. It reminded him of the first time he'd seen her standing on the side of the road. She walked toward him, and his pulse kicked up a notch. "Have fun."

He would miss her. "You, too."

As Zoe rubbed Denali's head, she leaned over to kiss Sean's cheek.

He didn't want another chaste peck. He didn't want to be dismissed like Denali, with a pat and a treat. He wanted a kiss. Even if it were only for pretend.

At the last second he turned his head. Her lips landed on his. He felt her tense, but she didn't pull her mouth away from him. Instead, she relaxed. He brought his arm around her.

The taste of her, all sweetness and warmth, seeped through Sean, making him feel better than any pain medication could. The best part, however, was that she kissed him back.

Her mouth pressed against his as her lips parted. She arched closer, her jacket crinkling between them until he felt the softness of her chest against him.

Probably for show, but Sean didn't care.

He'd wanted this. Needed this. Needed her.

Denali stood on the couch, stuck her nuzzle between their faces and pushed until Zoe backed away.

"Don't worry, Denali." Zoe laughed with pink cheeks and swollen lips. "I know who the number one girl is around here."

Sean steadied his ragged breathing.

A good thing she knew, because he wasn't so sure anymore. All Sean knew was he wanted to kiss Zoe again. Maybe he should see about getting some mistletoe.

Except…

He wanted more than kisses from Zoe.

Mrs. Hughes said once he's better you'll get married.

Marriage was too extreme, but Sean agreed with his mom on one point. He liked having Zoe around. The only problem was what would happen when he was fully recovered?

How would Zoe fit into his life then? Would she even want to?

Flushed with fresh air and excitement, Zoe entered the great room.

A fire crackled in the river-rock fireplace. Denali lay on her dog pillow with her head resting on a stuffed football toy. Sean sprawled on the couch where she'd last seen him. His long legs rested on the ottoman, his face a study of intense concentration. Kendall and Austin sat on either side of him. All three stared at the video game they played on the large screen television.

The whole scene reminded her of a family sitcom.

Zoe smiled impishly. "Hi, honey, I'm home."

Home. The word struck her with unexpected force.

The governor's mansion had never been like this. She had

lived there since she was eight, but it felt more like a museum than a home. The only time her family sat down together to play games or cards or watch a movie was when the press showed up to do a story on them. Most of the time she'd been on her own.

Zoe barely remembered the large estate, her childhood home, where she'd lived before her mother had been elected. The property had been sold after her father's death.

Denali rose, stretched and lumbered toward her.

Sean glanced over, returning Zoe's smile with one of his own. The sense of homecoming struck again, making her knees go weak.

"Hey, I missed you," he said.

She'd missed him, too. Even though she'd had fun with Jake, Bill and Tim, she'd worried about Sean, wished she could share her experience of cutting down her first Christmas tree with him. But now she was here, she worried even more.

Because this was not her home.

He was not her boyfriend.

And as soon as he was better, she would leave him and Mount Hood behind.

Her smile faded.

"Did you find a tree?" Austin asked.

Zoe cleared her dry throat. "The guys are trying to get it out of the truck."

Sean stood and made his way toward her using the walker. "Trying?"

The kids' aunt, Carly, came out of the bathroom.

"It's a big tree," Zoe admitted.

"This I have to see," Carly said. "Kids, you want to come?"

They were too engrossed in their video game.

Carly shook her head. "I'll be right back."

Sean looked at Zoe with an invitation in his eyes. "You didn't kiss me hello."

Zoe's heart fluttered. "We don't have an audience."

He motioned to the kids totally enraptured by their game.

"I think they count more as chaperones," she said quietly.

Sean grinned and held out his hand. "Did you have fun?"

She let herself take it, noticing how warm and strong his grip was.

"Yes." Zoe focused on being his caretaker, his friend. Anything else wasn't possible. She released his hand. "I only had to use one of my essentials."

"Which one?"

"The chocolate bar."

"Leave it to Porter to remember the most important essential." Sean laughed. "So you found a big tree."

She nodded. "Jake didn't think it would fit your tree stand so he stopped off and bought a bigger one. They're going to put it on outside."

"You better get the beers ready," Sean said.

"What for?"

"Getting a big tree into a stand is at least a two man production. Think lots of choice swear words and grunting."

Zoe was amused. "That sounds awful."

Sean grinned. "Naw. It's tradition."

Zoe arched her brows. "Really? For someone whose friends claim he's a Grinch, I wasn't expecting respect for tradition."

"Traditions are important, Zoe." Kendall said, the video game controller on her lap. "Especially at the holidays. Isn't that right, Sean?"

"That's exactly right," he said.

Austin nodded. "Last year, Sean brought back a Christmas tradition to save him from going stark raving mad at his parents' house and drinking too much and killing one of his cousins."

Zoe looked at Sean. "Oh, really?"

"A cousin twice removed." A sheepish smile crossed his face. "I didn't realize the kids were listening so carefully."

She laughed. "So what is this tradition that saves you from the insane asylum, detox and incarceration?"

Kendall inched forward until she was sitting on the edge of the couch. "Can I tell her, Sean?"

He nodded.

"Before my first daddy died on the mountain, he would take me snowshoeing with a bunch of his friends on Christmas day before dinner. They also used to do it before I was born. And sometimes my mom would go, too."

Zoe had met their mom, Hannah, when she dropped off a pan of lasagna last week. She seemed like a lovely woman with an almost-one-year-old baby boy in addition to Kendall and Austin. Hannah had seemed as devoted to Sean as her children were.

"That sounds like a wonderful tradition." It reaffirmed what Zoe had seen at the hospital, how much Sean was a part of the community here in Hood Hamlet. He not only attracted friends, but also knew how to keep them. She'd tried, but hadn't been able to sustain relationships that way.

"It's my favorite tradition," Sean admitted.

"What about opening presents from Santa?" Austin asked.

"Much better than presents," Sean answered.

Zoe remembered all the bouquets from women in the hospital. He'd admitted to only dating casually. Maybe Sean didn't sustain all relationships. Only friendships.

"Everyone waited six years until Aunt Carly came back to Hood Hamlet last Christmas to go snowshoeing again," Kendall added.

"We got to go with them," Austin said. "They gave us snowshoes. We had hot chocolate and cookies, too. It was awesome."

"Sounds like a wonderful tradition," Zoe said.

Kendall nodded. "I can't wait to go again."

As Austin stared at Sean's legs, the smile on the boy's face turned upside down. "Are you going to be better by Christmas?"

"No, little dude." Sean messed up Austin's mop of blond hair. "I'm going to have to sit this year out."

"But you have to be there." Austin stuck his jaw out. "Please."

"Oh, please, Sean." Kendall's eyes gleamed. "It won't be the same if you're not there. And Denali, too."

Zoe's heart ached for all of them. She fought the urge to reach out to Sean.

He gripped the walker. "If there was any way, you know I would be there."

"Maybe we can figure out something," Zoe offered.

"Yes!" the kids said in unison.

As they gave each other high fives, Sean motioned to his legs.

Zoe shrugged. "Christmas is still a couple weeks away."

"My mom says Christmas is a time of magic and miracles, especially on the mountain," Kendall said.

Zoe smiled at her. "Your mom is right."

Sean shook his head. At least he didn't say bah humbug.

"Ho, ho, ho," a male voice bellowed from the front door. "Christmas tree delivery for Mr. Hughes."

Jake, Tim and Paul entered wearing Santa hats and carrying in the Christmas tree. Carly followed with an old-fashioned red cap with white lace, the kind Mrs. Claus might wear, on her head.

Austin squealed with laughter. Kendall giggled.

The scent of pine filled the air. Denali ran to sniff the tree.

Sean whistled. "That is a big tree."

"Size matters, Hughes," Bill joked.

"Want to put my tree up next to yours?" Sean asked.

"I've seen your tree, Paulson," Tim said. "Better cut your losses now."

"I still can't believe you got that tree in the truck," Carly said. "Is it going to fit in here?"

Jake held the end with the tree stand attached. "Have a little faith in the magic of Christmas, beautiful."

"The tree looked so small compared to the others towering around it." When Zoe had seen how big it was in comparison to the truck, her heart had dropped to her feet. "But it will fit."

Please. She prayed for a little Christmas magic. Let the tree fit.

Tim and Bill righted the tree while Jake held the stand.

"It fits," Bill announced.

Zoe breathed a sigh of relief. "Told you so."

"You did." Sean smiled. "But I think we're going to need a lot more lights and ornaments than I have."

Carly leaned against her husband Jake and smiled. "It's lovely as it is."

"Beautiful," Kendall agreed.

"Perfect." Sean looked at Zoe, a smile still on his face. "You did good, babe."

She glowed at his praise.

This might not be her home, but this would be the only Christmas she ever spent in Hood Hamlet with Sean. Zoe was going to make it a Christmas to remember. She wanted to make sure Sean never forgot it.

Or her.

CHAPTER EIGHT

THE NEXT day ZOE crawled under the branches of the Christmas tree to check the water level in the tree stand. Almost empty. She tipped the pitcher awkwardly to refill it. "I never had to do this at my mother's. I can't believe how much water this tree needs."

"Cut trees drink a lot at first." Sean sat with his legs on the ottoman and a MacBook Pro on his lap. He'd been working a little each day in addition to his physical therapy and workout sessions in his garage gym. "But in a couple of weeks, it won't need much at all."

She wiggled out on her stomach and sat back on her heels to grin at him. "Sounds like you. Lots of care to start, and now look at you."

"Gee thanks," he said dryly. "I always wanted to be compared to a Christmas tree."

"Hey, I love this tree." Realizing what she'd just said, she blushed. "Because it's fresh. I mean…its size. Er, shape. The way it smells."

"It's a great tree," Sean said, rescuing her from embarrassment. "Better than the small one I had last year. It's only going to be tall trees from now on."

He meant next year, in the future.

Zoe's stomach clenched. She'd never given much thought to the future. That had always bothered her family, but now she couldn't stop the questions swirling in her mind.

Where would she be in twelve months? What would she be doing? Who would she be with?

She rose and returned the water pitcher to the kitchen. "Well, you wouldn't want Bill to have the biggest tree, would you?"

Sean laughed. "Are you ready to decorate?"

"Let's wait until you're on crutches and can help."

"You don't have to."

"I want to wait." Her gaze drifted from the tree to him. "The only trees I've decorated were little dinky tabletop jobs, and I had to do it myself. I want this tree to be different."

"Your family never had a big tree?"

The trees in the governor's mansion were always huge, but... "My mom likes themed trees so every year she hires a decorator."

"That must cost a pretty penny."

Nodding, Zoe thought about the different trees through the years. The bird one with turtle doves, French hens, calling birds and partridges had been her favorite. "My mother loves showing off her Christmas tree. No expense is spared."

"Everybody has their own priorities."

"Her trees are always gorgeous, but it's not much fun watching the decorator's crew put on the ornaments instead of getting to do it ourselves."

"You never got to decorate your family's tree?"

"Never," Zoe admitted. "Sad, isn't it?"

She tried to sound lighthearted, but failed.

"Let's wait then so we can decorate the tree together," Sean said. "We need to get more stuff anyway. Why don't you see what decorations are in the container so we know what to buy?"

Zoe carried the large green-and-red container that Hank had brought in this morning from the entryway to the great room. She placed it near the tree. "At least you have some things."

"Most were given to me, including the box," Sean admitted. "Christmas decorations aren't something guys put a lot of thought into. At least this guy."

"I'll Be Home For Christmas" played on the radio. As Zoe hummed along, she removed the lid from the container. She really did feel at home here with Sean.

A green-and-red tree skirt sat on top. Each triangular piece was made from a different fabric pattern. Stripes, plaids, gingham. Nothing too feminine, yet the feel wasn't too masculine, either. Perfect for a family.

Zoe's insides twisted. "This is nice."

"Aunt Vera made it for me," he said. "There are matching stockings."

Zoe placed the tree skirt on the container's lid. "The stockings are right here."

She held three quilted stockings in the air to see how they would hang. They were pieced together with the same fabrics used on the tree skirt. Sean's name was embroidered on the white cuff of one of the stockings. A smaller stocking had Denali's name stitched on it. "Who's the blank stocking for?"

Sean rolled his eyes. "It's Aunt Vera's not-so-subtle hint I should settle down."

"You weren't kidding when you said they were on your back about getting married."

"Nope. I should have never adopted a dog or built this house. Both gave my family the wrong idea."

"A four-bedroom house isn't your typical bachelor pad. It might give women the wrong idea, too."

"I'm upfront with the women I date. They know I don't have that kind of time to put into a relationship."

"That must go over well," she teased, but a part of her knew how those women must feel. His words reminded Zoe of her family. Work had always taken priority for them. And that had left her feeling like an outsider and alone.

"Not always, but they need to understand I have a lot going on. Normally, that is. When I'm not injured."

Zoe glanced at the tree and thought of how things would

be in a couple weeks. Sean would probably be in the office every day and working out when he wasn't. A big change from now. "Maybe if you meet the right woman someday, you'll want to make time for a relationship."

"Maybe." His tone suggested that was unlikely. "In the meantime, you can use the stocking."

She flushed. His Aunt Vera had made the blank stocking for his future wife, not his pretend girlfriend.

"I don't need a stocking." Zoe carefully placed the stockings on top of the tree skirt. "I haven't had one in years."

"You have to have one here."

"Why is that?"

"Stockings, especially handmade ones, are a Hughes family tradition," he explained. "Besides, if you don't have a stocking where will Santa put your presents?"

Zoe imagined her name embroidered on the blank stocking. She pushed the thought from her mind. "Don't you mean my lump of coal?"

"Nah, you've been a very good girl." He raised a brow. "But we still have a little time until Christmas Eve. If you want some help doing something naughty, I'm happy to oblige."

His words loosened the tight feeling in her chest. She wished he could oblige her.

No, Zoe reminded herself, she didn't.

She pulled out a box of a single strand of lights. "White lights?"

"I bought those myself," he said. "I grew up with multi-colored lights, but the white ones look like stars to me."

Her heart melted. "I can't believe your friends think you're the Grinch."

"I don't mind. I have an image to uphold." Sean struck a pose. "Gruff loner with a dog."

"Don't you mean overprotective mother hen?" she teased.

"I'll ignore that."

She pulled out a box filled with a dozen colored balls. Next came three silver stocking holders that spelled JOY, no doubt gifts based on the number. Finally she removed a large shoebox. "What's in here?"

"All the ornaments my cousins' kids and friends' kids have made me over the years."

Zoe opened the lid to find everything from paper ornaments scribbled with crayons to painted wood ones. "These are adorable. Maybe we could invite all your cousins' kids over to make more ornaments for the tree."

"If you do that, everyone is going to want to come."

"The more the merrier. We could make it a tree-trimming party." Excitement rippled through her. "I've always wanted to string popcorn and cranberries and make a garland."

Sean didn't say anything.

And then Zoe remembered with a pang. "You don't like family get-togethers."

"I didn't like family get-togethers when my family was breathing down my neck telling me to settle down," he admitted. "Now that I have you, it's not a problem."

"But…"

He smiled at her. "You said you wanted this tree to be different. Let's have a party."

Zoe jumped up, ran to the couch and sat next to him. "We'll need to call an event planner right away. Is there someone you normally use?"

"Event planner? Honey, this is a tree-trimming party in Hood Hamlet, not a wedding in… Where did you say you were from?"

Oops. No way could she tell him her hometown. "I most recently lived in L.A. I'll just call a caterer instead."

"Uh-uh. Try a potluck."

"Really?" she asked.

He nodded. "My family likes to cook. They expect to be asked to bring food to a party. Especially a family gathering."

She'd never been to a potluck in her life. "Well, I don't want to step on any of the Hughes's toes."

"One phone call to my mother, and your work will be done."

Zoe smiled uncertainly. Organizing a family gathering was not at all the sort of thing her mother would enjoy.

Sean eyed her. "What kind of parties are you used to, Zoe?"

"Not that different from yours," she hedged. "It's just we don't have an event planner in the family."

He raised an eyebrow.

"Your mother," Zoe explained. Now that she thought about it, about being surrounded by family, even borrowed family, for the holidays, her spirits soared.

He studied her. "Happy?"

"Very." She hugged him. "Thank you."

His arms circled around her. "You're welcome."

It was just a hug, a gesture between friends, but his warmth and closeness sent her pulse racing. She didn't want to let go. Sean didn't seem in any hurry to end their hug, either.

Zoe looked up at him, her face mere inches away.

He gazed down at her, his eyes full of desire.

She swallowed and glanced at his lips. It would be so easy to kiss him. All she had to do was lift her chin and move her head...

"Naughty?" he inquired huskily, his pupils dilated. "Or nice?"

Her heart leapt. Zoe struggled to breathe.

Naughty.

But if she kissed Sean and things went sour, she risked ruining everything she'd been working so hard to do and be. She wouldn't be able to stay here and care for him. She wouldn't be able to show her mother she'd learned to be responsible.

That wouldn't be nice at all.

Keep it light, Zoe told herself.

"I think we'd better both be good," she said. "I don't want either of us to wake up with..."

"Coal in our stockings?"

Zoe shook her head. "Regrets."

No regrets this morning. Last night on the couch with Zoe had been another story, but he'd gone along with Zoe's wishes again.

Sean made his way out of the orthopedic surgeon's office on crutches. He respected Zoe's decision to keep things all business while he was laid up. But his sutures had been removed. He no longer needed the air cast on his ankle or the stupid walker.

He was feeling stronger, more himself, more confident.

Sean didn't want to drive Zoe away, but it was time to test the limits.

"Let's grab some lunch." He wanted her to see him as a man, not a patient. "Then swing by my office."

The look of concern he'd gotten to know so well over the past two weeks filled Zoe's eyes. "Are you sure you're up for all that? You're taking some awfully big steps right now."

"I'll take smaller ones." Just like the small steps he wanted to take with her. Sean breathed in the crisp, cold air. "I'm up for it."

Zoe unlocked and opened the passenger door of his truck for him. "As long as you don't overdo it."

Sean slid in and stuck the crutches behind him. "Me, overdo it?"

"Overdo is your middle name."

He wouldn't mind being over her. Doing her, either. The little fantasy made him smirk. "I can't keep sitting around and doing nothing. It's totally against my nature."

"I know." She walked around the back of the truck and climbed into the driver's seat. "Why do you think I have to watch you practically 24/7?"

"My devastatingly good looks and charm?"

She turned the key in the ignition. The engine roared to life. "Sorry, but as your caretaker I'm immune to those things."

Zoe hadn't seemed so last night. In fact, she'd looked almost feverish when she gazed into his eyes. Just thinking about it raised his temperature. "Better be careful, oh caretaker of mine, I'm always up for a challenge."

Zoe sat at a small table across from Sean at a quaint little café. Celtic harp music played from hidden speakers. A server, clad in black, removed their plates and silverware.

It was the kind of place she liked to eat at, good atmosphere, delicious food, but hadn't had the chance to since striking out on her own with a monthly allowance to budget.

She raised her glass of strawberry lemonade and smiled. "Here's to you getting such a positive report from your doctor."

Sean lifted his glass of soda and clinked it against hers. "And getting rid of the stupid walker."

Zoe took a sip. "I'm happy your recovery is going so well."

"I'm getting better."

"You are." The realization made her happy, but a little sad that her usefulness and time with Sean had a definite end now. With his legs under the table and his crutches propped against the wall, he didn't look injured or like her patient at all. He looked whole and virile and tempting. Uh-oh. "Thanks for suggesting we stop for lunch."

"You're welcome." Sean slid cash into the leather folder and handed her one of the chocolate mints wrapped in green foil. "It's about time we had a first date."

She choked on her lemonade. "We're not dating."

"My family doesn't know that. If anyone asks what our first date was, we can tell them this place."

"Couldn't we just tell them we met at Timberline?"

"That wasn't a date. I didn't pay for your lift ticket."

He was teasing her. She was tempted to play along. Part of her wanted the fantasy that this was a date. A real one.

But Zoe knew better. Even if things were different, Sean Hughes didn't have the time to make a relationship work.

He'd said so himself. She was tired of being someone's afterthought. She didn't want to do that again.

She took another sip of her drink. The strawberry lemonade tasted bittersweet. "I didn't realize pretend relationships had dating rules."

"They follow regular dating rules, which reminds me—" Sean raised her hand to his mouth and kissed it "—official dates should include a kiss."

Zoe's hand tingled at the spot his lips had touched her skin. "Shouldn't you have to walk me to the door?"

"That's a given. We live together."

The way he said "together" sent a ball of heat zipping through her.

Not good.

She sipped her ice water. "So what's next?"

"How does taking my pretend girlfriend to work sound?"

"What if your real-life caretaker thinks you should go home instead?"

"I'd tell her I feel great," he said. "If that didn't work I'd remind her I'm the boss and the doctor said it was okay."

"Guess we're going to work, then."

Zoe was curious, interested to see the man, not the patient she'd been spending time with. Maybe what she learned about Sean would make her struggle to be responsible easier to handle.

She parked the truck at Hughes Snowboards and slid out. By the time she'd reached the back, Sean was waiting for her.

"You're fast on the crutches," she said.

He negotiated his way through the gray slush in the parking lot. "I've had some practice using them before."

Worry had her biting her lip. "I guess you've had a lot of injuries as a rescue worker."

"I've never been injured on a mission," he explained. "Rescuer safety is our number one priority."

"Then how did you get hurt?"

"I climb for fun and ride as much as I can. I'm careful, but stuff happens."

"Like equipment breaking."

"Or rock fall and a hundred other things." He winked at her. "Good thing I'm a fast healer."

"Yeah. A fast healer." Zoe tried to muster some enthusiasm, but failed miserably. The bad news kept coming. She'd thought Sean might need her help into January. Now she wondered if he'd need her past Christmas. As she followed him into the factory, she dragged her feet. "That's a very good thing."

Over the noise of machines and the buzz of fans, music blared from speakers. Snowboarding posters covered the walls along with brightly colored banners with Hughes, Catch Some Air and Ride printed on them. She recognized a couple of people who had visited Sean at the hospital and at home.

Sean waved at one employee. Another hugged him. Everyone looked happy to see him back. He smiled, looking alert and confident and in complete control, as if he hadn't spent the past two weeks sitting on the couch playing games, reading and watching television.

"This place is big," she said.

"Burton has nothing to worry about from us." Sean stopped to check a board being built. "We have a niche market, but we're seeing steady growth in a couple of sectors. We're adding new product lines and expanding old ones."

Sean had always come across as intelligent. They'd had long talks about politics, economics and a whole bunch of other subjects, but today he seemed so different.

This was one of the first days she'd seen him in clothing other than shorts and T-shirts. Aunt Vera had modified a pair of khaki pants for him to wear over his encased left leg. The colors in his long-sleeved shirt brought out the green in his hazel eyes. But the differences she saw went deeper than his apparel.

He wasn't Hank and Connie's son or a mountain rescue volunteer. Sean was a businessman, a successful one given the size of his factory and the number of employees who worked for him.

She was impressed and intimidated. "You love what you do."

"Best job in the world." He thought for a moment. "Except when the prototype binding I designed broke on Thanksgiving Day. That pretty much sucked."

"I know how that hurt you personally, but I didn't even think about how it could impact your business."

"Business is fine," Sean reassured her. "I've also gotten to spend time with you. So the accident wasn't all bad."

Zoe's pulse skittered.

His acceptance of what had happened and his reassurance to her was so different from her family's reaction whenever something went wrong. They would point fingers and assign blame. No one ever saw the silver lining like Sean.

Her respect for him grew.

"Let me show you the other building," he said.

Zoe heard the pride in his voice. Despite her worries he might be overdoing it, she wanted to see more of this side of him.

They exited the factory via thick double doors, crossed beneath a covered walkway and into another building, one that looked newer. She noticed the quiet right away. No music or machines. Poster-size snowboarding photographs lined the walls. Cubicle walls filled the open space with three offices along the side wall.

"We have a retail shop in Hood Hamlet that Tim runs," Sean said. "Everything else is sold on the Internet or by distributors."

"Argh! I hate pink," a male voice said. "Why don't they just buy Roxy or some other chick brand?"

"Excuse me," Sean said and made his way toward a cubicle near the back. Zoe followed.

Energy drink cans and candy bar wrappers littered a desk. A twentysomething guy with shoulder-length brown hair stared at a computer monitor. He looked totally dejected.

"What's up, Taylor?" Sean asked.

"This custom top sheet, dude." Taylor pointed to the monitor and a sorry-looking snowboard that resembled the color of medicine used to calm an upset stomach. "Customer wants something 'unique' for his seven-year-old daughter. She likes pink and princesses."

"Let's see what you've got." Sean stared at the monitor. "Okay, you've got the pink covered. The swirl of stars is a nice touch, but it doesn't say princess yet. Try to think like a seven-year-old girl."

Taylor groaned. "Dude, this is just wrong. It's like drawing with my own blood. It's killing me."

Zoe covered her mouth to hide her smile.

"Come on, kid," Sean encouraged. "You're my best graphic designer."

"I'm your only one since Cocoa left for Vermont."

"You can do it." Sean patted Taylor's shoulder. "The little girl riding this board could be a future gold medalist. Let that inspire you."

Taylor gave him a look. "Princesses don't shred, man."

Zoe pressed her lips together to keep from laughing. Poor Taylor. No doubt this was a galaxy—make that a fairy-tale kingdom—away from his comfort level. "Could I make a suggestion?"

Both Sean and Taylor looked her way.

Sean motioned her into the cubicle. "Taylor, this is Zoe. She knows more about princesses and the color pink than either of us could ever hope to."

"Do you have a piece of scratch paper?" she asked.

Taylor shoved white paper and a pen into her hands. "If you can save me from this misery, the first round of drinks is on me."

"Let's see if this helps." Zoe thought back to one of her favorite art classes from college. She sketched Taylor's basic star design and added in some wands, crowns, glass slippers and flourishes that matched the way he'd drawn the stars. She saw a set of colored pencils on the desk. Her fingers itched. "If I had more time…"

"Take all the time you want. Whatever you need," Taylor said.

Zoe opened the metal case of pencils and pulled out three different shades of pinks. With rapid strokes, she feathered in the design using all three colors, explaining as she drew. "Try starting with a softer pink. Overlay darker shades so you get a mix. That will add some texture, too. See?"

She showed them her drawing.

"Dude, that's totally rad." Taylor stared at the drawing. "I mean, Zoe. Thanks."

Sean stared at her with gratitude in his eyes. "Yeah, thanks."

"You're both welcome."

"Everything cool now?" Sean asked his designer.

Taylor's nod was barely perceptible. He was too busy working.

She followed Sean out of the cubicle.

"Do you have a background in design or does it come naturally?" he asked.

"I have a degree in fashion design, but no job experience," she said. "My family thought my major was a huge waste of time and effort, but I love working with shape and color. I figured since they'd eventually force me to attend graduate school for business or law, I could afford to indulge myself as an undergrad."

"I can't believe they didn't recognize your talent."

His words sent her confidence soaring. "My mother thought my designs were cute doodles."

"Unbelievable," Sean said. "The Christmas tree, the top sheet. You've got an incredible eye. You're good at what you do, Zoe."

"Thanks." Inside her suede boots, she wiggled her toes. "That's the nicest thing anyone has ever said to me."

"You've been hanging with the wrong crowd, then."

She stared up at him. "You might be right."

"You should think about using your degree."

The idea of working in design had never crossed Zoe's mind. She'd always believed her brothers had been right about her degree being worthless in the real world, the business world they inhabited. "Maybe I will once you're better and it's time for me to…"

"There's no reason for you to think about finding another job right now," Sean said.

She hadn't been thinking about a job. She'd been thinking about having to leave.

"I still need you," he continued.

Good. She liked him needing her. And until this moment she hadn't a clue what she might do once he no longer did. Getting a job couldn't be that hard. After all the fashion shows and benefits she'd attended over the years, she had contacts in the industry. Her notoriety might even come in handy for once.

Zoe glanced at Sean.

But finding a job would mean leaving Hood Hamlet, most likely Oregon. She didn't want to think about leaving right now. Not until after Christmas. Maybe not at all.

On Saturday, Sean couldn't believe this was his house.

"Jingle Bell Rock" played on his stereo. The scents of spiced apple cider lingered in the air. A buffet of finger foods and desserts lined the kitchen island.

Zoe supervised a bunch of kids making ornaments at the dining table. She was laughing and encouraging them, glue on her fingers and glitter in her hair. Sean smiled. She looked like his own personal Christmas angel.

Outside, his dad, uncles and cousins hung Christmas lights on the front of Sean's house and his back deck. But today, Sean didn't even mind being stuck inside. Today he could touch and kiss Zoe all he wanted. For his family's sake, even though it was really for his own.

Connie put her arm around Sean and gave him a squeeze. "I'm so happy Zoe and you wanted to do this."

"It was mainly her, Mom."

"But you could have said no." His mother gave him another hug. "Thank goodness you didn't listen to us going on about settling down. I'm glad you waited for Zoe. The two of you are good together."

Sean took a sip of eggnog. He'd been hearing that a lot today from his family. Aunt Vera had danced an actual jig when she saw the three stockings hanging on the fireplace.

Normally, his family's interference drove him up the wall. Yet today he didn't mind so much. Maybe it was the eggnog. Maybe, whispered a little voice in the back of his mind, it was Zoe. "She's a great girl," Sean said.

"Don't forget about your grandmother's ring in the safe-deposit box."

"Mom." He didn't really mind their interference. Not when their presence in his house made it possible for him to get his hands on Zoe. But they were still playing roles, he realized, with his family and with each other. He was getting tired of it.

"Just a friendly reminder." Connie's smile widened. "I'm not trying to push you into anything. That seems to be happening all on its own."

Sean couldn't disagree with her about that. He and Zoe were getting closer. Granted, they spent most of their waking hours together. Attraction simmered, yet they continued to only exchange chaste kisses and hugs. Mostly for show. Unfortunately.

"Oh, boy," Connie said. "Aunt Vera has a sprig of mistletoe and she's headed Zoe's way. You better get over there before someone else gets a kiss."

No one was going to kiss his girl. Sean gripped the handles on his crutches. "On my way, Mom."

"Oh, Rebecca." Zoe stared at the wood ornament covered in gold, red and pink glitter. "What a pretty star. I love it."

Rebecca, the six-year-old daughter of Mary Sue and Will Townsend, beamed. "It's for you, Zoe."

"Thank you." Zoe hugged Rebecca, the epitome of sugar and spice and everything nice. "Do you want to hang it on the tree?"

The little girl's brunette ponytail bobbed as she nodded. "I'll be right back."

"Here comes the mistletoe," Aunt Vera said in a singsong voice. "Who's going to get a kiss?"

Two young boys grimaced, as if kissing were the yuckiest thing that could happen. A couple of girls raised their hands, wanting to be picked.

Aunt Vera stopped behind her. "It looks like…Zoe."

Zoe looked up to see mistletoe hanging over her head. "Who shall I kiss?"

"It better be me or there will be blood," Sean said.

Anticipation quickly replaced the amusement in his eyes. Zoe knew exactly how he felt. She wet her lips.

"Stand up, girlie," Aunt Vera said. "The boy's on crutches."

Zoe rose.

Sean stood with his crutches pressed up near his armpits and held out his arms to her.

She went to him, knowing everyone was looking at them.

He'd made no secret of wanting her, but as long as she pretended to Sean and to herself kissing was for show, it wouldn't have to lead anywhere. As long as they had an audience, kissing him was safe.

Sean's mouth captured hers without a moment's hesitation. His lips moved with a tenderness that made her ache. Once again, he made her feel cherished, special, desired.

The taste of him made her drunk, as if someone had spiked the cider.

His arms circled Zoe. He pulled her closer.

She went eagerly, pressing against his strong, hard chest.

The kiss heated up. His tongue tasted, explored her mouth. She was awash in sensation. She struggled to remain in control, knowing people, children, could see them.

It wasn't easy.

Days, okay, weeks, of pent-up longing poured out and went into her kiss. Zoe's hands splayed his back. She could feel the muscular ridges beneath his shirt.

Her pulse raced. Her blood boiled. She didn't want to stop kissing him.

"Get a room," one of his cousins yelled.

The kiss came to an abrupt end. Zoe backed away from Sean at the same time he backed away from her.

Embarrassed by getting so carried away, Zoe stared at the floor. She could only imagine how she looked. She felt hot, as if someone had cranked the thermostat. Her lips felt bruised, swollen, tingly.

Her gaze met Sean's. The desire in his eyes sent her already-racing pulse skittering. He wanted to kiss her again. Good, because she wanted to kiss him again, too. And again. And again. And…

A sudden chill shivered down her spine. Her breath stilled in her chest. She couldn't pretend anymore, to Sean or to herself.

His family had returned to what they were doing. Decorating, hanging ornaments, eating. Soon they would leave. She and Sean would be alone.

Alone.

Free to do whatever they wanted to.

For real.

That made her realize how dangerous it was to be living alone with him. To her heart and to her mother's campaign.

"I'll have to leave the mistletoe here," Aunt Vera quipped.

Two of Sean's cousins nudged each other.

Zoe forced a smile. She glanced at the newspapers covering the table where the kids painted and glued. She could imagine the tabloid headlines if they found out she was living with Sean, not as his caretaker, but as his…

She couldn't bring herself to say it.

Staring deeply into her eyes, Sean tucked a strand of hair behind her ear.

Her heart went pitter-pat.

"We'll pick this up later," he whispered.

Oh, no. Her pulse pounded in her ears. Neither one of them was pretending now, but how could she admit the truth?

Zoe Flynn Carrington, party girl, wild child, governor's exiled daughter, was falling in love.

And she didn't know what to do about it.

But with her mother's special election and ultimatum hanging over her, Zoe couldn't let her impulses or her hormones plunge her into another scandal. No matter how she felt about Sean.

CHAPTER NINE

SEAN waved goodbye to his parents, the last ones to leave the party. He closed and locked the front door. Now he and Zoe wouldn't be disturbed if someone had forgotten something.

The mind-blowing kiss from this afternoon had been on his mind for hours. If not for his cousin's heckling, Sean would have kept kissing Zoe. He'd completely forgotten about their audience. He'd forgotten everything except her. He wanted to feel that way again. "I finally have you all to myself."

Zoe retreated into the kitchen. He followed her.

He'd been trying not to push Zoe into anything. He'd been good, patient, nice. Now it was time to be…naughty.

Sean grinned.

She picked up a serving spoon from the drying rack on the counter and placed it in the drawer. "I need to make sure everything's cleaned up."

He appreciated her work ethic. She made sure she earned every single dollar he paid her. He respected that. Her. But even the most stellar employee needed a…break.

Sean made his way toward her, not letting the crutches get in the way. He knew what he wanted tonight. "Later."

Her smile wavered. She looked uncomfortable. Nervous. "Don't want to wake up to a mess."

"Zoe, I'm done playing games. I want you."

He'd upped the ante. Finally said what had been on his mind for weeks. Hell, from the first day he'd met her. Now all he could do was stand and wait.

Would she check, call, raise or fold?

Zoe's brows furrowed, as if she were mulling his words over in her mind and trying to make a decision.

"I don't want to play games. I'm tired of pretending." Sean leaned against the counter. "Let's make something real out of this thing between us."

She picked up a silver cookie sheet and held it in front of her like a shield. "You need me."

"Damn straight, I need you," he admitted. "Come here."

Her cheeks turned a bright pink. "I meant you still need me to take care of you."

Not this again. He moved toward her. "Stop bluffing and pretending. We both know that kiss today wasn't for show. There's something very real going on here. It's time to take things to the next level."

Zoe clutched the edges of the cookie sheet until her knuckles turned white. "I wish I could."

"There's nothing stopping us."

"I'm stopping it," she said. "My role here is getting a little blurry. I like you, Sean. I can't believe how much I like you. But I can't accept a salary, live in your house and have a romantic relationship with you at the same time."

"Why not?"

"It's like you're paying me to…be here."

He was insulted she'd think that way about him. About them. About herself. "Is this you talking or your mother?"

A beat passed. And another. "Both of us, I think. I want to be responsible."

"Don't you think you're being overly cautious?"

"Better overly cautious than too impulsive."

He took a deep breath. "Okay. I hear you. But we're both adults. We can handle this."

She didn't look convinced. "For how long? You won't need my help much longer."

"Zoe, even after I'm one hundred percent recovered, I still want you around."

"That's nice to hear." Despite the warmth in her eyes, tense lines still marred her forehead and bracketed her face. "But…I remember what you said about dating casually. How long do your relationships usually last?"

Her question caught him off guard. "The past doesn't matter."

"Please, Sean."

"You can't judge our relationship by how I felt, or didn't feel, about someone in the past. You're different, Zoe. You're special."

"Are you sure about that?"

The vulnerability he saw in her eyes was like a vise gripping his heart.

"Yes," Sean said gently. He hadn't had a relationship with a woman that wasn't purely physical in years. "Usually I meet someone, we see each other a few times, and it's over. I've never spent time getting to know someone the way I've gotten to know you these past weeks."

"You said you didn't have time for a relationship."

"I'll make time for you."

"I want to believe that."

"Then believe it."

"It's not just you," Zoe admitted. "I've made a lot of mistakes in the past."

"It doesn't matter what happened before I met you."

She gazed into his eyes, as if she wanted to believe that, too. "This is the first time I haven't plunged headfirst into a relationship myself. It's been…nice."

"Frustrating."

"That, too." She smiled up at him. "I really like you, but I need to do this right."

"Be responsible."

"Yes," she said. "Could we wait a little longer until I'm no longer your official caretaker? Maybe I could find a job around here. A place to stay."

He'd hire her in an instant as a graphic designer. But that would only add another complication. He couldn't date an employee.

Her words nagged at him.

It's like you're paying me to...be here.

Zoe was right. He didn't want to put her in an awkward position. He would have to wait. Or he'd have to think of something else. Make some calls. Make an effort. Leanne had mentioned something about getting a roommate. "I'll do whatever it takes, Zoe."

"Thank you."

Sean caressed her cheek. Truth was he couldn't care less if she found a job or another place to stay. He was willing to give her what she seemed to need: a home, a big family and financial security. Those things were nothing compared to what she gave him. "I'm the one who should be thanking you."

She smiled up at him.

His breath hitched.

"But let's get one thing straight," Sean said. "You're not my pretend girlfriend. You're my real one. And I still plan on kissing you when we're with my family."

Her eyes widened. "You don't see your family all that much."

"Not usually, but don't forget—" he grinned "—it's Christmastime. You said it yourself, holidays are a time for family."

Retail therapy had always lifted Zoe's spirits. She enjoyed the noise, the energy, the glittering mall decorations. Still, she worried about Sean's ability to navigate the jostling Christmas crowd.

"Are you sure this was a good idea?" She glanced at Sean, walking on his crutches next to her. "I can't believe you wanted to come shopping."

He shrugged. "Everybody shops at Christmas. Besides, we needed to get out of the house."

Because of the limits she'd set on their relationship.

Not that Sean wasn't cooperating. They still enjoyed each other's company, the poker and video games, the discussions of work and family and even the weather. But as much as Zoe tried to keep things the same, there had been a shift in their relationship since the tree-trimming party and that kiss. The lack of physical contact was beginning to feel as false as their original ruse.

Sean Hughes was everything she could ask for in a boyfriend. Smart, funny, caring and giving. Strong, responsible, courageous, too. He didn't care if she could cook or made mistakes. He liked her for who she was or who he thought she was. She couldn't wait to take things to the next level.

As soon as Sean's leg was healed.

As soon as she told him the truth.

Her heart beat faster.

No. Zoe couldn't tell him the truth now. She didn't want anything to spoil Christmas.

Four singers, dressed in old-fashioned Victorian costumes, sang Christmas carols underneath a thirty-foot lit tree decorated with twinkling lights and big metallic ornaments.

She stared up at it, thinking of their tree at home. "This is all so bright and pretty."

"Very pretty," he said, looking at her. "Do you know what you want Santa to bring you?"

"I've already gotten what I wanted." Zoe smiled at him. "I get to spend a white Christmas in the mountains with you and your family. That's the best present ever."

"What about spending Christmas with your own family?" His eyes were warm, his tone suddenly serious. "Wouldn't you rather be with them?"

Her stomach knotted. She was touched by his concern. Panicked by it, too.

"It's not practical this year." Not possible, even if she wanted to be with them. She would have more fun here with him and his family. "Really, it's better I'm in Hood Hamlet. Trust me."

"Are you sure?" he asked.

"Yes," she said firmly. "I plan on calling my mother on Christmas."

"Do they have my address?" Sean asked. "To send your presents to?"

"No, but my family's not big on gifts," she explained. "They usually give gift cards or cash. That sort of thing."

"Unlike my family who are very big on gifts," he said ruefully. "I've got a huge list. We'd better get started."

Zoe noticed the crowd, the people carrying packages and shopping bags. She knew Sean well enough to know he would never complain or ask to leave. Not until they'd accomplished the—what had Bill called it?—objective. "What if you hang out in one place and be the keeper of the gift list? I can buy the items and bring them back here for you to approve and check off. That way you don't have to worry about walking around on your crutches and I don't have to carry everything at the same time."

Sean glanced around. "That sounds like a plan. It's more crowded than I thought it would be."

"Christmas is less than a week away." Zoe motioned to an empty table, pleased she could help him this way. She liked taking care of him, liked knowing she was needed. "Sit there. I'll get you a cup of coffee then hit the stores. We'll be out of here before you need a refill."

He sat. "Spoken like a true shopping expert."

The words sent a chill down Zoe's spine. She handed him his list.

When Sean finally learned who she really was, he would realize how close his words were to the truth. He would find out a lot more things about her, her family and her reputation. She hoped he wouldn't be too upset.

Swallowing a sigh, Zoe gave him a pen. "Be right back."

While Zoe shopped, Sean used his iPhone to buy her Christmas present.

It's not practical this year.

Maybe not. But maybe it wasn't practical because she couldn't afford to go home. No permanent address. No money for Thanksgiving dinner. No way to get back to her family if she wanted to.

He could fix that.

Sean knew exactly what to give Zoe—a plane ticket, an airline voucher actually, so she could visit her family when she wanted to. His finger hovered over the order button.

Sean worried she would think he was interfering.

Hell, he was interfering.

With good intentions, of course.

Just like his family always interfered with him.

The realization made him wince. But the thought of doing something nice, something selfless for Zoe trumped his momentary discomfort. She shouldn't be embarrassed about her financial circumstances. She had a job now. She was responsible. It was time to reconnect with her family.

He pressed the button to buy the voucher.

"Hey, Sean."

He saw a man dressed up as Santa Claus standing next to his table. "Do I know you?"

Behind gold wire-rimmed glasses, the man's blue eyes twinkled. "I know you, Sean Hughes."

Oh, the guy must have recognized him from the news. Sean got a lot of that after high-profile rescues, but news junkies and armchair climbers usually remembered him and liked to talk about certain rescues.

"Mind if I have a seat?" Santa asked.

"Go ahead." Sean guessed Santa must get coffee breaks. "Busy time of the year."

"The busiest, but it'll slow down soon enough." Santa sat and stretched his long booted legs out. "What are you searching for?"

Sean tucked his iPhone in his pocket. "I was just buying a Christmas present for someone I know."

"Someone special?"

"Yeah."

"Remember, only you can give her what she wants. Needs," Santa said mysteriously.

Sean thought about the airline voucher. "I just hope she likes her present."

Santa pushed his glasses back up his nose. "If you give the gift with your heart, she will."

"Is that a line from a greeting card or a fortune cookie?"

"You always say whatever's on your mind." Santa laughed, a boisterous, rich sound that stirred childhood memories of visiting Santa Claus at this same mall.

Sean looked closer at the guy. He looked a little familiar.

Nah. He shook his head. That had been more than twenty years ago. It was just the red suit and white beard.

Santa grinned, his cheeks a rosy pink. "I've always liked that about you."

Sean had the reputation for speaking his mind. That was why the press sought him out for interviews and sound bites. "Thanks."

"Before I go, I want to tell you something." Santa leaned over the table. "Life gives you presents you didn't plan for. All you can do is accept them. Zoe is a gift, Sean. Take good care of her."

"How do you know her—" before he could finish his question, Santa was gone "—name?"

Sean looked around. The sign in front of the North Pole Village where children had their picture taken with Santa said he was feeding the reindeers.

Odd, Sean thought.

"More presents to check off the list." Zoe appeared and set two more shopping bags under the table with the others. She studied him. "You okay?"

He nodded, even though he felt a little off after the visit with Santa.

She glanced at the list. "I'm almost finished. Two more stores, and we can head home."

With that, she bounced away, a spring to her step and a smile on her face.

Home.

Sean realized how much he wanted Zoe home with him. Not just for Christmas, but New Year's and Valentine's and…

On Christmas Eve, Zoe was surrounded. By the sound of the church choir singing, by a sense of hope, peace, and love…and by Sean's entire family, who took up three whole pews at the lovely rustic church. Young cousins and elderly uncles, Aunt Vera in a feathered hat, mothers holding babies and fathers wrangling excited little ones.

Zoe sighed with contentment. Sean sat beside her, his crutches laid flat beneath the rough-hewn log pew in front of them and his arm around her. It felt good, warm and right. Connie was on the other side, her hand clasped with Hank's resting on his thigh.

Zoe loved her family. Being exiled from them had shaken her world. But at this moment, in this church, she was thankful her mother had banished Zoe from home and threatened her trust fund. Otherwise, she wouldn't be here tonight.

With Sean.

Where she belonged.

It wasn't even December twenty-fifth yet, but this had already been the best Christmas ever.

The organ rolled out the opening chords of "Away in a Manger." Anticipation rustled through the pews. Zoe looked inquiringly at Sean. With a smile, he nodded toward the back of the small church.

Zoe caught her breath in delight as children dressed as characters from the Christmas story filed down the aisle. First came the animals—curly haired sheep, cows with little faces peeping out, two older boys stuck together as a camel. Sean chuckled at a shepherd, dragging his tiny toy sheep behind him like a dog on a leash. Wise men in paper crowns and turbans and bathrobes followed. Next, a choir of angels in white dresses with gold wings on their backs and garland halos on their heads floated down the aisle. One angel was sweet little Rebecca, who had made Zoe the star at the tree-trimming party.

All the white reminded Zoe of a wedding, of the floating fabric from a bride's gown. She imagined herself walking down the aisle dressed in white with a lace veil flowing behind her.

A lump the size of Rebecca's halo formed in Zoe's throat.

What was going on? She had never once pictured herself as a bride. Not when she'd been a bridesmaid. Not when the tabloids had claimed she was engaged to someone she'd never even met.

But here… Now…

Her heart stuttered.

Zoe could picture it so clearly. And she knew why. She turned her head to gaze up at Sean.

She wasn't falling in love with him.

She'd fallen.

I love him.

She inhaled deeply and exhaled slowly.

Zoe had come to Oregon running from her past, escaping scandal, stinging from her family's rejection. Determined to prove her mother wrong and regain access to her trust fund, the last thing on Zoe's mind had been romance, let alone finding love and commitment.

But in some ways, her mother had been right.

Zoe had needed to learn to be responsible. In taking care of Sean, she'd learned to take care of herself. In helping him until he could walk, she had learned to stand on her own two feet.

She admired his commitment to his work and family, his connections to the community, the volunteering of his skill and time with OMSAR, his hard work and careful preparation as well as his sense of fun and adventure. Even when he was injured and in pain, he managed to be generous, caring, strong.

She loved that about him.

She loved him.

And he wanted her.

Her heart sighed.

She was glad they'd taken their relationship slowly, getting to know each other. She could be sure this wasn't just another infatuation or mistake. But in striving to be responsible, had she let caution overwhelm her instincts too much?

As the donkey, Mary and Joseph walked down the aisle, Sean looked down at her and smiled, and she knew.

"If a pregnant woman carrying the son of God can't find a room at the inn, there's no hope for the rest of us," he whispered.

Zoe giggled softly.

Contentment welled inside her. Sean accepted her for who she was. She didn't need to change. She could still follow her heart. Only now she would be smarter about it.

She was done pretending, through with playing roles or games. Her pulse raced. She didn't want to keep putting it off. She wanted to tell Sean the truth.

Trepidation grabbed hold of her.

Maybe not the whole truth all at once. He would be shocked and probably hurt. Her real identity would raise certain issues and questions. She had no idea how he would react, but she didn't want protracted explanations about scandals, campaigns and trust funds to overshadow the magic of this special Christmas.

But she would share the most important fact, the most important gift, of all.

Her love.

She loved Sean.

And it was time to tell him so.

Tonight…

No, she'd wait until tomorrow. Christmas day.

Christmas morning dawned with a shower of snowflakes. Sean smiled. A white Christmas for Zoe.

As Denali bounded through the snow outside, he added a

log to the fire. He thought about the long kisses he'd shared with Zoe last night in front of this very fireplace.

Real kisses without an audience.

It had been more than he'd expected. Sean could have pushed for more. Zoe had seemed willing, but he had remembered what she'd said about working for him and being paid a salary. That had made him pull back. He wanted everything with Zoe to be special, to be perfect.

This was new territory for him, and like the times he wanted to climb a new peak, he needed to be ready. Oh, he might not need a topo map, climber beta, weather reports and avalanche forecast, but as with climbing, he wanted to limit exposure, minimize risk and stack the odds in favor of a successful summit attempt.

As much as Sean wanted Zoe, he had to be prepared.

Denali stood at the door. Zoe waded through the wrapping paper from their stocking stuffers strewn about the floor. "I'll let her in."

As Zoe wiped the dog's paws, the fire roared back to life. Colorful flames crackled in his fireplace, vying for attention with the yule log and carols playing on the television screen. Sean sat on the couch with her present on his lap.

"This one's for you," he said.

Her smile lit up her face like the white lights on their Christmas tree. She sat next to him and took the box. "Is it fragile?"

"No."

She shook it. "I don't hear anything."

"Open it."

"If you insist." She ripped off the bow and tore through the wrapping paper.

Sean couldn't remember a better Christmas, not since he'd gotten his first snowboard a couple decades ago. Back then he hadn't realized what an impact that gift would have on his life. Maybe today would be the same with Zoe.

Denali lay on her big floor pillow, chewing on the bone she'd found in her own stocking. Empty plates from their breakfast, cooked by him so the fire department could take it easy this morning, sat on the coffee table.

Zoe stared inside the gift box. "An airline voucher? Not to take this the wrong way, but do you want me to go away?"

The confusion in her eyes belied her attempt at humor.

"I want you to go home and visit your family. Emphasis on visit," he said. "I gave you a voucher because I have no idea where they live so couldn't buy you a roundtrip ticket. I also wanted you to be the one to decide the right time to go."

As she read the voucher, tears spiked her eyelashes. "This…" Her voice cracked. "You didn't have to do this."

"I wanted to," he said. "Now there's nothing to stop you from going home."

"Thank you." She cuddled against him, one hand on his chest, and looked up at him. "Maybe you could come with me?"

"I'd like that."

The lyrics of the Christmas carol mentioned home and family. That sounded good to Sean. He held her in his arms. Man, he could get used to this.

"Have you called your mother yet?" he asked.

"No." She snuggled closer. "But I will."

His pulse kicked up a notch as she pressed against him. "Don't forget, it'll be crazy at my parents'. It takes hours to open all the gifts."

Zoe sat up. "I'll call home before we leave."

"I'm interfering."

"Yes, but I understand." She squeezed his hand, sending a tingle up his arm. "It runs in your family."

He laughed.

She glanced at the clock. "Your present will be here in a minute. It's not something I could wrap, but I hope you like it."

He rubbed her back. "Having you here is the best Christmas present."

"I can say the same about you. Though the airline voucher is a very thoughtful gift."

Denali raised her head. She dropped the bone.

"Is someone here, girl?" Sean asked.

The dog trotted to the door.

"Come on." Zoe jumped off the couch. "It's your Christmas present."

As he followed her to the front door, he heard bells jingling. Must be on the television.

As she rested her hand on the door handle, her eyes brimmed with excitement.

"Close your eyes."

Sean did. He felt a rush of cold air, as if someone had opened the door.

"You can open them," she said.

He stared out the front door at a horse-drawn sleigh in his driveway. A large black horse pulled a red-and-green sleigh decorated with a garland. Two old-fashioned lanterns hung off the front. A driver with a stovetop hat and forest-green frock coat held the reins with gloved hands. Denali had already jumped into the sled, ready to go for a ride.

Zoe touched her lips gently to his. "Merry Christmas, Sean."

"Wow. I never would have expected this."

She pulled back to gaze into his eyes, hers wide with hope. "You like it?"

"I love it."

I love you, he thought. But he wasn't ready to say the words just yet. He framed her face with his hands. "This must have been really expensive."

"You're worth it."

"Thank you," he said, choked up. "Thank you so much."

Denali barked from the sled.

Bubbling with excitement, Zoe pulled a bundle of his clothes out of the coat closet. "Put these on."

Insulated pants, down jacket, thermal socks for his feet. "Where are we going?"

She grinned. "It's a surprise."

Soon, they were on their way. Even Denali looked thrilled.

The sleigh took them on a tour around town. Sean cuddled with Zoe under thick wool blankets. He brushed his lips across her forehead. "This is a fantastic way to spend Christmas. A sleigh ride through our own winter wonderland."

"Just wait. The best is yet to come."

Sean didn't doubt it. His parents and family thought she was the perfect match. He had to agree with them. He'd never felt so close to another woman. He'd never wanted to settle down until Zoe. She'd come into his life exactly when he needed her.

He could imagine what would come next—a life together, more stockings hanging on the fireplace. He was ready for the future, a future with her.

CHAPTER TEN

TWENTY minutes later, the sleigh pulled up to a trailhead where a group of snowshoers stood around a bonfire. Sean took a closer look. Not any snowshoers—Jake, Carly, Kendall, Austin, Leanne, Bill and Tim with his young son, Wyatt, in a baby carrier. Just like last year. From their flushed faces, Sean could tell they were just back from their walk.

Maybe we can figure out something.

He'd completely forgotten what Zoe had said that night when the Christmas tree arrived, but she hadn't. Her gesture underscored what he loved about her—her warm, generous heart, her impulsive nature, her understanding of how to have fun. He could only imagine how much she must have spent. She'd probably blown an entire paycheck on this.

On him.

You're worth it.

A lump formed in his throat. Sean couldn't speak.

Zoe held his gloved hand in hers and squeezed. "I know you would have rather gone snowshoeing with everyone, but I hope you don't mind hanging out and having hot cocoa and cookies."

Sean cleared his throat. He felt an odd tingling in the pit of his stomach. "I don't mind."

She smiled.

A good thing he was sitting down, she would have knocked him down with that grin of hers.

He remembered what that Santa guy had said at the mall.

Zoe is a gift, Sean. Take good care of her.

She was a gift, one Sean wanted to cherish and keep.

A ball of warmth settled at the center of his chest. He squeezed her hand. "This is such a special Christmas present."

A satisfied smile lit her face. "Jake helped me with some of the arrangements."

"But it was your idea."

She nodded, a little shy.

"Thank you." He kissed her. "I can't wait to see how you top this gift next year."

Her eyes widened again. Her breath caught. "Next year?"

Did she understand, Sean wondered, that he wasn't joking, wasn't pretending, wasn't playing games any longer?

She smiled. "I'm sure I'll come up with something."

Sean thought about not only spending next Christmas with Zoe, but also the 365 days in between.

"But I still have something else for you this year," she said.

"You've given me so much already."

"I want to give you this." Zoe took a deep breath and another. She gazed deeply into his eyes. "Sean, I love you."

His heart jolted. The air rushed from his lungs. A fire lit in his gut.

Best Christmas, ever. Hands down.

He touched her cheek. "I love you, too."

She grinned, the blue of her eyes sparkling. "Just remember who went all in first."

Zoe had told Sean she would call her mother. She knew she needed to, but still she hesitated. A part of her worried what her mother would say.

Christmas had been perfect so far. Sean loved her. She didn't want to ruin everything by having to hear her mother's disapproving voice.

But it was Christmas. Zoe had to call. She picked up the telephone only to set it down again.

Pathetic.

If Sean and the rest of the Hughes had taught her anything this past month, it was the importance of family. She needed to do this.

No more pretenses. No more being who she wasn't.

Despite their differences, she loved her mother. And that meant sharing a few basic, important things with the governor. Like phone calls on Christmas.

Or the fact that Zoe had fallen in love.

She called her mother's personal number. The phone rang and rang.

Relief mingled with disappointment. She continued to let it ring so it would switch her over to voice mail. At least she could leave a message.

"Vanessa Carrington," a stately female voice said.

Anxiety shot through Zoe. "Merry Christmas, Mother."

"Zoe. How good to hear from you," she said. "We got your presents. It was very thoughtful of you. You'll see some extra money deposited in your account. We all thought that would be more practical than gifts."

Zoe smiled wryly to herself. She thought about the number of presents under Connie and Hank's tree with her name on them. But Zoe knew her family meant well. "Thanks."

"How are you doing?" Vanessa asked with genuine concern.

"Fine." Zoe hesitated. "But Mother...I've met someone."

"A man?"

"Yes." She held her breath.

"Zoe."

The disapproval in that one word made her cringe. "It's not like that, Mother. I know I'd say that anyway, but he's different from the others. His name is Sean Hughes. He owns a snowboarding company in Oregon. I met him on Thanksgiving Day. He broke his leg. I've been taking care of him."

"Well, I... Are you living with him? In his house?"

"Yes, but it's not what you're thinking," Zoe explained. "I'm working for him. With a salary. Under the circumstances, we haven't… We've kept that part of our relationship professional."

"I don't know what to say."

"Maybe…that you're happy for me?"

"I am, of course, but Zoe…do you need money?"

A familiar frustration gnawed at her. The old Zoe would have cringed or slammed the phone down. Not the new Zoe. "No, Mother, that's not why I called. I'm fine. I've earned enough that I haven't had to touch my allowance this month."

"That's very responsible of you."

"I'm learning," she admitted. "It isn't easy taking care of somebody. Or myself. Maybe now I have a better understanding of what you must have gone through with me. Especially after Dad died."

"My goodness. You sound different," Vanessa said. "More mature. If this is the influence of your…new man, I approve."

"Thanks."

"I mean it." Her mother's voice warmed. "Merry Christmas. Perhaps, since you've learned your lesson, it's time you come home."

"I'm staying in Oregon."

"Why would you want to do that?"

Zoe thought about the smile on Sean's face when he realized the second part of his present. Or the way he kissed her while they sat at the bonfire with his friends. Her friends now. Or the way he planned on her being with him next Christmas. Joy overflowed from her heart. "I'm in love with Sean."

The line went silent.

Zoe gripped the receiver. "Mother?"

"Love?" her mother's voice rose two octaves. "You can't be in love. When did you say you met him? Thanksgiving?"

"I'll admit it hasn't been that long, but I know what I'm

doing," Zoe said firmly. "There's nothing that will make me change my mind."

"Nothing?"

"Nothing. Not even my trust fund," she reiterated to drive home the point.

"Because of this man? What's his name?"

"Sean Hughes. Yes, it's because of him, but it's also because of me. I finally know who I am. What I want."

"He could be after your money. I'd hate for you to have your heart broken again. I'll have him investigated."

"There's no need, Mom," Zoe explained. "Sean has a successful company. His family has lived in the area forever. They're very well-known, liked, down-to-earth. No skeletons in the closet."

Only a lot of ex-girlfriends.

But she had her share of ex-boyfriends.

"This sounds serious." Her mother sounded more concerned than ever. "Why don't you bring him home so your brothers and I can meet him?"

"He's still recovering from his fall, Mom," Zoe said. "He has a tib-fib fracture. It's healing, but traveling might be too hard on him."

"You are more responsible."

"I'm trying to be, but I'm still me, too."

"Well, you," Vanessa said. "It sounds like I need to come to you, then. How does the twenty-eighth sound?"

Zoe gulped. "That's only three days away. Why don't you wait until after the holidays?"

"I don't want to wait. E-mail my assistant your contact info," Vanessa said. "I'll let you know when all the arrangements have been confirmed."

"Sure."

"Dinner's ready so I have to go," Vanessa said. "Have a Merry Christmas, Zoe. I love you."

"I love you, too, Mother."

Zoe hung up the phone.

Her mother, the venerable Vanessa Carrington, would be here in three days.

What in the world was Zoe going to tell Sean?

Talk about a magical Christmas.

Sitting in his parents' living room, Sean smiled at the scene around him. Flames crackled in the fireplace. The scent of ham lingered in the air. Colorful ribbons and bows lay strewn on the carpet. Kids ran around with their new toys and smiles as bright as the lights on the nine-foot-tall Nobel fir tree. But his favorite part was Zoe.

She'd seemed nervous, a little distracted, after her phone call with her mother, but all of that seemed to disappear once they'd arrived here and his family pulled her into their holiday craziness.

He put his arm around Zoe. "Enjoying yourself?"

Her blue eyes sparkled, matching the new knit scarf she wore around her neck. "This is the best Christmas ever."

"Yes, it is."

Not even his mother's not-so-subtle hints about how special it would be if he proposed right there at the Christmas celebration bothered him. Truth was, a marriage proposal didn't seem like such a crazy idea any longer.

She loved him. He loved her.

More mistletoe appeared over them, compliments of Aunt Vera. There was no longer any awkwardness about kissing under it, no more pretense or lies. This was for real. He'd never felt so relaxed and happy.

Sean kissed Zoe firmly on the lips, as if they had been together forever, not just since Thanksgiving.

She stared at him with suddenly misty eyes. "I wish today didn't have to end."

"I know, but New Year's is only a week away." Sean had a lot of work to do between now and then. He cuddled with Zoe. "Why don't you come with me to the Rail Jam Extravaganza so we can ring in the New Year together?"

* * *

The next morning, Zoe stood in the bathroom. She stared at her reflection in the mirror.

"Sean," she said aloud. "There's something I need to tell you. Flynn is actually my middle name. My last name is really Carrington. My mother is Governor Vanessa Carrington. You may have heard of her. And me."

Lame. Zoe shook her head.

Thank goodness her mother didn't arrive for two more days. Maybe by then Zoe would know what to say to Sean.

"Zoe." His voice sounded different. Urgent. Anxious.

She hurried down the stairs. "Are you okay?"

Sean nodded once. He stood on his crutches. "The call for a rescue mission just went out. I need to head to the base camp and help."

Just for a moment, she wondered what he thought he could do with two bad legs. But she bit her tongue.

"Sure," Zoe said. "Let's go."

"I can hop a ride with Jake."

"No. I want to be there. With you," she said, so there could be no misunderstanding. "This is an important part of your life. I want to know what you do up there."

A muscle flicked at his jaw. "I won't be up there."

Hearing his frustration, she touched his arm. She knew how important his rescue work was to him, how responsible he felt for the men and women he worked with. "Not today, but with the progress you're already making, you'll be up there soon enough. It'll be better if I have an idea of what's going on before that happens."

Some of the tension left his face. He tugged on her braid. "Come on."

"Do I need to bring anything?"

"Patience," he said. "Maybe some prayers. A book wouldn't be a bad idea, either. It could be a long day."

She stared up at him, her heart full of love. "As long as I'm with you, it won't matter."

He shrugged on his OMSAR jacket. "Oh, didn't you want to talk to me about something?"

"Yes," she admitted. "But it can wait."

"There's another weather system moving in." Sean, acting as the PIO, public information officer, spoke to the media at the base of rescue operations. He would rather have been on the mountain. But he was happy to contribute in any way he could, and he was comfortable in the public eye. Good thing, too, as the number of microphones and cameras kept increasing as more information about the missing climbers was released. "According to NOAA, the winds will increase to eighty-five miles per hour. The rescue teams on the mountain have a turnaround time of two o'clock to make sure they're out of danger."

"What about the missing climbers?" a local news station reporter asked. "Won't those winds be dangerous for them?"

"Rescuer safety is our first priority," Sean explained. "We are attempting to regain contact with the missing climbers."

He glanced at the back of the room for Zoe, but she had slipped away. He didn't blame her. The media storm was pretty intimidating for anyone who wasn't used to it.

"So to confirm what we know," a radio reporter said. "A father and his two teenage sons, ages seventeen and fourteen, are missing somewhere on Mount Hood."

"Correct," Sean said.

"Do you know if both boys are injured?" a journalist for the Portland daily paper inquired.

"We are still trying to confirm the extent of the injuries for each of the subjects." Sean noticed the IC, incident commander, gesturing to him. "The teams will continue their search until the turnaround time. We'll have another briefing at fourteen hundred. Thank you."

He hurried over to the IC and waited while the man ended a cell phone call. "Any word?" Sean asked.

"No, all the snowfall overnight is making it hard to see anything," the IC said. "This is going national. CNN, FOX, MSNBC."

That meant phone interviews until they got their crews out here or piggybacked with one of the local news affiliates.

"It's going to turn into a real circus," the IC added.

"No worries," Sean reassured him. "It's nothing we haven't dealt with before. Or won't deal with again."

The lines of IC's face relaxed. "Nice to have you down here for once, Hughes. Though I know you'd rather be up there."

Sean thought about the teams up there. Yeah, that was where he wanted to be, too, but until he was a hundred percent recovered, he would only be a liability. At least his effort down here freed an able-bodied person to do the real rescue work. "Happy to help out where I can."

"I need to go and check with the safety officer."

"I'll prepare for the interviews." Sean sat at a table with notes about the mission objectives, the number of teams in the field and the three subjects. A steaming cup of black coffee appeared in front of him. "Just what I needed."

Zoe placed her hands on his shoulders. "Caffeine works wonders."

He leaned back against her and felt the beating of her heart. "I wasn't talking about the coffee."

She kissed the top of his head. "Just tell me what you need."

"That's easy." Sean wished he could send some of the warmth he felt right now to the teams in the field. Up on the mountain, the risk of frostbite was high. "All I need is you."

All he would ever need.

Sean wasn't about to let Zoe get away from him. He would have to see about getting his grandmother's ring out of the bank safe-deposit box. Just to be prepared...

A traditional girl like Zoe deserved a traditional proposal. That would take planning and preparation. Right now, he needed to focus on the missing climbers and rescue mission.

She massaged his shoulders. "Things are tense around here."

"With the weather changing again, the teams will have to come down."

"I can't imagine what that father and his two sons must be going through up there. Injured. Stuck on the mountain." She shivered. "I can't shake the sound of that teenager's voice during the 911 call."

"The kid's keeping it together given what happened," Sean said, impressed with what he'd heard in a call from the fourteen-year-old. "Now that we've lost contact… You know, I was the same age the first time my dad took me up Hood. I remember what he told me as we were preparing for the climb. He said, 'Son, there are old climbers and there are bold climbers, but there are no old bold climbers.' Climbing with your dad is great, and it should never turn out like this."

"They'll find them." Zoe pressed against him. "It's only the twenty-sixth of December. There has to be some Christmas magic left on the mountain."

Sean turned and kissed her quickly on the lips. "Maybe we can send some of our magic up to them."

"Your kisses are pretty magical." She smiled. "So is the way you handle the press. They adore you. I have a feeling a photograph of you hugging the boys' mom will be on the front page of the paper tomorrow."

"I didn't know you were watching me." He took a sip of his coffee. "Every time the press appears, you disappear."

"Just trying to stay out of the way."

"Well, I'm really glad you're here."

"Me, too." Zoe smiled at him. "I'm getting an idea of what you do, and the precautions you take to make sure everyone stays safe. I'm impressed."

Her willingness to lend a hand, do whatever needed to be done, warmed and impressed him. "You'll make a fine associate member."

"That's what Will said." He had been working here at the

base, too. Not for OMSAR, but the sheriff's office. "He also said cooking wasn't a membership requirement."

Sean laughed. "A good thing in your case."

"Hey, I can learn," Zoe said. "Remember, I got five cookbooks from your family for Christmas."

"And two fire extinguishers."

She grinned. "Well, you like to be prepared, and your family is getting to know me well."

A loud commotion sounded. Streaks of light flashed. The noise level rose exponentially.

Zoe looked at him, her nose crinkled. "I didn't think you had another press conference scheduled until later."

"We don't." Sean rose. He would have heard if the status had changed. "I better find out what's going on. Come on."

"I don't mind staying here."

"Humor me."

Zoe pulled her ski cap so low he could barely see her face. "Okay."

"There's no reason for you to hide." He tugged on her hat. "Unless you're wearing something that says OMSAR, even someone as pretty as you is safe from the media frenzy."

He entered the cafeteria to see Will, in full deputy's uniform, escorting a stylish older woman.

Will motioned to him. "This is Sean Hughes, Governor."

Governor? Not of Oregon, that was for sure. But the woman's face looked a little familiar. Still, Sean couldn't place her.

"It's so nice to meet you, Sean." The woman's wide smile reached her blue eyes. "Zoe's told me a little about you."

"Zoe…"

"Mother?" Zoe sounded horrified. "What are you doing here?"

Mother? Sean's gaze darted between the two. He could kind of see a resemblance. Straight nose. Full mouth. Maybe that accounted for the familiarity of her face? But Zoe and her family were estranged.

"Visiting, dear," the woman said.

"You said you wouldn't be here for two more days."

"I know, but I wanted to see you so I decided to come today."

"You left Maxwell's house early to come see me?"

The surprise in Zoe's voice, the hope in her eyes, nearly broke Sean's heart, even though he was really confused and still reeling from their introduction. What did Will mean calling her Governor? Governor Flynn?

The woman nodded. "I wanted to see you and meet Sean."

Zoe ran to her mother's open arms.

A flash captured the moment.

Zoe drew back as if she'd been covered in acid, not light.

"Don't worry, dear," her mother said gently. "It's okay."

Not wanting to interrupt, but needing to know what was going on, Sean cleared his throat.

"I'm Vanessa Carrington." The older woman extended her arm. Her nails were polished. Her skin soft. "It's so nice to meet you, Sean."

Not Flynn. Carrington. He knew who Governor Carrington was. Most people did. The then-wife-now-widow of a multi-millionaire who'd decided to give politics a whirl. The mother of a flighty socialite. He'd seen the stories on *E!* and in the tabloids at the supermarket. Sexy blond party girl Zoe…

Carrington.

He stared at Zoe, hoping for some other explanation.

She hunched her shoulders. "Flynn is my middle name. I'm really Zoe Carrington."

The missing socialite. The wild child. The other woman.

But that couldn't be the same sweet brunette who burned food, danced in the snow, walked his dog and played with his cousins' kids.

No way. Not his Zoe. Someone had to be pulling a prank.

He looked again from the governor's well-preserved jaw-line and expertly made-up face to Zoe's. He could still see that resemblance between the governor and her. Around the nose and mouth.

Sean glanced at Will, who looked as surprised as he was.

"I was planning to tell you, but…" Zoe glanced at the curious media with a look of fear in her eyes.

Sean might be confused, but Zoe was scared. Trembling. He needed to protect her. "Hey, baby, it's going to be okay."

It had to be okay. This was the woman he wanted to spend the rest of his life with.

"Look, it's Zoe Carrington," someone yelled.

"She's with Sean Hughes," another shouted.

The media rushed forward like a wave about to pound the shore. Will stepped in front of the governor, placing himself between her and the horde of reporters while her security detail scrambled to get closer.

"I'm so sorry, Sean," Zoe mumbled.

"Let's just give them what they want." Governor Carrington smoothed her jacket and adjusted her scarf. "Then they'll leave us alone."

Sean didn't think a sound bite or two would satisfy that hungry crowd.

"Whatever you think best, Mother." Zoe sounded different. Polished. She readjusted her hat, combed through her hair with her fingers and pinched her cheeks to give them color.

He stared in disbelief at the sudden change in her.

"Ready, Sean?" Vanessa asked.

Will gave him a sympathetic look.

Zoe's blue eyes implored him.

Sean would do this for her. "Sure."

Will raised a hand to quiet the mob. "Governor Carrington will take a few questions now."

The press jockeyed for positions. Flashes blinded them. Lights blared down on them. Cameras rolled. A bouquet of microphones was shoved toward their faces.

Sean wasn't a stranger to the press, but all this was rather disconcerting. The governor acted as if this were nothing. Zoe stood as still as a statue.

"Good afternoon," Governor Carrington announced to the media. "Our prayers are with the missing climbers, the rescuers on the mountain and all of their families today."

"You're in the middle of a tough campaign for a coveted U.S. Senate seat," a woman reporter asked. "What brings you to Mount Hood only a few weeks before the special election?"

"My youngest child. My daughter, Zoe, has been staying in Oregon." The governor smiled at her and Sean. "I'm here to support her and someone who is very special to the Carrington family."

Sean stiffened at the implication of her words. Okay, it might be true, but he didn't like the way she'd announced it to the world. His arm slipped from around Zoe's waist.

"How long have you been in Oregon, Zoe?" someone shouted.

"Since mid-November." She flashed a flirty smile. "I've been staying in Hood Hamlet for almost a month now."

A reporter scribbled a note. "Right under our noses."

No, right under his. Sean stared at her.

"Well, I'd hoped it was the one place you wouldn't suspect, and you didn't." Zoe was transforming before his eyes from the sweet woman who took care of him to first daughter without the slightest hesitation. He was stunned by the way she handled the media like a pro, teasing and flirting as if she'd done it her entire life. It was weird and unsettling to see her act this way. "Though I had to hide when some of you interviewed Sean at the hospital."

So that was why she hadn't been in his hospital room, he realized. One question answered, but more kept surfacing.

Where was the woman he'd fallen in love with? Who was the woman standing next to him?

Sean felt totally blindsided. He wanted answers. He wanted them now.

"You could have told us, Sean," a reporter he knew well said.

Survival and self-preservation instincts kicked in. "I wanted to keep Zoe all to myself."

"I don't blame you there."

"He also has been a little preoccupied with his recovery," Zoe added.

"And you?" someone yelled from the back of the crowd.

Zoe smiled coquettishly.

Talk about the press conference from hell. Sean gripped his crutches so tightly his knuckles turned white.

"What are your plans, Governor?" a woman shouted.

"Well, I want to spend a little time with my daughter." Vanessa smiled at Sean. "And I'd also like to see if I can convince Sean to fly back east and join us on the campaign trail for a few days."

Join them where? Sean's temper flared.

"What do you think about that, Sean? You ready to leave the mountain for politics?" a radio reporter asked.

Hell, no, was how Sean wanted to answer, and he would have except he didn't want to hurt Zoe. Instead, he motioned to his crutches. A perfect excuse. "I'm not sure I'd be much help in my current condition."

Zoe stared at him with gratitude in her eyes. "But once Sean's back at one hundred percent, there'll be no stopping him."

"What about Lonzo Green?" another reporter called out.

The married actor? Sean looked at Zoe.

She held her head high. "You should talk to his wife if you want information about him, not me."

A reporter held a digital tape recorder. "How do you feel about Zoe's colorful past, Sean?"

"The only thing that matters is the present," he answered.

"Governor? Any comment?"

Vanessa Carrington beamed. "Of course, I'm delighted

with Zoe's choice. Sean's going to fit into the family just fine."

His jaw worked. So, Zoe had an interfering mother. So did he. Sean could live with that. But at least his family's expectations had always been expressed in private. He'd never expected—he'd sure as hell never wanted—some media-savvy governor presenting him to the press as some kind of "first-son-in-law" and wanting to take him on the campaign trail.

Sean motioned to Will, who stepped in and called a halt to the press conference. "That's all, people."

"What is going on?" Will whispered, as the media dispersed.

"I have no idea," Sean said grimly.

The deputy glanced at Zoe, who was huddled with her mother. "You didn't know?"

"Nope."

"Damn."

That was putting it lightly.

Zoe walked over to him. "Are you ready to go home?"

Sean's pride was hurt and his faith in his judgment was shaken. He felt used by both Zoe and her mother.

"The mission is still going on," he said tightly. "I can't leave."

She stared up at him with wide eyes. "But…we need to talk."

"Not now. I don't have the time."

"But—"

"Three climbers are missing." He couldn't control his temper any longer. "I have a responsibility here. A role. This is what I need to focus on right now. Not this. Not you. Go home."

"I can't leave." She touched his arm. "You need me."

"No." He jerked away. "I don't."

CHAPTER ELEVEN

ZOE DELAYED taking Denali for a walk until the rescue was reported on FOX News. A rescue team had found the missing climbers, a father and two sons. The three missing climbers were suffering from frostbite and broken limbs, but at least they were alive. A happy ending, the anchor concluded joyfully.

A last moment of Christmas magic, Zoe thought.

Standing in the snow with Sean's dog, she blotted her eyes and blew her nose, grateful and miserable at the same time.

Her feelings were hurt, but she knew Sean had a tendency to overdo it; however, with three lives on the line, his preoccupation was justified. Still she needed a sprinkle of that Christmas magic herself right now.

You need me.

No, I don't.

She whistled for Denali and headed back to the house.

I don't need you.

"Sean's back." Vanessa met them in the foyer, her usually severe face sympathetic. "I'm going to be in the study checking my e-mail and making phone calls so the two of you can talk."

"Thanks, Mother."

With a deep breath, Zoe walked into the great room to find Sean sitting on the couch. But the man who'd needed her help getting to the bathroom or washing or dressing was gone, replaced by an almost stranger with a determined set of his jaw and hard lines on his face.

She'd done this to him. To them.

The realization clawed at her heart.

Zoe walked toward him intent on making things better. She sat next to him. "I'm sorry, Sean. I've been meaning to tell you the truth. That's what I wanted to talk to you about."

"You should have told me." Sean shook his head. "I felt ambushed today."

"I know." She stared at the floor. "I wanted to tell you the truth right away, but I was afraid someone might find out who I was or where I was. My mother threatened to cut off access to my trust fund if I didn't straighten up and be more responsible."

"Trust fund? I figured out your family had money, but I didn't think you did. So you needing a job, a place to stay, were more lies."

"No. I wasn't lying about any of that." Zoe lowered her voice. "My mother put me on a limited allowance. I had hardly any money left when I met you. You really helped me out."

"I thought we saw each other for who we are." He stared at the fireplace. "But I haven't a clue who you are."

"I'm still me. Zoe. My last name doesn't change that." She scooted toward him, but he moved away. Her heart felt as if it had cracked. "I figured out who I was being here with you. The real Zoe. One I like and am proud to be."

"The real Zoe?" he repeated. "Everything was based on a lie."

Under the hurt, she felt a flash of temper. "I agreed to be your pretend girlfriend. Continuing the charade for your family was your idea."

"Exactly. My idea. I knew what was going on. We both knew what we were getting into." He grimaced. "You agreed to the lies we told my family, but I never signed on for this."

"I didn't lie to you. I just didn't tell you everything."

"I trusted you. Do you know how it felt not to know who the

woman standing next to me at the press conference was? She looked like you, but she sure as hell didn't act like you."

"My mother has been governor since I was eight," Zoe tried to explain. "Everything from my father's death to my brothers' weddings has been covered by the press. I was taught to act that way when I was a little girl. It's second nature. I can't help it."

He rose. "What else don't I know about you, Zoe?"

"What do you want to know? My secrets? The lies printed about me in the tabloids and gossip blogs?" Tears pricked her eyes. "Who I've been with you is who I am. I just didn't know it until coming here. Listen to your heart. You know me, Sean."

"I'm not so sure anymore."

Her heart split open. "I love you."

The three words spilled from her lips as if they could make this all better, make things go back to the way they were this morning.

He didn't say anything.

"Sean…"

"You're asking me to accept a completely different vision of you with short notice and no preparation." He used his crutches to cross the room, to get away from her. Denali followed him. "You've sprung this on me at the worst possible time. I'm just getting my life back on track. Recovering. Working. I can't be distracted right now. I have the Rail Jam Extravaganza on New Year's. That's a priority for me."

"And I'm not." Zoe fought the urge to say something hurtful and run out of the room. Her insides trembled and tears welled in her eyes, yet she remained in control. She wasn't that same, old Zoe. "I've heard that before."

From her mother, her brothers, boyfriends and friends. Zoe wanted to believe Sean wasn't like the other people in her life. She wanted to be his priority, but maybe that wasn't possible right now. Still, she knew he needed her. Not to take care of him because of his injuries, but to love him. The way she needed him to love her in return.

"You need time," she said.

He nodded.

"Fine." Zoe's heart ached, but she would give Sean what he wanted. "You gave me time when I asked for it. I can give you that now. Time and space so you can focus. I'll go home with my mother."

And wait.

Who the hell was Zoe Carrington?

Three days later, Sean was alone with his thoughts and his dog. He'd sent his family away, rejected his friends' offers to come over with beer and sympathy. Not even work was filling the void. He hadn't realized there'd been a black hole in his life until Zoe left. Sean wanted to be alone to nurse his leg and his grievances.

He stared morosely into the empty fireplace. Was this how the women he'd broken up with felt? He'd been a player. Zoe had played him good.

He grabbed his laptop, went to Google and searched for her name. Over sixteen million results appeared, everything from evocative images to a wikipedia entry.

Some of the entries made him sick. The coverage of her and the married actor that seemed to catapult the guy's career to A-list. An NFL quarterback who claimed she'd stalked him only to whine when he heard she was dating someone else. Car accidents and run-ins with the paparazzi that resulted in confidential, out-of-court settlements.

No doubt there were two sides to each story. He couldn't bring himself to believe the woman he'd been living with for the past month was capable of the motives attributed to her by the media.

Sean remembered Zoe saying she'd been dealing with this since she was eight. No wonder she'd developed ways to cope.

He selected News.

One headline read Governor Carrington to Host Final New Year's Eve Ball.

He scanned the article about the term-limited governor's last big hurrah, her final New Year's party to be held in the governor's mansion. The story mentioned Zoe was expected to attend the highly anticipated soiree.

Other stories mentioned only Zoe's name, nothing about what she'd been doing or where she'd been. Even the gossip bloggers posted that Zoe continued to keep a low presence since returning home from her "travels."

Strange. If Zoe was such a wild child, why hadn't she returned to the same party scene she'd left in Los Angeles? Why wasn't she hanging out with her old friends making up for lost time?

Sean focused on one image that had caught his eye. A picture of a blonde climbing out of a cab in front of a club back in September, but superimposed on her face were the eyes, the smile of the woman he loved. He tried to reconcile the party girl in the skimpy green dress with the woman he knew.

Zoe Carrington. Zoe Flynn.

Blonde. Brunette.

Homewrecker. Homebody.

The two women were supposedly one and the same. Yet…

Who I've been with you is who I am. I just didn't know it until coming here. Listen to your heart. You know me, Sean.

Zoe's words swirled through his brain. He stared again at the photo, into her eyes, remembering what the Santa guy had said at the mall.

Life gives you presents you didn't plan for. All you can do is accept them. Zoe is a gift, Sean. Take good care of her.

She had accepted him, but he hadn't done the same with her. That was when he realized…

Her last name didn't matter. Her last name didn't change anything.

He did know her.

Sean looked around the room and saw the big, tall

Christmas tree with all the homemade ornaments she'd helped the kids make. His gaze focused on one in particular, a star that Rebecca had made.

He knew Zoe's compassion, her creativity and her ability to stand up to him when needed. He also knew her heart, her giving, nurturing thoughtful heart.

She'd accepted his past while he…

What had he done?

Zoe, no matter her last name, was everything he needed. All he needed. The woman he loved.

But his pride hadn't let him see it.

For weeks the two of them had talked about everything, but when finally faced with the fact Zoe had a life outside of their little world, Sean had shut down. He hadn't wanted to listen to her.

He'd been upset. Hurt. Stupid.

He had to go after her. Apologize. Make her see that she didn't have to be Zoe Carrington or Zoe Flynn. She could just be Zoe. His Zoe. Zoe Hughes.

But how?

Sean dragged his hand over his face.

He thought about what Zoe might have done in this situation. She would have followed her instincts, acted impulsively, made a grand gesture.

Like the sleigh ride on Christmas day.

He needed to take a page from her playbook and do the same thing, to go all in even if he wasn't holding the right cards and sure he would win.

Sean thought for a moment. He remembered reading about a New Year's ball. That would be a grand gesture, but he had the Rail Jam Extravaganza to attend at the same time. He was the face of Hughes Snowboards. He'd built his business by making that kind of public appearance a priority.

And I'm not. I've heard that before.

He stared at Zoe's image.

She'd said enough about her past for him to realize her

family had never made time for her. He didn't want to be like them. He couldn't be like them.

Zoe deserved better.

He'd never made time for a woman before, but Sean wanted to convince Zoe that she was a priority in his life. No matter what it took.

Sean rose, tried to take a step and fell back onto the couch.

In his hurry to make things right, he'd forgotten about his crutches, about his leg.

He couldn't do this on his own. He was going to need help to pull this off. Sean picked up the phone and started punching in numbers.

On New Year's Eve, Zoe eyed the enormous clock set above the stage in the ballroom, counting down the hours and minutes until midnight. The band tuned up. Ice sculptures dripped and gleamed. Fragrant and colorful flower arrangements decorated the linen-covered tables. Everything was in place for a spectacular start to a Happy New Year.

But Sean wasn't here.

He hadn't contacted her in the five days since she'd left Hood Hamlet. Not a word, a voice message, an e-mail, a postcard.

Zoe worried how he was doing, whether he was taking care of himself or overdoing it, and if he'd hired someone else to help him out. She hadn't really expected to hear from him with the Rail Jam Extravaganza coming up, but still, she'd hoped.

She was being mature, but she wanted to pout like a child. She wanted to be a part of his life, but he'd made it clear she wasn't an important part.

A lump formed in her throat.

She had agreed to give him time. Maybe now that she'd left Hood Hamlet, Sean had decided he didn't have time for a relationship. He wanted his life to be like it was before his fall.

Her heart squeezed.

"Can you believe it's New Year's Eve?" Vanessa Carrington sashayed toward her across the shining ballroom floor in the governor's mansion. "I know this has been a difficult week for you, Zoe. But I'm happy you're home and here tonight."

"Thanks, Mother." Zoe forced a smile and pressed her cheek to her mother's powdered and perfumed one. "The room looks wonderful."

"Thanks to you. I'm so pleased you spoke with the event planner. You really have a good eye." The echo of Sean's words touched Zoe's heart. "And speaking of lovely..." Vanessa motioned for her to spin around. "That blue is very flattering."

"Thanks."

The look in her mother's eyes softened. "I know you miss him, but it's New Year's Eve. I hope you'll try to have fun tonight."

Zoe had to laugh. "I can't believe you're telling me to have fun."

"Well, I am." Vanessa placed her hands on her hips. "Don't think about Sean. We can deal with that later. You've worked so hard on this party. It's time you enjoyed yourself."

Zoe had thrown herself into the party because she didn't want to think about all she'd left behind in Hood Hamlet. She missed the small town, the people, even the mountain.

Mostly, though, she missed Sean.

Still she couldn't put her life on hold indefinitely. Once, maybe, but not now. She had plans to make. He had taught her the value of that. As soon as the holidays were over, she was putting her résumé and a portfolio together. She'd be prepared whether she heard from Sean or not.

Maxwell, her oldest brother, appeared. He wore a black tuxedo. With his hair slicked back, he looked like the scion of politicians that he was. "The guests are starting to arrive, Mother."

"Thank you, dear." Vanessa extended her hand to Zoe. "Shall we?"

Zoe straightened, smiled and took hold of her mother's hand. "Let's party."

The limousine drove through a neighborhood of large, old houses covered with colorful lights and inflatable decorations in the front yards. The homes might have been bigger, but they made Sean think of Peacock Lane, a Portland neighborhood that took decorating for the holidays to the extreme.

"I don't know about you guys." Bill sprawled out on the backseat of the limo. "I might look like a million dollars, but I feel like a penguin in this monkey suit."

Tim adjusted his bowtie. "Well, you look like a monkey."

The limousine turned left and drove through a gated entrance. Sean stopped toying with the cuff links on his white, starched shirt and stared. A mansion, set back, was lit by thousands of white, twinkling lights.

His heart pounded in his chest.

"Get a load of that." Jake whistled. "We're a long way from Hood Hamlet, boys."

No kidding. Sean stared at the house—it didn't seem a big enough word—where Zoe had grown up. At one point, he'd thought she was homeless. He would have never imagined she'd spent the past sixteen years of her life living in a modern day palace.

"Too bad Will isn't here in case we get into trouble," Tim said.

Bill nodded. "No 'get out of jail free' card for crashing the governor's ball."

"We aren't crashing," Sean said.

Three pairs of eyes turned to him.

"I called in a few favors, gave away a couple boards," Sean explained to their surprised faces. "It wasn't going to do us any good to show up at the door and not be let in. We're on the guest list."

"Always prepared," Jake said.

"Team leader extraordinaire," Tim agreed.

"Cool, now we can eat and drink and not feel guilty," Bill quipped. "Joking."

"You ready, Sean?" Jake asked.

He nodded, still staring at the house. Zoe was inside, somewhere. His objective—to find her. "That's a lot of area to search."

"Don't worry," Tim said. "This is nothing compared to a few of the places we've had to look."

"True that," Jake agreed.

"I still can't believe your wives let you come." Bill fiddled with buttons. The television turned on. The lights dimmed. "On New Year's Eve, no less."

"Carly told me she'd never forgive me if I didn't help," Jake said.

Tim nodded. "Mine said the same thing and added I'd better not screw this up for Sean."

The limousine stopped next to the front steps. A uniformed attendant opened the door.

"Let's do this," Sean said, as if they were about to head into a whiteout rather than a black-tie, by-invitation-only event.

The four of them exited the limousine, feeling like fish out of water. Their normal tools and uniforms were on the other side of the country. No backpacks, helmets, ropes, ice axes and well-worn boots. They had to make do with tuxedos, cuff links, bowties, cummerbunds and shiny, tight shoes.

"No matter what happens." Sean adjusted the crutches under his arms. "Thanks for backing me up on this, dudes."

Jake patted him on the shoulder. "Our pleasure."

Bill rang the doorbell. "Gentlemen, it's showtime."

Inside, women in fancy, long dresses and guys in tuxedos mingled. A real live band—with brass and plenty of soul—played from an elevated stage at one end of the room. Guests sat at linen-covered tables, eating, or stood and drank.

"I don't see her." Sean scanned the crowd. He had no idea if Zoe would still be a brunette or have gone back to blond or some other color. "Let's split up. We can search a larger perimeter that way. Rendezvous back in fifteen minutes."

Fifteen minutes later, no one had seen her.

Jake met his eyes. Shrugged. "No luck."

Sean needed luck. His chest tightened. He needed… Christmas magic.

"It's a big place," Tim consoled him. "Let's expand the search area."

"Zoe would be at the party if she were here." He looked around once more. Still nothing. "Grab a drink and some food. I'm going to make one more pass before calling it."

The others headed to the bar.

Sean rounded a corner and bumped into Governor Carrington.

Her eyes widened when she saw him. "Sean?"

"Hello, Governor."

"Vanessa."

"Vanessa," he corrected.

"Well, look at you." Her once-over made him feel as if he were on display at a fashion show or something. "Not quite the mountain man today."

Sean shrugged. "When in Rome…"

"You fit into Rome quite nicely."

"Uh, thanks. I came to talk to Zoe, but I can't find her."

Vanessa glanced around. "She's here somewhere."

Sean straightened, every nerve ending stood at attention. "Zoe may not want to talk to me."

"Oh, she'll talk to you." The governor motioned to two large doors. "Zoe might be out there. She used to hide on the balcony during parties when she was a little girl." A soft smile formed on Vanessa's face. "She's still my little girl, Sean. But I hope everything works out the way you want it to."

"Even if it means I take Zoe back with me to Oregon?" he asked.

Vanessa nodded. "Even then."

"Thanks."

Sean glanced at the big clock over the stage. Almost time.

With a deep breath, he propped open the balcony door and swung outside on his crutches.

Standing on the balcony on the chilly, overcast night, Zoe ignored the goose bumps on her arms and how cold her toes were. Instead, she stared at the lights twinkling in the nearby neighborhood. They reminded her of stars.

Stars.

Her breath caught in her throat.

I grew up with multicolored lights, but the white ones look like stars to me.

Sean.

Her chest constricted.

She remembered the glittery star ornament little Rebecca had made for her. Zoe had left it on the tree, thinking she would be back.

If only she could wish upon a star now for what her heart desired....

But Christmas was over. All the magic had been used up. No more miracles to be had.

She clutched the railing, disappointed and hurting.

That time on the mountain was over. She was back in the governor's mansion, back in the public eye. She was happy to be reconciled with her mother and brothers, but she couldn't go back to being the same old Zoe. Even if her wish for love didn't come true, she had a brighter future ahead of her than the one she'd dreamed of.

She had Sean to thank.

Because he had believed in her, depended on her, she could believe in and depend on herself.

Tears pricked the corners of her eyes.

Even if he didn't need her anymore.

A noise sounded behind her.

Uh-oh. Someone had found her favorite hiding spot. No doubt her mother or one of her brothers.

"I'll go back inside," she said, not turning. "I just needed some fresh air."

"Don't rush back on my account."

The familiar male voice sent her pulse racing. She turned slowly, afraid she was imagining things.

But she wasn't.

Her heart leapt. "You're here."

Dressed in a black tux and looking devastatingly handsome, he made his way toward her on crutches. "You look gorgeous, absolutely stunning, like a real-life princess in that gown. Though I must admit to being partial to you in wet, clingy pajamas."

Zoe's heart melted at the compliment, but she forced herself to straighten. "Aren't you supposed to be at the Rail Jam Extravaganza?"

"I sent two of my employees who I'm sure will rise to the occasion," he said. "You're my top priority, Zoe."

The air rushed from her lungs. No one had ever said those words to her before.

Standing in front of her, he tucked a piece of hair behind her ear, the gesture so tender her eyes stung. "For years, I've told myself I didn't have time for a relationship. I wouldn't listen to my family, to anyone. Then you came along, and all I could see, want, dream about was you. I should have never let you leave. I'm sorry, Zoe. I should have believed you when you told me who you were. Not Zoe Carrington or Zoe Flynn. Just Zoe. But I was too stubborn to realize it."

She swallowed, hoping to find her voice. "I'm sorry, too. I should have trusted you with the truth, Sean, but so many times people I've known have run to the tabloids to make a quick buck…"

"We both should have done a lot of things."

Her heart bumped. "All I've ever wanted is to be loved and accepted for who I am. Not what my family or friends expect. I just want to be me. I'm not going to settle for anything less."

"I don't want you to settle." Sean held her hand. "I love you. Only you."

The sincerity in Sean's eyes and voice told Zoe his words were true. She smiled. "I love you."

"Do you think we could try again?" he asked. "I want to take you back to Hood Hamlet, back home."

Her heart fluttered. "I'd like that."

Sean lowered his mouth, pressing his sweet lips upon hers. He swept Zoe against him with one arm, her skin tingling where he touched her.

His lips moved over hers. Tasting. Caressing. Loving.

She melted into the kiss, drinking up the taste of him. His warmth and his strength danced through her veins.

Zoe gave in to his passion, returning his kiss with a desire all her own. She didn't know how long they stood there, how long they kissed. The only thing that mattered was this time. This man. This love.

Slowly, with a heartrending tenderness, Sean drew the kiss to an end.

Zoe stared at the man she loved. The affection in his eyes matched the way she felt in her heart. Every kiss, every touch they'd shared had brought them to this moment. "So you're going to be my real-life boyfriend."

He shook his head, a quick, decisive gesture that stopped her heart.

"I want to be more than your boyfriend. We've had only one official date, but being with you these past weeks has shown me it will work. I want you to know I'm committed." Sean swung backward, tried to move, then stopped. "Damn crutches."

She let go of the breath she'd been holding. "What?"

"I can't go down on one knee because of my leg, so this will have to do. Marry me, Zoe Flynn Carrington. Be my wife. Be my partner. Be my everything."

This was everything she imagined it would be and more. Joy overflowed. "I'd be honored to be your wife, Sean. Yes. Yes, I'll marry you."

Inside, the people started counting down to midnight.

He pulled out a velvet ring box, opened it up and, as the

horns blared the ringing-in of a new year, slid the ring onto Zoe's finger. A perfect fit.

She gazed at the intricate filigree and diamonds, a feeling of family and home and tradition welling up inside her. "Your grandmother's ring?"

He nodded. "We seem to have been fated from that first day we met, but if you don't like it—"

"I love it," she said. "But not as much as I love you."

Sean grinned. "Happy New Year, Zoe."

He brushed his lips across hers once more.

A feeling of contentment flowed through her. It was as if this was the moment she'd been waiting for, but it wasn't the ending. Only the beginning.

"Happy New Year, my love," she said.

Zoe stared up at Sean with stars in her eyes and his ring on her finger. She smiled. There had been some Christmas magic left after all.

MILLS & BOON®
HAVE JOINED FORCES WITH THE LEANDER TRUST AND LEANDER CLUB TO HELP TO DEVELOP TOMORROW'S CHAMPIONS

We have produced a stunning calendar for 2011 featuring a host of Olympic and World Champions (as they've never been seen before!). Leander Club is recognised the world over for its extraordinary rowing achievements and is committed to developing its squad of athletes to help underpin future British success at World and Olympic level.

'All my rowing development has come through the support and back-up from Leander. The Club has taken me from a club rower to an Olympic Silver Medallist. Leander has been the driving force behind my progress'

RIC EGINGTON – Captain, Leander Club Olympic Silver, Beijing, 2009 World Champion.

Please send me ___ **calendar(s) @ £8.99 each plus £3.00 P&P** (FREE postage and packing on orders of 3 or more calendars despatching to the same address).

I enclose a cheque for £ _____ made payable to Harlequin Mills & Boon Limited.

Name ....

Address ....

.... Post code.............................

Email ....

Send this whole page and cheque to:
Leander Calendar Offer
Harlequin Mills & Boon Limited
Eton House, 18-24 Paradise Road, Richmond TW9 1SR

All proceeds from the sale of the 2011 Leander Fundraising Calendar will go towards the Leander Trust (Registered Charity No: 284631) – and help in supporting aspiring athletes to train to their full potential.

All the magic you'll need this Christmas...

When **Daniel** is left with his brother's kids, only one person can help. But it'll take more than mistletoe before **Stella** helps him...

Patrick hadn't advertised for a housekeeper. But when **Hayley** appears, she's the gift he didn't even realise he needed.

Alfie and his little sister know a lot about the magic of Christmas – and they're about to teach the grown-ups a much-needed lesson!

Available 1st October 2010

www.millsandboon.co.uk

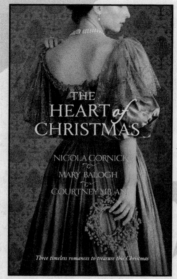
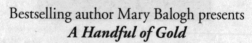

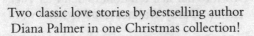

"Did you say I won almost two million dollars?"

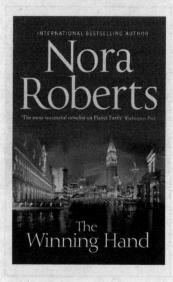

Down to her last ten dollars in a Las Vegas casino, Darcy Wallace gambled and won!

Suddenly the small-town girl was big news— and needing protection. Robert MacGregor Blade, the casino owner, was determined to make sure Darcy could enjoy her good fortune. But Darcy knew what she wanted; Mac himself. Surely her luck was in?

Available 3rd December 2010

www.millsandboon.co.uk

2 FREE BOOKS
AND A SURPRISE GIFT

We would like to take this opportunity to thank you for reading this Mills & Boon® book by offering you the chance to take TWO more specially selected books from the Cherish™ series absolutely FREE! We're also making this offer to introduce you to the benefits of the Mills & Boon® Book Club™—

- **FREE home delivery**
- **FREE gifts and competitions**
- **FREE monthly Newsletter**
- **Exclusive Mills & Boon Book Club offers**
- **Books available before they're in the shops**

Accepting these FREE books and gift places you under no obligation to buy, you may cancel at any time, even after receiving your free books. Simply complete your details below and return the entire page to the address below. You don't even need a stamp!

YES Please send me 2 free Cherish books and a surprise gift. I understand that unless you hear from me, I will receive 5 superb new stories every month, including two 2-in-1 books priced at £5.30 each, and a single book priced at £3.30, postage and packing free. I am under no obligation to purchase any books and may cancel my subscription at any time. The free books and gift will be mine to keep in any case.

Ms/Mrs/Miss/Mr _____ Initials _____

Surname _____

Address _____

_____

_____ Postcode _____

E-mail _____

Send this whole page to: Mills & Boon Book Club, Free Book Offer, FREEPOST NAT 10298, Richmond, TW9 1BR